THE

Blue Orchard

JACKSON TAYLOR

A TOUCHSTONE BOOK
Published by Simon & Schuster
New York   London   Toronto   Sydney

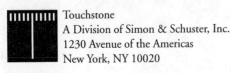
Touchstone
A Division of Simon & Schuster, Inc.
1230 Avenue of the Americas
New York, NY 10020

This Touchstone hardcover edition January 2010

TOUCHSTONE and colophon are registered trademarks of
Simon & Schuster, Inc.

For information about special discounts for bulk purchases,
please contact Simon & Schuster Special Sales at 1-866-506-1949 or
business@simonandschuster.com.

The Simon & Schuster Speakers Bureau can bring authors to your live event. For more information or to book an event, contact the Simon & Schuster Speakers Bureau at 1-866-248-3049 or visit our website at www.simonspeakers.com.

Designed by Joy O'Meara
Illustration from iStockphoto.com

Manufactured in the United States of America

10 9 8 7 6 5 4 3 2 1

Library of Congress Cataloging-in-Publication Data

Taylor, Jackson.
  The blue orchard : a novel / Jackson Taylor.—
    p. cm.
  "A Touchstone book."
    1. Nurses—Fiction. 2. Middle-aged women—Fiction. 3. African American physicians—Fiction. 4. Abortion—Pennsylvania—Fiction. 5. Harrisburg (Pa.)—Fiction. I. Title.

  PS3620.A946B58   2010
  813'.6—dc22   2009011381

ISBN 978-1-4391-8668-8
ISBN 978-1-4165-9684-4 (ebook)

For little Brad, little Lisette, and
the one without a name . . .

THE

THE
Blue Orchard

Prologue

Since my name has appeared in the newspaper following our arrest, my entire moral character is being drawn into question. In town, at the Market, I notice people finger-pointing and whispering, and upon quick return to my car on Broad Street, I see one enterprising soul has broken an egg on the windshield. Now I'm reluctant to even go downtown. Over the years I've always drawn a bit of attention, the oddball stare or squinting curiosity; there's speculation, a certain notice of my clothes, whispered gossip. They might even know I'm a nurse.

People who don't know Dr. Crampton might imagine him as some kind of back-alley butcher in a bad part of town, slicing open unfortunate women lying naked under a bare lightbulb. The truth, however, is that Dr. Crampton has for over half a century been our city's leading Negro citizen. His widely respected medical practice opened in 1904, and prior to our arrest, no lawman would have dared tamper with him, for he is also a full-fledged member of a political machine as proudly crooked as any in the nation. He is the state's deputy secretary of health and a vice-chairman of the Republican Party.

Yes, Dr. Crampton has always played his cards right, moving about town in king-sized late-model Lincolns, chauffeured by men who are sometimes as shockingly white as the gloves they wear. I've witnessed firsthand how Dr. Crampton throws money around; he greases big wheels, plays Daddy Benefactor, buys flowers, medicine, mortgages, baby carriages, and Negro votes, which for decades have been delivered to his Republican friends.

Not only is Dr. Crampton the undisputed leader of the Seventh Ward, which is colored, but in 1919 he founded the Negro YMCA, and he also sits on the governing boards of any number of banks, churches, medical groups, and charities. For me, it's been an honor to work for this astonishing man, to attend the many tributes and testimonial dinners held on his behalf, where citations from governors and senators are bestowed. In fact, his commanding presence is such a certainty of life in our city that on the morning of the 14th of November the whole town gasps when we are arrested.

The police ransack his well-furnished yellow townhouse, root out the ground floor's medical offices, then climb upstairs to his private quarters, where his closets are emptied, his dresser drawers dumped, his fine wardrobe tangled: silk ties, shoes, shirts, suspenders, and spats. In every room hand-knotted Persian rugs are heaved up and piled into mountains, leather-bound books are swept from mahogany shelving, and his collection of French portraits and American landscapes are pulled from the walls and stacked like firewood. Even the furnace in his basement and the meat in his kitchen freezer are examined.

A short time later the police proceed uptown to my own house at 2311 North Third Street. In their report they describe it as a three-story, red-brick dwelling with pillared porch and mansard roof. Recently our city's ill-conceived Capitol extension project has caused many great houses in Harrisburg to decline, as angry displaced Negroes without the means to make repairs move farther uptown with every passing month. But everyone knows that if you live above MacClay Street, as I do, the neighborhood is unlikely to change. It will remain elegant, wealthy, and white. The police rarely have business here.

Dewey, my husband, answers the knock. The tough voices at the door alert me.

Trouble.

I quickly lie down on one of the beds in the dining room, pull a cover up over my clothes, and pretend to be ill.

The men enter. I can see the cops silently glance at each other as they count the number of beds in the downstairs rooms.

"You Verna Krone?"

I nod.

"You work for Doctor Crampton?"

"I'm a licensed nurse," I answer.

"Well, you're under arrest for illegal surgery."

I lie back as if too sick to move and let them search the house. Dewey follows them around like a bellhop waiting for a tip.

Left alone for a moment, my wits gather and a guise of tough calm overtakes me. I can't believe they've stated the crime so obliquely, but of course they can't make an arrest without making some kind of charge. "Relax," I whisper to myself. "Relax into the conflict." Isn't that what Dr. Crampton would do? From the hallway closet upstairs, one of them removes enamel basins—a full dozen—several cartons of sanitary napkins, and some freshly sterilized syringes. It all gets lugged downstairs. "Why all the Kotex?" the fat one asks.

"Is there a law against menstruation?"

They cringe. Female stuff. My belligerence irritates them.

"Why all these syringes?"

"I'm a nurse. I make house calls," I say, sounding plenty peeved to be answering such questions. Meanwhile I'm relieved to see they've found nothing of significance. The joke's on them. A day earlier and the house would have been full of women.

They want to take me downtown, but I tell them I am too sick to travel. They're puzzled, demand to know what ails me.

"I've got a serious condition with my vertebrae," I say. "My orthopedist has prescribed total bed rest. Take me downtown and you'll cause permanent injury to my spine."

They don't like it but are afraid to call my bluff.

"We've got orders," the taller one stammers.

"Well, you'll contend with Harvey Taylor if you try to move me," I say, making tough, like I could wrestle and hog-tie both of them.

The detectives are dumbfounded. Harvey Taylor runs the state and these boys know it. For the time being my lie works. They exit.

The night drags. I lie awake and speculate, afraid to use the phone, afraid to leave the house, afraid to fear the worst. Early the next morning the detectives are back and, spine or no spine, insist I accompany them to the courthouse, where Dr. Crampton has been sitting up all night waiting to see the judge. My condition requires me to put on quite an act of pain, suffering into my black cashmere coat and fox-fur collar, hobbling out to the car, wincing at every step. It's all for show, but if I keep it up, maybe it will allow me to return home and not be placed in a holding cell.

When I enter the courthouse, Dr. Crampton lifts his gaze to look at me. His lips press together in the faintest recognition. I nod, almost imperceptibly, pretend to barely know him. Our courthouse isn't segregated, but on that day it might as well be, for I take a seat on the far side of the waiting room, as far away from Dr. Crampton as possible.

If I had it to live over again, I'd do it differently. I'd find my courage, sit beside him, renounce the detachment, wide as an ocean, that pulls me from the dear man who is losing everything. But on that day—after being arrested—I will not stir. I will not admit to feeling anything for him: no good can come of it.

Our arrest is teaching me the limits of my daring. Even now, it surprises me how before that day I never really accepted that Dr. Crampton was colored. I preferred to view him as the sole member of a separate species, unique, unbound by the conventions and problems of ordinary Negroes. But of course he's not white either, and now trouble shows his skin growing ever darker and affirms the folly of my self-serving vision. Dr. Crampton is being stripped of his special privilege, and it's time to recognize that he is a Negro, and I am white.

Till the day I die, I will regret that day, and how the safety of my own race seduces me to disengage from his, to suddenly follow previously ignored codes. The change is subtle, almost unnoticeable; only he can detect it. The notice gets chiseled on his heart: *Let your ship of misery pull away, I am staying ashore.*

In America we are born knowing a Negro can pull a white woman down simply by association. And a Negro on his way down? Well, perish the thought.

It isn't done. It isn't done. It isn't done by me.

Affections for a Negro man that run as deep as mine are not appropriate. They menace. Imagine what can come of them. Probably a majority of people believe our relationship is or was romantic or sexual. They assume he lusts for me and I for him. They wink at the notion of a professional partnership, a collegial cooperation between a Negro man and a white woman.

By the time we see the judge, it's late in the day and I've been named as codefendant. My brain slows like cold molasses, stuck with one thought: Are we in for a soft rap on the knuckles or a real prison sentence? No one seems to know.

"Not guilty," I say, following Crampton's lead, trying to sound confident. Once the bail money has been posted, we are free to go. Late-night phone calls go out to Dr. Crampton's friends, but now, suddenly, few can afford to take his call. The situation is too dangerous.

Pending the trial's outcome, and because of the unpleasant attention I drew at the Broad Street Market, I've retreated here to the farm, where I'll stay until all this has been decided. It's a fruit farm, one hundred acres, less than an hour north of Harrisburg, with a breezeway connecting the main house to a small stone summer kitchen. Inside is a big black range, where in warm weather I cook and do the canning—and at any time of year come to sit when I need to brood on something.

Crampton has always warned me not to keep records and maybe he's right. Maybe I should've just written our business down in the dirt and let the rain settle it. But now, after the arrest, I'm glad a record exists, hidden in the summerhouse under the walnut dry sink, a dishwashing stand no longer used in this day and age. Here two gallon jugs of vinegar rest on a slab of soapstone, and when all that's taken out, two boards can be lifted to reveal a false bottom.

The ledger stored there measures five by seven inches and sits more than an inch thick. The cover is worn and battered from fifteen years of duty. Moisture and passing years have warped the paper, but each page lists the names of nine patients, complete with addresses and phone numbers—front and back make eighteen—the entire book holding more than five thousand names. Each woman was also required to list a person we could contact in case of an emergency. When you add those names in, ten thousand people are listed. The book is a map not just of Harrisburg but the entire state: Main Line mansions near Philadelphia, shacks in the coal regions up north, missions on skid rows everywhere. Sometimes, in the margins, I note who referred a particular girl, inking in senators, congressmen, and clergy. Harrisburg is only ninety miles from Washington, D.C., and a handful of referrals have even come from White House administrators working under Roosevelt, Truman, and most recently Eisenhower. Can anyone on this list get our case thrown out of court?

Some people live without compasses, and for years I've counted myself among them, roaming whatever moral direction I pleased, changing course if and only when it suited me. But the arrest brings uncertainty. On the one hand, I've always believed discretion for our patients to be sacred. On the other, I didn't expect to retire so soon. Why should we take the fall when ten thousand others are complicit? The ledger is a dangerous double-edged weapon. It can be guided to favor our case or turned to give evidence against us.

I leaf through the book and remember the faces, the horrible stories: incest, beatings, rape—and ordinary housewives who just didn't want another baby. Every case was different: girls under twenty, wide-eyed and frightened, women over forty, tired and drawn, career girls, sensible and sure, tough girls who often cried more than the others, bad girls who were foulmouthed and mean, the sick, the abused, the adulterous, the jilted, the lovelorn, the mentally infirm, and of course the damned. We saw every religion, every educational background, and every size of bank account.

Some of the women hemorrhaged, and there was that lone woman from Lewiston, an attractive bookkeeper, the only patient in fifteen years we ever lost. She bled to death.

Some of the women befriended me and over passing time still send me Christmas cards, grateful to have been in the hands of a good doctor and not left to one of the butchers. Other women came and went and are long forgotten. Our practice was the place where women's terrors intersected women's dreams. And would I have cared about any of it if I hadn't also been making piles of money?

I'm forty-four years old, and suddenly I see how I've blinded myself to the many small, regrettable qualities I possess—pride and greed foremost among them. Over the years a series of tiny transgressions has led to even greater ones, and now I'm left to weigh the stone I carry around where my heart used to be.

I've never been good at keeping a diary. Looking back, the age and experience I've acquired seem to heighten my naiveté and ignorance. I read my old words and feel stupid all over again, and like many people who keep records, I've grown obsessed with hiding this one, always fearing the secret reader who will stumble across it and snoop on me. Yet now I realize I've always written with just that person in mind. Many times I've thought of tearing up the book or placing it in the fire, but I've held on. I stare at it and somehow its pages lay my life bare. Herein I see myself as others might.

Still, this ledger cannot replace what I remember, for now I see that what one doesn't write is often more important than what gets written. Perhaps none of this matters to anyone but me, but I am someone, and suddenly it seems important not to forget that lonely, dirt-poor girl I once was—if only to know how I ended up here, to know how I became Verna Krone.

BOOK

One

When Miss Castle comes up the hill, the sun has already baked the road white and the hem of her dress is caked with dust. It surprises everyone that she's walked out here in the hottest part of the day. An early heat wave has struck, unusual in this part of Pennsylvania, and we've taken the kitchen chairs outside and set them under the beech tree hoping to catch a breeze. Hazel and I take turns sitting in the straight-back chair with the plank bottom, trading it for the more comfortable black one with the broken cane seat. Mom is feeding Myrtle and has taken her apron off. Her dress is spotted with milk and porridge and I know she feels ashamed at not looking washed in front of a schoolteacher.

Miss Castle tells Mom I am her best pupil and asks if my leaving school can't be put off. She says I'm good with numbers and have a way with words far advanced for a girl of fourteen. It makes my face warm to hear the praise, but I know it's true. Mom shifts the baby on her hip. "Try to remember you're not the only blade of grass in the meadow," she reminds me.

Mom explains how she was lucky to find me a job housekeeping. Pop's condition has worsened. He hasn't worked in almost a year. Miss Castle looks across the yard to where Pop is sleeping on an old cedar plank pulled from the barn. You can see she is taken aback by how much older Pop is. Whatever Irish charm or silver-tongued sweet talk he used to attract Mom I'll never know, but he was fifty-four and she was nineteen when they met and that was more than fifteen years ago.

Hazel holds a bit of string over Pop's face, tickling his mustache. Miss Castle says not to disturb him on her account and asks if he's seen a doctor. Mom tells about the one who came out. When he saw we didn't have the two dollars to pay him, he never came back. "We're not common," she says. "We always paid our way or did without, but he was coughing up blood."

Miss Castle nods. Then we all stand there looking at the ground, the angry sun beating down. The freshly turned fields seem to absorb the heat, and the air is fragrant with the smell of lilac. Mom offers Miss Castle some tea but she only takes a dipper of water. I can see both of them struggling to stay calm.

Miss Castle comes over to where I stand. Her closeness, and the surprise of her kneeling here in our yard, suddenly makes me realize that we might never see each other again. I fight to keep tears from spilling down my cheeks. From inside her bag, she takes out a cloth-bound journal. "You've got to be your own teacher now. Write in it every day and you'll never be lonely," she says, handing me the book. Then she puts her arms around my shoulders and hugs me tight. Mom turns her head away. Our people don't hug or kiss.

After Miss Castle has departed, the knowledge that I'm really leaving here makes me notice every detail of our cabin, the funny way Hazel and Myrtle bunch the hems of their flannel nightgowns to kneel on them when they say their prayers, how they stand on tiptoe to help pull back the bed, how they sleep with their warm bodies pressed against mine while I lie awake with the hurt of leaving like the hand of God pressing down on my chest.

In the morning, Mom and I take the two biggest twig baskets and go out to cut spinach and rhubarb. The dry grass crackles when you walk on it, and it makes my ankles itch. As we bend over between the rows, I ask Mom how come Buckley doesn't have to leave school like I do. "Buck needs to study so he's prepared to raise a family of his own," she says.

Raise Cain is more like it, I think. I've heard women say that you always favor a boy, and the thought makes my blood boil. Buck thinks he's special because he's the only one among us born in St. Louis. He brags about it. Pop was married before. His first wife died and he left a daughter in St. Louis. I've heard he went back out there around 1907, after he took up with Mom, and that Mom followed him. Mom is so pale and withdrawn, she can barely get herself to ride the buggy seven miles to New Bloomfield—it's unthinkable for me to imagine her heading to the depot, buying a ticket, and chasing Pop all the way to St. Louis. And where did she get the money? But that's all I know of it, scraps I've overheard, and how Buck was born out there. I live to wonder about the rest.

This season the garden is sparse again. Pop never plants enough, and two grown-ups and four kids have appetite. What spinach there is will cook down and disappear, so Mom sends Buck and me out to pick dandelion to stretch it. The dandelion is big and tough and we have to go all the way down beyond the lower meadow to find some fit to eat. I do most of the picking while Buck runs off like he always does when work needs doing.

Once I've filled the sack, he returns to pluck a few leaves and take full credit. Coming home, Buck follows the tar road the county put in last spring. Crossing the bridge, he looks down and sees a big mama snake in the shallow part of the creek, her babies swimming all around her. Of course he can't leave her be no matter how I beg. He piles some rocks by his feet and begins to throw them over the side. The first few miss. The snake could swim away and escape, but she stays to scoop her babies up into her mouth and swallows them. The next rock lands on top of her and pins her down. "Leave her be," I plead, but he won't listen, his face alive like it always is when he's doing something mean. The snake keeps wriggling about, and I'm worried we'll be late for supper and get whipped. Finally her coils slacken, and he goes down the bank to tie a string around the body. It stretches almost a yard long.

Coming home, Buck pulls the snake and I walk behind watching the damp line it leaves in the dust. Then all of a sudden, something makes me skip forward to step on the snake's tail. He yanks the body, and the skin stretches shiny and taut, hanging suspended like that for a full second before the head splits right off. The babies held there fall about and lie wriggling on the tar road. Buck gets so mad he swings his fist to hit me, but I run ahead while he stays back to stomp them out. I look over my shoulder and see his cheeks flushed with an anger that's also his pleasure.

If Mom favors Buck, Pop on the other hand favors me. He likes me because, he says, I act like I'm bought and paid for and proud of the bargain. He also likes that I'm trying to write in a journal. "Dip your pen in the ink of truth," he says, "and for God's sake don't describe things better than they are."

"We don't own a bottle of ink," I tell him. And it's true. In school, Miss Castle once gave us the address of a factory in Philadelphia where we could write and order some India ink very cheap. She said ink promoted good penmanship. But Mom wouldn't hear of it, saying, "What if it rains and the ink washes off the card?" It was a foolish point, but a point nonetheless. So any writing we do still gets done with a large graphite pencil Mom keeps in the kitchen drawer. Before my journal, it only got brought out every blue moon to scratch penny postcards to Aunt Varnie detailing the date and time of some visit.

Mom cautions me against too much writing. "We're not the kind that can sit around with our nose in books," she says. Pop hollers that's nonsense, that people from all backgrounds benefit from books and that no one has proven that more than the Irish. He goes on and on about our mettle, the battles of Aughrim and the Boyne, the Irish kings. Mom hunches her shoulders with disgust. "Big talk from a man who can't earn wages enough to support his family," she says.

And she's right. Pop is a horse trader. Being a horse trader is as close to vagrancy as one can get without going to jail. Horse traders often travel in pairs, and Pop used to partner with a small, red-faced brute named Fielding O'Malley. They'd roam around exchanging one swaybacked mare for another, hoping to gain some advantage, better hooves, better coat, better teeth. But it's a shiftless life because nags are never thoroughbreds. We haven't heard from Fielding O'Malley in some time and Pop says he probably died on his back in a henhouse.

Pop isn't a good provider but he sure can talk. In the evenings, on the porch, his voice will get slow and solemn as he sweeps his hand across the sky. "With the evening clouds the rapturous shade of violet you see before you now," he'll say, "we'd scan the land to evade some gun-eyed farmer—then lash! O'Malley would snap the buggy whip round the head of some stray chicken, hauling it up into our laps as we'd leap and ride away."

After they've stolen the chicken, they stop for the night, build a fire, pack the dead bird in mud, feathers and all, and then bake it in the embers. Once it is done, they crack open the hardened clay, and the skin and feathers peel clean off, leaving only hot, juicy meat against the bone.

I've heard this story many times, but tonight, maybe because my leaving tomorrow has made me sore, I say, "That sounds like the most rotten way to eat chicken I've ever heard." Mom starts to laugh and drops her knitting; she covers her mouth with her hand and has to leave the porch. Pop doesn't get angry but I know he's injured. He draws a long, slow, wheezy breath and says, "Girl, never knock a man who's scouting out the best times of his life."

2

To reach the Wertz farm from here takes a walk of several hours—up over the mountain, down through the gap, then across Cumberland County. They say the Wertz property is really owned by a well-to-do family named McCormick. We learned about Vance McCormick in school because he went to France with President Wilson to put a stop to the Great War. There are wealthier families in Pennsylvania—the Carnegies of Pittsburgh, the Biddles of Philadelphia—but the McCormicks do all right. Pop says they own the ironworks in Harrisburg along with a steel mill and about twenty outlying farms. The farms are prosperous and Mom says most men would give their right arm to oversee a McCormick farm. Pop needles her, saying, "A one-armed man would have a heck of a time threshing." "It's an honor," Mom snaps back. "It says he's trustworthy." Pop snorts with irritation. "The rich get richer."

I've only ever seen Mr. and Mrs. Wertz once, in New Bloomfield, climbing into their buggy. The skin across his face was tight and handsome in a way that comes from hard work. They say he's an industrious plain-vanilla man with good character. Her face was full, with dark brown eyes, and I remember admiring a yellow hat pin she wore made to look like a bumblebee.

I don't have enough clothes to pad a crutch—two dresses, a cotton nightgown, a petticoat, a few pairs of stockings, and some undergarments—but Mom lets me take the leather box Pop used to carry when he was horse-trading. The thing isn't heavy, which is good, as the walk over there will take almost four hours.

The Wertz farm has a hundred and forty acres, rocky but rich and dark, with a lot of acreage set aside for cows. Mr. Wertz meets me at the gate and introduces himself. He shakes my hand and says, "Oh, you're a big-boned girl." My cheeks grow hot. He tells me how Mrs. Wertz has gone to the farmer's market in Carlisle, where she peddles eggs, butter, cream, and vegetables. She'll be back by evening. "We hope you'll be at home here," he adds.

The house is not as fine as you might think after seeing the two of them in town, but it's built of long, cool bricks that defy the weather. The kitchen sits in back, far bigger than any I've ever seen. The countertops are oak but worn down with knife cuts. I guess they never heard of cutting boards, which even we have. You can see why they need a hired girl: the knobs on the cupboards are crusty, an open barrel of oats sits right by the door, and the dishrag smells sour.

Beyond the kitchen door stands a milkhouse, and inside, on its wall, a two-year-old calendar hangs, its pages curled and yellow, specked with fly dirt. He sees me notice it. "Mrs. Wertz wrote down all the birds she saw in the garden that year and now she can't seem to part with it," he says, like we both agree it's odd to care about such a thing.

The parlor is well-appointed—an upright piano and some glazed candlesticks, pottery vases, a grandfather clock, and a morris chair with doilies pinned to it. Four good-sized bedrooms are upstairs. He and she share one, another is for sewing, and one is for their six-year-old daughter, Penny, who sits on the floor playing with a gallon jar of buttons. She's small for her age, with dark hair, a red snot nose, and blue eyes so pale they look like bottle glass. "Are you from far away?" she asks.

"Over the mountain," I say.

The fourth bedroom has the curtains drawn. He pulls one panel aside and I can see the room faces the back, overlooking the stream. I am disappointed when he says it's only for guests.

My room is in the attic—hot as blazes. The sun can be felt baking the tin roof, and though they are heavily coated with pitch, the inside seams burn to the touch. He shows me four roofing nails tapped in the wall for hanging my clothes, then he leaves so I can unpack. I sit for a moment with a hollow feeling in my chest. The mattress is hand-sewn ticking, and flat. It hasn't had fresh stuffing in some time. That's one thing Mom is particular about, and we change the straw in our mattresses every fall.

I'm scared to be living with a family that's not my own. I miss Hazel and Myrtle. We've always slept in the same bed. When you've helped wash and feed babies since they were small, you can't help but feel they're like your own. It's so hot, but I'm not about to cry.

I put the leather box beside the bed like a table. I hear Mr. Wertz pumping water in the yard and from the tiny window in the gable see him put his head under the spout and soak himself.

I comb my hair, put on my apron, and compose myself. Once downstairs, I start by giving the kitchen a good scrub. Earlier in the day Mr. Wertz had killed a chicken and left it hanging over a basin to drain the blood. Without any instruction I know what to do—

clean and dress it, roll it in a bit of flour to keep the juice in, then roast it for supper. A set of dirty blue and white plates are stuck in back of a cupboard; farm scenes and animals are painted on them. I wash them off and the chicken looks nice on them. I make gravy like Mom used to when we had chickens; it comes out nice and smooth. Mrs. Wertz returns home from the market just before six and is pleased to find I have supper ready. "I can see I needn't have worried," she says, taking off her bonnet and shaking my hand.

Mr. Wertz sits at the head of the table, pours gravy on his plate, and eats biscuits like a wild man. His chair is made from hickory and the only one with arms. The rest of us sit on side chairs made from beautiful pecan wood. Six of them. The chairs and table match, and they're so smooth I keep running my hands over them.

There is little talk during the meal, but they do say my supper is good. Afterwards, while I do the dishes, a terrible lonely feeling comes over me. Warm soapwater on my hands always makes whatever is inside me want to come out. Later Mr. Wertz enters from the porch and gives me a rusty kerosene lamp to take up to the attic. "Don't burn the house down," he says. I wash off the glass chimney. Without the soot and grease it will offer better light.

3

I rise early, and Mr. Wertz shows me the barn and gives me a lesson in milking. "Hold your arm out away from your body and pretend your hand is the cow udder," he says. Then he takes some milk fat from a burlap-covered bucket and greases my fingers. He grips my pointing finger tight at the knuckle and brings pressure downward.

"Pinch the top closed before you squeeze down," he says. "Your hands got strength. That's good!"

It appears to amaze him when I sit down on the stool and go to work. Not to seem a know-it-all, I'm too polite to let him know that on more than one occasion I've helped Aunt Varnie milk cows.

Here we milk twice a day. Seven cows are mine. Mr. Wertz does ten, and Otis, the hired man, has hands so tough that he can do twelve in the same amount of time. Afterwards, I scald the pails and strainers with water boiled in the washhouse. Then we come inside, where Mrs. Wertz has breakfast ready. She's not much of a cook; her bacon's underdone, and you could shingle an outhouse with her pancakes.

Mrs. Wertz's face is finely featured, pretty, but gone plump with age. The weight that she carries in her hips makes her the kind of person who in a house fire might not get to where she needs to go, but despite this her feet are surprisingly nimble.

Later, when Mrs. Wertz hauls herself up to the attic to see how I've arranged my room, she shows me how to tie an old sack on the end of a broom to pull the cobwebs down from the rafters. "This heat is scorching my hair," she says with alarm, and carefully navigates herself back down the stairs.

There is a lonely quality to Mrs. Wertz. Like she's mourning the girl she used to be. I've never been delicate or pretty like her. Mom says I'll outgrow my baby fat, but hope is fading. At least I'm not as big as that girl who lives down at the foot of Polecat Road. She must munch pie in her sleep to get that size.

At night, in the darkness, from the floor below I can hear their bedsprings squeak. I know that means he's loving her. In the morning, I watch him through the lace curtains, an easy stride—hasn't a care in the world. Only the shadows under his eyes give him away.

Back to work. Dredge the catfish in cornmeal, brush my fingers, rinse the dishes, and head out to the garden to hoe the lettuce beds. At supper, Mr. Wertz compliments my fish fry. Mrs. Wertz folds her lips in like she's sucking on a peppermint.

Another wave of heat strikes. Pop would call the attic a sweat-box, and it leaves my body tired, like I've never been to bed. The hot sun couldn't care less and just keeps baking the air. In the barn-yard, the smells grow putrid, and in the evening, I tell Mrs. Wertz that we used to set our chairs outside under the trees. Her face looks shocked. "I wouldn't dream of putting my good wedding chairs in the dirt."

This morning when I came down, I saw that the bed in the guest room was unmade and reckoned he slept there. Why? It's a mystery, as a few nights ago they were so cozy. Later, when I go up-stairs to wash up, I see she's made his bed but has left the rest for me to do.

While cleaning rhubarb, I feel a spell come over me. The mira-cles Pop talks about, eggs from chickens, flour from grain, the way cows eat grass and clover and turn them into milk, which in turn gets churned to butter—for the first time I understand what he meant, "the confoundedness of it all," how everything in a room, including the room, can be traced back to something else, the daily miracles taken for granted. My left hand holds the eggbeater. I open it, close it, open it, turn my head away. I can still move my hand even without looking—a miracle, taken for granted. My other hand runs along the edge of the mixing bowl, the smooth, cool stone-ware, clay pulled from the earth. Then my mood darkens. Pop talks of miracles because he can't provide anything else. Then I know the voice of Mom is passing through me and I feel ashamed. Pop has always been good to me.

The lack of rain means the water in the well is so low it tastes like cold earth. We haul buckets from the pond to put on the gar-den. Penny tries to help, her mother's idea, but at her age the best she can do is make a lot of slop. Mrs. Wertz acts blind and says, "Isn't it wonderful how Penny lends a hand?" But every time I turn my back, she's eating bugs or has her fingers out over the hog pen. Otis takes a mason jar and traps a bee in it. The lid gets punctured with an icepick for air. Penny carries the jar around all afternoon, long after the bee dies. Only when she falls asleep can the jar be taken from her room. Mrs. Wertz whispers to me that Otis spent close to ten years in the state penitentiary and shouldn't be trapping things.

No doubt she'd have preferred to make that remark to Mr. Wertz, but he's out, busy with a mare that's lying on the floor of the barn after eating some bad hay. Earlier we looked in on him and he was deep in concentration, smoothing his hands gently up the mare's tensed-up rib cage.

In a day, the mare makes a full recovery, and on Sunday they hitch her to the wagon and drive to church. They say I can come with them or go home to see Mom and Dad. I opt for the latter and jump down at a bend in the road heading for Sterretts Gap. I sing to make quick time with my feet.

Climbing the hill, it shocks me to realize how small our house is. Myrtle and Hazel see me in the distance and come running. Buck is out hunting and I'm glad to visit Mom and Pop in his absence. I tell them all about the Wertz farm, how the plants are holding up and how I've never seen such bounty. Mom shows surprise to hear Mrs. Wertz isn't much of a cook. "Well, who'da thought." I tell how they've got an electric lightbulb hanging in the kitchen and that Mr. Wertz said it cost more than a hundred dollars to run the wire out from the main road. Mrs. Wertz says on an overcast morning in winter, the golden light is worth every dime. Pop says the McCormicks probably footed the bill. Both Mom and Pop seem satisfied that I've made a good start. He seems less tired, and Mom says he's having a better time of it. Hazel is doing a good job of keeping his handkerchiefs clean.

By midafternoon, the sun is red-hot, and I'm already dreading the return. We take the girls down to the creek to sit on the cool moss, put our feet in the water, and recite all the poems we know. I try "The Frost Is on the Pumpkin," by James Whitcomb Riley, but Mom interrupts and says, "That's an autumn poem, not right for a hot day."

Pop spends the afternoon sitting on the edge of the porch with a cool rag on his head. He only eats a small dish of rice pudding for supper. Heat always did make him lose his appetite. He tells the story about how he met Mom at the hotel in New Bloomfield. "When I walked into that dining room and saw your tight-waisted mother bustling between tables, it was the mist of morning and she was like a vision from God." He was there to partake of a breakfast he'd earned by shoveling manure in the stables. The owner had let him sleep there for the night. He was just getting to the best part, about how years don't matter when you find true love, when Mom puts down her needle and says, "Thirty-five years is too big a difference for even true love." Bitterness hangs in the air like a fog.

Pop sinks together. Cold eyes reveal his pain. But failure is only failure if you want someone to feel sorry for you, and he's the one always telling me not to describe things as better than they are. He used to have a temper that wouldn't allow such bossing or sass. Once he pulled an axe on Mom in the middle of the night when she said she was leaving.

4

I'm scalding the milk strainers. He comes in and stands behind me, as though to check my work. I pretend not to notice. He'll laugh if he sees his attention makes me bashful. He doesn't like to go unnoticed.

Mrs. Wertz brings lemons home from the market. I make a lemon sponge pie, pleased to follow Mom's recipe from memory: 1 cup sugar, 1 tablespoon flour, 3 egg yolks, ¼ cup lemon juice, ½ teaspoon grated rind, 2 tablespoons melted butter, 3 egg whites (beat), 1 cup milk. Blend everything, fold in the egg whites, add the milk last, and bake in a crust. The secret is adding some extra lemon juice, and to open the oven door from time to time so the top doesn't brown too quickly.

Mr. Wertz goes on and on about how good it is. It's a wonder he's been able to keep himself fit on her cooking. When I go home I'm going to get Mom's recipe for angel food cake. The strawberries are so abundant here I don't have to be spare with a sauce, and I dream about bringing some home for the girls.

Then Mr. Wertz enters the barn, where I've set my stool by the flank of a cow, places his hands on my shoulders, and says, "The girl who did the milking before you enjoyed my company."

I shake free and don't look at him. Mrs. Wertz isn't back from taking berries to market, but if she was, I wonder if his big talk would amuse her. I'm ashamed that Otis is within earshot, but if he overhears anything, he pretends he doesn't and just keeps working.

Two days later, at dawn, Mr. Wertz climbs up to the attic. His wife is downstairs percolating coffee. My bed is made and I'm already washed. There isn't time to pull my dress over my head, so I hold it up in front of me. "I just wanted to make sure you didn't oversleep," he says, all foxy. I'm speechless and can't believe it as he stands there looking at me for way too long.

I'm hopping mad that he can pull such shenanigans. I'll wear my clothes to bed from now on if I have to.

The milking goes on as usual. Otis and Mr. Wertz talk. I come back into the kitchen, wondering if his wife senses anything, but her face is blank and unknowing. She comprehends only how lucky she is to have him, talks about him all the time, the way he likes his noodles cooked, his shirt starched, his pipe cleaned. If I were her, I'd do the same.

The next day, Mrs. Wertz and I are out digging taters when an aeroplane flies over our heads. It's going due west. She hollers for Otis and Mr. Wertz and they come running out from the barn, where they were sharpening knives. After it's gone, we're so excited that we take a break from chores, go to the house, and drink cold ginger tea on the porch. We keep a watch on the sky but the aeroplane is not seen again.

A few more days pass, and after a good soaking rain the lower meadow is suddenly green, dotted with dandelions and wild onions. To think, only yesterday Otis was saying the stream was so low the fish were getting freckles. He and Mr. Wertz plant broom corn. They're about ten days behind. The regular corn was harrowed last month and some little green sprouts are already visible.

Penny and I sneak away, lie on our backs in the meadow, and watch the clouds drift by. I hold on to an apron of fresh-picked peas. She lifts her arms and tries to touch the sky.

In the afternoon we ride with Mr. Wertz to the smithy to watch old Pose, the sand-colored workhorse, get shod. The smithy gives us each a handful of peanuts his brother brought up from the South. He teaches us the words to "Under a Spreading Chestnut Tree, the Village Smithy Stands."

I've begun to teach Penny all the songs I know. She likes "Cucumber Doll." We almost cry when we sing it because the poor doll gets left out in the rain. Otis taught us "The Wreck of the Old '97," about a train that was going round the bend at ninety miles an hour. At the end it warns the ladies, "Never speak harsh words to your true-lovin' husband, he may leave you and never return."

Mom always liked "Mary and the Wild Moon," another sad one about a baby who freezes to death, and Mrs. Wertz is teaching us one about an Indian maid called "Pretty Red Wing." We're still learning this one but there's a line about the "pale moon shining," and then it says "she was sleeping, her sad heart bleating." I think that's wonderful, to describe her heart as bleating. I told them all how before Pop took sick he was partial to hymns, especially "Amazing Grace," and how in stormy winter weather we'd prop our feet up on the stove and sing to keep warm.

5

The traffic is heavy on the road on account of a three-day camp meeting over in William's Grove. Some women come for Mrs. Wertz, and so Penny and I get to tag along. I've been to camp meetings before with Aunt Varnie and Mrs. Darcey. Otis thinks I'm crazy when I say I find them uplifting.

The tent is jammed with people singing and listening to the gospel, their faces lit by lanterns hammered to the tent poles. Up in front a man in a brown velvet vest stands with a white dove chained to his forearm. He's telling everyone, "Rest in the Lord, and find your way to Christ." Two rows in front of us, a woman falls to the ground between the folding chairs, her body writhing to and fro like it's being shot at. Her dark dress picks up the sawdust that is spread around, while the muscles in her throat tighten like ropes. Then she begins to speak in tongues.

As the mayhem grows, Penny gets frightened and begins to wail. "I want to get her blessed," Mrs. Wertz calls out, but the crowd moving forward is too thick, and when Penny won't stop her caterwauling, I'm instructed to forget the blessing and to lead her home at once. It annoys me to no end to have to leave early and miss the rest of the show. Walking back to the Wertzes', I do not speak to Penny. When we enter the kitchen, I tell Otis what happened. "Bible thumpers," he says with disgust, and retires out to his shack beside the barn.

The weekend blossoms with beautiful weather, though a bit on the cool side, and while on my way home to visit Mom and Pop I stop at the general store. It's named Shad's for the man who owns it. He's got bolts of fabric and dry goods and a ready selection of tools in the back. I buy licorice whips and banana taffy for Hazel.

When I get home there are four wagons standing in the lane. It must be some kind of husking party but it's not the right season for that—and on a Sunday? Pop is in the kitchen, lying on top of the woodbox in his good suit, a clean horseblanket wrapped around his legs. He died Saturday afternoon. The skin on his face hangs sallow and stiff and some flies are already on him.

"There was no one to send for you," Mom says quietly. "I prayed you'd come along."

The house is stifling and I run outside and lean against the back wall. The logs are warm from taking in the sun. I cross my arms over my chest as tears shiver through me. Buckley and Pop's best friend Abe are down by the barn. I watch them prop planks onto two sawhorses, nailing pieces together to make a coffin. Buck has carved a board with dates and he waves it in my direction. "Don't cry," he hollers. "Eighteen fifty-one to nineteen twenty-four—most men would be glad for them numbers."

Later they take the short-handled shovel up to the ridge to dig a hole. They return and carry the coffin into the kitchen. Mom stays in the other room with Aunt Varnie, and everyone else waits in the yard, hot from wearing black clothes in the sunshine. Finally the men come out carrying the box that now holds for eternity the body of my pop. They all go up the hillside and I stay behind to look after the children, who sit in a row alongside the house. The men stop once to rest under the weight of the body, their shadows like specks on the ridge. I try to hear their words, but the sound won't travel, so I sing "Amazing Grace" to the restless children.

Pop's death doesn't seem to make a difference to anyone but me.

When they come down from the ridge it's afternoon. Mrs. Darcey has brought a whole shoebox full of fried chicken, and Aunt Varnie baked a raisin pie. "A couple more weeks and the cherries would have been in season," she says. Mom keeps rubbing her hand over the wood grain in the table boards while we eat. Her lovely red hair is mostly gray now. Nobody says anything about anything.

When evening comes, Aunt Varnie coaxes Mom to write a post-card to Delia in St. Louis. "With all their money, the least they can do is provide a proper marker for the man."

"Most likely we are wasting a good piece of copper on the stamp," Mom says.

Then they talk about asking Grandma Peffer for help with money and decide no good will come of it. "I'm sure she'll say if we don't know how to provide for our children, we shouldn't have had any."

Mrs. Darcey says it's getting late and that she'll post the card at Shad's and see that I get dropped off near the gap road to Wertz's. "Your mom sure is lucky to have you working," she says.

I nod.

As I come back over to Cumberland County, the air on the mountain has a couple of cold spots, like someone pulling back the blankets on a chilly morning. Though it is June, I haven't felt warm all day.

Inside the house, I tell Mrs. Wertz that Pop passed away. It's the first time I've said the words out loud, and it is a struggle not to cry. She heats me up a plate of soup. I eat it and am rinsing out the dish when Mr. Wertz comes in and says, "Please accept our condolences." I thank him and, once he's back outside, go right up to the attic.

The next day I disappear. I lie in the upper meadow among the wildflowers. Maybe it's the heat, but I don't care. Let her look after her own child for a while. The ground is hard against my stomach, my arms are close around my head to block the light, and I breathe in the dark smell of earth. No one is alive but me.

Later, in the middle of the night, I wake. Someone is sitting on my bed.

Heart pounding. The hair on the back of my neck stands up.

I hear breathing and I think of the earthy meadow.

Then someone rises and slips back down the stairs.

For a long time I lie awake hoping I imagined it, that the darkness is playing tricks on me.

In the morning, in the washhouse, I'm doing laundry. His slow walk. The wet clothes. Then he's up against me. Pressed tight. He's strong. I smell the sweat of work on his overalls. My heart is a hammer. He lifts my hand to touch. I flinch when I feel his leg. "Wanna hold you," he whispers. "No one will know." Through the window, his wife is at the line pulling wet sheets from the basket, a mouthful of clothespins. He doesn't love her.

In the evening he gives me a book of poems including some by Gerard Manley Hopkins and Elizabeth Barrett Browning. "I remember you saying you like poems." Half dead from work, I leave the lantern on as long as I dare, but the words are impossible to comprehend. I think of Pop's body underground, restless like sprouts growing in a sack of potatoes. There are some doors that should never be opened. I blow out the wick and pray, God, please don't leave me. I don't want to be alone in the dark.

· **6** ·

Mr. Wertz has gone to Newport, Mrs. Wertz is upstairs lying down, and I'm left alone to deal with the strange man who comes to the gate in a rickety flatbed wagon. His skin is dark like the leather on my shoe, and I know Pop would say that he is one of Mr. Lincoln's citizens. He stands by the porch waiting, doesn't knock or even put a foot on the steps, just stands there waiting.

Penny and I look through the lace curtains and he smiles at us. His brown face is like an old twisted tree. After a while I get to thinking that even if it is the devil himself, I'd better see what he wants.

He bows real deep as I open the door, but he doesn't come up on the porch. "How do, ma'am," he says. No one has ever called me that before. He takes a shiny skillet from his satchel and says, "With Christmas coming, you might consider making someone a gift of tinware. You might even buy it for yourself." That he is speaking to me about such things leaves me so surprised I can't utter a word, not to mention that he's talking Christmas in July.

"They never leave me no money," I finally sputter. He gives a smile and nods, puts his cap back on his head and says, "Before I move on, may I have a drink of water?" I go and get him a glass, then stand by the pump while he drinks three times. Then he takes the bucket and gives a drink to his horse, an old worn-out nag that looks like it can't wait to leave this world.

I've seen colored men in New Bloomfield only a couple of times. They come through on the logging crews. But I've never spoken to one or seen one up close. The backs of the man's shoes are trod down sideways—many miles have been walked since they were new—but I'm surprised to see they're well polished. By now I'm no longer afraid, and the man is quite friendly. He tells me that in his lifetime he's been to five states—Pennsylvania, Maryland, Virginia, New Jersey, and Delaware.

"My daddy was well traveled," I tell him. "He went as far as Ohio and Missouri."

The man smiles, nods, and gets ready to leave. He picks up the reins to the old horse, then turns one last time. "You wouldn't by chance have some leftover bread you were thinking of pitching?"

"No. We don't," I say. "Mr. Wertz wiped his eggs with the last piece at breakfast, and we're planning biscuits for supper."

"Thank you kindly just the same." He tips his hat and goes off down the lane.

When I come back inside, Mrs. Wertz is up. She's been watching from the window and is in a fury. "How could you give a drinking glass to a man like that? You don't know what diseases he has or what he might do. And telling all our private business, and using Mr. Wertz's name." She makes me take the glass out back and smash it, says it isn't fit to use no more.

Afterwards, I go by myself to the upper meadow. My throat and rib cage ache as I lie under the sky; the clouds moving above me are sadder than any song. I feel lost like the cucumber doll and wish somebody would wrap their arms around me.

When I come back to the house, Mr. Wertz is standing on the

porch drinking a glass of water. Is this a mockery? No? He's thirsty. Beads of sweat glisten on his temple. Penny is playing outside by herself and it's time to mix the biscuits. Nothing more is said, and I'm grateful when I realize Mrs. Wertz didn't mention anything to him.

The next day all is forgotten. Mrs. Wertz gives Penny and me an errand: she wants us to go over to the grist mill to see if we can find one of her pale yellow work gloves. She dropped it there last week.

The miller's wife scours the ground with us, but the glove is not found. We're back on the road headed home when the sky darkens, and before we can take shelter a summer shower is suddenly upon us. Out of nowhere, Mr. Wertz appears in the buggy. "Get in," he yells.

We ride halfway home and when we come to the covered bridge that spans the lower creek, he stops like I knew he would. "Let's wait for the rain to ease up," he says. He lets Penny scramble down to look for frogs. "Stay under the bridge and out of the rain," he warns her. Then he and I are alone.

Neither of us speaks. The air is chilly. My skin is goosefleshed. The heavy rain pounds the roof overhead. His hands are cold. His mouth is over mine. I don't know if I want him to hold me, but his arms are warm and I get still and let him. "Slide over here," he whispers, and lifts my legs. It doesn't mean anything to me, but I hold him like it does. The light is dim, but I wish it were dark. When the pain comes, he puts his left hand over my mouth, then he keeps smoothing my hair with his right. "Don't worry," he says. "Don't worry."

I do worry, and hope that Penny won't notice the buggy rocking. He finishes. Arranges himself. Squeezes me tight. Then jumps down to find his daughter. When we get home Mrs. Wertz is standing at the kitchen door. Penny and I leap from the buggy as she unlatches the screen. "What took you so long?" she asks.

"We stopped inside the covered bridge to wait. Penny wanted to look for frogs."

"Did you find my yellow glove?"

I shook my head. "No, I'm sorry," I say, and hurry up to my room to wash.

· 7 ·

It rains too hard to do field work, rains for days. We're all cooped up. Otis goes out and drives some stakes in the mud and finds it hopeless. Mrs. Wertz can't move her bowels and splashes back and forth across the yard to the privy. She's getting on her husband's nerves. She and I make underpants from some flour sacks she bleached out. We trim them with bits of lace. They're as fine as any from a store.

For supper we make chicken and waffles. I burn the bottom of the gravy. Then I burn my hand on the skillet trying to save the whole mess. Mrs. Wertz brings a cool cloth to put on the burn. They eat the gravy anyway, and no one mentions it.

If only they had some books to distract me, to drive out the shameful feeling I get whenever I think of us inside the covered bridge. It gets so bad I read the *Farmer's Almanac*, and it just keeps raining. The last time he came upstairs at night, just before the storm, I pretended to be asleep, motionless like I was dead. But it didn't matter to him. He'd lie down with a ghost. Does she hear him in the quiet house? If she wakes does she think it's field mice scratching under the attic floorboards? He's taking chances. The rain makes everything worse.

Day after day, she and I keep sewing. We cut apple green cotton to make sunbonnets. In the center, long thin pockets are sewn with strips of cardboard slid in so the hats can be bent to fit our faces. Penny helps.

In the afternoon Mr. Wertz brings some gears in from the shed, and we clear the kichen table so he can spread them out to wipe them down with oil. He keeps getting up, pacing to the window, and each time she follows him with her eyes. She makes idle chatter, which I know he hates. She warns me about boys. "Try to pick a husband who's a good provider."

I nod, and keep my eyes on my needle and thimble.

At supper he talks more than usual, goes on and on about halting the thresher in the lower field on account of the rain. "God knows we'll need an ark if this keeps up," she says, more than once. She bakes him a lemon sponge pie for supper, using my recipe, and when she puts it on the table in front of him, he thanks her. You can see how tickled she is to get that kind of attention.

Finally Sunday comes, and the weather breaks to glorious sunshine. I head for home, stopping at Shad's to buy some candy. Orange taffy in my hand, the last hill behind me, my feet walk through the fern glen and jump over the swollen creek, muddy from all the rain. I catch my breath and then my heart stops: a dark motorcar almost as long as the porch is standing in front of our house. It startles me because nothing as elegant as this has ever been up here before. It must have breached the stream. I long to run my hands on the creamy leather seats, the shiny dark blue paint, the polished headlights, but I don't dare in case someone sees me from the window.

Inside the house, a woman in a green straw hat and a man in a brown suit stand as I enter. I'm dumbstruck to realize it is John and Delia traveling all the way from St. Louis. "We got your ma's postcard and came to pay our respects." They both shake my hand while I gape in amazement, then I join them at the table.

Mom rummages through the cedar chest and brings out a tintype showing Pop seated on a barrel chair, leaning back in a natty three-piece suit and a pair of scuffed-up boots. His hair is still dark. Behind him, his first wife stands. "I hardly knew my mother," Delia says, studying their faces. She is beautiful when she speaks, her brown hair tucked at the nape of her neck, an amazing light dust of powder on her cheeks.

Mom fiddles with her apron pockets. "I can't believe that's his likeness. He'd been unwell so long I almost forgot how fetching he was."

I can't stop looking at Delia, her pale green suit with little narrow jacket, the pattern too fine to be homemade. Woven in the handiwork around the collar and lapel is a piece of black velvet ribbon that makes a loop at the bodice to fit over a single black button. Oh my, it is elegant.

"I wish there was something of his to give you," Mom says, "but the truth is he didn't have nothing. He brought a nice glass cake plate when we took up housekeeping, but it broke the last time we moved."

"We didn't come to take anything," Delia says.

John is mostly quiet, but when he speaks his voice makes him sound like an important somebody. "Well, now as I recollect . . ." he says, or "One has to admit now . . ."

He and Delia ask me questions about school, then how I like my job.

"Verna's had longer schooling than most," Mom interrupts, as she brings forth a small pot with some mint tea and a saucer arranged with slices from an apple she probably picked up from the ground. Delia's tea is poured in the bone china cup kept on the curio above Mom's bed. Pop bought it at the World's Fair in St. Louis, years before he and Mom met. I've never seen anyone drink from it before. Delia stirs her sugar with a spoon and her movement is smooth, like smoke curling from a pipe. My own hands look like paws beside hers.

"Did you drive all the way from St. Louis?" I ask.

"The train," John says. "That car is rented from the hotel in Harrisburg."

Mom offers to fry them up some mush. They say they have to get back to town before dark. A silence falls. "If I'd known you were coming, I'd have cooked a real meal," Mom says. I wonder what she'd make it from.

If only I could speak, to ask if the stories Pop told are true. That John works for the steel man's union, that he had to skip town, leaving Delia behind because some men threatened to shoot him, and that he hopped a freight train with nothing but the clothes on his back. Pop said he scolded Delia, saying, "That's what happens to girls who take up with Catholics." But John was true, a man of his word, and Pop had to eat his words when after several months John finally sent for her.

But Mom would have a fit if I brought any of that up, even though it seems like they've run out of things to say. Then Myrtle starts wailing and they get the feeling Mom's holding up feeding her on account of their visit. "You sure you won't stay for supper," Mom says, with weakness in her voice. They both rise and make excuses about not wanting to drive over country roads in the dark.

Outside, John holds the automobile door open for Delia. What must it feel like to ride in an automobile like that? As they maneuver the big machine back down the hill, Mom says, "What a shame Buckley isn't here. I told them he was out trapping with Artie Sledge." Buck will be mad to have missed seeing the big car parked up here.

A few days later they return to put Pop's gravestone down. Though it's Thursday, Wertz lets me take off after the morning milking. When I arrive, John is already up on the ridge with the stonecutter from New Bloomfield. We all go up to see the marker, a nice square white stone that Pop would have called a waste, but we like it. "I still think of odds and ends I want to tell him," Mom says, her voice faint. Delia puts her arm around Mom's shoulder and says a sweet prayer. Her face looks beautiful against the yellow light. Then she notices the tiny wooden cross standing neglected and forlorn to one side of Pop's grave. After three years the pine is quite weathered and the carving has worn away. "If we'd have known, we could have bought a second marker," Delia says. Mom tries to pretend she's above feeling anything. "He was so small, we never got to know him."

Delia lifts her head and gazes outward. "You never forget a child you've buried." John, watching, reaches in his pocket for a roll of bills the likes of which I've never seen, pulls a few off for the stone-cutter, and orders a child's marker to be made.

"The baby's name was Patrick," I tell them. Mom looks like she'll start weeping and thanks John for his benevolence. His shoulders shrug.

Back at the house a kettle of chicken corn soup is waiting. Where Mom got the chicken is a mystery. After we eat, Hazel helps me wash dishes, while the rest of them gather outside on the porch. Then all at once, I notice their voices have hushed. Whoever is in the white rocker has stopped moving. I strain to hear. I think my name is mentioned, then the word *education*, and then my insides grow alive because I know they're talking about bringing me to St. Louis. Not a hair on my head moves as I wait for an answer. Then I hear Mom say that with Pop gone, "there's no way to get along without Verna. I need her to stay here."

John asks if there isn't some way for Buck to take charge. Mom answers John as though he's selling store-bought soap. "Buck can't be saddled with us," she says. "He's saving for his own family."

A short while later, we bid good-bye to John and Delia and watch their automobile go down the hill for the last time. How sad and uneven it all is.

8

Mrs. Wertz and I pick the bulk of the black cherries, taking turns climbing the ladder. I don't tell how sick I feel. We can them all and also put up thirty jars of strawberry jam and twenty jars of rhubarb. I'm so tired, I don't wash up properly, and in the morning ants are all over the kitchen. At supper she lets me cut the cherry pie; my lattice crust comes out perfect.

The next day it's the same, more cherries, more canning, more sickness. To pass the time Mrs. Wertz asks me about my family. I tell how when Mom was only nine she lost her mother. How all three daughters were called to the deathbed and given something. Varnie got a hairbrush with an ivory handle, Ida got a china brooch with painted flowers, and Mom got her mother's Bible. I don't tell how a few years later Granddad married Grandma Peffer, a hateful stepmother who refused to take his name. When Mom was fourteen, Grandma Peffer in a pique of anger took the heirloom Bible and threw it into the fire. Imagine, burning the only thing a girl has to remember her mother by. Despite this, Mom and Aunt Varnie still visit the old witch.

I'm sick every morning without fail. On Sunday I stop by Shad's and he's talking to a man in a plaid flannel suit. "That girl visits every week for candy," Shad says quietly. "She must want to keep herself sweet for Wertz." They laugh so hard I can smell the whiskey on their breath. I pretend not to hear. I know at times in my old dress I must look ignorant. Just then, a gray-haired woman steps out of a buggy on her way home from church. I know they won't act foolish in front of her. I pick and pay for jellied spearmint leaves, frosted with sugar and almost too beautiful to eat.

As I cross over the gap, the view on either side is grand. To gaze out over the valleys and wonder how many farms are stretched out there as far as the eye can see; how many horses; how many children; how many bales of hay? It makes one feel small.

Buckley comes in toward evening and acts half-decent for once. He and Artie Sledge have set up a camp and are trapping animals for a living. Must not be much of a living, because he nags Mom for a dollar. He would beg a chaw of tobacco from a dead man's mouth. I only make three and a half a week, and it hurts me to see her finally give the dollar to him. He's a piker if there ever was one.

On Monday morning I count it up and it's been forty-two days since Pop died. A dreary feeling hangs over me all day. Otis is too ashamed to show his face at the table, for on Saturday he cleared some brush to set some walnut fence posts, and the brush turned out to be poison. Now he's covered with a rash from head to foot.

With Otis laid up, Mr. Wertz and I do the milking alone. "Are you happy working here?" he asks.

"It's nice," I say, and lean over to wash dirt from a cow's udder. The other cows chew hay, their velvet brown eyes staring out. Scared he'll be angry, I don't know how to make him understand that I won't ever do it again.

The heat has made the flies worse. The manure draws them. We unlatch the privy door and they fly off and then buzz right back to where they started. Sometimes Penny and I race across the barnyard to outrun them. Other times, in the afternoon, if the sun is just right, the whole barnyard shines purple and green and the ground looks like it's moving.

In the evening the Wertzes send me up to the Hanlan farm to borrow a particular wrench that Otis needs to repair the gasoline engine in time for shelling corn. Up there and back takes me more than an hour, and I'm annoyed to be sent so late in the day after I've milked and cooked supper too. When I return they're all huddled in the dining room, and then I see that they're standing around cranking a tub of vanilla ice cream beside a black walnut birthday cake. Mrs. Wertz has taken butcher paper and cut out a snowflake shape and sprinkled powdered sugar through to make the cake top look like lace. They sing happy birthday and I'm beet red though I had mentioned my birthday to Mrs. Wertz the day before hoping for something like this.

After we partake of the confections, Mr. Wertz picks up his fiddle and Mrs. Wertz accompanies him on the piano. I watch his fingers on the strings. The music brings something out in him, something he doesn't want me to see. He asks her to sing but she declines. He badgers her, but no matter, she still won't put her voice to song. All of a sudden he falls into a sulk. He packs away his fiddle, like nothing is of any concern to him.

In the morning I'm sick again. It's so hot Otis says the hens are laying hard-boiled eggs. If that isn't enough, Mr. Wertz tastes the milk we've wrung out and spits it to the ground. "It's tainted," he mutters, his lips still white. One of the cows must have found a patch of wild garlic and it went all through the milk. We empty the offending buckets into the hog pen. Now we have to taste milk from each cow to see if we can recognize the criminal.

Otis says its mankind's job to force its will over nature. Seems to me nature is a lot tougher than people. Working a farm wears people down, especially the women. I begin to think Pop had the right idea in wanting to roam the world instead of tame it.

On Sunday Mrs. Wertz sends me home with two jars of last year's peaches for Mom. We've been canning the new crop and she wants to clear the shelves. Mom pours the peaches and syrup into a flat cake pan, drops biscuit dough across the top with a spoon, and bakes a cobbler. While we wait for it to cool, the cabin is quiet, just the old wall clock ticking. Mom lets out a couple of deep sighs and turns in my direction.

"Are you in trouble?" she asks, out of the blue, peering at me with squinted eyes.

I stay still. To speak a word will shame us all.

"Are you sure?"

"I'm sick every morning."

"Is it him?"

I nod.

Mom turns away. Then she pulls herself up from the table and goes to sit in the rocker for a good long while.

"I never would have thought he was the type to pester," she says, her voice low like an injured animal's. She's scared but trying to solve the situation in her mind. All of a sudden she rises, picks up the cobbler, opens the door, and throws it pan and all out on the porch. Hazel and Myrtle stare wide-eyed. Mom begins to sob, she just sobs and sobs. I cry too, for I'm to blame. When she's cried out, she blows her red nose in a handkerchief and goes out to scrape the cobbler off the floorboards of the porch before the raccoons can get it. There's no joy in it now, but we eat it anyway.

Once the girls are in bed, she takes out the washtub, her face grim. "I know some who have been helped this way." In the darkness I make three trips to the well for water that she boils on the stove. She throws handfuls of rock salt in the tub and tells me to undress and get in. "It'll be a shock to your system," she says. I follow her instructions and put a rag between my teeth. She takes two pot holders, lifts the kettle, tips it, and pours scalding water onto my stomach.

·   9   ·

Finally someone's using the guest room besides him. Two of Mrs. Wertz's sisters visit from Emmitsburg. We cook a capon with all the trimmings and eat early like it's Thanksgiving. I'm hurt when they ask me to serve. Mr. Wertz makes a big fuss over the sisters, laughs at their stories, tee-hee, haw-haw. I think I hate him now.

The skin on my stomach is sore and red. Whenever possible, I keep my hands in my apron pockets to keep the material away from my body. Sunday night, I walked in that position the whole way home. Pop always said our blood was rich with Irish rage and for the first time I think I know what he means, for despite all our efforts, I'm still sick every morning.

After supper, Mrs. Wertz plays piano and he accompanies her on the fiddle.

> *Took my girl to a dance one night*
> *Was a social hop*
> *We danced until th'lights went out*
> *An' th'music had to stop*
> *I took her to a restaurant*
> *The finest in the state*

She said she wasn't hungry
But this is what she ate:
A dozen raw, a plate of slaw,
A chicken and a roast
Some applesass
And asparagass
Soft shell crabs on toast.
A box of stew, and crackers too
Her appetite was immense.
When she asked for pie
I thought I'd die
For I had but fifty cents.

Of course I wasn't hungry
And didn't care to eat.
Expecting every moment
To be kicked out in the street.
She said she'd bring her folks around
Some night an' we'd have fun.
I gave the man my fifty cents
And then the fun begun.
He punched my nose
And tore my clothes
He hit me in the jaw.
He gave me a prize
Of two black eyes
And with me swept the floor.
If you've a hungry girl
Take my advice
Don't try it twice
If you've got but fifty cents.

After the morning milking, frying breakfast, and making all the beds, I come around the corner of the tractor shed and spy something moving in the shadows. I approach the doorway and see the older sister is bent over and he's behind her. The way he grips her hips as he pushes reminds me of the way animals carry on, rabbits or dogs, boys showing off their peckers after school. His head begins to turn in my direction, but I am already gone.

The day is agony. I'm too busy cooking and serving them to think. In the evening Mrs. Wertz descends the stairs dressed in a too-tight pink taffeta dress, carrying sheet music under her arm. Supper's a blur. Then they all go into the parlor. It's a fine party. This time it's the younger sister on piano with him on fiddle, a bottle of whiskey and a shot glass by his foot. My eyes pierce him like two blue pins.

Then Mrs. Wertz stands nervous in front of us all and begins to sing "Oh, Promise Me." Her voice is rich and pure. Everyone claps when she is finished. They goad her on to sing "Hearts and Flowers." They say her voice hasn't lost a thing, and I learn that as a young woman she studied music for a summer in Baltimore. At that time they talked of her going on to New York, and when she was nineteen, she was supposed to sing at a concert in Harrisburg, but two weeks before the program, the opera house burned to the ground.

The last song she sings alone is "After the Ball Is Over," and it's beautiful but sad. At the end of that one we all join her in "Auld Lang Syne."

It's past ten o'clock when we finally get to bed. He stays downstairs drinking whiskey and sometime after midnight I hear him creaking upstairs to the attic. He gets mad when he can't get the door to open, and stands outside cursing a blue streak under his breath. I lie under my quilt, terrified that he'll wake the house, and they'll all discover how I've jammed the lock with a bent horseshoe nail. His attempts to open the door are clumsy and unsuccessful. Eventually he goes back down.

In the morning, sick with shame, I dress and go to do the milking. Otis and I work alone. Afterwards Mr. Wertz enters the kitchen as I make breakfast. "Think you're smart," he hisses, but I'm too sick to look at the food, let alone him. I keep working. He goes out and slams the door. Once the ham and eggs are fried, the sisters come down in their traveling coats, their bags packed. They're leaving a day early and pass me without looking at me or speaking a word.

Mrs. Wertz does not come down and he does not come in to eat with them either; instead, he hitches up the team. I stay in the kitchen and when the sisters leave they make no good-bye.

Mr. Wertz doesn't return until evening. We're not sure where he spent the day. He plans to sit by the fire and looks all over for his good pipe.

"Penny, have you seen it?"

"No."

"What about you?"

"No," I say, cool as ice.

"You both sure you haven't seen it?"

"Nope."

But inside, I'm dancing. His pipe is rotting in the woods where I threw it.

·　10　·

When I arrive home, Mom is in bed with a wet cough and a fever. Hazel and Myrtle are in their nightclothes, their hair in tangles, everything a mess. They haven't had a hot meal in days.

I cook onion soup and every four hours spoon Mom a dose of tonic from a brown bottle Mrs. Hampton sent over. It seems to help her sleep. I write a postcard to Mrs. Wertz and say my mother is sick and that I'm needed here for the next week or so. Abe comes by and takes it to Shad's for mailing.

Abe visits the next day with a rabbit and again the next day with some trout. He quietly slouches in the cherry rocker at Mom's bed-side while I cook. He's not the neatest man to look at, has the man-ners of a lop-eared mule, even keeps his dusty hat on in the house, but he's got a kind heart, and knowing Pop has died, he feels a stew-ardship over us.

"You women are alone," he says, "so I ought to cut up some wood." He takes a log from a stack behind the house and drags it through the frozen mud and spends all afternoon chopping and then stacking the wood on the porch. My gratitude makes me al-most hug him.

On the fourth day, Mom wants her hair brushed out. That means she's feeling better. "Is there anything you're wanting for?" Abe asks when he visits. "A hundred dollars," Mom replies, and her kidding is a sign she really is feeling better. I wish I could say the same.

A week passes. The tonic bottle is empty so that means a trip to Mrs. Hampton, an hour's walk. Abe would go but I decide the exer-cise and fresh air might do me good, besides the path back through the mountains is too steep for his sled or wagon; even in summer it's chilly, with cold pockets of air lodged there. Pop used to say that mountain air had a bite that could freeze fire. When I arrive at Mrs. Hampton's, I peer through the chicken wire windows of a rabbit hutch built on her porch. The poor rabbits press their gray pelts against the rear wall of the warrens for what little heat the house gives off.

"Come in, puff-a-muffin," Mrs. Hampton says when I knock. She touches my hands, then leans in to study my eyes. "Mom's get-ting better," I say, handing her the bottle.

Mrs. Hampton's son is scrubbing dishes at the sink; he doesn't speak and his heavy-lidded gaze wanders off in odd directions. I'm relieved when she says to follow her down to the mossy cellar. In the dark, on the stone steps, strange, musty things brush the top of my head, and when she swings the lantern up, it is possible to see dried plants hanging from wires pegged to the beams. On one wall, shelves hold mason jars, lined up and labeled with strips of butcher paper fastened with drops of candle wax. The jars are labeled with neat handwriting—burdock, nightshade, elm bark, plum stone.

She talks the whole time she works. She asks about school, if I have a boyfriend, and is surprised when I say I no longer attend and that I don't know any boys. "Isn't there a fella?" she asks, using a funnel to refill the brown bottle with liquid from a glass jug. "This'll bring your ma back to health," she says, corking the bottle.

Then she turns her face to mine. "Now, I've been a country midwife long enough to recognize a girl in trouble. I felt the heat in your body the moment I opened the door. How long has it been since you last had your lady's day?" she asks.

"A while," I say, shocked by her plain talk. And if she can see my trouble, can everyone? She scurries about to gather some more ingredients, which she mashes into a paste. "I never ask a girl how it happens. There's no point in knowing. All love stories are the same." She scrapes the paste into a glass jar, only this one is blue, and hands it to me.

Walking home, I keep our medicines in separate coat pockets, and upon returning, give Mom a dose of hers. Before bedtime I put a teaspoon of my own thick concoction in the center of a handkerchief and twist it to suck on it for a while. Mrs. Hampton says that will give steady release, giving things a chance to work. I pull back the covers and crawl in bed beside Hazel and Myrtle.

·   11   ·

By the way everyone acts when I awake, I'm scared to ask what happened. I don't recall a thing. Apparently I've been gripped by a fever so bad even Buck says he never thought I'd live. "Whoever thought you'd slim down," he adds.

It shocks me to learn almost three weeks have passed.

It's clear Mrs. Hampton's remedy has done its job but also caused some kind of havoc to my health. She's come by almost daily. "Don't say anything about 'the cure,' " she whispers to me. "They have no idea." Instead she dispenses strange medical advice, saying Mom ought to rub goose fat on my chest to get rid of the cough. She doesn't offer to say where we might get a goose. My mind is confused, and my strength is sapped. I spend most of the day in sleep.

Aunt Varnie visits. She says threshing has begun on the neighboring farms but that the yield is low on account of the dryness. Uncle Mose struggled to bring in four loads of hay by himself and is hoping for help. Mom doesn't want to go but feels she has to.

"What about my job with Wertz?" I ask, suddenly rediscovering the obligations that have been lost in the cloud of fever. Last week, they tell me, Mr. Wertz came by in his buggy. He brought a bushel of potatoes, a quart of kerosene, and my leather box, packed with all my things. He said they found a new girl to do the milking. I open the leather box. Neatly lying on top is Mrs. Wertz's lone, pale yellow work glove, the match to the one we were looking for that day he picked me up in the buggy. Did he put it there to remind me? Did she?

The next morning Abe drives us over to Aunt Varnie's farm. Though I'm still weak and sore, I'm expected to pitch in. Of course, Buck is nowhere to be found. By noon the threshing comes to a halt after the thresher hits a fieldstone and breaks a blade. The gasoline engine can't be used until a new blade arrives. We're behind schedule, so Uncle Mose hitches up the team and we do it the old backbreaking way, sun so hot you see spots in front of your eyes. At night we crawl exhausted into our makeshift beds on the hard kitchen floor. Abe sleeps in a chair near the stove.

Aunt Varnie is good, but when she touches my arm, her hands are like ice. There is also something new in her attitude toward me, like she's figuring out how to perform her "aunt's duty" to straighten me out. One night while we do the dishes she actually says, "I could barely believe it when your ma told me that you were in trouble. You always seemed like a leader in your family. I guess you discovered the hard way that a girl who's sneaky finds consequences. One sin leads to another."

Sin? Which sin? Does she mean what happened with Wertz? Or what happened after? Did Mom tell her about the scalding tub of rock salt? Is that what she's referring to as sin? I want her to explain so I can explain, but then I remember those lonely moments when a hug, even from Mr. Wertz, felt welcome. I cannot bear the thought of discussing such details with Aunt Varnie or anyone. No. No. Better to keep quiet about it all. For what if there was a slipup and she found out about Mrs. Hampton's remedy? Wouldn't that be another sin? No. No. The only way out is silence. And to accept responsibility for my fall with the hope that God himself will forgive me.

Finally the threshing is done. We stay long enough to pull some pumpkins and cauliflower from the field, then filling our skirts with potatoes we pile into the wagon. The last of Indian summer is passing.

The next Sunday, Buck shows up at our cabin with a girl. She's dark-haired with freckles, and not at all coarse like I'd have imagined a girl of Buck's would be. We roast sweet potatoes and serve them in their jackets with hot tea. The girl's name is Liz. I'm dying to ask her what she sees in Buck, though I suppose he's not bad-looking if you don't know him. I'm tempted to tell her how he used to hold Pop's rifle on me and pretend to fire, and about the time he lifted the gun at the last minute, pulled the trigger, only to find the gun was loaded. After the gun went off, his face went white. He'd shot a hole in the ceiling. If he hadn't lifted the gun in the last second, he'd have shot me. Mom and Pop never knew. Pop saw the hole a few days later and said to Mom, "Look, one of them kids pushed the broom handle through the ceiling"—one of those times when we knew better than to call attention to the truth.

Buck struts around all afternoon like a pheasant, and even offers Liz more tea. There is a part of me that wants to pull Liz aside and say, "Run, girl, while you still can." Nonetheless, when they leave,

Mom and I can't stop laughing over the thought of Buck fetching anything for anyone. "She'll be able to handle him," Mom says.

The weather grows frigid. In the morning I go out and bring firewood in. Mom does some wash and jams the green coverlet in the wringer. By the time I see she needs help, she's got half the cover in the washtub, the other half in the dirt where it's dragging. Fingers violet from the icy water, she stubbornly tries to pry the wringer open. It takes more than half an hour to unscrew the handle and free the bunched-up material.

We come inside cold to the bone, but there's no relief. The house is chilly, our food is running low: there's nothing to cook. That night we eat a cold supper of pig souse and cheese.

A few days later a big snow falls. It clings to the trees and porch rail. Mom is ill again and takes to her bed. At one point she wakes feverish and bawls that she's tomato hungry. I'm at a loss for what to say; it's months before tomatoes will be in and we've used all the jarred ones we've put up. In the afternoon Abe comes by to visit, and he has sense enough to fib and say when the sun comes up he'll find Mom some big, vine-ripened Brandywines.

The sky looks to be clearing. Abe goes and cuts more firewood, stacks it on the porch, and as he is leaving, I wrap a blanket around me and hurry out and say, "There'll be no Christmas for the girls this year, unless I find a way to get to New Bloomfield to buy some candy." Abe is agreeable to taking me to Weaver Brothers Emporium and motions to his sled. My savings are almost eight dollars. I tie the money in a handkerchief.

In town, the cold streets are packed with hardened snow, and the sled glides easily to the door of the store. While I look around at all the wonderful things, my eyes travel up to a shelf behind the notions counter, where a row of exquisite dolls is lined up. Something reckless swims over me—a sort of unexplainable and impractical surge—and I hear myself say to Mr. Weaver that I'd like to see a doll. I handle it with care, taking in its fine-tailored clothes and delicate face. It takes three dollars, but I must have it. To spend so much money on myself is both thrilling and horrible at the same time. Mr. Weaver wraps thin sheets of white paper around the doll. My heart beats fast as longing and fright race through me.

I end up buying the girls some rock candy, and two nice oranges for Mom, and then go outside to meet Abe. As I approach the sled, I'm too bashful to tell him that at my age I've bought myself a doll. So I lie and say the doll is for Hazel. "What about Myrtle?" he says. And then the next thing I know, I've gone back inside and am asking Mr. Weaver to wrap up another doll, this one for Myrtle.

It gets dark early, and when Abe drops me off, the moon shines upon the snow. How will I ever face Mom? Six dollars! On dolls! If only it had occurred to me to leave some of my savings at home.

I don't show Mom my purchases but stow them in the cupboard by the kitchen table. My stomach shakes just thinking about it.

Christmas is a sorry affair. Mom's illness means we can't go to Aunt Varnie's, and they aren't about to come here. No one knows where Buck is. In the morning the girls are spellbound with the dolls but Mom is inconsolable and forbids them to be played with. She needs to resell them. The dolls sit on top of the sideboard and stare down at us—ruining any cheer we might feel for the day.

At noon Abe comes by and with a victorious smile hands us a wild duck. He apologizes for its gauntness and says, "I hope it isn't sickly. It's the only one I saw for miles." I clean it and it is indeed bony but in good health.

At last the cabin smells like a holiday with the duck roasting—a few turnips, potatoes, and carrots sliced in with it. But when I pull the iron roaster out of the heat, none of us can believe how the oven has shrunk the bird. As Abe divides it with the carving knife it skids around on the platter, yet somehow, its emaciation renders it even more delicious. Though it tastes a bit fishy, we're hungry and we've eaten worse. I'll make potato soup with the carcass.

12

New Year's Day has come and gone and Abe hasn't been seen for more than a week. Mom grows worried and to appease her I strap on Pop's old winter boots, stuff the toes with rags, and stomp through the snow into the valley to find him. An hour later I'm at his little ramshackle outpost. Apparently he'd had a job doing day labor at the Dietrich farm when one of their dray mares bit him in the thigh. His leg is enormously puffed up, but he says the swelling is already subsiding. "You should have seen it two days ago. I thought I might lose it."

Even without an injury, the snow saps the strength in one's legs and a horse is out of the question. No wonder we haven't seen him.

Abe gives me an extra bag of mush meal and tells me where he has some deer meat buried out in the snow. I stay through the afternoon, wash out some of his clothes, and cook up a big batch of stew. I leave him most of it but pack two mason jars full for us.

When I return home, I see that one of the dolls on the sideboard is missing a big chunk from her lovely china face. While Mom was napping, Myrtle clambered up on a chair to take it down. It slipped from her hands and hit the floor. Her failure shames us all, and I can't keep myself from bawling because we've never been able to keep anything nice.

Worse, we are running out of food, there's still no sign of Buckley, and Mom is out of tonic. Her gums are bleeding and all night long she weeps because she's still tomato hungry. I must leave home and look for work. There is no other way. Again, Pop's old winter boots are put to work. As I trek through the snow, wind whipping through the trees, my face stings with cold, the snow is up over my boots and in spots as high as my knees. It takes me several hours to reach the gap. Down in Cumberland County I walk up the miserable lane of every farm along the way but no one needs help. How nice it would be to have a real winter coat as opposed to walking around wrapped in a blanket.

· 13 ·

The next day, in Hogestown, going west toward Carlisle, I find a job at a roadhouse. The man who runs the place is named Murphy. He's nice-looking with thick dark hair and big ears.

I'd spent the night huddled in a barn and in the morning was lucky to procure a ride with the driver of a mule team. When we arrived in Hogestown, it was he who spotted the cardboard help-wanted sign in the roadhouse window.

When I enter, Murphy is standing behind the counter reading the newspaper. "You're only the third person who's come in here all day," he says. "Only cabin fever could bring someone out in this weather."

He's surprised when I tell him I've come about the job. I can see him quickly eyeing my blanket and boots.

"Well . . . I need a counter-girl," he says. "It's fairly simple, if you don't mind cleaning, serving lunch to customers, and helping to put gasoline in the cars when I'm busy. The pay is six dollars and fifty cents a week."

He asks me where I live, and when I tell him I just rode over from Perry County, he takes a cigarette from his frayed pocket, leans his elbows on the counter, and says, "I'm afraid I can't hire you. Perry County is too far to travel every day."

"Mister, I've already been pulled from school," I say. "I've got a pair of children and a sick mother to feed. I can do it."

Murphy ponders this. Just then a rickety black automobile pulls in and honks its horn. It's clear Murphy doesn't like to be honked at. He pulls his jacket from a coat hook and says they must be crazy to drive in this weather. Through the curtains I watch him tip his cap, then crank a fuel pump to fill the automobile. When the driver prepares to leave, his tires hit a patch of ice and spin. I run out and help Murphy rock the black machine and push against its cold fenders until traction can be regained. Finally it heads down the road with the back swinging to and fro. "We better get back inside and warm up," Murphy says when he sees me shivering.

Across the counter, he serves me a steaming cup of coffee and a piece of custard pie from under a glass lid. It's the best pie I've ever tasted. I ask him if his wife makes it.

"I do my own baking," he says. "And I can tell from your face you don't believe me." Then he shows me the kitchen and the sawed-off broom handle he uses to roll the crust.

He seems to understand I have no place to go. "I wasn't looking for someone to live here," he says, "but maybe we could fix you a cot in the storage room." He points to a doorway with a faded piece of calico hanging from a wooden rod.

The next evening, walking back over the gap, my feet are like blocks of ice and I've got two dollars in my pocket for the two days I've already worked. I go to the store. Shad comes in from eating his supper, napkin hanging from his sweater. "I need two weeks' worth of food for four people," I say.

"Your credit is used up. When you gonna pay?"

I lay my two dollars on the counter, and when he learns I have a new job that pays more than six dollars a week, he agrees to give me four dollars' worth of credit.

I unpack the crate of groceries at home, after carrying them over the frozen creek and up the hill. "Please, please make supper," Mom says. "I haven't the strength."

The next morning the weather is warmer, and I return to the roadhouse. My route is direct, and with the help of a couple of wagon lifts, I make good time. The business sits on the main road between Carlisle and Harrisburg, where a good bit of automobile traffic passes—sometimes two or three cars at a time. Murphy teaches me how to crank an engine, then prime the gasoline pump, and soon I also know how to change oil, put water in the radiator, and check air in the tires. I only pump gas if Murphy is busy. Mostly I work the luncheon counter.

Lots of people come in, don't even take their coats off, and just have a cup of coffee. The wind never stops blowing, but the heat from the griddle and range keeps the joint warm and the steam on the windows is like a curtain of fog. We don't charge to refill coffee and I keep the glass lids sparkling clean so the pie looks tempting. When I talk up the pie, many decide to try a slice, and once in a while a customer, usually a trucker on his route or another man lucky to have a job, leaves a penny or two for a tip, which Murphy lets me pocket.

Murphy is an honest-injun type and seems to know what I'm thinking even before I do. I'm not homesick here like at Wertz's, but he nonetheless offers me some notepaper to write my family. In the evenings, when the roadhouse closed, it was difficult to read because Murphy was shutting off all the lights. Electricity is expensive, and since I've learned you don't get rich selling pie and coffee, I didn't want to ask for anything extra. Eventually he noticed me reading by the streetlight coming in the window, and rather than admit he's doing it for me, he says, "I hope you don't mind but I need to leave the lights on tonight." He himself doesn't care about the darkness because in the evening he stays out in the garage bent over the engine of an old rusted car. A lone lightbulb that he moves around gives him vision, and he keeps warm with a fire burning in an old oil drum. That's just his way. He says he'll take me for a ride when the weather improves.

14

There is no snow for over a week, so I go home to visit Mom. Abe Lease comes by and brings a piece of bacon rind that I cook up with some dry beans. Mom likes having Abe come by. He's decent, quiet and respectful, and knows much about animals and nature. He owns a big book of medicine for animals and he's brought it over so I can look at it. Abe's the first man I ever heard admit that he's not sure about God. He says most people are either disgusted by religion or fall for it too hard.

I make a pie for supper and teach Mom to crimp the edge like Murphy does. She is pleased with the outcome. Murphy's been letting me practice pie making but I've got a long way to go to match his.

I tell Murphy how much I miss school. So when business is slow he has me take a paper placemat and copy things from the radio onto both sides. Other times he'll read a news article out loud and then has me write down everything I can remember about it. When I've exhausted all I can recall, he reads the article aloud again so I can hear what I missed. He calls it the "roadhouse college," and says writing down what you remember hearing is a form of critical thinking. It surprises me how much stuff I learn this way. Sometimes in the morning when he's baking, I sit in the kitchen and read news articles to him. Nine times out of ten we get interrupted by a car blowing its horn for gas.

Last Saturday he learned I'd never seen a moving-picture show, so we closed the roadhouse early to attend one in Carlisle. His automobile is held together with leather straps, and after wrapping ourselves up in blankets for warmth, we bumped along so hard our insides shook. In town, we entered a barnlike building with wooden benches and a sheet stretched over the wall at one end. A beam of light began to cast pictures there, as a piano played. There were views of city streets, various men, a woman with a baby, a man on horseback chasing a locomotive. In between, cards with poems on them appeared. After working all day, my tiredness grows, and I decide to skip the poems and just watch the pictures. In the darkness, with the music, my body relaxes, my eyelids droop. It is suddenly the end, and a man and woman are hugging in a rowboat.

There's an intermission. More people enter. Murphy buys popcorn in a brown paper cone. "How did you like the story?" "Good." My teeth chatter even with the blanket. "Do you think the man really loved her?" What's he talking about? "Seemed like it." "Do you think the girl's uncle was too strict?" "Which girl? What uncle?" "Verna? Didn't you follow the story?" "What story?" "Didn't you read the cards?" "I was too tired to read poems." Murphy smiles. "You have to read the cards to follow the story." Then he starts to chuckle. Then he starts to guffaw. Then that turns into a full-out belly laugh that is worse because he's trying to hold it in. He tries to contain himself but his shoulders shake and a couple of people turn around to see what's so funny.

My ignorance is on full display.

The second picture starts, silly scenes of men doing crazy things, building a house and hitting each other in the head with hammers. It's funny. But I'm not in a laughing mood. There are no cards to read. Then a longer picture begins. I read the words; a band of outlaws talk to each other about a bank robbery someplace out west. Big deal. I see now how everything is connected and feel stupid for not catching on sooner. But it's all very tiring.

Coming home, Murphy keeps after me to know why I'm so quiet. Finally I let him coax my feelings out. "You can poke fun at me," I say. "And you can think me ignorant. But I can't take it when you laugh at me."

He is silent. "I'm sorry," he says. In a minute I begin to feel bad about making him feel bad, and when we get back to the roadhouse we sit and eat a piece of pie in the kitchen together. Nothing more is said. I let bygones be bygones.

15

When spring arrives, the grass along the sides of the roadhouse sprouts bright green while purple crocuses push up. With the break in the weather the mud is terrible. Some cars stopping for gasoline are coated. You have to scrape it off with a piece of cardboard. Business picks up as more people take to the roads with the better weather, but money worries plague Murphy.

I manage to save twelve dollars. At night I lie on the cot behind the calico curtain and dream of what my life might have been like if Mom had let me go to St. Louis. How Delia and I might have worn fine clothes and sashayed up the avenue spending John's money.

One afternoon Murphy brings in an old Victrola he's bought at an auction of household objects belonging to a farmer whose land was taken over by the bank. "Spending money on such foolishness is probably what caused him to go broke," I say. Murphy says everyone in America is on the gravy train, but that farmers are still being left out. Buying a Victrola is his idea of helping them and he refuses to say how much he paid for it.

At home, Buck is set to marry Liz. She says the wedding will be held at her father's farm in Boiling Springs, and after ruminating about the hymns she's choosing, she asks if I'd like to sing one at the ceremony. "Heavens no," I say. "I can't sing. I can only whistle." We laugh at the idea of a whistling wedding. I tell her how I like music if it's catchy, and about the Victrola, and how when there are no customers and Murphy's not around, I put on "Shakin' the Blues Away" and dance around the roadhouse. She thinks that is funny and isn't at all scandalized.

Later Mom joins us and wants to be part of the conversation. Liz reveals nothing. With the girls, we take a walk through the woods and then west to the railroad tracks. Years ago we used to go back there a lot to visit Mom's friend, Gladys Strong, who lived with her father in a yellow house by the crossing. During the big war, Mom used to take us there to watch the troop trains go by. We'd wave at the soldiers. Gladys was bold, and the thought of all those young men going overseas moved her. Whenever she heard a train whistle approach the crossing, she'd run out and blow them kisses.

One hot July a train held up for a few minutes and a soldier leaned out the window and spoke to her. He wrote his name and address on a small pack of soda crackers and threw them out the window. She decided to write him care of his parents' farm in Minnesota, and they forwarded the letter to his battalion overseas. He wrote her back from France and it got to be a regular thing. After Armistice Day, he returned to look for her. They fell in love and he took her away. Gladys was the only friend Mom had for miles, and when she went to Minnesota, Mom cried for weeks. Gladys wrote two letters saying how happy she was, but Mom, ashamed to report how her own life was miserable, never answered. Pop always called Gladys the "soda cracker girl," like she was a bit fast. But I admire her resourcefulness. She used to say, "If there isn't a way, we'll make one."

I wonder if I'll ever marry. Boys don't notice me and I have to worry that one who likes me will find out I'm not untouched. I've been combing my hair over to one side like a woman wore hers in one of the movies, but only Murphy and one regular customer notice.

16

It rains for days, and there is little road traffic. Above the cash register a worn-out photograph hangs. Seven women, laundresses, stare out, eyes dulled by work. They don't smile; their hair is pulled tight; their hands are wet, with the sleeves of their shirtwaists rolled up to the elbow. They stand amid piles of clothes soiled by people they have never met, steaming washtubs, a shelf of cook starch. The one farthest left has the same dark eyes as Murphy—his mother. When the roadhouse is quiet I study her, handkerchief tucked in blouse, hand resting on hip. Will I end up like that?

My savings are up to fifteen dollars but I wish it was thirty. Money is on everyone's mind. Murphy wrote his sister down in Reading and asked her for a small loan for taxes. He doesn't know I know, but he left the letter on the counter while he tended someone's automobile and my eyes fell upon it by accident. Murphy's sister must have said no to the loan. He had a letter back from her and has been agitated ever since. The county is demanding tax payment in full by the due date.

In the evening I go over to the Dunkel farm for eggs and cream, and returning home between the cabbage rows, I spot a fox lapping up water in the pond to my left. He is rust-colored in the late sun, and sleek, and I can just see his pink tongue breaking his reflection in the water. The fox senses me and inches backwards with a limp and a wounded look, then scurries through a fencerow of privet. I wonder how he was injured.

The next morning we attend the wedding of Buck and Liz. I wear my new handkerchief dress that I've sewn from a stack of navy blue paisley handkerchiefs. They come eight to a package, and it took two packages, much cheaper than fabric cut from a bolt, and stylish too. Mom threads a new ribbon in her summer hat and wears a lovely bottle green dress that Aunt Varnie got for her. A Packard pulls in beside us, driven by Aunt Mae's son Jeb. He's in his final semester at Carson Long military academy and wears his uniform. If he wanted to arrive in style, his plans were ruined because someone made him stop and pick up Grandma Peffer. When her fat legs step out onto the running board, it's clear the years are catching up to her. She holds a cane in one hand, a bag of apples in the other, which is all the wedding present she plans to give.

Inside, Liz comes down the stairs and steps into her mother's parlor, and one look in her clear eyes brings grace to the ceremony.

Vows are exchanged, and afterwards we go out to the yard in back where barrels, crates, and planks have been put together to make tables and benches. Liz's father has roasted wild rabbits and ducks that Buckley shot, and there is ham and sausages from the smokehouse. Many neighbors bring side dishes; one woman baked six rhubarb pies. The party should be brighter, but there's a hushed sound to the whole affair, people eat and drink quietly, and I get the sense that more than a few of them think Liz is marrying beneath her. Some of the men get up now and then and go back to the woodshed. Grandma Peffer says they're breaking the temperance law, but none of the other churchgoers makes a fuss.

The real trouble starts when Jess Cabot brings out his fiddle. A man and woman start to dance. They aren't our people. Someone says they're cousins of Liz's father. The dancing makes certain people edgy. Others join in—though none of us. At dusk someone lights a bonfire. That does it. "Drive me home, Jeb," Grandma Peffer says. "I've had enough of these devils on parade." It irritates Jeb to have to leave, and he stands by helpless while Grandma Peffer, though she has a full smokehouse of her own, grabs most of the leftover ham and wraps it in a dish towel to take home.

Once she and some of the other objectors leave, the party relaxes a bit. Personally, I think the dancing is beautiful, the pretty skirts spinning, the men stomping their boots, the sound of the fiddle and banjo. And long as I live I'll never forget what happens next. Mom shocks us all by rising from the table and swaying with the music. The light from the fire makes her skin glow, and for a moment the beauty that was once hers is glimpsed again. Her hair comes loose and we stare with awe as she begins to dance by herself, slow and with reserve as though weary of this life. All around her the June bugs light up the air, and all of it—the beauty, the dance, the season—will last such a short time. When the song ends, Mom stands lost, like a child left at the county fair. She begins to weep. Abe gently takes her arm and escorts her into the house. "Our people never did mix well with strangers," Aunt Varnie says. The music has ended, the yard grows still, and the empty sound of crickets is all that remains of Buckley's wedding.

· 17 ·

It's official. The roadhouse must close. We've struggled all through the summer and now a man from the bank comes and says they have a buyer for the property who will not wait. "Tell me the name of the rat forcing me from my livelihood," Murphy says with frustration. The man from the bank leaves in a hurry.

On Sunday Murphy offers to drive me home to Perry County for a visit. Abe Lease stops by and in another man's presence he grows talky and tells how before he came to work at the tannery he was a raftsman for a lumber outfit, part of a crew that would fell large tracts of trees up north. The men would lash the logs together, forming rafts a couple of dozen feet wide but hundreds of feet long. A shack would be built on top for cooking and sleeping and they'd float downriver. A regular crew, composed of between five and thirty men, would chain up at night along the bank and make a camp. When the logs finally reached their destination, which could be a railroad depot as far south as Philadelphia, the crew would return home on foot, stopping in Harrisburg to blow their pay. Most of the money would disappear in the hardscrabble district, and after a few wild nights the rafting men, broke but well spent, would head north again for another run. Railroads put an end to rafting, and recently Harrisburg tore down all the hardscrabble bars and flophouses. "They built a sunken garden in its place," Abe says, shaking his head. "An Eden as low as low can be."

Abe's entire rafting story gets told while Mom is down at the creek bathing with Hazel and Myrtle. Upon her return any talk of highlife is cut dead. Murphy tells us how he's had another letter from his sister down in Reading and that there seem to be jobs down there. He offers to take me along. Mom makes it clear she doesn't approve of the way we've been keeping house together.

My face grows red with embarrassment not only because what she believes to be between us is untrue, but because in my ignorance it never occurred to me that she might think that. Murphy does a good job of reassuring Mom that he is honorable, but when we arrive in Reading a few weeks later it turns out his sister Ruth thinks the same thing. She tells us our room is upstairs, and Murphy lets her know right away that I will need my own room and bed. They quickly agree to give me a small storage room off the kitchen. I can see how the idea of a man and a young woman traveling together even for work puts ideas in people's heads.

Ruth runs a Bible-selling business from home, advertising in newspapers. She ships them from the post office but also sells them door-to-door, and on Tuesdays and Saturdays from a booth at the market.

As we unpack our car, she stands in the doorway, thick-knit sweater wrapped across her fleshy bosom, and watches to take inventory of our things, never offering a hand and hardly shifting from the doorframe as we bring our possessions inside. "How long will they stay?" is written all over her face, along with a shrewd look that asks, "Is there anything of value?" Yes, where money is concerned Ruth has itchy palms.

Her house is set in the middle of a block-long row, with a little porch that sits a foot off the ground enclosed by an iron railing, a style they say is unique to Reading. The front door faces Buttonwood Street, which runs downward for several blocks ending at the railroad yard where some enormous factories are built.

Murphy and I rise early and go around looking for work. It's a big town, with prosperous stores and grand houses on the hill. The main street climbs up a mountain where on the east side an oriental building called the pagoda looks out over everything. They say it's a nice place to picnic. In the evening we return and Ruth is annoyed we haven't found any jobs. "Did you try the factories at the end of the street?" she asks.

"I don't want Verna doing factory work," Murphy says.

When Ruth looks directly at you, which is rare, her eyes pinch with scrutiny. She displays a creased brow and wiry hair held in place by thick bobby pins that she bites open. At home she often lets the hair hang loose and from time to time it shows up in our food. She believes in the gospel, and in Christ, and prays to inspire others with her strength, drawing power from her private suffering with God. Sometimes, from the sidewalk, she'll cast her hard eyes at the neighbors, studying every household on the block, noting who hasn't swept their walk, or painted their porch columns, while at the same time cataloguing the history of their faults, trials, missteps, not to mention their riches.

I try to help around the house, but Ruth is suspicious of my cleaning, worried I might move something. The floorboards of the house are uneven and slope to a steep staircase that leads up to their bedrooms on the second floor. There is junk everywhere, closets full of old clothes, musty panniers and crinolines that no one has worn since the last century, boxes of strange items, everything from rusty ice tongs to bath brushes with the bristles worn down, boxes of sand where fresh flowers can be dried (a previous business before Bibles), odd rolls of wallpaper, worn-out boots, a cherry stoner, and empty soda bottles.

In a nod to Abe, Murphy finds day work at a lumberyard feeding enormous logs through a saw to make planks. He returns at night with hands stained from tree sap that leaked through his work gloves. "Scrub that off before you come to the table," Ruth scolds. Poor Murphy's shoulders curve forward with irritation.

My cooking is far better than hers, but Ruth guards the kitchen and the pantry, and even when I do something as dull as peel a potato, she hovers by my shoulder to make sure I haven't cut away too much. She makes a big commotion about shooing houseflies out the window and I once see her put a drinking glass over a moth to usher it back out to the garden. "I can't tolerate suffering in animals, insects, or plants," she says, and she even forces me to agree that spiders might have a soul. But humans don't make her list for consideration because the debt of original sin is high.

Ruth prepares the most meager amounts of food possible, one small fried potato and two slices of toast, each topped by a gravy ladle of cream chipped beef. "You must chew your portion more, Verna," she advises, and sets an egg timer on the table in front of me. "Measure your pace of eating against the sand of the hourglass." After the plates are scraped and wiped to a shine by our still raw hunger, she'll say, "See, once again I've made just enough food."

"Murphy is a fine baker," I say. "Maybe he would make a pie for us this weekend."

"Sweets can only tempt us to want more," she says.

Murphy does not join in any table talk as Ruth shunts all discourse to a dead end by spouting her narrow, solid opinion on every topic. She doesn't seem to notice his silence and only hammers him with questions that require one- or two-word answers.

"Will the sawmill have work next week?"

"Not sure."

"Do you recall the name of Father's first cousin? The one who ate three slices of kidney pie at Father's funeral?"

"Tommy Nickles."

"Did you know the water was left dripping in the upstairs sink this morning?"

"Are you sure it was me?"

"Who else?"

I get lucky and find a job in the stockroom of the Viceroy shoe store, filling in for a woman having a baby. Three days a week I'm expected to work late, and I stay in town pleased to take my dinner at the drugstore, finding joy in their delicious grilled cheese or fried egg sandwiches, and discovering how dining out makes meals seem like a banquet.

Murphy also takes a late shift and Ruth is delighted that our absence allows her to stretch the food even farther. The months pass.

Ruth finds the way Murphy has taught me to copy things from the newspaper to be a waste of time. She has me copy things from the Bible instead. The more I write, the more questions crop up. "Wouldn't God want Adam and Eve to have knowledge? Wouldn't he welcome their desire to know more?"

"The fruit was forbidden," Ruth says, annoyed.

"But if God is so powerful, why would it matter so much whether small, weak humans obeyed him or not?"

"It's part of his plan. It's measuring the faith of mankind."

"But doesn't measuring faith make God seem kind of petty and small?"

Ruth shakes her head and notes that my education is sorely lacking in wisdom. I stupidly tell her how Grandma Peffer threw Mom's Bible in the fire. Ruth opens her mouth aghast and for once no sound comes out.

One evening the windows in the whole house rattle as Ruth rushes in bursting with excitement. The Bible company that she represents is coming to town for a weekend of lectures and they've asked her to deliver one. Her eyes glitter at the topic she's been assigned: what it means to be like Christ.

Over the next month the project consumes her. She jots down ideas on index cards and every morning scans the paper to find examples of Christian acts. Stories of disaster beckon; a family whose house burned down is given a box of donated clothes, or a boy whose foot was cut off by a train is carried to school every day by his brother, a nun who in an act of empathy maintains a prayer vigil for a man whose wife died in childbirth. Ruth always reads her findings aloud, and I'm forced to agree, "Yes, that certainly is a Christian act," and "Yes, I wish we could be more like that too." She adds these news stories to her ever growing list and then calibrates them in order of sacrifice and selflessness.

Murphy meanwhile grows more miserable with every passing

week. It angers him when Ruth takes his Victrola and sells it for ten dollars to the junk man. At first he is silent, but I can see a storm is brewing. Ruth pinches and nags and suddenly his temper flares and he says, "Christ, Ruth, you treat me like a schoolboy!"

She chastises him with great personal affront for using such language under her roof and denies she treats him this way. Then she adds that until the day comes when he begins to show more responsibility, she has no choice but to remain vigilant after him.

"Christ, Ruth! The hair on my balls is turning gray," he shouts.

Now, injured more by the repeat of crudeness than the wrath, she runs upstairs to her room. He feels like even more of a failure when a short while later he has to go up and knock on her door to apologize. He's growing more tightly wound.

One evening Ruth invites Mrs. Simpson, the old lady next door, and her daughter Corrine over to sit in the parlor and listen to her practice her speech. "It's another opportunity to spread the message," she confides in me. Mrs. Simpson shuffles in and sits, her behind crammed in a foundation garment and sticking out like a tire on the back of a truck. Her daughter Corrine has a blank face, a slapping face as Pop used to say, with a mouth of crooked teeth that she tries to hide. Her eyelashes are almost white, and they blink incessantly as she takes one of the small cups of lavender tea with milk and sugar that Ruth has me pass around. There is also a small pressed-glass plate holding some thin slices of fruitcake that Ruth has been hoarding since who knows what Christmas, and Mrs. Simpson sets to work munching on those.

Ruth stands under the archway leading to the vestibule and begins to deliver her speech, referring to a pack of notecards from time to time. As she moves along, her ability to convey ideas through language actually impresses me, especially at the end when she lists all the different names there are for Jesus: Son of God, Prophet, Emmanuel, Savior, King of Kings, Fisher of Men, Shepherd, Teacher, Healer, Redeemer of Mankind.

The talk ends and Mrs. Simpson rises and shuffles toward Ruth, hands clasped and clutched to her breast, her feet unsteady from squeezing into high-heeled shoes that are too small for swollen feet. "Thank you, thank you, thank you," she cries. "You really are a messenger from heaven."

Corrine stays seated, her hands pressed between her knees. We are both grateful that Mrs. Simpson is expressing enough appreciation for everyone. Eventually I also tell Ruth how fine her lesson was but keep to myself that something makes me uneasy about the idea of her speaking in public.

18

The crowd at the auditorium in West Reading is larger than expected. Farmers arrive from all around Berks County with food baskets on their arms, set to make a day of it. Across the rows of folding seats and to the back, I see Murphy enter. He's handsome with fresh clipped hair, and I know he has only come because he recognizes this is an important day for Ruth.

The founder of the Bible society opens the program with a prayer, asking a special blessing for Calvin Coolidge and our country, and when he introduces Ruth, he notes how she's been successfully representing the Bible company for almost three years. There is polite applause as Ruth moves to the lectern, wearing a purple dress that only last week was a terrible shade of puce. I helped her dye it and also advised her to sew a big mother-of-pearl button on the bodice. Framed in the lamplight the whole effect looks good, and Ruth's face shines in the heat as she leads us in a second prayer, asking for guidance and strength. The rhythm of her talk is different than at home; it's more earnest, more humble, and people are riveted by her words.

The talk lasts for thirty minutes, people nod as they recognize some of her newspaper accounts, and when she ends by listing the many names for Christ, she says it shows us how there are many avenues from which to serve.

People give her tremendous applause and there are even a few cheers. Then when the room quiets, Ruth begins to take questions. "What do you think Christ would make of modern science—the way it challenges our belief?" one man asks.

Ruth pushes the combs in her hair. "Believing in scripture is an act of faith, and faith works for those who have it. Let us not forget that Mr. Clarence Darrow, who has so eagerly attacked the Bible on this subject, is an agnostic. I myself prefer to be linked to God and Adam's rib than to a monkey. If you doubt in your heart that the gospel is true, I'd suggest you pray to God for an answer, then ask yourself if your life is better with faith or without it." The audience applauds Ruth's reply.

Next comes a question about the nun who kept the prayer vigil. A shriveled woman in a brown dress is wondering to what order she belonged. Ruth apologizes, saying that information wasn't mentioned in the newspaper.

Then a small, balding man with sad dark eyes and a drooping mustache rises, and his manner is ominous and almost menacing. "Excuse me," he says, in a voice that's high and thin. Several people chuckle; one woman whispers, "Now *there's* a real ape-man." An uncomfortable pause grips the hall as the man seems to struggle to collect his thoughts. Finally he continues with his question. "Miss, can you give some examples from your personal life of how you are like Christ?" He emphasizes the word *you*, in a way that sounds like it could be slightly mocking.

Ruth smiles and gazes down. For the first time I feel a degree of warmth and compassion for her. It can't be easy to face ridicule in front of a crowd. "Every talk has its weak points and you've located mine," she says with gentle humor and modesty.

The man looks disturbed and grows more challenging. "But

how can you expect us to believe—when you don't share any of your own experience in these matters?"

Discomfort ruffles the crowd. "Sit down, Muskie," a woman's voice calls from a few seats over. The Bible Society founder steps to Ruth's side. "I'm sorry," he says. "We have to move on. Perhaps we can talk with you afterward." From the look on Ruth's face I can see fear begin to grip her: she's worried that the man's question will ruin the credibility of her talk. "Wait," Ruth says, "I think this is important to answer." The Bible Society founder shoots Ruth a look of displeasure, then backs away.

"Perhaps it is as false to never sound one's own trumpet as it is to sound it all the time," she says. "So let me try to tell you more about myself." Her voice is steady and calm as she begins a list of her Christian practices. "I pray, I try to help others, I give Bible discounts to elderly people who need them, I try to spread the message." Then with the keen sensitivity of a bat, Ruth feels the audience determining the answers to be pale and thin; they want more than talk of happy deeds. Shrewdly, she perceives the audience's disappointment, and though the crowd's bite is probably mild, she worries that they no longer love her as much as they once seemed to. Pleasing them becomes a drug that grips her.

"Perhaps you will benefit from a story about my own family," Ruth offers up. She's now a runner who has finished the race but can't stop running. "I have a brother whom I've taken in to live with me. He's always been a black sheep. As a ne'er-do-well young man he got into trouble, went to jail more than once, and just had a time of it. His marriage wore out and recently he was forced to close a roadhouse he was running. He wrote to me for help, and I've since opened my home to him and a young girl who worked for him as a waitress. They've been with me quite a few months now and I've found love in my heart for both of them. He is like a prodigal brother. And the girl is actually here today. Stand up, Verna, so the people can see you."

In horror, I hear applause and almost swoon. "Stand up!" Ruth implores again. All eyes turn in my direction as Ruth points me out. My face flames red. I rise and quickly sit back down, consumed with embarassment.

"That's Verna, the girl I told you about. She comes from a family in Perry County where her mother threw the Bible in the fireplace. But here, in Reading, among you all, she is being educated and redeemed."

Now I'm really burning. On fire. My mind grows so small. I can't move. There is more applause. For me? For Ruth? I quickly glance back over the sea of curious eyes to where Murphy was standing, but he's disappeared. Blood pounds in my ears. He must be beside himself. People rise and mill about for a break. One man pats my shoulder: "Don't worry, Missie, you'll find your way." One woman tries to engage me in conversation and I'm forced to nod in numb agreement that "yes, it is a blessing that God sent Ruth to me."

Outside the hall, there's no sign of Murphy. I walk around the entire building looking for his car and decide it's preferable to walk home than to go back inside for more pity. Ruth might be annoyed that I've bolted, but I don't care. The walk is dreary—houses with ash cans out for pickup, leaves and sludge congealing in the gutters, half-empty trolleys sliding by in the distance. I feel most upset that Ruth has gotten the facts of the story wrong. It wasn't Mom who threw the book in the fire but Grandma Peffer, and as Granddad's second wife, she's not even a blood relative, and the book wasn't thrown into a fireplace but a woodstove.

More than anything, I want to see Murphy, to find comfort in him. To let him know that I wasn't shocked to hear he'd been in jail, and that to me it makes no difference. I suddenly hate Reading as much as he does, the black railroads and factories, the gloomy mountains. And I hate Ruth too.

Back on Buttonwood Street there is no trace of him. The sun is setting, I'm nervous and jumpy and can't sit still. With nothing else to do, I get the wash pail out and begin to scrub the kitchen floor using all my fury. Under my gripping hands the rag arcs wide across the planks from the deepest muscles of my back. It feels so good to rid myself of some of this fury. The task goes quickly, and the floor is almost finished when I pause and feel someone watching me from the doorway. I turn and Murphy stands there with his dark hair falling over his forehead. One look is enough to let me know he's been drinking. It seems like we're both too exhausted to speak.

His feet move slowly across the wet floor as I rise and I feel his hands take ahold of my elbows. We stand there, in stillness looking at each other. The pressure of his fingers makes me want him so bad my knees almost give out. He feels it too, for he leans down and puts his lips over mine. His kiss is wet with the taste of corn liquor. Then he hugs me to him and a crestfallen sob escapes from deep within me.

"It's okay," he says, and strokes the back of my neck, his head bent into my shoulder.

"No," he whispers. "No, you're too young."

We stand there another moment, then with great remorseful resignation, he lets me go, steps back, turns and goes back out through the kitchen door into the garden. By the time I can come to my senses and follow him he is gone.

So, I go back inside, empty the wash bucket into the commode, wring the rag out to dry, and then, so as not to have to see Ruth, I retire to my room and lie on my bed, still shaking inside from my encounter with Murphy.

In the morning Ruth comes down to the kitchen, granting me a cheerful good morning. "So much excitement," she says, her voice light and artificial. "I dealt with Bible sales all afternoon. One church in Campbelltown is taking fifty copies!" Her eyes move around the room but avoid my direction, like a guilty dog trying to pretend he hasn't been chewing on your best boots.

Ruth puts the kettle on, and in a small saucepan dumps two flat tablespoons of farina into some boiling water. "I hope you didn't mind my calling you out like that," she says at last, needing to address my silence. "But you looked so nice, and that man so rattled my nerves I couldn't think straight. Afterwards you were nowhere to be found."

"I came home."

"Well, again, I hope you aren't upset."

"I'm over it," I say as curtly as possible.

Ruth slides the kettle onto the back burner. "I'm just glad Murphy wasn't there to hear me make a fool of myself."

"But he was there," I say. "He came to hear you."

For a split second Ruth's hands stop their activity. She flinches one of them up to straighten her hair but stops in midair. "Murphy was there? I didn't see him."

"He was in the back."

The side of Ruth's jaw clenches. Then she turns toward the stove with a bitter frown. "Well, maybe it's time he realized how much I've done for him," she says. "I've always tried to help, though he's never so much as even said thank you. He likes to think of himself as the only honest man. The only honorable soul. Our father was like that too. Well, going bankrupt is not a badge of honor. Sometimes you have to skim some cream off the milk to survive."

I tell Ruth I have to leave early for work.

Days pass with no sign of Murphy. Ruth and I keep a plate of food on the back of the stove for him. Finally, one evening, I'm in the kitchen when I hear him come in the front door and go up the stairs. Ruth meets him on the landing. I listen from the bottom hallway.

"Where have you been? You've had us sick with worry."

"I've found a job up in Pottsville," he says, and it sounds like he might have been drinking. "I've taken a room there."

"Oh fine," Ruth sneers. "Waste money on a boardinghouse and leave Verna behind for me to worry over. It's so kind of you to come by at all."

"I came to get my things."

"I suppose this is all my fault," Ruth says, her voice rising. "I suppose that's how I deserve to be treated after taking you and Verna in and giving you a home?"

"You'll get your reward in heaven," he says.

"Don't you worry," Ruth snaps with fury. "And from now on

don't expect good old Ruth to stand here and take you in when your dreams don't pan out. It's always the same. Good old Ruth, she'll provide—a bed, a meal, a five-dollar bill. Then when you're ready to roll you needn't even say good-bye? Well, this time, good old Ruth has had enough!"

"Why don't you nail yourself to a cross," Murphy says.

"Don't you dare use blasphemy under my roof!" Ruth screams. She begins to sob. I hear her feet move across the floorboards and the door to her room slam shut.

And now Murphy changes his tone. He grows soft and understanding. Through the door he apologizes for speaking rough and says he's grateful for all that Ruth has done. There is awkward silence. "I just came by to tell you the time has come for me to move on."

The change in his tone seems to annoy Ruth, not console her. Through the closed door I hear her shout. "And what about Verna? You're just leaving her here?"

"I'll see she's provided for."

His footsteps are slower coming down the narrow stairs under the weight of a suitcase. I jump back behind the swinging kitchen door and pretend to fold dishtowels. Murphy sets his bag down and comes in. "Hey, kid," he says. "I guess you heard us upstairs." I nod, afraid to speak or the tears will come. "I don't have a phone in Pottsville, but if you need to find me I'm working at the Harvest meatpacking plant. I'm sorry that nothing's working out."

"It's okay," I say. "You don't have to adopt me."

Murphy takes my hand and presses a ten-dollar bill into my palm. "Buy a ticket and go home to your people," he says. I glance at him, then look away, my eyes welling up. He puts his arm on my shoulder. "Come out to the car," he says. "There's something I want to give you."

At the curb he reaches into the backseat of the car and brings out a rolling pin. It's made of ash, long and smooth, without handles. "I won this in a card game off a Frenchie baker," he says. But I know he's made it himself. "It's more refined than a broom handle."

I'm so upset that later I can't recall if we even hugged or said good-bye or anything. We've been like kin to each other. I lie awake at night and weep over his departure.

·   19   ·

It's strange to be back in Perry County, where autumn is coloring the hills. The sunshine warms me as I walk and my bones begin to relax from the pressure of failure. You can tell winter is coming from the smell of wet leaves and a draft that moves through the cabin like a ghost, rustling the curtains even with the windows shut. The place seems to have grown smaller, the girls bigger, and they are now accustomed to having the bed to themselves. Witnessing Mom's dour life up close is also a burden. I miss the pace of city life.

Aunt Varnie has learned that I'm back, and I'm relieved when she sends word that she can use my help with butchering the hogs. The morning I arrive at her doorstep, the frost on the fields looks like sprinkled sugar. Aunt Varnie fixes me a plate of waffles and we chat while I eat. "I'm so glad you turned your life around after what happened with Mr. Wertz," she says at one point. Hearing that name again is like burning my hands on the hot griddle.

That evening a light skiff of snow falls and suddenly we are all eager to begin butchering, mouths watering for some fresh pork. In the morning Uncle Mose unbolts the barn door and the warmth of the cows being closed in all the long night greets us with its rich, heavy air. We have just finished the milking when five men from neighboring farms show up to help slaughter. Aunt Varnie brings me back inside the house, and even there, the sound of squealing hogs grates upon our nerves.

After a couple of hours the noise finally stops, and together Aunt Varnie and I bring the men a kettle of bean soup and a shoofly pie. Poles and hooks have been set in the barnyard and the plump pink bodies hang with their snouts to the ground, their dead weight causing them to shift now and then in the cold breeze. Once the men have eaten, we take the dishes back inside. The rest of the afternoon, they flop carcasses down onto worktables and scrape the bristles from the skin. One man has brought his son, a boy of eleven, whose job it is to sort the insides into different buckets. His small hands are raw from rinsing the dirt from the intestines. The messiest stuff will get cooked down for scrapple.

With long, sharp butchering knives and heavy hacking cleavers, the men work until dusk carving the flesh and singing:

We'll be having sausage and dumplings when she comes!
We'll be having sausage and dumplings when she comes!
We'll be having sausage and dumplings,
We'll be having sausage and dumplings,
We'll be having sausage and dumplings when she comes!

We store all the meat in the springhouse and over the next few days we prepare it piece by piece for smoking and curing. All the fat scraps get boiled and rendered, and the scent of cooking lard permeates the whole house. When you handle a dishtowel, slip on an apron, or press your face against a pillow, the smell of pure hog fat stays in the fabric. Aunt Varnie gives me two dollars to help grind sausage, which she'll be able to sell at market. The rest of my pay will be in meat, which I'll bring home to Mom. Over these days, our hard work yields mountains of fresh pork and we cook and dine like kings. What we can't preserve or consume ourselves, we share with the neighbors.

During the second week, a light snow falls overnight, and Aunt Varnie says I better get started on my trip back home before the real snow comes. At the breakfast table, she gives me a small package with my name on it. Inside a nice pair of mittens is folded. I feel bad at not having something to give her in return.

I walk all the way home wrapped in a blanket, toting a heavy burlap sack weighted down with meat, soup bones, and some dry beans. When I unpack it at home, Mom claps her hands together at the sight, but the girls will barely look at me when they see I haven't brought any candy.

In my absence they've been playing with the remaining china doll, taking it to bed with them. You can definitely see it's not new anymore and probably not worth trying to sell. As bad as things are, I'm secretly relieved that Mom hasn't gotten around to it anyway. I don't scold the poor girls about the doll because cooped up indoors the temptation must have been great.

Over the next few days we make some lovely meals, while I contemplate my future. Winter is upon us and I can see that we won't have enough provisions to see it through. One morning I get up and tell Mom I am going to Harrisburg. Her face is shocked but she sees I am determined, not the same girl she once knew. All her objections yield quickly to my strong will. I hope I am as capable as I pretend to be.

My journey begins on foot but after a few miles I manage to hitch a ride to Duncanon, then another down the river to Enola, then another down to Lemoyne. From there I walk across the Walnut Street Bridge to Harrisburg, which lies on the opposite shore. The dome of the Capitol rises among the buildings with curved beauty and grace. Its green tiles glisten in the sun and form a reflection on the river. I marvel at the trolley cars that swing around sparking electricity. At a lunch counter off Market Square, I buy a newspaper. By the end of the day I've found a job as a live-in housemaid, working for a certain Mrs. Meyer, who lives in a well-appointed townhouse on Second Street. My pay is six dollars and twenty-five cents a week.

20

I spend the next several months elbow deep in dishwater. Mrs. Meyer is a Jewish woman whose family came from Germany. She has two sons, one a lawyer, the other a businessman, who come to dinner every night, and she keeps two sets of dishes for their meal. My prowess in the kitchen is soon noticed, and when the cook leaves, I get promoted with an extra dollar a week. A tough taskmaster, Mrs. Meyer has a sarcastic streak. If in a day a thousand things go right, she'll harp on the one thing that goes wrong. But under her scorn and watchful eye I learn to poach salmon and make perfect brisket, gefilte fish, and matzoh ball soup.

I also learn the correct way to greet a guest, answer a telephone, serve cocktails, and polish silver. The first time I do the laundry, I hang her big old brassiere out on the clothesline near the kitchen. She is furious. "Maybe in the country you hang personal wash outside where only squirrels can see it," she snaps. "But in the city, it's hung in the attic or inside a pillow case."

Her personal habits interest me. After wearing furs, she likes them aired on a small screened-in sleeping porch on the second floor; her brown eyebrow pencil is to be cut back but never pointed so she can draw thick, wide eyebrows with a single stroke; every morning before I ever see her she's tightened into her corset, zipped in her day dress, and adorned with an assortment of chunky bracelets, earrings, and pins. She never takes anything for breakfast but a small glass of Epsom salts and the bottom half of a grapefruit, where she says more juice collects. When grapefruits go out of season she eats stewed prunes or whatever fresh fruit is at the market.

At around eight o'clock, the breadman Charles Dennis comes to the kitchen door and brings warm loaves of rye, marble rye, and white from a good bakery back on Cameron Street. He compliments my hair, my eyes, the color of my apron. I know he's full of beans but his words please me nonetheless.

Charles is almost twenty-six, and I'm closing in on seventeen, when he asks me out on a date. My first, if you don't count running to the movies with Murphy, which wasn't a date at all. He takes me to a Gloria Swanson picture and puts his arm around me in the theater. He's the first person to tell me I'm pretty. My head soars like a helium balloon. He actually likes my freckled skin and blue eyes. It's fantastic that a man is willing to pay for food or movies. At the end of the date he kisses me with an open mouth. It worries me that more time should pass before that is allowed, but his lips are smooth and the feel of his tongue shocks me down to my toes. His chin is rough, a man's face, and when I'm away from him I can't wait to see him again.

The weeks pass, people comment on how good I look. I lose weight and pay more attention to clothes. Even when I'm in my kitchen apron or uniform, men notice me at the Broad Street Market and on the trolley car.

Sometimes I complain to him about Mrs. Meyer and tell him that when you live in someone else's world you learn all about them but have little chance to develop yourself. Charles tells me about a doctor at the Polyclinic Hospital with a family who is looking for a housemaid. After a year with Mrs. Meyer I'm ready for a change and Charles helps me get the job. When I tell Mrs. Meyer I'm leaving, she softens. "You're a good girl," she says sweetly. "How can you do this to me after all I've taught you?" She offers me an extra dollar a week but I decline. Still, in parting, she gives me a linen handkerchief with an embroidered border. The gesture touches me, and I learn something about not waiting too long to let someone know you appreciate them.

Dr. Gibson and his wife are undemanding. He leaves for the hospital at six in the morning and requires nothing. She practices simple habits, arises at eight, and likes a pot of tea and toast brought to her room. They go out to many dinners for charity or with friends, so cooking isn't an every night obligation. They have a couple of dinner parties every month, eight or ten people, but they hire an extra girl to help. We serve rack of lamb or a standing beef rib roast.

Their two daughters are away at Albright College. Mrs. Gibson says living alone with the doctor is like a second honeymoon. On weekends the daughters sometimes visit with bulging suitcases. Their heavy flannel skirts and luxurious silk blouses are strewn about on the bed for me to put away. My hands caress the fine fabrics with envy. God does indeed provide better for some than others.

Charles meets me on my day off and we take drives, pointing out a particular white swan on a slate gray lake, or an interesting tree, or the light on the pink horizon. He takes class on Tuesday night, studying accounting and tax appraisal. He's a man with a future.

One Sunday we drive out to Perry County to see Mom and are met by yapping dogs and screaming children who run beside the car. Aunt Varnie and Aunt Ida just happen to be there, wrapped in aprons, elbow deep in flour, using my French rolling pin to make apple dumplings. "Pleased to make your acquaintance," they say bashfully, welcoming Charles and shooting me curious, eyebrow-raising looks. The gossip will keep them alive. They've brought along a big Sunday dinner, and we sit around the table to eat.

Charles is a good listener and everyone approves of him. Just as he did with Murphy, Abe tells Charles about his rafting days. Later Buckley comes by, leaving Liz at home with the new baby, and even they find common ground, talking fish hatchets and bale hooks. Buck explains how an Indian fellow he met taught him to tie green cowhide to the bottom of his boots to keep them from getting sucked down by the river. I don't believe the story. The part about meeting an Indian is probably pure hogwash.

In August the Gibsons leave for a trip to Atlantic City. It's a glorious weekend, warm and tranquil, and we spend it at a summer camp Charles knows of, up in Dauphin County, where he teaches me to play miniature golf. Standing behind me with his elbows flexed, he places his feet on either side of mine, and their narrow delicacy surprises me. He shows me how to swing the club, and after the game we sit in the shade, cut a pear, and feed each other crescent slices. His dark eyes are all over me and I feel dizzy. We check into a cabin at a motor court and in a short while stand naked before one another. His attitude is respectful and patient. We have all the time in the world. The breeze from the window is balmy and carries the sound of an afternoon baseball game somewhere in the distance.

The shadow of his hand moves across my belly, and my senses come alive. I know he will soon be my husband.

Afterwards, every physical sensation in me is heightened—the Turkish towel after a shower, the heat from the mug of complimentary coffee he's gone to fetch from the camp office, the table's rough wood grain beneath my fingertips, the cold water I splash on my face. His naked feet are indeed delicate and fine-boned and quickly become my favorite part of him. What joy—the man I've come to love, whom I'm destined to marry, sleeps beside me under the same cover. All the weight and worry are lifted. For once I'm happy, as we lie in the moonlight touching for hours.

The next night, my eighteenth birthday, he takes me dancing to a honky-tonk club on the outskirts of Carlisle. His forearms hold me with confidence, and I, who freeze whenever my physical appearance is appraised, am suddenly a tall woman moving across the wooden dance floor with effortless grace. "It's a foxtrot," he says, and I feel his warmth and ease as we keep step with the other couples.

The Gibsons return at the end of the week and bring me a box of saltwater taffy and a small bottle filled with beach sand. I begin to imagine living in my own home with Charles. We'll budget his pay, and I'll do some kind of work to bring in extra money. But my days of fitting to the form of another woman's household are nearly over.

21

In the last days of October, the stock market crashes. Everyone is nervous but me. The Gibsons give me three days off while they go to a medical college where he is delivering a lecture. Charles picks me up and we return to the tourist cabin, only this time the room is chilly and unheated, so we press against each other for warmth. I yield to him, building our history for the date when we will marry.

The stock market crisis worsens, but with Charles to love, nothing worldly frightens me. The economic events bother him a bit, the uncertainty of it all, but he is still the same man. It is I who am different. One Sunday we take a trip to see Mom. When we get to the top of Sterretts Gap, I ask him to pull the car over so I can share some news. "We're expecting," I say.

His face is overjoyed as he takes my hands and breathes warmth onto them and says, "Don't worry, everything is going to be fine." I ask him about getting married. "Don't worry," he says, "we'll take things step by step." He kisses my fingers.

"I'd like to tell my mother," I say. "It would be nice to tell her we're getting married." He discourages me from speaking about it. "Verna, I need to get used to the news before we spout it everywhere," he says. "Let's just wait until we have our plans more firmly in place."

At the table I have no appetite and wonder if the women notice. But they just talk about how as winter approaches they already miss the garden and how flowerbeds are the surest sign to tell if there's a woman living in a house. Mom remarks that pansies are her favorite and have little velvety faces that look up at you. Charles catches my eye and I know he is thinking of the baby, same as me.

Uncle Mose wants to know what Charles thinks of the crash. "It'll straighten itself out," Charles says, "provided people can hang on to their homes and the factories don't start shutting down."

Uncle Mose notes that farmers have had little economic benefit in the boom times since the war ended. "It's not unpleasant to think that a lot of rich people are learning a lesson and losing their money." Charles says the market is just adjusting itself to gluttony. Uncle Mose says he and Varnie have always relied on God's mercy to deliver good weather and growing conditions, and businessmen will have to learn to do the same.

Who cares about all this? I think. I'm going to have a baby and can't even tell my mother.

By dusk a miserable wind cuts across the valley and makes it hard for Charles to crank the car. His overcoat flaps behind him. I shiver for a moment and realize that perhaps hard times are just beginning. How could that be? The drive back to Harrisburg is silent. We hold hands and Charles whistles a tune under his breath. The wind buffeting the car and the intensity of the emotion from earlier in the day have worn us out.

My mind keeps returning to Ida and Varnie and how they looked out the window at Mom as she walked across the yard to the privy. Their nodding and muttering were odd. Hmm. Hmm. As sisters, they always scrutinize Mom, but this was different. All at once it dawns on me. The realization feels like someone has thrown a stone at my head. I suddenly understand. Mom is also with child. It's true, her middle-aged face and figure were fuller. What a fool I am for not noticing. I do the math in my head: 1888 to 1929. Mom is forty-one.

No wonder nobody paid attention to me.

Pop used to say if Aunt Varnie or Aunt Ida happened upon a person whose clothes had caught fire, they'd apply themselves with utmost urgency and do everything in their power to douse the flame. However, if they happened upon a person whose mind was on fire, aflame with gossip, self-pity, injustice, anger, or regret the excitement would consume them too and they wouldn't be able to keep from adding kindling and kerosene. "It's the Irish way," he would say. "Nurse a grudge so it grows hotter and can't be extinguished."

Will Mom marry Abe?

22

It's Thanksgiving and I'm awake with nausea and discomfort every morning. By Christmas I begin to show. I wait patiently for Charles to propose. "Getting married on New Year's Day would be nice," I say, when he stops by to deliver the bread. He looks stricken. "Verna, please don't corner me like this when I'm at work." He gulps his coffee, glances at his watch, and looks out the window at the idling truck like an escaped convict. The need to pin him down is overwhelming, but I know he won't propose under those conditions.

On a cold, rainy Wednesday in January, we meet at the Magnolia Spot Tea Room and he shakes a set of keys to an apartment that a friend has lent him. My heart beats with anticipation, knowing the time has finally come. But as soon as the apartment door is locked he begins to try and remove my clothes. I feel self-conscious about my figure and the weight I'm putting on. "When are you going to marry me?" I say through tears, and flinch from his kiss. "I'm beginning to show now."

"Verna, I love you so much," he says. "To be with you every day is all I think about. To know I've made you cry kills me. I never want to hurt you." He places his arms around me and I give in to his embrace.

"I'm upset because Mrs. Gibson has been acting strange," I tell him. "I think she's noticed my condition."

"I understand," he says. "Please know I'm doing everything in my power to get my ducks in a row."

My mind flashes from the pain in my heart. I'm in love with someone who does not deserve it. But I can't let him know that or then he'll never marry me. I slog through the afternoon but eventually unfold myself under his tender caress. Afterwards I make the bed, smoothing out the wrinkles in the chenille spread.

Two more weeks of rushed morning visits and he makes no mention of his plans—of putting his ducks in a row. My nerves fray. He's undependable. Not grown up. Selfish. Still a child.

The friend who lent him the apartment remains away, so we return there. This time all the ugliness of the place comes alive—dirty cracked linoleum, dingy curtains, chipped furniture, and yellowing walls.

I don't want to end up here.

I imagine women like me waiting, waiting in towns all over the country, all over the world, alone, grim about the mouth, upset at the horror of waiting so involuntarily.

"I want to leave this place," I say, and know a quarrel is brewing.

"We just got here, Verna."

"This place is a dump," I say. "Let's leave."

"You're being silly," he says. "We don't have anywhere else to go."

How can I find the phrase that will pay him back for his selfishness? "I can't expect you to be considerate of me or my feelings. But the least you could do is find a decent place for us."

His face grows red. "When did you turn so dainty?"

The desire for a fight rises up in me and I can't suppress it. "I was respectable before I started carrying on with you." My voice is sharp—a knife. "You don't care about me. You don't understand what I've been through. Why don't you tell the truth and admit that you don't love me."

For a moment the horror is upon me. I have failed to keep myself in check.

"Verna," he says, "you're behaving like a spoiled child."

"You're the spoiler," I shout. "You come around here and tell me you love me and want to be with me. I'm completely in your power. In your lies. Is it too much to want our baby to have a mother and a father who are married? Can't you see I'm sick of waiting?"

"Well, I'm sorry," he says, voice dropping low, like he's the injured party. "I'm still trying to figure things out."

"Like what? Putting your stupid ducks in a row! Don't you see what your indecision is doing? Is there someone else? Maybe you'd rather be with her?"

"I'm not continuing this conversation until you calm down," he says, standing and moving to the door with his hat.

"Where are you going?"

"Out to walk around the block."

"Don't go. I need you," I say, and tears begin to stream down my face. "It's all so confused in my head."

I apologize to him and tell him I don't understand what I'm saying, that the three months of waiting have been more than I can bear. I apologize for being such a burden. I apologize for wanting so much from him. I apologize for my anger. "But please," I say, "please do the right thing by the baby."

We are both silent for a long while. He puts his hat down and comes over to sit beside me on the bed. Now the moment I have so long been waiting for has finally arrived. My hot words are embarrassing, but they have done their work. From the look on his face I can see he is making up his mind to propose.

"Verna." He pauses. "I'm sorry but I can't marry you." Another pause. "I'm already married."

There is a spot of color on each of his cheeks as he looks away. I sit and stare at the linoleum and wonder if I will ever be able to move again.

·   23   ·

On a weekend when they are home from Albright College, Mrs. Gibson's two daughters corner me in the kitchen after overhearing their mother speaking to her husband. Like girls who gossip in the last pew at church, they want to know not only if it's true but also how it happened.

"He's a regular fellow," I say. "We plan to marry."

"A wedding!" they squeal, clapping their hands together with excitement. "When is it?"

"Well, he's had to go on a trip," I say, uncertain because the lie is getting bigger. "He won't be back until after the baby is born."

Their faces grow more composed as if to hide themselves, eyebrows tilting in with a certain upper-class concern. "Your poor mother must be beside herself."

"Oh, she understands," I say. "She's also expecting."

Stupidly misguided in my intention to sound grown-up, I just blurt it out. I blurt it matter-of-factly, believing they will simply accept it as a fact, as if to convince them that none of this worldly business is a concern to anyone, least of all them and their family. Maybe by recognizing how commonplace the phenomenon of expecting a child is, so commonplace that Mom and I both do it, they will easily accept my situation.

Their confused expressions show the terrible mistake I've made. They know my father is dead and suddenly I'm stuck trying to explain Abe Lease and how he stays at our place. My temples throb, my head is full of sand. I look at the clock and tell them I have to get busy to get supper ready in time. They cease further inquiry and smile graciously as they drift away.

As soon as they leave the kitchen, I can tell that something has changed in the way I'm being perceived. My ears burn imagining the whispered conversations taking place in their well-appointed bedrooms. "Do you think she's a slattern?"

The next morning Mrs. Gibson calls me into the library for a discussion. She sits upright in a chair by her writing desk, so upright her spine is as straight as a statue. "Will you marry?" she asks, in a matronly but firm manner—a curious combination of sympathy and disgust. I shake my head. "I feel bad about this, Verna," she says quietly, "but I have no choice but to set a proper example for my girls. People will talk." A new maid arrives within the hour and says she'd been hired the day before. Mrs. Gibson gives me an extra week's pay.

• • •

As the weather warms, Mom and I both move around the cabin, our stomachs pushed out. We hardly ever speak. Mom goes into labor a few weeks ahead of me. Lantern in hand, out into the June night Abe flees to fetch Mrs. Hampton. At midnight, a baby boy pushes his head through, then out into this world his slippery body follows. I'm fascinated but almost sick at the thought that my own body will soon be contorting with the same chore.

The next morning we awake and Mrs. Hampton is pouring buttermilk for us to drink. "Where's the baby?" I ask. Mrs. Hampton goes about her task with an unnatural efficiency. She says it died in the early morning and that she's put the body out in the springhouse until Abe comes by to dig a grave.

Mom is washed out and doesn't seem too upset over losing her baby; she may even be relieved. I wonder if what Mrs. Hampton said is true. Pop used to say no one knows more tricks than a country midwife. For weeks I wake up in the middle of the night and think I hear the baby crying out in the ice-cold springhouse where Mrs. Hampton left it.

In the morning, Abe Lease comes by and says he's got a two-week job digging roads for the county. He asks if he can leave his horse and wagon for us to look after so he can work unencumbered. Of course we agree, and after he's gone Mom gets a wild look and hitches up the wagon. "There's not enough of anything to feed these kids much longer," she says. "If we ride to Grandma Peffer's maybe we can persuade her to give us something from her smokehouse. Even a few soup bones would help."

I'm tempted to remind Mom how Grandma Peffer didn't even bother to come to Pop's funeral—and I know word was sent—and how unpleasant she was at Buck's wedding. I also debate whether to remind her that Pop said I never had to go back to her place again. But desperation or cabin fever or some other madness has given Mom unusual determination, and the wagon is already hitched.

Pop took my side completely the New Year's before last when Grandma Peffer lied and said I stole money from her. The trouble started after lunch, which Pop always called her famous thin soup with no meat. It didn't matter to me what she served, I could barely eat there anyhow. Her kitchen always smells rancid, like somewhere there is stashed a plate of fermented corn fritters.

They left me to do the dishes while Grandma took everyone outside to show off her smokehouse and the hams hanging from the rafters. God forbid she'd give us a slice. She's got that selfish streak that runs through a lot of people around here. And so, while stacking the freshly washed dishes in the cupboard, I see a chipped shaving mug on one shelf with some half dollars inside. I never touched them. I wouldn't have dared.

Then a month later we learn from Aunt Varnie that Grandma has been telling everyone that after she fed our whole family, I repaid her by lifting two of her half dollars when her back was turned. "There's nothing worse than someone who steals from her own people," Aunt Varnie reports her saying.

My face burns. I tell Pop I'm going to go over there and spit right in her eye.

"You've been falsely accused," he says, all grand at the injustice, like he's a Tyrone king in a court of law. "That old woman has drawn trouble all her life. She can't see a bedsore without sticking her finger into it."

Mom is having none of it but Pop finally prevails. "Verna need never go back there ever again," he decrees. Then he insists on repaying the dollar, making a great show of passing it to Uncle Mose for safe delivery. Now there's a dollar less for groceries—and Grandma Peffer has the nerve to say *I* stole from *my* people!

Now, in the wagon, all of this is being relived in my mind and I'm growing ever more angry to be accompanying Mom and the girls in the bumpy wagon, which is not a good thing for a girl in my condition to be doing anyhow. About a mile from Grandma Peffer's lane we pass by the ruins of an old stone house. My stomach is sore with the baby and my mouth feels like I've been chewing on coffee grounds. "Stop the wagon," I say with a voice that means business, and Mom actually obeys. I climb down and puke by the side of the road.

Then a hardness that I've never felt before arises in my chest. "You'd best go on," I say. "I'll wait here for you to return."

Mom's face is stunned. My declaration isn't a question, or an order. It's just clear I'm stating a fact.

"You can't sit here all day . . . outside," Mom says.

"Either I wait here or there's going to be even bigger trouble." My voice is strong and sharp and comes from a deep, new place.

"But what will I say?" Mom asks.

"Don't say anything. Or tell her I'm ill. Or better yet, say that since she didn't see fit to come pay her respects to my pop—I won't come pay her any."

Mom holds the reins and I can see her knuckles are white. I go and sit on the garden wall by the ruins of the house and keep my gaze down at my shoes. Mom holds the wagon to the spot for a good long minute. Finally, I hear the sound of a lap rug being thrown down, followed by the creak of wheels as the wagon moves on. My head stays down until the creaking grows faint and disappears.

At last I look up. The trees are glowing from the sun shining through the leaves and the ground is shaded. It's a beautiful day but you can tell we're on the upside of summer. After a while the lap rug seems welcome and I go and pick it up, and wrap it around my shoulders. An apple is on the ground nearby, which Mom must have also tossed down. I slip it into my apron pocket and then wander around the ruins of the stone walls imagining where the rooms once were. In some places the foundation is completely grown over with wild grapes.

Suddenly I feel tired from the weight of the baby pulling on my back and from the day's strong emotions. I lie down on some leaves and listen to the sound of the woods. I think about the house. What happened to the people who once lived here and called this place home? Were there any babies born here? If I ever had a house as fine as theirs must have been, I'd never leave it. The wind is shifting the trees, and I pull the lap rug tight around me. Somewhere a stick snaps under a deer and then I'm asleep—my first really deep sleep in weeks.

When I awake it's to the sound of an elegant horned owl flying through the trees with its wings spread wide. I imagine it as an angel watching over me. It's almost evening now and as I begin to eat the apple, I hear the sound of the wagon coming back down the trail. Mom picks me up and we head home. I see the wagon is empty and nothing is said about meat or soup bones the entire way. We make the last part of the journey in the pitch black darkness. I finally jump down and walk the horse to guide it with the lantern so it won't stumble. Last thing we need is a horse with a broken ankle.

My own labor begins on a strangely cool day in mid-July. Sam is born that night. My body produces more milk than he can consume and my left breast is beset by an infection. It aches unbearably. Mrs. Hampton treats it with camphor, and Sam howls at the scent. My body feels like I'm turned inside out, and I can tell the other women have limited patience for my slow recovery and that soon there will be noise about getting back into the saddle of chores. On my third day in bed, Mrs. Hampton says, "Life's affairs drag from bad to worse if you let them." Mom cuts parsley for the soup: "It's not like you've got a provider." Aunt Varnie is direct with her curiosity: "What became of that nice fella?" Mom is particularly annoying. After her many years of helplessness, she's hardly to be mistaken for someone who knows how to get on with things. But still she says, "It's not like we can expect others to carry our burden."

"Well at least I helped you with your burden," I snap back. The noise stops. Everyone looks at me as some sort of ingrate.

When I'm alone with the baby, I sit and really look at him. He's cute and I feel drawn to cuddle him, but Mom comes back in and I make up my mind right there and then that there is no way I can afford to let this baby into my heart—or the pain of leaving it will kill me.

In the morning Hazel and Myrtle head off for school and I get dressed, gather my things, and pack the leather box. I hold the baby for one last moment, kiss it, then quickly put it back in the cradle, knowing if I don't hurry I will never get away.

Mom is out back weeding the meager vegetable bed with a rusted hoe. She straightens up as I come out of the cabin dressed for travel and carrying the box. Her lips prune.

"Somebody has to go and earn wages," I say. "Somebody has to."

She blinks back the tears that begin to overwhelm her. "Not again."

I hold my own. "I'm useless here looking after a hungry child. Useless. But I can go and make money. I know how to work."

Mom lets a rush of air pass between her teeth and looks over her shoulder as though there might be someone there to consult. Then her head turns back to face me again. "Please don't do this," she says.

I feel the back of my throat grow warm with emotion but I will not cry. "I know a lot of people will hate me for leaving my baby. But I've got to go do something."

Mom grips the garden hoe until her knuckles are white. "You won't come back."

"I will."

Mom leans into the handle. "You won't. I know it. I'll be left to look after that child. I can't do it, Verna. I can't." Sobs begin to wrack her shoulders.

"There's no point going on this way," I say, my voice hoarse with emotion. "Just take one look at this situation."

Mom pulls away and takes a handkerchief from her pocket. "Well, dear God, I should have known. You're as bullheaded as your father. He always blamed me for ruining his life. Never stopping to think that he sure as hell ruined mine. They tell you that they love you. Then they turn and run."

We hear the baby begin to cry inside the cabin.

"I have to go," I say, my throat full of tears. "I'm sorry."

Mom turns her back to me and slowly begins to walk toward the house, the garden hoe dragging from her hand. "So long," she says, over her shoulder. "Glad to have met you."

24

The Great Depression is the first historical event in my life that seems aptly named. I spend days sitting on the hard wooden bench of the employment office in Harrisburg, find a few days' work, then come back to sit some more. I work as a cook, a maid, a dishwasher, a babysitter, a charwoman, a seamstress, and even for a season as a chambermaid at the Penn Harris Hotel—where I wander the carpeted hallways pondering which room John and Delia might have stayed in when they came from St. Louis a decade before.

The hotel gives a checklist to work with: first strip linens, second sweep the floor, third wash and polish the bathroom, fourth put everything back again with furniture wiped and dusted and beds remade. Often the women leave face cream and makeup on the towels, but the worst task is cleaning the mirrors over the dressers after a salesman has stayed there, for it's their habit to wash out their handkerchiefs in the sink and then to press them flat on the mirrors to dry overnight. The hankies peel off the glass in the morning smooth and wrinkle-free, ready for folding, but the mirror is terribly smudged and in need of scrubbing with ammonia water.

Though I send every dime I can home to Mom and the children, she is so behind on the cabin's rent that the owner has finally asked them to leave. He's never really had much respect for us to begin with, but since Mom and I were both pregnant at the same time, and he notices Abe Lease is always hanging around, he probably figures that it's time to cut his losses. Mom, with Abe's help, travels all over Perry County looking for a new home, but everywhere she goes her reputation precedes her.

One day I run into Charles Dennis. Usually I snub him, but this time, not knowing where else to turn, I plead for help. Through him I locate a small wood-frame, three-bedroom row house in Cumberland County, and he helps me get favorable terms on the rent. Despite Mom's protests that she'll be too far to see Abe, I move her, lock, stock, and barrel with Myrtle, Hazel, and Sam to Mechanicsburg. Three weeks later Abe grows so lonely he boards up his shack and crosses the gap to join them, and I'm glad because though they are terribly crowded, his tiny pension from the tannery helps defray the expenses.

During the first six years of Sam's life, I see Charles Dennis a half dozen times—and extract from him a total of seven dollars and twenty-eight cents toward raising his son. On one occasion, Sam's fifth birthday, I trick Charles into coming along to visit our boy, and as he bears no gift, Charles, the big spender, flips Sam a quarter. Though I'll never trust Charles Dennis again, there is still something between us. For a while I imagine him leaving his wife for me, but she's a Catholic, and then I realize that even if he did abandon her, I wouldn't want him under those conditions.

A few months after Mom has moved to Mechanicsburg, Grandma Peffer drops dead in her yard while digging at a thistle with the heel of her shoe. Franklin Moore, the dapper man who runs the Penn-Harris, hears about the death from my supervisor. He calls me into his office and says the hotel would like to give me a paid grieving day. I almost faint with gratitude and surprise.

Heavy rain makes travel in every direction a mess and Aunt Varnie says it's just like the old witch to die when conditions are at their worst.

"Now that she's dead," Mom says, "you shouldn't call her a witch anymore."

"That's what you call someone who dabbles in hexes," Varnie replies.

Sam plays at Mom's feet the whole time and doesn't come to me even when I extend my arms. "Does it bother you the way he's taken to your mom?" Varnie asks, a hint of salt for the wound.

"Of course not," I say. "He's better off with her."

I hope my voice displays no hint of the anguish I feel at such thoughts. To make the moment worse, Buck is there with Liz and overhears the whole exchange. But they seem to be having their own troubles. He looks tough from being out of work and she looks strained, her pretty freshness gone with the Depression. And we all just know Buck is drinking.

At the Penn Harris I meet another chambermaid named Olive Hopper and to save money we share a room in a flophouse. Olive says I've got a good head on my shoulders and once these hard times are over she's sure I'll go places. She's impressed that I fish newspapers out of the waste bins and copy out articles on my lunch break. Olive talks nonstop about returning home to Philadelphia. "Why, in Philly we've got dozens of jobs that are just begging for people to take them," she says. "Why, there's one restaurant where we can make twelve dollars a week—double what we make here." Olive is smart, fast-talking, and streetwise. "I've been around the block more than once," she boasts. "And not always in the best neighborhoods." Her nasty insights about the hotel guests and her observations on the dumbness of Harrisburg citizens in general demonstrate a worldliness that, coupled with her slow, loose-limbed walk, makes me admire her. Hard times have toughened Olive up, but she found the answers long ago. I feel lucky to be in her company.

I'm scared to death of Philadelphia, but at the same time I'm excited when one day we finally decide to pack up and go there to give that city a try. From its magnificent brand-new train station we can see a river, and well-dressed crowds of people seem to be going every which way. But then we take the trolley car pretty far out to a shabby section of row houses where we will live, and it shocks me to see how run-down everything is. Many of the houses only a block away have been taken over by scores of colored people. The men are mostly idle and stand around looking crusty and shiftless with their hands in their pockets, while many of the women go off and work. It seems like the women that stay behind spend a lot of time leaning out upon their windowsills with their hair tied up. They yell at their children with voices like I've never heard, or they kid and laugh with the idle men. I'm glad Mom can't see me walking down the street here or she'd think I was trash for sure.

It turns out the restaurant Olive talked so much about has room for only one girl. Naturally, Olive takes the job. I try some other places but no luck. Now Olive and I share a room on the top floor of a boardinghouse for women that's only a match away from being history and where the rent is far from fair. No cooking is allowed, but we hide a hot plate at the bottom of the dresser and make coffee and boiled eggs in the morning. Olive says all the women do it.

Olive is a swell gal and after a week manages to get me a job in her restaurant after all. On the evening before my first day of work, she helps me cut my hair. It's very straight with bangs, modern like Constance Bennett's, but I'm not thin like her.

Crane's Restaurant has a terrible kitchen, steaming, filthy, and full of swill. Their notion of cooking is to heat vats of lard and drop chicken, breaded fish, potatoes, bacon, and anything else they can think of into it. On the plate, you're left with a big greasy mess, and our clothes and hair always smell deep-fried. They offer a special of calf's liver, which is cheap—and thankfully fried in big cast-iron pans—and often I sell thirty or forty of those a night. Even in these hard times the customers are better dressed than by Harrisburg standards, the men in jaunty ties and the women often in fur pieces, but they still seem coarse and lack manners. Some of the women actually smoke cigarettes at the dinner table. The customers aren't friendly either, especially for a city priding itself on brotherly love. Still, I'm grateful to Olive for the chance to make money.

Leaving through the alley at the end of the work shift, we see big rats trample over one another. Sometimes, after closing, the cooks will trap one, its grisly tail twitching, and throw it into the deep fryer for laughs.

Our uniforms are beige with white cuffs, apron, and hat. At first I think they are smart, but they require much care and have to be scrubbed and washed after every shift. Olive is usually going out on a date and gives me a dollar a week to wash hers. I carefully stash the money in my savings purse, which I keep hidden in the bottom drawer of my nightstand.

I don't know where Olive finds the energy. It takes forever to get to work on the streetcars, and at night I can barely copy things from the newspaper because I'm half-dead from work.

The tall, middle-aged woman who manages Crane's is named Veronica McDonald. She has terrible grammar, dyes her hair orangey red, and wears tight girdles, fancy collars, bows on her shoes, and lots of perfume. The waitresses are tough and smart-alecky like Olive and frequently say things behind Veronica's back that I'd be ashamed to think—like how she learned her grooming habits on her knees in a whorehouse.

They cut each other down too. "I need a cherry for the top of this banana split," one of them calls out in the kitchen. "You ain't had a cherry in years," another hollers back. "Or a banana either," a third chimes in. For customers, particularly the men, Veronica wears her most magnanimous smile and dips her voice in honey. "Oh—I haven't seen you in a while," she'll say, seductively helping them off with their coats. Then once they're seated she minces away in her bow-topped shoes and glares at us. "Move your ass," she snarls through gritted teeth.

We are constantly having our speech corrected by her: we are supposed to describe a meal saying, "It is served with mashed potatoes" instead of "It comes with." Also, after someone's finished eating, she wants us to say, "I'd be happy to bring you coffee with your dessert," even if the people haven't said they wanted any dessert. That takes gall.

Veronica looks down on me because I'm from the country, and when a party is seated with certain male customers considered to be high rollers, she doesn't trust me and I'm ordered to swap tables with a more experienced and smiley waitress, like Olive, who knows how to lean over to show off her bosom or tell a flirty joke. I'm grateful, for I grow red-faced and bashful handling these wisecracking men.

Veronica indeed recognizes that I'm not as jaded as the other girls, and at times she speaks to me with more reserve and the occasional bit of advice. "Always make whoever it is that is giving you their order think they are the center of the world," or "When serving dinner plates to a man and a woman who've both ordered the same thing, it's important to give the bigger piece of meat to the man," she says.

"That's the opposite of what she learned in the whorehouse," one of the girls whispers as Veronica exits through the kitchen's swinging door.

Two boyfriends keep Olive's social life from getting dull. The older one is close to forty and Olive says she dates him "to pay for things." The other one is in his midtwenties and "made for love." It's embarrassing to watch Olive manage two boyfriends while I can't procure one. It dawns on me that Olive is fast. She lacks conscience.

Then late one night I return home from Crane's to find that Olive has moved out. At first I think burglars have struck—the topsy-turvy room in disarray—then I notice Olive's things are gone. Waves of sickness wash over me when I see she's ransacked my things too and stolen my savings. The landlady says Olive took off with her suitcase in the morning, just after I left for work. How could I have been so dumb? How could I have trusted her? I'm ill with grief.

I'm obsessed with tracking her down. She has a sister in Allentown. But with no address, how can I find her? How can I travel there when now I have no cash and can barely afford to take the streetcar? Would her sister even give me the time of day? The only other kin I know about is the scofflaw brother selling land in Florida. Olive recently confided that he's fallen in with bootleggers who sell cut-rate alcohol labeled as the real thing.

Self-pity keeps me up at night. I weep from anger. There is no way I can pay the monthly bill at the boardinghouse. My insides feel like I've swallowed burning embers. The morning sun comes, I dress for work like a snail. Nobody there seems shocked at Olive's disappearance. A few of them smile, shake their heads, and say, "That Olive's a case."

Their amusement and indifference upset me; it's almost as if thievery is to be expected against someone as young and dumb as I am.

My work is affected; I'm slow and in a daze. By the end of September Veronica McDonald calls me into her office to give me my pay. "You need to go back home," she says, and from a patent leather clutch produces an envelope that contains a one-way ticket to Harrisburg. She must have visited the Thirtieth Street Station before work to buy it. "All the girls chipped in," she says. How embarrassing to find that my failure in Philadelphia is rendering me a charity case, but I don't refuse. Veronica isn't the kind of woman who likes being seen as soft. I stand there tongue-tied and try to express gratitude. "Aw, don't get all sappy-eyed about it," she says, and seems glad to rid herself of me.

· 25 ·

Back in Harrisburg, jobs have grown even more scarce; my lodgings change almost as often as my work. I take a room with a widow on Fifth Street, who shows me hand-tinted photos of her husband and son. "Both of my men died of cholera within a few days of each other," she says, sniffling.

In really lean weeks I stay at the mission house for women or on a cot in the community room of the Catholic church, or in warm weather, to pinch pennies, I sometimes sleep fully clothed on a park bench, making sure I'm not in a colored section, or I sleep at the YWCA or hole up like a squirrel in a gasoline-smelling room over someone's garage, and more than once I skip out on rent in the middle of the night. I'm not the only one. Across the country there are hundreds like me flat broke and desperately hunting jobs.

I do a stint as a waitress in a nickel-a-drink chop joint, and when one of the customers asks me out, I almost drop my tray. His name is Norm Trexler and he drives an oil truck. We go on a couple of dates and he tells me he's heard of a housekeeping job for one of his oil customers, a woman named Mrs. Parrish, and he arranges an interview for me.

Her house is on Front Street, large with six bedrooms and the most stylish company rooms I've ever seen. She herself is an elegant woman wearing a burgundy dress with knife pleats, her voice cultured and refined, her taste impeccable. When she hears I've worked for her friend Franklin Moore at the Penn Harris Hotel, she phones him, then hires me on the spot.

All kinds of modern conveniences make her kitchen a gold mine for learning—gas range, modern electric refrigerator, percolator, waffle iron, and toast maker. In her dining room there's a double-door closet with long poles set in the wall. Her tablecloths don't get folded but are rolled so they have no creases.

I study everything Mrs. Parrish does, and her closets of clothes, many with labels from New York (Bonwit Teller, Henri Bendel, Hattie Carnegie) and from Harrisburg (Worth's and Mary Sachs). On Thursday afternoons she attends a ladies' card party and luncheon. When it's her turn to host she tells me she wants to serve Waldorf salad. I'm unwilling to admit that I don't know what that is, so I go down to a bookseller off the square and look it up: apples, celery, walnuts, and mayonnaise—big deal. My resourcefulness is growing.

Once I start working for Mrs. Parrish there's a change in my relationship with Norm. He doesn't seem to want to let me forget that it's him who got me the job, and at times he seems almost jealous that I've adapted to the work so well. In the evenings, after Mrs. Parrish and her guests have taken dinner, Norm often drops by. He sits in the pantry and I fix him a plate of food, which he eats while I wash up the kitchen.

He knows I have a son who will soon turn six and that he lives with my mother, but when I try to explain how, as a parent who only shows up for holidays or the odd weekend, I have no rights, he doesn't seem to understand. "If I notice things that need better tending," I try explaining to him, "I must keep silent or it looks like I'm criticizing Mom."

Norm misses the mark every time. "Well, it sounds like you've got yourself a bout of girlie melancholy," he says, or "You're as sensitive as a lost kitten." Sometimes, even worse, he'll say, "You don't know how to think positive," or "You can't see the sunny side of life." It's difficult to explain, and I give up trying. You can't explain things to a numbskull.

It's ironic that although Norm helped me secure this job, he hates my long hours and begins carping that I deserve a better life. He reads workers' pamphlets, the kind given out on the street, and picks up their phrases and ideas. "What you have is an inferiority complex," he says, or "That's why you're content doing housework for a living." Then he goes on about how only modern factory jobs uphold the dignity of the free citizen and that if I intend to continue slaving for rich people, I might wise up and cut corners in my chores, or even spit in their soup. He can harp on something longer than a Baptist preacher and pays no heed when I say it isn't in me to be slouchy or bad-tempered, and then I remind him that it was he who helped me get the job.

He says the richer the people are, the later they eat, and that it's my right to be done with work before they finish such folly. It riles him that my schedule includes only one free day every other Sunday and that I don't have my own place. What he really wants is for me to have a job where I return home by 5:30 every evening to fix his supper—stand at his range and make tapioca pudding to satisfy his mama-boy sweet tooth. He gets so wound up over the need to improve my life that he even mocks the fact that I'm praised for my skill at cooking.

Then one day Norm hears of a job with union benefits at a big sock factory in town. "I'm gonna get you in," he says. He tells of a friend who knows a fellow that knows a fellow who knows the foreman there. It makes me uncomfortable to think of quitting my job with Mrs. Parrish. Still, I'm so tired of bickering and maybe Norm is right, maybe it's time to take a risk and break the routine.

Just as I'm beginning to talk myself into calling the factory man Norm has procured, there's a crisis at home. Abe Lease is rushed into the hospital for an emergency operation on account of his high blood sugar. A large portion of his left foot has to be removed, leaving only his big toe. His system is in shock because of the poisons in his blood. This is frightening for Mom and for us all. If he dies, we'll need every extra penny to pay the rent. Much to Norm's annoyance, I put off making the call requesting an interview at the factory. When I visit Abe in the hospital, he is improving, but his feet are pale, with skin soft as bread dough. The doctor hopes it won't be necessary to cut more away. To think, two weeks earlier he was still pitching horseshoes in a dusty field down by the scrap yard.

Mom is enduring pretty well, considering, and Mrs. Parrish is generous in allowing me to visit them two mornings a week. But when Abe comes home, Mom can't stomach changing his dressings. I show Hazel how the doctor said it should be done, but Hazel is distracted. She's twenty-one now and seeing this fellow named Joe, who seems like a solid citizen. He speaks of his job in the grocery business, saying, "It's a field with a future." Apparently, more and more stores rely on stuff that's already packaged in factories. "You get accurate measure that way and the stuff is fresh and free of bugs."

Abe's recovery is slow. His breathing is irregular, and the metal can of Power's asthma powder that he used to keep in the outhouse is brought inside. Every few hours he lights some, breathes in the smoke, and starts a hacking cough until yellow sputum comes out of his lungs. In a couple of hours, the wheezing worsens and he begins the process all over. The smoke from the powder has a horrible stench and lingers through the entire house.

One evening Norm enters Mrs. Parrish's kitchen and notices I'm wearing my yellow cotton dress with the light blue cuffs. "Why have you changed out of your uniform?" he asks all foxy, and can't understand it when I explain that after working all day and serving supper, I don't want to sit in my uniform the rest of the evening. "You were planning to go out, weren't you?" he questions. I explain and explain, while he challenges, until finally, like a dog grown tired of chewing on a meatless bone, he lets it drop.

We take a cold drive south along the river and stop at a ramshackle inn down between Shipoke and Steelton. The joint is owned by an old woman, who serves nothing but some stale coffee and a nip of whiskey. She joins us for the first nip, and then we each have two more shots. I'm so worn down by it all that this time I agree to go and speak to the factory man about the job. We head back to Harrisburg, and when Norm kisses me, his mouth is wet and sloppy on account of the liquor.

Despite the nest of butterflies in my stomach, the interview with the foreman at the sock factory goes well. The man's name is Rufus Collins; he's burly with a red beard. He asks me a few questions, wants to know where in Ireland my people come from, and is annoyed that I don't know. His people hail from Cork. Despite the disappointment my ignorance and indifference to my Irish heritage causes him, he says I can have the job if I want it.

I give my notice to Mrs. Parrish. The news saddens her and she seems surprised that I'd want to leave her fine home to work in a factory. I feel like a heel leaving the job after all the off time she's given me to help with Abe. Norm comes by in the evening and helps me move to a boardinghouse just west of Cameron Street. I'm unhappy at spending money on rent, but at the same time, my new prospects are exciting. Norm takes my hands in his and says how much he cares for me, how he wants me to have a better life. Outside the sun is setting and the orange glow fills the sky.

Later, with my new freedom, we visit Sam, arriving after dark. He has chicken pox and Mom says that tending both Sam and Abe is a terrible burden. "Maybe Myrtle could help for a change," I say, but Myrtle is out for the evening hanging around some churchgoers. Lately her head has gotten really big and she's developing a holy snobbery as if her discovery of faith is setting her apart from the rest of the human race. When she returns I remind her how Pop used to say, "Too much virtue can hurt you." She looks at me like I'm a Philistine.

In the morning I arrive early and the foreman puts me to work on the line folding socks into matching pairs—easy enough. I wear my pale green linen dress with the lace collar. The other women come with do-rags on their heads and old housedresses that button up the front. I feel sorry that they don't have a fine dress like mine—until we start to work. Cast-iron stands—flat in the shape of a foot and heated hot as blazes—are bolted to the table in front of us. Wet socks get taken from a bin and pulled down over the hot metal to press them flat. Then we fold them into pairs. The noise deafens. Steam shoots out. Sweat runs down my body in buckets. If you aren't quick you scorch the socks or burn your fingers on the blistering foot-stand. I notice the hands of the other women— nothing but scars and calluses from years of seared flesh. All I can think about is Mrs. Parrish's nice home with its fine things. I work hard to keep up with the other women, my sense of dread growing. It's clear, a terrible mistake has been made.

When the lunch whistle blows, I take my pocketbook and flee like I'm crossing over the river Jordan—no explanation to the foreman and no paycheck. My first day at the sock factory is also my last. Those wilted women on the line must have had a good laugh over how the sock dye ruined my lovely green dress. I can never wear it again.

As soon as I'm away from the building, I start fighting the tears. I walk past the warehouses on Cameron Street, and from a coin-operated telephone, I call Norm. Luckily he is in the office between deliveries. "Get down here and pick me up," I say, my voice filled with hurt. The sound must alarm him. He's there in ten minutes and drives me away. For a good hour I sit in the oil truck and bawl like a baby. How am I going to pay for a boardinghouse? How stupid it was to quit my nice job. Since I have nowhere else to be,

Norm lets me accompany him while he makes the remainder of his oil deliveries. I sulk all afternoon. In the evening he drops me back at the boardinghouse. He knows it's his fault.

Though it won't help my reputation, the next morning I move in with Norm, but only until I find another job. In the weeks that follow I do all I can to generally make Norm's life hellish, harping on how stupid he was to make me quit a good job in the middle of the Depression. He reminds me that I have free agency to leave, I am no beauty queen, and most guys will have nothing to do with me because I have a child.

Hard times generate hard times.

I play my errors in my head again and again. How I wish I'd used my savings and gone to St. Louis instead of to Reading with Murphy. Now it's too late. Perhaps Pop's daughter Delia and her husband struggle with money these days too? Or does she still ride in fine automobiles? How I wish I'd never met Olive Hopper. On and on.

I look in the phone book and dial Charles Dennis. If his wife answers I'll quietly set the receiver back down, but it's evening and he picks up. I cry and say that Sam is sick and needs medicine. I don't tell him it's just chicken pox or that he's already recovered. Charles sounds unwilling to get involved so I plead with him. It's difficult to be polite but I remind him that his son is coming up on six years, and that I've just lost my job. I never thought I'd be one of those women who cry to get things out of men, but here I am.

The next day Charles meets me in front of the Harrisburger Hotel. I tell him how I've spent the past few weeks sitting in the employment office with no prospects or money, how I even swallowed my pride and went back to Mrs. Parrish to ask for my old job. She was polite but my place was already taken. I don't tell him about Norm and oddly he doesn't ask where I'm staying.

A week later we meet again and Charles says he's heard of a housekeeping position with a family named Larson. In another week, following a steely interview, I've moved in with them, and though the job is challenging, I don't care because it gives me a way to move away from Norman's anger and his name-calling and jealousy.

Still, there's no class in the Larson household and nothing to learn but bad habits. They have three horrible, bratty children who scare me to death. They're also tight with money. My second day there she counts the cubes in the sugar bowl to see if I've helped myself to any. They only grant me one Sunday and one Wednesday a month off and she makes comments that imply I'm a charity case. "It must be nice to have a decent house to live in when so many people across the country are doing without."

In the evening Norm stops by. I don't dare feed him so much as a slice of cheese. She might weigh it. One evening, while the Larsons are out, I bring him up the service stairs so he can see my dark, moldy room under the eaves in the attic. For once he doesn't open his mouth about the dignity of the free citizen.

26

On my monthly Wednesday off, Charles Dennis and I will occasionally meet in the afternoons. He keeps his guard up but provides me with stingy bits of money. We usually take a small cabin at a motor court outside of town—which he also pays for. One week it's late and raining hard when we drive back to Harrisburg. There's an odd feeling of gloom in the air and I'm relieved that Norm hasn't come around looking for me. The weather worsens. We sense trouble in the way it pounds down hour after hour. Too much water is falling too fast.

The next day is St. Patrick's Day. Mrs. Larson and I are on guard—eyeing the river's edge from the curtained windows. We actually hear the crack of debris scraping across Front Street as the Susquehanna leaps its bank to come gurgling up between the old trees. Norm Trexler is suddenly banging at the kitchen door in a yellow slicker and boots, shouting, "Get out! Get out!" Water swirls under the front door and streams across the lovely inlaid floor of the foyer, then into the living room with its expensive rugs. We escape out the back door, splashing through a foot of water to the alley where Norm's oil truck waits, motor running. We cram the two-seated cab with the three children, a tight fit made worse by adding ourselves and the two furs—a chinchilla over a mink—Mrs. Larson insists on wearing. Somehow the truck escapes the alley and the flood zone, while Mrs. Larson holds her jewelry case and bawls over her ruined house. Everywhere, mothers and babies are stranded on rooftops, but she can't acknowledge our lucky rescue.

With the bridges to the West Shore closed (everyone worries they might collapse), we head east up State Street to Allison Hill, where Mrs. Larson's sister lives in a large Spanish-style house. There we crowd around the living room radio and drink cocoa. The announcer at WKBO says the Pennsylvania Railroad has closed the entire main line between Harrisburg and Pittsburgh. That means no one on the eastern seaboard can get to Chicago, let alone further west. Miles of track lie under water, bridges wash away along with stone retaining walls, causing landslides. The railroad declares an emergency, calling for hundreds of men to help with relief. In Harrisburg they are to report to a warehouse near Cameron Street. They also call for women to volunteer—cooks and nurses in hastily erected tents to aid the workers and people who've lost their homes. The announcer is barking that hundreds of miles of telephone poles and wires are also down. When our own power goes out, the radio's voice is silenced.

The next morning the water slows, and Norm hurries by to say they desperately need help at the Harrisburg Hospital. Mrs. Larson's sister says, "I'm taking Verna and going."

"But who will look after the children?" Mrs. Larson cries.

"I guess you'll have to do it yourself, dear," her sister replies, "so stop sniveling." I bite my tongue to keep from laughing.

Norm delivers us to a spot just above the flooded station, where we climb into rowboats. We see a group of colored men standing waist-deep in water, then it deepens and we pass a city bus and dozens of automobiles completely submerged. On Market Street, many of the plate glass windows are broken and ruined store merchandise floats in water that in some sections has reached fifteen feet. By the time we disembark at the hospital, people are looking out the window at the swollen Susquehanna, wondering if the Walnut Street Bridge will hold against the rushing force and the debris collecting at its base.

With no power, the hospital elevators don't run, and we line the staircases passing food trays up to the higher floors. It takes hours. A woman named Dora is assigned to the step above me, and as I am taller than her, we're almost on the same level, making it easy to talk. During our break, we sit together. "I came here," she says, "because I've always wanted to be a nurse and thought some hospital experience, even this kind, might help me get hired. I tell people I want to become a nurse," she confesses, "but don't know if I can cut it."

"Well, getting ahead is never easy," I say, realizing too late how much I sound like Mom, a voice that knows its limits. Nursing? No education. Impossible.

By evening the floodwaters have crested but there's still no power. Dora and I play cards by candlelight and sleep with the others on the tiled floors of the hallway. The next morning we again work side by side, and a strange thing starts to happen: the more Dora talks about *her* desire to become a nurse, the more the notion begins to excite *me*. When I confide that I only have an eighth-grade education, she shrugs it off. "You don't need a diploma to study 'practical nursing,' " she says. "And there's a school right on Derry Street that does the training."

By afternoon the flood waters have begun to recede. Mrs. Larson shows up, annoyed to find my help is still being needed and also to see I've found a friend. "I'm not paying you to socialize," she says. Before hurrying off, she lets everyone in earshot know her sister is married to a doctor.

"Does she always speak to you that way?" Dora asks. I shrug, but Dora says I needn't put up with it. "I know of an old lady on Boas Street who is looking for a girl. She's also impossible to work for, but at least she has manners, and her son pays nine dollars a week for help. If you gotta take guff, why not go where you can make a few extra dollars?"

"Why don't you work there yourself?"

"I did. I just left because I couldn't cut it. But I bet you can."

Such magic words. "I can."

In the morning of the next day I slip out of the hospital and find the address Dora gives me to meet Mrs. Nelly. Her son Tom is the county commissioner and he happens to drop by to check on his mother, taking a short break from inspecting the flood's destruction. They like my qualifications and hire me to start as soon as my stint at the hospital is over.

27

Norm meets me at the hospital, curious to know where I've been. He says Mrs. Larson is furious at my absence and that I'm to join her on Front Street immediately where she is already surveying the damage to their home. As the water departs, the river is leaving a foot of horrible silty mud behind, and Mrs. Larson acts like a hysteric when I say I won't be staying to help with the cleanup. She says, "Forget a letter of recommendation," and that I'm showing my weak character with such disloyalty. I hurry up the back stairs to my room, for once grateful that in her house the maid's quarters are high and dry on the top floor. I gather my things and depart. No doubt the major participant in Mrs. Larson's cleanup effort was to be me, and so happy am I to be free of the backbreaking task, and her and the band of horrid children, that I even walk away from the pay she owes me.

I spend the next two days with Norm, going back and forth to the hospital until at last the power comes back on. Then I head over to Mrs. Nelly's, walking along Front Street, where the curbs are littered with furniture and rugs ruined by the flood. In many of the mansions, the curtains were tied in knots across the windows to raise them off the floor. Sometimes they were high enough, and sometimes the muddy water spoiled them just the same, leaving sopping dirty panels of velvet and two-colored silk. I pass discarded objects, gilded chairs, inlaid cabinets, entire libraries. One house has a waterlogged grand piano outside. On Second Street the damage isn't as bad. On Third there's a rumor the trolley will be dismantled.

Upon my arriving at Boas Street, my first task is to help Mrs. Nelly dress. "I never dreamed I'd have a new girl starting so soon with all the havoc from the flood," Mrs. Nelly says. "I told Tom this girl must have spunk."

She is bony and slight and not inclined to need a lot of corseting, but she likes her petticoats and any number of patterned blouses—polka dots, stripes, plaids, anything but florals, which she says on an old woman reek of death. Whoever worked for her last autumn left her summer clothes well tended and stored.

That night I lie in my bed, cozy and dry, so grateful to be in a house untouched by the flood and not in the hard hallway of the hospital or scraping out the muck at the Larsons'. I sleep like a baby, the first good rest I've had in days.

· 28 ·

Mrs. Nelly's house is cleaned on a weekly schedule. Monday is wash day; Tuesday we iron and clean the bedrooms; Wednesday I tackle the stoop with a scrub brush, polish the brass on the front door, and even polish the brass water spigot that comes up from the basement. Friday we clean the downstairs rooms and shine the silver for the weekend. Saturday is marketing day and we clean the kitchen. She checks everything. Luckily there is a laundress.

On Wednesdays she sends me down to the big Catholic church on State Street to bring her a vial of holy water. The church is beautiful but I never linger. If Pop saw me walking into a Catholic church, he'd turn in his grave.

I haven't had news from Murphy for a while, so I write and tell him about the flood and my new job, knowing he'll get a kick out of me making nine dollars a week. A few days later the letter comes back marked return to sender. He must have moved, so reluctantly I send it on to Ruth, hoping she will know his new address.

A few weeks later the weather warms, and I visit Mom and Sam in Mechanicsburg. The whole town is celebrating Jubilee Day. At the festival, Norm has volunteered at a concession that sells funnel cakes for Irving College. His stand swarms with customers and he gives Sam a free cake. I wait while Sam sits at the makeshift counter and eats. A nice-looking fellow with a wide-open face comes and stands nearby and I recognize him. It's little Johnny Potter's brother who used to be in Miss Castle's class at the Pomeroy school. He remembers me too and a happy conversation begins. "Tell me about Johnny," I say.

Johnny's brother is about to answer when Norm hollers over the counter, "Verna! Stop flirting with every blade that comes along."

At first it seems he's kidding but then it grows clear he isn't. Everyone turns to look. Johnny's brother apologizes and says he didn't intend harm. I could crawl into a hole for shame. This isn't the first time Norm has shown his jealous streak and it's getting worse. When the festival is over, Norm finishes work and picks me up at Mom's house to drive me back to Harrisburg. "I'm sorry for sounding off," he says. "But I like you so much, and the thought that someone else might want you makes me crazy." I'm still plenty peeved, and still Norm doesn't believe me when I say I wasn't flirting.

The next time I visit, Mom hands me a letter that she's received with my name on it. It's from Ruth. I tear it open. It says several weeks ago Murphy was in an accident. He drove his car off the road and into a tree along the bank of the Schuylkill River. He was able to bring the car home and put it into the garage behind the house where he was renting a room. Apparently trying to keep anyone from seeing the damage, he was working on the repairs with the garage doors closed. Poison fumes from the exhaust pipe overcame him. He was found lying on his back on a roll board, a wrench still in his hand. I put the letter in the envelope and stick it in my handbag.

As I'm serving supper that night Mrs. Nelly asks me what's wrong. I say, "A man I knew has died." For some reason she assumes it's Sam's father and I don't bother to correct her. It's a convenient lie. More than ever I wish Murphy was Sam's father.

The next few nights are sleepless. I'm fiery hot and full of memory. I get up, gaze out the window at the sliver of moon, and remember how Murphy once kissed me, his dark hair falling over his forehead in a way that made me weak. I would have done anything he wanted. But because of my age he protected me. There is no substitute for character and you never know where you'll find it. I weep at how many deaths we all endure before our own takes us.

29

In the months that follow, Mrs. Nelly is kind. She takes me under her wing. Meanwhile Norm announces it's time we finally marry. It's the same old speech, and the more he tries to coax me, the less appealing the idea becomes. Over the years his persuasions have ranged from saying Sam needs a father to saying it would make me respectable again. The "again" part really irks me. At times he pleads, pouts, and mocks. The worst times are the badgering periods: "You oughta do this. You oughta do that." I want to say, "I'm a grown woman and think I know what I oughta do." Hazel says I've been on my own for too long and that I have to practice letting a man take the lead. I point out that she doesn't let her husband do that. She says it's different once you're married. I tell her it's not that I'm against marriage. I just don't want to marry *him*.

A few weeks later Norm takes me to Mechanicsburg and we join Mom for a lunch that includes large plates of vegetable soup she has made. Norm brings Sam a rubber ball and in no time Sam disappears from the stoop and is lost somewhere down near the railroad yard where he shouldn't be playing. Hazel finds him knee-deep in coal dust, the red ball missing. I wonder how many times things like this happen and I just don't hear about them.

Later, when Mom and Myrtle are out of earshot, Hazel whispers, "Liz has finally taken the children and left Buckley. She's living with her father down near Boiling Springs."

I persuade Norm to drive me over to Boiling Springs. It takes us a while to find the farm as I was only there once for the wedding and can't remember exactly where it is. The afternoon grows windy and when we finally pull in Lizzie is wrestling the wash on the line. She straightens up when she sees me and comes out to the road. She looks thin and played out. I can count her ribs through her cotton dress when she hugs me. She brings us inside and prepares warm cups of sassafras tea.

"I couldn't take it anymore," she says. "He stayed out drinking. The table was bare. With three children to feed, I sat there with only an icebox full of beer. I begged him not to bring it home. One night I got so angry, I opened the beer bottles and poured them out behind the house. He came home later, drunk, and had a fit when he saw the empty icebox. To show me who was boss, the hog unzipped his pants and pissed right into the refrigerator. Any woman who stays after that is crazy."

Toward evening her father and mother come in and sit with us. I feel ashamed for them to know I'm from the same family as Buck. It is a scary thing for a woman to leave her husband but Liz says her mother has been understanding and won't hear of her going back. Lizzie walks us back to the car and looks so peaceful that for a moment in the soft, fading light hints remain of the beautiful bride she once was. I shiver when I realize how the same thing is happening to her as happened to Mom.

30

The Pierce School of Nursing occupies the rooms of an old Victorian house sitting behind a hedged garden on Derry Street. I attend their biannual open house to learn more about a career in practical nursing. The ground-floor parlor is lined with wooden chairs. Dora sits in the second row. As soon as we see each other it's like we're long-lost friends. "I kept hoping you'd come," she squeals.

When I first saw Dora without the disorder of the flood, she looked a little strange in a moth-cut, green plaid coat and scruffy daydress missing two buttons. I also noticed that the air around her smelled like lemons. Later I learn she has a love of perfume, and being too poor to buy any, she makes her own from lemon peels. An old Italian woman taught her how.

Dora and I have a lot in common. Her folks never owned their house either; she too quit school during the eighth grade and started working; her father is also dead, though he gambled everything of value first, whereas ours never had anything of value to gamble. I share with her the things Mom would say to me if she knew I was attending the open house—"Twenty-eight! That's too old to go to school! You're lucky to make a living keeping house. Schooling won't teach you as much as real life and it costs money." I tell Dora how Pop used to call fear of advancement "the Irish link between cradle and grave."

"Our people come from Eastern Europe," Dora says, "and it's the same thing there."

Since Dora first suggested it, my desire to become a nurse has continued to strengthen, and the open house is like a new beginning. The information is exciting. A woman wearing a white uniform and duty shoes speaks about learning to go after something we want. Her hair is crowned with a crisp white nurse's cap—a ship anchored to a sea of marcel waves—and how we yearn to earn sails like those.

"Close your eyes and imagine a red dress," the nurse continues. "Can you see it in a shop window? Now, don't say, 'I can't have that.' Say instead, 'I can work to earn that dress!' then set about to make that dream come true. One of life's most difficult tasks is asking for what we want. People who know how to ask for what they want have an easier time getting what they want. But you can't *ask* for what you want if you don't *know* what you want."

An underground spring of desire bubbles inside me; suddenly it bursts to the surface like a fountain. I know the woman is speaking directly to me and that I've been born with an uncommon personal power. I can use it to raise myself.

Tuition is fifty dollars a year. It might as well be a million. Five cents buys three pounds of chop meat and ten cents a small chicken. A burlap sack of root vegetables costs a quarter and feeds our family for a week. Fifty dollars is several years' worth of savings from sixteen-hour days that leave your body aching and your mind too exhausted to dream or learn anything.

But secretly I continue to think of the example offered by the red dress, and I envision my own desire. Before I go to sleep at night I imagine a wallet full of money, then I imagine a cigar box full, and finally a whole dresser with every drawer crammed. I imagine a fine house, and fine clothes, and having Sam come live with me.

But my visions of prosperity and a better life are soon put to the test. Reality has a way of mocking my aspirations. One Sunday Norm drives me over to visit Aunt Ida. Her oldest boy, Cleveland, takes Sam outside to swing from an automobile tire hanging from a maple tree. I'm in the middle of helping Aunt Ida fix supper when I hear Cleveland hollering at Sam. "You're nothing but a bastard."

Wiping my hands on my apron I hurry outside and grab the smart aleck by his ear. "Don't you ever call my son that again," I say.

Then Aunt Ida appears and says, "Cleve isn't wrong in saying that—because that's what Sam is."

"He's only a child," I say. "It's not fair."

"Well, you should have thought of that before you got into trouble." Her voice is like a hammer hitting nails.

I go inside, retrieve my hat and gloves. Norm is out on the back porch talking to Uncle Jess. "Let's go," I say. "I'm not staying here."

Aunt Ida follows me, scolding. "Verna's living in a dream world and it's high time someone pointed out the facts."

I take Sam's hand and we go and sit in the car. My upset grows because I realize that my desire to protect him has made things even worse. Norm scurries over and places his foot on the running board. "Now, what's going on?"

"We're leaving because we aren't welcome," I say.

"What about supper?"

"Can't you ever think of anything besides your stomach? To hell with supper! There's no way I'll sit at that table."

Driving back to Harrisburg, Norm is sore because we have to stop for hot dogs at a roadside stand and he has to pay. My upset procures no sympathy. "By now you ought to know what people think of these things," he says. "Especially if they're churchgoers."

"Well, I'd expect that sort of talk from strangers," I say, "but not from my own flesh and blood—or from you."

•   31   •

As the summer grows hot, Mrs. Nelly decides to visit her sister down in Asheville, North Carolina. During that time, her son Tom arranges a temporary job for me with the government works administration. I continue to reside at her house to look after things but work in the office during the day. The idea that I might learn something new is exciting, and to think I've been deemed fit enough to work in the Capitol. Before she goes, Mrs. Nelly buys me two navy cotton day dresses. Wear navy every day, she says. "You'll always look trim and no one will wonder if you have other clothes."

Her own leather-bound trunk is packed with black linen skirts, which even in summer she wears to the ankle in the old style. Like the tablecloths in Mrs. Parrish's house, they have been pressed and rolled for packing to avoid wrinkles.

Now I can visit Sam every weekend, and when I see Myrtle her face holds a cold, jealous look that I'm working in the Capitol. I tell no one that my days are spent sitting on a hard maple stool filing index cards. The seats are flat and backless and by lunchtime you feel like your spine will snap in two. The rooms have enormous electric fans on either side and we keep all the windows open but the air this year is already so sultry it doesn't help. By afternoon it's all I can do to keep from lying on the floor and taking a nap. The skinny girls seem to have an easier time of it, perching on the edges of the seats like wrens. My hips are too broad to perch and when I lumber on and off the stool I feel like a hippopotamus.

The index cards belong to the Veterans Administration and have veterans' war records written on them in pencil—what year and rank they entered the service, what branch they were in, any languages they speak, where they were overseas during the war, and when and at what rank they left the service. I've seen some names I recognize—Norm's cousin Andy; a colored man named Schappy who used to live up on Jefferson Street and be a driver for Mrs. Gibson and finally Mr. Tewkes, an old man who lives across the street from Mom in Mechanicsburg. In order to be hired we had to sign a paper saying that to protect the people mentioned in the records we would agree never to speak about our work outside the office.

It's the first week of August when I receive a call from Tom Nelly saying that Mrs. Nelly has taken ill after eating southern catfish. As soon as she can travel she's leaving Asheville and will railroad home. This means I won't have to work at the Capitol much longer and it feels like I'm getting out of jail. I'll cook and bake and take care of Mrs. Nelly until she's got her health back.

The next weekend Mom holds a letter addressed to me in Murphy's handwriting. It bears a Pottsville postmark from more than a year ago and arrives accompanied by a letter from the post office saying the letter was lost and has taken that long to catch up with me. It's eerie getting a letter from a dead man. In it Murphy tells how he's back at the meat-packing plant. He asks me if I could send him the names of any employment agencies in Harrisburg, as he's thinking of heading back this way. He says he misses me. Poor Murphy, he must have been desperate. How bad I feel not to have responded. I can't shake my melancholy the rest of the day.

At around noon I ride to the depot with Tom Nelly. His mother's train is delayed and he treats me to a bacon sandwich and coffee in the station dining room. He doesn't eat but runs over to the Esquire Bar for a snort. The politicians and judges congregate there and the bar doesn't admit women. Tom returns just as the train pulls in.

Mrs. Nelly is the last one off, so frail she can hardly climb the stairs up from the platform. "Tom, promise me you'll never eat catfish," she says.

When we get home I give her a bowl of chicken broth and she goes right to bed. Later I bring her plain toast, egg custard, and some noodle soup. Tom stops by and I can see he's upset. The doctor comes and says she must have picked up some strange Carolina parasite.

Thanks to Tom's influence, Liz is able to assume my job at the Capitol. As a way of saying thanks she gives me two jars of mixed pickles. She says the job suits her and that her spine, unlike mine, feels okay at the end of the day.

A week later Mrs. Nelly slips and breaks her wrist. She's failing fast and Tom hires nurses to come in. I steady myself for yet another death. The first nurse is efficient and very knowledgeable, but she only lasts six days before she takes a permanent job somewhere else. The next one is a sloe-eyed fool, and so gruff her voice could strip wallpaper. Mrs. Nelly doesn't like her, but her weakened condition prevents her from saying much. Every day the nurse leaves small tasks undone and I step in to fill her place. It's good practice. Watching this lazy woman shuffle around actually gives me confidence and makes me realize what a fine nurse I'd be; something in my nature is geared for it, the very thing that has eluded this woman, despite her fine uniform and cap.

But no matter what efforts we make, Mrs. Nelly is not improving, though her eyesight remains sharp. "I see a cobweb in the corner of the room," she says between naps, and sure enough a spider is there.

The next morning I find her body propped up in her reading chair, glasses still on her nose, her sewing chest on her lap, embroidery hoop still in hand. The last of the old school, a woman who never cut her hair or wore her skirts above her ankle.

Tom holds a real Irish wake, with corned beef, whiskey, and fiddles. The formal service takes place in the same Catholic church on State Street where I'd fetch her holy water. Tom's friends from government pack the pews. "A real Republican send-off," one man says. Everyone is impressed that even the big boss Harvey Taylor comes to pay respects.

I stay on for a few days at Tom's request and one afternoon Mrs. Nelly's niece comes by and removes a rocking chair and a mirror from the house without so much as a "how do you do?" I go down to the courthouse and let Tom know his mother's things are being taken. I want to be sure he knows it isn't me taking them. He says he gave the niece permission to go and pick something out to remember his mother by. "She should have told you about speaking to me," he says, and thanks me for my service. "You made the last months of mother's life so pleasant," he says, his face pale. "Verna, I knew the end was coming but I never expected it to hurt so much."

"I know," I say. "It always hurts."

To change the subject, he asks what my plans are.

I stumble over my words, hoping he won't try and land me another government job. "I've been thinking that since I like to help people, I'd like to go to nursing school, but the course takes a year and costs fifty dollars—twenty-five each semester. So until I have that saved, I'll probably work in other homes where people are sick."

Tom leans back in his chair, his fingertips touching, like he's deep in thought, then out of the blue he says I should follow him. To my surprise we actually leave the courthouse and go to the Dauphin Deposit Bank. Tom withdraws a hundred dollars and gives it to me. "Fifty of it is for you to keep for looking after mother so dilligently, and fifty is a loan. You can pay me back when you get your first nursing job."

32

Dora's mother has found her a cheaper nursing school down in York and won't give Dora her father's measly insurance money unless she comes home and helps on the farm. Dora is upset so Norm and I load her up and drive her down. Seeing the small farm where she grew up makes me pity her. The wind has removed every scrap of paint from the outbuildings and the whole place looks like a hog pen. She's miserable and weeps when we say good-bye.

On my first day of training at the Pierce School, I wear a plain oatmeal-colored dress with a wide collar and matching belt. A square of crimson fabric is tied around my neck like a scarf. I've seen Claudette Colbert wear one that way in a movie and I think it looks citified.

The large Victorian house undulates under the ivy, geraniums, hanging ferns, and climbing roses, all shaggy in the September sunshine.

Mrs. Pierce stands on the other side of a great set of doors shaking hands with each of us as we enter. "Welcome," she says, "welcome." She does not budge from her post until all twenty-three new students are present and accounted for. She wears a lavender blue dress with lace sleeves and a blue brooch at the neck. Her white hair is swept up in sparkly combs. I immediately like Mrs. Pierce.

Because it is the first day, four teachers stand before us clad in crisp white uniforms that we all long to wear. They talk about the courses to come and how until the Civil War nursing was a male profession. They hand out wallet-sized cards with the nurse's oath printed on them, which Mrs. Pierce leads as a group recitation:

> *I solemnly pledge before God and in the presence of this assembly, to pass my life in purity and to practice my profession faithfully. I will abstain from whatever is deleterious and mischievous, and will not take or knowingly administer any harmful drug. I will do all in my power to maintain and elevate the standard of my profession, and will hold in confidence all personal matters committed to my keeping and all family matters coming to my knowledge in the practice of my calling. With loyalty will I endeavor to aid the physician in his work, and devote myself to the welfare of those committed to my care.*

Just the way she articulates a sentence makes me thrill. "Now ladies, this pledge will be read by one of our staff every day at the start of classes. On the day of your graduation you will publicly take the pledge from memory and deliver yourselves through the portals of the nurse's occupation."

In the large dining room a delicious buffet lunch is spread: ham, roast beef, and silver bowls with fresh fruit. I am overcome. This gracious table has been prepared with me in mind. Some of the other girls from the country have never eaten off china plates, and again I'm glad for the experience I've acquired working in better homes.

Following lunch we are given a syllabus with a list of books to buy. On a blackboard the teachers list the first month's curriculum: ethics, hygiene, ventilation in the sickroom, pressure sores, burns, allergic diseases, pulse, temperature, respiration, enemas, douches, and the use of syringes.

At four o'clock a small bell rings and we assemble in the dining room again, where a tea cart is rolled out. No one can believe that this too has been prepared for us. We are asked in the future to bring our lunch from home, but the tea trolley will remain a daily four o'clock ritual and each student will take a turn to bring cookies.

After the first week, attending class in the white uniform of our profession becomes mandatory. No prodding needed—we rush to the uniform shop in Pomeroy's Department Store to place our order.

In the morning I step from my door, hushed by the rustle of a muslin underskirt. I carry my sweater on my arm so as not to ruin the effect my starched, white appearance has on others; men step aside and tip their hats, women nod and smile, and children stare in wonder. I realize a nurse is like an angel, a sacred thing.

The students are extremely excited and fill the hallway, posing in its long mirror. "Oh, my dear, you look professional," Mrs. Pierce compliments. "How nice. How clean."

In the big classroom we take notes as her silver diction sets us a challenge. "I would like each of you to now think in terms of acquiring skill. Good skill helps you move more freely in the world.

Skill is your confidence. Skill is your protector. Skill is your friend. And this above all else—skill is a legitimate form of power. Did everyone hear that? A legitimate form of power! The operative word here is *legitimate*. Skill is not the realm of the fascist or the bully, or the weak and dependent. Skill allows us to mitigate those qualities in ourselves and in others. Hone your skill. Acquire skill. Practice it. Never stop learning. Skill will set you free."

33

As it turns out, it isn't Mom who raises the most opposition to school, but Norm. It annoys him that I've never mentioned my desire to practice nursing, as though I've been holding out on him. "Girlie, you've got yourself some big ideas," he says, standing in the living room of his mother's house, sipping coffee with extra cream and sugar.

How to explain that the dream of getting paid to help people makes my teeth ache with hope?

Norm says, "At your age, with so little schooling, you may as well forget nursing."

I stare away from him with blank eyes and a sudden dislike because I know that he cannot stop me no matter what ridicule passes his lips. For the first winter of my life, I don't wake in the cold, dark dawn, feeling down with the blues. I jump from the bed, elated to dress in my uniform, to head for the bus.

At school we learn about diet and nutrition. As practical nurses we are expected to walk into a patient's home and know how to cook. There are rigorous lessons on meal planning for sick patients, how to peptonize milk, beef, or chicken—a chemical process that duplicates pancreatic extract and aids digestion. Solid foods are mashed and pureed and, depending on a patient's constitution, mixed with lime water, arrowroot water, oatmeal water, albumen water, barley water, or rice water to form a gruel that can be easily swallowed. We make a beverage with lemon juice, cream of tartar, sugar, and boiling water called an "imperial drink." For those who've lost too much weight or are weak we make eggnog, chocolate eggnog, milk lemonade, koumiss, bonnyclabber, junket, beef tea, beef gruel, oyster broth, clam broth, orange albumen, and homemade custards. For the constipated we make delicious warm bran biscuits.

We make liver dumplings, liver soup. We serve nephritic diets. We learn about oxalic acid in foods, as well as alkali-producing foods. We learn about the purine content of food, as well as calcium, iron, and about how acidosis results from eating too much sugar and starch.

Norm comes by and wants to take me to Hershey to a snow-flake dance. "I need to study," I say, and he grows petulant, sitting on the sofa, nervous as a catbird, watching me read. Finally I say, "Please, just go to the dance without me." He leaves in a huff and says, "This isn't the kind of dating I had in mind."

We learn how to nurse around contagious diseases—scarlet fever, measles, whooping cough, diphtheria, erysipelas, tuberculosis, venereal disease, general fevers—and what can be done to relieve them.

Bandages: how to wrap them, wash them, roll them.

In January we learn about massage, stroking, friction, kneading, vibration, percussion, artificial respiration, sunstroke, frostbite, burns, and injuries to the eye. Also apoplexy, epilepsy, hysteria, shock, nephritis, gout, headaches.

February is spent on obstetrics and pediatrics and what to expect at every stage of a baby's development. Then there is a brief lecture on the moral implications of stopping a pregnancy. The nurse lecturing says, "I'm sure none of you will ever be involved in such terrible doings, but the state requires that we cover this."

Abortion

This means the interruption of pregnancy before the seventh month. The child is not viable before the twenty-eighth week.

Symptoms: Abortion may be only "threatened," that is, the woman has light uterine contractions, miniature labor pains, and a little bleeding from the uterus; abortion may be "in progress" when the pains are strong and regular, bleeding more free, and the cervix beginning to open for the exit of the ovum; it may be "incomplete" when the fetus has been expelled, but more or less of the placenta is retained. The term "septic" abortion is used when the process is complicated by infection. It is a dangerous combination. "Missed" abortion means that the process, having started, stops, the child dies, and is retained in utero. It may be thus retained for months and be mummified, or for years and be calcified—"stone child" or lithopedion—or it may become infected and be the source of serious disease. . . .

Diseases of the uterus—infantilism, retroversion, endometritis, and cervicitis (infection)—are well-known causes of abortion. Women with general infections—typhoid, tuberculosis, syphilis (here usually after the fifth month) and other chronic maladies, heart failure, Bright's disease, pernicious anemia, etc. —are likely to have miscarriages.

Malformations of the fetus are frequently discovered in abortions. Evidently nature determined they were not fit to live and thus eliminated them. A woman should never be told she has produced a monster—it hurts her finer sensibilities, and she will always be apprehensive that the monstrosity will recur in subsequent pregnancies.

Then we are told that to interrupt a pregnancy is a crime and means we will certainly go to prison. It is a great sin. My head is dizzy. Do I look guilty? Is the woman speaking to me when she says, "Now some of you may have even heard of women who involved themselves with such procedures. You can be certain that

they are damned." These are plainspoken facts, and they upset me
for I did not have this information and hadn't realized how awful
these actions were. Surely God will forgive my ignorance?

We begin the study of how the female body develops. There is
so much I did not understand and it is one of the most shocking
things we have read to date:

> *Puberty . . . may be defined as that period in the life of the
> individual when it becomes capable of reproduction. The
> changes are more rapid and marked in the female—indeed, her
> sexual life is more intense and plays a greater role in her exis-
> tence. Madame de Staël said: "Love is only an episode in the life
> of a man, it is the whole story of the woman."*
>
> *The girl passing into womanhood changes physically and
> psychically. The hips broaden, the limbs round out with fat, and
> the angularity of the body is replaced by graceful curves. The
> general carriage of the body is more womanly and dignified.
> The breasts enlarge, become more prominent, fuller, and firmer,
> the result of the growth of the gland tissue and the addition of
> fat; the nipple becomes more prominent; the primary areola de-
> velops. The skin shows marked changes; its activity is increased,
> that of the sebaceous glands particularly, so that not infrequently
> comedones and acne result. The hair takes on more luxuriant
> growth, and it also develops on the mons pubis and axillae;
> striae—fine lines—sometimes appear on the thighs, and espe-
> cially on the breasts. These striae are due to the stretching of the
> skin with deposit of fat. They at first appear as purplish lines,
> but after several years turn a silvery white. The external genita-
> lia grow larger, darker, more vascular, have more secretion, and
> emit a faint characteristic odor. The thyroid enlarges, the larynx
> changes, especially in the male. In the female the voice is also
> altered, becoming fuller, lower in scale, and more melodious. In
> brunettes the tendency is toward contralto; in blondes, towards
> a soprano range.*

The mind undergoes alteration in its three parts—the will, the intellect, and the emotions. The will especially, during the change, becomes uncertain, and the girl loses to a good extent her control over it. Hysteric manifestations are quite common. The intellect broadens; new perceptions give a grander conception of life. The girl feels that a great transformation is taking place in her being, and the pride of womanhood and of anticipated wife- and motherhood swells in her. The emotions during the period of change also become unstable: the girl laughs and cries often without reason, is happy, gay or sad, and melancholy without cause. The inclination towards the male increases, while at the same time a sense of modesty and shyness appears.

This transformation is the outward expression of the changes occurring in the internal organs of generation and in ductless glands led by the hypophysis cerebri. The uterus is developing rapidly. The vagina and the tubes grow longer, the ovaries take on a special activity, the Graafian follicles enlarge—ova develop. With ovulation comes the ability to reproduce, but the girl at puberty is unfit to bring forth children. Cases are on record where girls of nine or six and a half years, bore large children. Plato set twenty years as the best age for the first child, and Wernichm from a study of the development of the children of young women decided on the age of twenty-three as best. At this time, also, the pelvis has achieved its full development; the bones are still somewhat elastic, the joints supple; the coccyx, particularly, can be pressed back, and the genital tract is soft and elastic, while the woman is also more fully evolved morally and psychically.

The time of the advent of puberty, and with it, the menses, depends on many conditions. Warm climate seems to develop the female early, the equatorial women having their periods before the twelfth year, while the Laplander is free until the seventeenth to the twenty-third year, and some of the Eskimo women menstruate only in summer. Girls living in luxury and amid

stimulating surroundings menstruate early—the poor girl, the
country girl, the tuberculosis—late.

I read these passages and dwell on memories of my own body at this time, how information was nowhere to be found to explain what was going on. My body changed so much those first few weeks that I was with child and then afterwards changed back again. I wonder if what Mrs. Hampton dispenses is considered a drug. Is she damned? Is Mom?

At night I pray to God to forgive everyone. "My mother is ignorant," I plead. "She didn't know any better." But how did she know about the rock salt bath? Who told her of such things? I pledge to God that in repentance I will dedicate my life to being the best nurse possible. In penance, I promise to study as hard as I possibly can.

I stay up and copy ever more passages from the different nursing books and try to hold all the information in my head. Study, study, study. No time for anything else. I practice Latin. New long words: *urticaria, volsella, scopolamine, nymphae.* Waiting for the exams to come.

Meanwhile Norm is angry. Mom is angry. Myrtle is angry. Buck is angry. The world is angry. But for once I'm not. My pledge to atone cleanses me. I have a newfound purpose. I will redeem myself through nursing. There's no money coming in, but I don't care. When Mom says, "We aren't the kind of people who should bother with education, we'll only have to labor anyway," I don't hold that against her anymore. She's not acting out of malice. It's just what she knows, and now I know more.

There are tests every week and quizzes every day.

Disease!

Medicine!

In the final weeks we learn about surgical postures, burns, embolisms, thrombosis, how to sterilize instruments, how to sterilize gloves, how to sew wounds with horsehair, catgut, chromic gut, and linen thread.

We learn about urine analysis, lumbar puncture, vaginal irrigation, gastric lavage, pharyngeal irrigation, colonics, ear irrigation, how to give insulin, intravenous infusions, and finally catheterization.

We study day and night for our finals—written, demonstrative, and oral. I fret and worry and work and improve and love it.

On June 12, 1939, a tent is erected in the garden behind our school and our commencement is held. I stand proud and tall and tears roll down my cheeks as I recite the nurse's oath with the other women. Each of us goes up to the podium where a crisp hat is placed on our heads by Mrs. Pierce, who's grown as emotional as we are. A nurse's pin with the Pierce School logo is affixed to the bosom by one of our teachers and we are handed a diploma. In the afternoon a photographer sets up a display and each of us takes a turn posing for our portrait, which will be colorized and sent to us in the mail.

Everything about the ritual and ceremony is special. Mom comes with Hazel and Myrtle. For the occasion, they wear new hats—black pillboxes with flowers and ribbon which Mom pays for using money from Abe's tannery pension. Norm stops by and cheers when he hears my name called. I'm touched that though he worked in the morning, he dashed home to change into his suit.

BOOK

Two

1

It is mid-July.

Here at the state hospital it seems like Dora's the only one I can really talk to. At the same time, sometimes she gets on my nerves so bad that I have to go to my room to be alone.

If you compare what Dora learned about nursing with what I learned, it's clear my training at the Pierce School was far better. She never learned to give shots or to assist in surgery, and when she first saw my nursing manual, she couldn't believe it had drawings in color.

So with all this advantage, how did I end up here beside her? Is this another form of penance? I can't convince myself to believe that. Not after all that work. How could I have been so short-sighted? This isn't what I thought nursing would be like after studying so hard with so much sacrifice, and yet I ought to be grateful to Dora for putting in a good word to the head matron and getting me the job. Turns out they are always looking for help. I can't blame Dora for not tipping me off; she really thought things would get better if I joined her. It's a case of misery wanting company.

Dora is a practical nurse who isn't all that practical. Tuesday she let a patient bring a water glass from the cafeteria back to the ward; they can cut themselves or us. But she is very humorous and has a good heart, which counts for a lot with the people who live here.

I should stop torturing myself and step outside for some fresh air. A lot of acres are needed for this place as a buffer zone because nobody wants to live next to an asylum. Behind the smokestacks of the laundry is an enormous vegetable garden: squash, new potatoes, limas, and even some corn. The ordered rows are weeded and the beans and tomatoes staked. Growing vegetables saves the state money and it's a vocation for the patients. Too bad the vegetables end up in the hospital kitchen; they may as well run over them with a freight train. The tomatoes are ripening and I pull a straggler for Dora and myself to eat.

I try not to let on as to my disappointment or that I too have been scanning the want ads in the paper to look for a private job. I'm also planning to use the pay phone in the lobby of the main building to call Mrs. Pierce and say I need a new situation. Maybe she'll hear of something.

A small woman named Etta has begun to act as my assistant. Her head trembles from side to side with some kind of muscle spasm, but she always helps me wake the patients to take them in groups to the bathroom. Once they're up, we help them dress, and as we make the rounds she carries the needle and thread to fix a button or mend a tear. I look at her and can't help thinking how pretty she'd be if her hair weren't cropped, but they say it has to be cut or she pulls it out.

In the evening she helps collect the shoes, in the morning helps pass them out again. The state buys the shoes oversized so they fit as many people as possible, and all the laces are removed. The state fears they might swallow them or worse. How seriously Etta and I took the shoe distribution at first, lining and stacking them in the closet; it took an hour to get it right. Then one night the head matron for all the wards comes by. "Save time 'n' just pitch 'em in, honey," she says. "They don't need the same pair every day; they don't know the difference." We follow her orders but it bothers me to treat human beings this way. Seeing her hardness is even more of an incentive to get out of here before I become like that. Why do women in power so often begin to act tough like men?

I'm not trained to be a psychiatric nurse, but there is some advice in the nursing manual that I've copied several times and try to obey:

The aims of the true psychiatric nurse are fourfold. Briefly they are:

1. Recovery of the curable.
2. The amelioration of depression and of the loneliness and sense of detachment in the lives of the mentally ill.
3. The prevention of (or if too late the overcoming of) pernicious habits. This habit-acquiring tendency of mental patients makes 75 per cent of our work.
4. Building a foundation for future mental health and permanent emotional stability, wherever there is possibility of recovery.

The requisites are:

1. Firm, genuine, and unfaltering interest in the patient (not sham).
2. Adaptability to the personality of the patient—the art of companionship.
3. Poise and quiet self-confidence.
4. A realization that the voice has a peculiarly marked influence over all nervous and mental patients.
5. Optimism—it is the *mental sunlight* these patients so sorely need, but it must emanate from abiding faith and hope, not from some ostrichlike tendency to ignore misery as nonexistent.

A few suggestions for the psychiatric nurse:

1. Treat the patient on the basis of his *sanity*, not his *insanity*.
2. Remember that appreciation is invaluable *when rightly used*. Nothing stimulates the growth in a good patient like the knowledge that you are looking for good in him.
3. Avoid thinking in terms of "punishment." Pernicious habits are not broken by punitive measures. When correction ceases to be *curative* it should no longer be used.
4. Avoid ridicule—one of the cheapest and most devastating of weapons.

5. Avoid hysterical sympathy, which sacrifices ultimate good for temporary ease.

6. Do not "coddle" patients, giving them weakening attention.

7. Never agree with, humor, or verbally combat delusions—either meet them by diversion or substitution.

8. Never ask anything of a patient you would not do yourself.

9. Learn to reproduce in writing the peculiar sayings of your patient.

In the broad sense our ideals may be summed up in this picture of a psychiatric worker, published several years ago in a sketch called "The Jungle of the Mind" and characterizing a woman physician, working in a State Hospital: ". . . That is what she does—thinks human beings, thinks them back to original fitness and confidence. She takes tattered nebulous bits of intelligence and welds them whole; ragged souls and mends them with true feminine patience. She re-creates."

I've tried to practice these ideas but in a room with sixty or a hundred people it's almost impossible to think myself into fitness, let alone the patients. The size of the whole facility is baffling. Whoever wrote these manuals ought to come here for a few weeks.

·   2   ·

On Saturday Norm picks me up and we drive over to Mechanicsburg to have dinner with Mom. Abe Lease has had another operation, only this one on his other foot. The wound where his toes were removed is healing nicely; with a cane he's even able to go up the stairs.

After we eat, Mom lets Sam run outside to play, and when we are done she tells me that the children at school have been calling him names because he doesn't have a father. She's told him not to leave their block but when I go out later he's nowhere to be seen. I find him playing down in the cinders by the railroad tracks with some older boys. He comes running as soon as I call his name. I don't scold him, but I tell him he should listen to his gram.

Together we walk down to Market Street and I buy him an ice cream. While we walk back licking our cones I say, "I've heard some kids at school have been calling you names." He doesn't speak, just walks along eating his ice cream. I feel so uncomfortable, like I'm talking to a stranger. In his eyes I probably am a stranger. "Well, don't pay them no mind," I say. "My dad used to say to me act like you're bought and paid for, and proud of the bargain." And then it hits me. I'm giving advice from my father to a boy who has no father. And it's probably bad advice anyway, just one of Pop's old saws. How miserably I've failed this boy.

When we leave Mechanicsburg, Norm wants to go to Wildwood Park. I'm pensive and not in any romantic mood. The sight of parked cars that have the daily newspapers opened and attached to their windows annoys me. Norm jokes that you see more newspapers being read in Wildwood Park than anywhere else in the city. Once, last summer, we too tried making a curtain with the *Telegraph*, but the windows had to be rolled up to hold the paper, and the air was so humid, the car became unbearable.

"Better someone see a flash of titty than they find us suffocated," he said with a laugh, finally removing the papers and opening the windows.

"They'll be more likely to see your backside than anything of mine," I said, and immediately regretted being vulgar. Norm thought it was hilarious.

3

A small woman with spectacles and a plain hat of navy cotton trimmed with three pink rosettes comes looking for Etta. "I'm her aunt," she says, quite touched to learn Etta is acting as my assistant. "If there's ever anything I can do in return," she says, "please let me know." From her I learn that Etta's parents died of influenza when she was small. The aunt and uncle raised her until she was twelve. One night they awoke to the dogs barking, a sharp cracking sound, and a strange light at the window: the hayloft of their barn was on fire. The uncle bolted out to open the doors to let the horses and cows run free, while the aunt rang the dinner bell. Any farmer knows if you hear the dinner bell in the middle of the night there's trouble. Those within earshot rang their own dinner bells to spread the word, then went tearing across the fields in nightshirts to help their neighbors in distress.

Etta ran after her uncle with a pail of water. She fell in the doorway of the barn, cutting both knees, then scrambled to her feet and took two steps inside as the entire roof collapsed. Sparks shot fifty feet in the air. The uncle had already made it out through the side door, but Etta was buried under fallen rafters. The fire never touched her but she was trapped without air for a while and that caused damage to her brain. "If she'd only fallen sooner," the aunt said ruefully, "or been killed inside. I'm ashamed to say it but sometimes I don't know which would be worse."

It's difficult not to look at Etta now and wonder what her life might have been—husband, children, a bungalow somewhere with curtains she would have sewn herself.

The season's changing. I keep looking for work and hoping the Pierce School will call. So far there's nothing. The air grows chilly and the cell-like rooms overheat. I'm sure the state of Pennsylvania feels we are lucky to be drawing paychecks.

Every evening, determined not to fall under the spell of this place, Dora brings a notebook over to my room and we copy lessons from the nursing manual and quiz each other.

Some evenings Dora goes a bit wild. She's not the only nurse who sneaks cigarettes in the broom closet, but she also keeps a little mason jar of hooch hidden up in her room's toilet tank. She stands on the rim of the tub to reach it. When she drinks, it's always the same; first she's real talkative, then comes a period where she adopts a sort of high-pitched laugh that's very funny, but when the laughter fades, watch out. Her mood dives and the drink makes her sullen, and she storms off to bed. But still, I'd rather be around that than some of the other dames I see working here. Dora says the hospital has two kinds of nurses, those like us who endure it because we need the money, and those who do it because they like it. Bossing retarded people around gives the latter group a sense of importance and reminds me of what Mrs. Pierce meant when she spoke about legitimate power.

One evening Dora sees a photograph of Sam, taken in July on his ninth birthday. I tell her it embarrasses me not to have a father for him to look up to. "There's no need to feel ashamed around me. You know I practically had my Judy in a ditch by the side of the road." I tell her part of my story and imply that Murphy was the father and that he died before he could marry me. I make it sound like his death was the event that put me on the road of hard luck. It usually works, and people feel sorry for me. I have to be careful not to say that when Mom or Myrtle is around.

The other secret I carry is that I see Charles Dennis from time to time. He's still married and I still won't ever trust him again, but something exists between us that I can't explain. I try to tell myself to keep an open mind where he's concerned, that it's important not to hate somebody you've once loved.

Dora tells me she once had a baby who died. The name of the baby's father is never mentioned and I don't pry; next thing she'll start putting the same kind of questions to me. She also tells me the story of a woman she knew who jumped out of a window at a hotel in Lancaster because she was pregnant.

Dora has met Norm Trexler and doesn't approve. She's asked me several times what I see in him. How to put it across? At thirty-nine, he's ten years older than me, still lives with his mother, and his belly hangs over his pants from too many sweets.

I tell her men aren't lining up for a woman with a child. "That's a poor excuse," she says. "Sam lives with your mother; he's not in the way." Dora reminds me that men who like sugary things are always mamma's boys at heart.

She's right. But so what?

The next day the tall girl with the lovely brown hair gets sick in the dining room. I've finished serving lunch, chicken potpie with cherry gelatine for dessert, and everyone has just gotten their food trays when she grows ill. Vomit flies over four other trays, and though Etta and I work as fast as we can, a couple of the patients don't have enough sense to stay out of it. An old woman from Ephrata keeps eating from her plate like nothing has happened and that's enough to make two others start retching. We order everyone to stand away from the table and begin to wipe everything down. What a mess. Dora stays while I wheel the cart back to the kitchen to replenish the trays for those who hadn't finished eating. The head cook has already put everything away and says she won't take it out again. "But some of them haven't eaten," I explain. "Too bad," she says. "If I had to reheat potpie every time one of these crazies up-chucks, I'd never get home."

The whole disaster lasts until two o'clock, and I divide the food on my staff tray among the ones still hungry. Dora says to keep a sense of humor or we'll go mad and be living here ourselves. "It's like a W. C. Fields picture," she says, but I worry that laughing will just harden us further. "Can I get you some more potpie?" she jokes to me for days afterwards. And the laughing is irresistible. We can't stop for the rest of the afternoon.

But every day the big question poses itself—what is my purpose for staying in this job? Seeing the hardness of the nurses who've been here more than a year leads me to think about how to get out before I become like that. Dora's the only one who seems to understand. She says that if the war comes, nurses will be needed and they won't care what kind of training you have. Everyone says we're getting ready for war in Europe. The paper is loaded with it and bad stuff about Roosevelt. The newsreels too. The Navy is tearing down Irving College in Mechanicsburg and is building a depot there, and the Army has built another depot down in New Cumberland. Soon the new turnpike to Pittsburgh will open and a lot of people say it's intended as a direct military supply route.

One morning the girl on our ward with the birthmark on her face strikes Dora in the head. I see the whole thing. The girl's face is twisted like an old floor mop being wrung out. Rage turns her birthmark from red to purple. We quickly restrain her and call the doctor, who is down in Harrisburg at the Polyclinic. By the time he gets up here she is calm. "Only send for me if it's a real emergency," he says, and gives the girl an injection anyway. Afterwards the head matron comes by. She is getting ready to leave for the day and has changed out of her uniform. Her dress is printed with flowers that make her look as big as a meadow. She scolds us for not following proper procedure. "You aren't supposed to phone the doctor without calling me first," she says. Dora has a knot on the side of her head big as an egg. She is furious.

The matron is shocked when Dora curses her out. I pull Dora by the sleeve, put my arm around her, try to muffle her hollering, but nothing works. It's too late. Now the matron is yelling. Telling Dora to pack her junk and hit the road. She stands in the doorway while Dora packs, then follows her to make sure she is gone. The door slams behind them.

Without Dora there really isn't anyone here to talk to.

4

The cook outdoes herself and makes a large tray of apple fritters for the staff. They're greasy but I take three. My appetite can't be satisfied. Then I see the head matron cut to the front of the line, her big thighs rustling back and forth like a pair of dirigibles as she walks. She piles her plate high and suddenly I'm not hungry. I wrap a couple of fritters in a napkin and bring them back to the ward for Etta. She is tickled. She eats them in the linen closet so the other inmates won't see.

The frost has rendered the gardens dormant and to walk among the bare furrows in the brisk afternoon is a bit soothing, but somehow I can't shake this feeling of melancholy. I'm seeing the light at the end of the tunnel—a boyfriend like Norm, a job like this. It's not daylight but an oncoming train.

At nursing school they said private service has wonderful advantages, but I also ponder downsides—families that interfere and criticize, heavy lifting, patients who live in a rat hole. You can't depend on old people not to get sick, need hospitalization, die. Lord, how many have I already buried? Your future is always uncertain. People don't hire nurses until things are bad. Sometimes they wait too long.

The next day I get a letter from Dora. She's taken a small apartment on Fifth Street in a row of stone houses not far from the Capitol. She's found work with a doctor on Forster Street. Her letter says it's time for me to leave the nuthouse and that I should come stay with her.

A week later I give my notice to the head matron, who sits behind her desk on a wooden bench because her rump is too big for a chair. She leans onto her meaty forearms bulging like two legs of lamb. "You know you're giving up pension and retirement," she says. "Yes," I nod, understanding how that stuff is just a carrot they dangle so that they can keep you in the race. If I stay, my death will happen long before any retirement kicks in. I'm truly sorry to say good-bye to Etta, but I'm not sure how much she understands.

When I arrive at Dora's she opens her door with a cigarette in her mouth and says, "I'm a hillbilly chain-smoker from old Raleigh." She hugs me and shows me where she's made a daybed for me just off the kitchen. "I'd give you the small bedroom," she says, "but I need it for patients."

The next day a woman arrives and stays hidden in the extra bedroom. I know there's something fishy about her being here but I don't know what it is. I have a feeling she may have had the clap.

General Consideration of Venereal Disease

A nurse must never let the patient know that she has discovered such an affection. She should tell the doctor. In some states it is obligatory to report such cases as in other contagious diseases.

It must not be thought that because a patient has venereal disease it must have been acquired in illicit relations. Physicians and nurses have acquired syphilis in the course of their work. Men have acquired it in the barber's chair; washwomen, from washing infected linen; children from using another's slate pencils; anyone from drinking from the same cup as a luetic with mucous plaques; patients in the dentist's chair or under operation, from infected instruments. A physician, using a eustachian catheter, infected 35 patients with syphilis!

Similar possibilities exist with gonorrhea. Guarded speech, therefore, is obligatory on the nurse, as scandal is easily started and endless domestic woe may be inaugurated by the nurse dropping the merest hint regarding the nature of the malady. If she is questioned regarding the manifestations of disease, she should quietly but firmly refer the inquiry to the physician. Nor

may she speak of the disease or of its symptoms to any of her
friends or other physicians, as they may recognize the description
and connect it with the patient.

"He who tells even the smallest part of a secret loses his hold
on the rest."

Right now Dora is guarded on the subject, and I'm not going to pry. I have other things to worry about.

A few days later Mom roasts a capon with yams and mince pie. She's pleased to afford these things. The food is on the table and she calls up the stairs for Abe to come down. He doesn't. We find him sitting upright in bed, still warm, but he's passed from this earth.

All the food gets hurried back into the kitchen, the capon is pushed back in the roaster, and Norm runs out to fetch the doctor. An hour passes before the doctor arrives with the undertaker in tow. In the meantime I have Abe washed and laid out like they taught us in nursing school, a rolled towel under his chin to prop his mouth closed, his rectum packed with cotton, and his penis tied to prevent leakage. It's strange but he's not Abe anymore—just a corpse. The men are taken aback. "I'm a nurse," I tell them. They nod. "You must be a good one," the undertaker says approvingly, and everyone hears him.

After the body is carried away, our growling stomachs lead us to take a plate of food, but we don't really enjoy it. In the evening Myrtle comes home from the five-and-dime where she works, and the news about Abe so upsets her, she runs to her room with a great emotional display. Later she goes to use the privy and comes back in bawling; she holds Abe's can of Power's asthma powder. "He must have used it just before he died," she says. Her theatrics annoy me.

On the day of the funeral, Norm is kind and takes the day off from work to drive me up to New Bloomfield, where the service is to be held and where Abe will be buried. Mom doesn't bawl or anything, she's just withdrawn. Aunt Varnie and Uncle Mose arrive late and tell how on the way a curtain of rain descended on their buggy and huge gusts of wind made it impossible to hold the oilcloth tar-paulin over their heads to keep dry. The rain stopped spilling as quick as it began, but not before they were both soaked to the skin and had driven off the road to seek shelter in a bed of spruce trees. Uncle Mose says that he intends to get a car. Aunt Varnie says he's too old to learn to drive and that she never saw pine needles so fresh and green as on their detour—like angels were guiding them to look at God's handiwork.

"I intend to get a car," he says again.

Hearing all this, I think Mom's relieved to live in town now and not up in Perry County anymore. The three sisters, as they often do, sit and reminisce about all the funerals they've seen, counting how many years since Pop and Grandma Peffer passed, retelling how she fell and died after digging at that thistle in the yard.

Driving back to Harrisburg, Norm seems irritable. The truth is he's been growing ever more controlling since I left the state hospi-tal. It annoys him that I'm rooming with Dora and not him. "You oughta do this, you oughta do that," he begins too many sentences. I tell him, "I'm a grown woman and think I know what I oughta do."

5

In the newspaper it says that an ocean liner in the middle of the Atlantic requires five miles in order to turn around. Maybe I too need that many gallons of water to change. I'll see the ocean some-day, on my terms.

I know Dora is in the process of turning around. She's pulling in quite a bit of money working for the doctor on Forster Street. We don't talk about it, but I've never seen her so nervous, always looking between the blinds to survey the street, always whispering to her patients—all women—and carrying strange basins to and from the bathroom.

We recently counted all the jobs we've had since we started working: twenty-seven for me and thirty-four for her. She's never stayed at a job for more than a few months. Her favorite jobs were a dress factory up in Elizabethville and a peach-canning plant in Adam's County where they cooked the kernels inside the pits to make a syrup that flavored custard ice cream.

A few days later I go downtown to buy some underwear and socks for Sam. I also get him a pack of licorice whips, his favorite. On the square, coming out of Kaplan's, I bump into Liz. Her manner of talking and dress are as plain as when I first met her. She looks rested, her ringed eyes still pale as an owl's. She doesn't mention Buckley nor do I. Hazel says Liz has a new fellow over on the West Shore, but again I don't ask.

Liz congratulates me on getting my nursing license and then we both get sort of bashful like we don't know what else to say. Maybe she's on to a new part of her life and the less she sees of Buckley's people the better.

Mom's face is like a stone when I tell her I ran into Liz. Mom and Myrtle are both of the married-for-better-or-worse school and like to badmouth Liz because she left Buckley. There's never been a divorce in our family and they believe she's brought shame on all our heads. I say it's Buck who shamed us.

I have barely spoken a word to Buck in years. Somehow he found out I had visited Liz at her father's farm. "You bitch," he shouted across the kitchen of Mom's house. "You're trying to break up my marriage!"

"You don't need my help for that," I shot back.

"No wonder Sam's father wouldn't marry you." He stormed out and slammed the door so hard the glass cracked.

"Poor Buck," Myrtle cried. "Poor, poor Buck."

"The last thing he needed," Mom said, "was to be undermined by his own kin."

6

A photograph of Dora's doctor is printed in the sports section of the paper today.

"My God," I say with shock. "You didn't tell me he was colored."

Dora doesn't bat an eye. "What difference does that make?"

"I've never heard of a colored doctor before," I say. "Wouldn't working for one ruin your reputation?"

"I don't have a reputation to ruin," Dora says. "Besides, he has other whites working there." She goes on to tell me some of the men who drive him around town are white.

My heart pounds as I study the photograph. Dora is making her own rules. Underneath my reservation, there is excitement. It surprises me. Is it because Dora is getting away with things in a way that I can't? But how would I ever tell my mother I'm employed by a Negro? What would Pop have thought? By now, having lived in town, not to mention Philadelphia, I've seen plenty of colored people, but they seem pretty well separate from us. Their ways are different.

I study the photograph even harder. In the picture, the doctor is seated on a chair surrounded by twenty boys probably eleven or twelve years of age, all of them white. One of them has his shirt off and the doctor is checking his chest with a stethoscope. Underneath the picture it says: *Dr. Crampton measures the heartbeats of future Tiger gridders.* Dora says he's the medical physician and trainer for many of the sports teams in the city and that the players adore him. I've never heard of such a thing.

Dora also says his medical practice is quite large, with many white patients coming because he only charges a dollar a visit and dispenses free medicine. Being colored, he isn't permitted to practice at the hospitals and so must refer his serious cases to white physicians. But if a sick patient is too poor for the expensive doctors or hospital, he sets them up in private homes with practical nurses.

That's where Dora comes in; she tells me it's not that easy for him to find nurses willing to let sick people stay in their homes.

I ponder the idea of working for a colored man. Maybe those who do it just don't tell anyone. I decide to read up on home care and find this passage to copy:

> *The nurse has peculiarly favorable possibilities as a health teacher. She lives or visits in the home, can observe how the laws of health are being observed or neglected, and her close association with the family enables her to correct evil habits of living and instill good ones. . . .*
>
> *Compare the advantages of the surgeon in his capacious operating room, with good light, sterile utensils, many nurses and assistants, with the plight of the home attendant nurse. Compare all the conditions in which the hospital nurse works and those to which the nurse in the home practice must adapt herself. Thus it is not far to go to explain the existence of evils referred to in the above paragraph. . . . the nurse must learn how to imitate hospital conditions in the home, how to utilize such utensils and materials as she finds at hand, and how to carry out asepsis in the hovels of the city, the farmer's cottage miles from town, as well as the perfectly appointed homes of the rich. It would be well if her training could comprise a course in the outpatient department of some hospital. Such an experience will be all the more valuable to the nurse since, besides giving her actual practice, it will develop her character spiritually. She will get a glimpse into how the other half—the lower half—lives, and this will surely unfold in her breast the spirit of social service.*

There is nothing about the responsibilities of a nurse taking patients into her own home. And a deeply sympathetic heart? I'm not sure I have that. Dora's patients are a puzzlement. They don't seem poor at all. Every Monday and Wednesday she has a new one; they stay exactly two days and then are recovered enough to go home.

There's something suspicious about this precision. Can that many women all have venereal disease? Surely not. I'm afraid to ask Dora, and for once she's being tight-lipped.

A few days later the Pierce School finally calls and refers me to an old man named Clarence Zimmerman over in Marysville. He's retired from the railroad, collects model trains, and has been bed-ridden for a month. I take a liking to him right away. He lives in a neat little bungalow three blocks back from the river and away from the soot of the Enola freight yards, and you can see that his garden must have been well tended until just recently.

He can no longer climb the stairs, so two neighboring men come and move his bed down to the living room. I turn it into a clean hospital facility, following the instructions in the nursing manual: wrap the ironing board in a sheet, use it to lay out medical supplies, take the curtains down and just use shades—much cleaner—and wipe down everything with ammonia water. What a relief to be working again. I also instruct the neighbors to move the radio over next to the bed so he can reach the dials. He likes Kate Smith and says my voice reminds him of hers. "I can't sing," I say. "Well, you're still cheerful like she is."

When I return home in the evening, Dora is in a state. The patient staying here has been doubled over with cramps and has a low-grade fever. She calls the doctor but there's no answer. I enter the bedroom and stay with the woman while Dora keeps dialing the phone. I take a cool towel and press it on the woman's forehead. She moans. After about fifteen minutes she says she needs the basin, that she can't make it to the bathroom. I position it under her and she begins to pass clots of blood. Then all of a sudden a last bit of pulpy matter comes through. I've never witnessed anything so shocking. It's about the size of a baby bird—head, body, arms, and legs.

When Dora comes in I can smell the alcohol on her breath. She looks into the enamel basin and confirms that it is indeed a fetus. And then I know. Dora and her old colored doctor are breaking the law. I am abetting them. We could all go to jail.

The woman begins to breathe more regularly. Her cramps stop. From the bedroom closet, Dora takes a glass jar with a clear preserving liquid and transfers the fetus. "The doctor needs to examine the complete tissue to make sure it has completely passed. Otherwise she could get infected and go into shock. If the fetus is not completely torn away, he has to do a D & C."

Dora speaks as though it's all just matter-of-fact. She shows no thought or concern that what we are doing is illegal or against our nursing oath. I realize she probably thinks I've known all along. I'm in a fog but don't want to speak of it in front of the patient. I take her temperature and the fever is coming down. She's resting comfortably now, and the crisis is over.

Later, when Dora's in the kitchen, I get out my nursing manual. Dora doesn't want to listen but I tell her I need to discuss this, need to warn her. She is on dangerous ground and must be clear about her decision. She sullenly settles on the kitchen step stool and agrees to pay attention as I read aloud:

> Perhaps the saddest commentary on our "modern civilization," on our "higher thought," on our "ethical movement" is the increase in the practice of criminal abortion. Nurses are not long in training before they see how alarmingly this crime has spread, and they see, too, the lives lost and the homes wrecked by it. A nurse should never be party to such a procedure. It is always murder, and in several states legally punishable as such, and often suicide, and by gentle counsel she should dissuade the woman from entertaining the thought of its commission. . . .
>
> The causes of abortion are many, injury, usually criminal interference, heading the list. It is very sad to contemplate the thousands of delicate little lives destroyed each year by criminal abortionists, and, too, the maternal deaths they cause—to say nothing of the life-long invalidism that follows in the wake of these ugly operations. Falls, blows, overexertion, mental shock, etc., seldom cause abortions unless the patient is predisposed by

disease of the uterus or some general malady. A slight jar may
bring on a miscarriage in such a woman, and a great shock may
not do it in another—e.g., a milkmaid was tossed by an angry
cow over a fence and terribly lacerated by a horn penetrating the
vagina, but she did not abort, delivering a fine child at term.
Lack of thyroid, of corpus luteum, of vitamin E may kill the
fetus—result, abortion.

As our medical knowledge increases the necessity for thera-
peutic abortion is growing less and less, and now it is only in
rare cases that the accoucheur feels that the best interest of the
mother, the family, and the community are served by this sacri-
fice. The operation however awakens sentiments of the greatest
delicacy; it includes heavy and painful responsibilities, and no
physician will perform it without the counsel and moral support
of at least one of his confreres. It is not sanctioned by the Catho-
lic Church, and in Catholic families the nurse should suggest
that a priest be consulted.

Dora grows angry. "A milkmaid thrown by a cow!" she snorts.
"That's nothing compared to what some guys do to you. And that
part about homes being wrecked! What homes? I grew up on a farm
where even the pigs tried to run away. They oughta write about
that. And they oughta have a chapter for men—instructing them to
share responsibility for intercourse. And why doesn't the church
teach men to stop taking women by force, to offer money and support for the children they leave behind? Judy's father, that son of a
b., disappeared during the second month I was pregnant."

"I didn't mean to make you angry," I say. "I'm just confused."

"Well, you've never been in my shoes. Sam's father died. He
didn't run off and leave you. Imagine being pregnant with no husband or money, not even any prospects. Imagine being desperate.
This is the first job I've ever had that gives me a chance to save so
that one day Judy can come live with me. Ask yourself why you
aren't with Sam. Ask the churchgoers about that and they'll say that's

what you get for putting out. Ask whoever wrote that goddamned nursing manual if they've ever tried to hold off the brute strength of a man who pins you down your first time out with him."

I nod and shudder, queasy and ashamed that I haven't told Dora the truth about Sam's father, that I haven't told her the truth about what happened with Wertz. I'm a coward for not wanting to ever recall let alone speak about the night I sat in a tin tub of scalding water and rock salt while my poor frantic mother tried to help me with an old wives' tale, or how it was Mrs. Hampton's remedy that finally settled my score. No, Dora is indeed the braver soul. She tells the truth.

I begin to think about the nursing manual. It has two authors, Joseph B. DeLee and Mabel C. Carmon. He's an MD and she's an RN. They both had careers at the Chicago Lying-in Hospital. Maybe Dora is right. Did either of them have to leave school like I did? I've learned firsthand how God provides better for some than for others. I try to calm Dora by telling her that though the whole idea shocks me, I just need some time to get used to it. She sulks anyway.

When Norm drops by later I don't breathe a word, and worrying that he might notice something, I get him out of the house as quickly as possible. The next day a heavy rain falls and Norm has to go down to Lebanon on company business. He'll be riding the company's truck, and so, instead of my taking the bus, he lets me borrow his car to visit Mr. Zimmerman.

I fix Mr. Zimmerman's breakfast, wash him down, and check for bedsores. His legs are womanly pale; he's a far cry from the thick-muscled man whose picture stands on the mantle. He listens to the news on the radio and says before the year is out we'll be at war. "The Germans are running all over again." He tells me about his son, who served in the ambulance corps in 1917. "Did you know the price of land in France is the most expensive in the world? It cost a thousand men a yard—including my son."

I stay with him until noon, cook him some porridge, empty the slop jar, fix his lunch. As I pull away from the curb I decide that since I'm on the west shore I'll go back to Mechanicsburg and pay a visit to Sam. The roads are a mess on account of the rain, and Sam comes home two hours late from school. Mom says a pack of older boys have taken him into their fold and he runs with them even when she forbids it. "Talking to the parents of the other boys might be of benefit," I say, but Mom says that they're mostly factory hands too bone weary to raise kids anyhow.

I scold Sam and he stares at the floor. I realize I'm not around enough for him to listen to anything I say. By the time I leave, it's close to suppertime, and when I return the car, Norm is already home. "Where have you been?" he asks, standing in the living room eating a sandwich stuffed with Lebanon bologna washed down with a cup of coffee, extra cream and sugar. The need to account for my activities and whereabouts annoys me. "You left this morning. Where have you been?" Wearily I go over the day's events.

"I better go out and make sure the car is locked," he says.

"You just want to check the dashboard to see how many miles I drove," I say.

"Well, it's my car," he says. "I got a right to check it."

"I'm sorry I ever borrowed it," I say. "I'm sorry I kept it so long. I'm sorry I thought you could be decent about it."

He goes out and returns with a balled-up chewing gum wrapper. "Someone left this in the backseat."

"No one was in the backseat," I say. "No one rode in the car but me."

"Then where did this come from?" he says, and holds the wrapper in the palm of his hand like he's a big detective in a movie and I've just been caught with some secret gum-chewing lover.

"How the hell should I know?" I say. "Oh, why didn't I just take the bus?"

"Well, Mrs. John D., why not take a hired car? I suppose you know we got a depression on. Your mother can barely keep a roof over her head and looks after your son. I thought I'd be nice since it was raining and all." His eyes want to punish me. To make me see the world his way.

"What do you know about rent?" I say. "You live with your mama."

"I pay my share. I pay more than my share," Norm sputters, his face now congested. "You keep your mouth out of my business. I'm trying to help you out. To set you straight. Not to let you waste your life on foolishness." He goes on to tell me how lucky I am that he let me use his car and that the last thing he deserves is a hard-hearted act from me. He reminds me that I am being foolish.

"I'm not a fool," I say, suddenly angry. "I'm not a fool." I stare at him and then turn my gaze toward the window, fixing on a spot below the sill where yellow water stains have ruined his mother's wallpaper.

Norm turns and gives a snort of disgust. He asks me when I'm going to stop playing him for a sucker. He reminds me of how good he's been to me, that he treats me better than most men would treat a woman who doesn't even know who her child's father is.

My hands curl. "Why don't *you* keep your mouth out of *my* business?" I say, determined not to be conquered this time.

"You've had it good with me, girl. I've been good to you." The tendons on his neck stand out as he slams down his coffee cup. "A man can only put up with so much."

I feel my own temper rise. "And I've been good to you."

"Hah," he snorts again. "You ain't no better than a gold digger. You can't show love for anyone."

A red-hot poker sears my insides. I stand up from the table and face him. "And you're nothing but a goddamned mama's boy."

His face contorts with rage and before I even know it, his palm flies against my cheek. My spectacles go flying.

"You hit me!" I scream. "You hit me." I hide my face behind my hand and begin to cry, not because it stings but because I'm so furious.

His mother opens the door to her bedroom and stands in the dark hallway wearing her nightgown and a hairnet. "Norm?" she says. "Let her go. Can't you see she doesn't want to get married?"

"Go back to your room, Mama," he says, his voice shaky. "I'm just trying to talk some sense into her. She's wrecking our lives."

"I never want to see you again," I cry.

"What?" His eyes are wild, like a coward's. "What did you say?"

"Norm!" his mother cries. "Please, Norm, let it go."

"Why can't *she* let it go?" he says.

"Because I've done nothing to be ashamed of," I say.

His mother comes closer, and I can sense she is being tactical, strategic. She suddenly tries to be the voice of reason and calm me down. "Now, now . . . it's all over and done with," she says.

I regroup and look at her with scorn.

"Mama. Let me handle this."

"No, Norm." His mother's voice has an edge now. "Let her be."

Silence descends. Five seconds. Ten seconds.

"What do you want me to do, Verna?" he says, his voice softening with a plea. I know that he is suffering inside, because his mother is a witness to his crime, and that she probably taught him any man who hits a woman is not a man.

"Leave me alone so I can find my glasses," I say.

He begins to search along the baseboard. "Here they are," he says, and stands studying the frames. "They got bent." He pushes the wire back into shape and I pull them behind my ears. They are crooked. That and the skewed angle of the lenses bring unavoidable tears to my eyes. "They cost fifteen dollars," I blubber.

His mother shuffles toward me and extends her hands. "Let's go in the kitchen. I'll make fresh coffee. We can have some cookies."

"There's no way I can do that right now," I say.

"I can make coffee pretty fast," his mother urges.

"No," I say. "I've got to be going."

"I don't know what you want me to do." Norm smooths his hair back in frustration. "Please listen to reason."

"I'm an adult. Don't tell me what to do."

"Norm. It's dark and still raining," his mother says. "Why don't you drive her home."

"No," I say, and wipe my eyes with my fingertips. "I want to be alone. I'll catch the bus."

"Norm, just go with her."

"No," I say. "I'm not scared." With trembling hands, I gather my raincoat and pocketbook.

"I'll put the light on for you," his mother says. "God bless you, honey. God bless you." She knows I'm leaving for good.

·   7   ·

Funny how many things you worry about never come to pass. I used to lie awake and fret over going to the shore and what Norm would think of me in a bathing suit. Now we'll never know.

Two weeks pass. He calls, sends letters and flowers for forgiveness. I get lonely, miss the big bands at the Chestnut Street Dance Hall, the car races. But I won't ever be seen with him again. Not just because he hit me; after all, my words were meant to injure him. I pretty much accused him of not being a man. Words can hurt as much as a slap. No, I don't want to see him anymore because I've changed and want something different from what he wants.

Dora keeps asking me what happened. I don't explain anything but say I need to move on. Normally she'd hound me, but I change the subject and we discuss abortion. I tell her I'm afraid, for her and for the patients. I tell her I agree that the people who wrote the nursing manual are privileged, but we ought to be able to govern ourselves and discern right from wrong. I remind her of the nursing oath. I tell her what she is doing with that colored doctor is wrong. We go back and forth debating for more than an hour. She weeps, tells me how she only wants to bring Judy to live with her. "If I depend on a regular job, Judy will be fifty. I'll never swing it." Then she tells me the doctor pays her fifteen dollars a patient. In one week she makes thirty dollars. If she had a bigger place she could make even more.

I'm silent after that.

In bed that night, all I can think about is money. My head swims with multiplying equations that keep increasing. In the face of such an avalanche of cash, even if it is only imagined, my moral objections grow faint.

Dora comes to me a few days later and says the doctor will assign her two patients on Monday, who will stay with us until Wednesday, when we take them back for checkups. Then afterwards she'll get two more who will stay until Friday. Her earnings will double. She'll make sixty dollars a week. The only catch is the doctor says it's too risky to transport the extra women by bus, and he wants Dora to get a car. I can't believe it, but she can already afford a car and doesn't even know how to drive.

We visit the car dealer and she buys a '29 DeSoto with a rumble seat and I give her lessons. I try to practice the gentle way Murphy taught me about the clutch and gears, but when I show Dora, each lesson leaves her more shaken than the last. She backs the car too far to the left or too far right; frequently the fender tags the edge of the porch and she has to stop, get out, and have a cigarette.

Another day of bad weather, and Dora is beside herself at having to drive to Dr. Crampton's. She rattles around all morning chain-smoking and chewing her lip. When I finally volunteer to drive her she hugs me with relief. The patient, a young woman with a fine suit and impeccable manners, is dressed and ready to go.

We drive to the doctor's house at 600 Forster Street—at the corner of Sixth, a street of mostly working-class white families and a small pocket of homes owned by well-to-do Negro families. Through the rearview mirror I see Dora and the patient admitted through the back door by an old dark woman, whose body curls over like the tip of a fern. Her name is Frances, she's the secretary, and she suffers from curvature of the spine.

I sit in the car, parked in the side alley, rain streaming down the glass. My vantage point includes the doctor's brand-new Lincoln, license plate MD-600, echoing his street address. On the left side of the alley is the Messiah Lutheran Church; at the rear of the property is another alley, which means you can park on three sides of his property—very convenient.

A light shines from inside the church, and the stained glass windows throw patches of color that reflect the wet car. I wait, sheets of rain drumming the roof.

Dora stays inside for about an hour. When she finally comes out she's accompanied by a new patient, an older woman this time, looks pretty well-to-do, fox furs and clip-on earrings that sparkle. They hold umbrellas and wear drizzle boots to protect their shoes. We quickly drive away.

In the morning I go to the Broad Street Market. When I return, Dora has left a note on the table saying she's gone to lunch with Ed Ames, a fellow she only met a week ago while having her shoes repaired. The note asks me to keep an eye on the patient. It's hard to believe she just left the woman alone. What if I hadn't returned? It bothers me that strangers can wander around, rifle our things, or find themselves in need of emergency medical help, with no one there to protect them.

I check on the woman, chat with her a bit. She's from Chestnut Hill in Philadelphia and already has three grown children. She says she is worried for her health.

In the nursing handbook, it says in the United States 23,000 women die each year in childbirth, 85,000 babies die in delivery, and another 85,000 die in the first four weeks of life. This is three times as many lives as were lost in the Great War, and the infant deaths are largely preventable.

When Dora comes home she hands me five dollars. "That's for helping out and for driving yesterday." She sets about making supper but I don't feel like eating a bunch of cigarette ashes in my food from the smoke that dangles from her lips, so I take over.

A couple of days later Mr. Zimmerman slips into a coma and dies. An older brother comes down from Lewistown to make arrangements. He's an old country gent and is most grateful when I fix him some food. He tells me his brother had a crush on me and said I was a crackerjack nurse. Now I'm out of work again.

8

We begin to take in two women at a time. They share the bedroom and we hang a blanket down the middle for privacy. It's far from ideal. The schedule remains, two new patients on Monday evening, return them to the doctor for a final examination on Wednesday, then take two more who stay until Friday. We're off Saturday and Sunday, though on a couple of occasions a woman has stayed with us over a weekend. We don't mind the extra money. From the fifteen dollars Dora gets per woman, she gives me five. I'm making twenty dollars a week with very low overhead.

She and I continue to debate. "Do you think that people would say that what we're doing is a sin?" I ask. "Even the Hippocratic oath says don't do it." I'm careful to say "we," but what I really mean is "you." By simply driving and giving a hand with the laundry and watching when Dora goes out, I allow myself to maintain that I'm not really involved.

"Well, doctors may take the oath," Dora says, "but a heap of our referrals come from them, and they're damn grateful to have someone decent doing procedures. That way they don't have to do them themselves. They know how well connected Dr. Crampton is to the hospital if anything goes wrong. Doctors know everyone in town who's doing them. The SOB down in Steelton is so notorious they call him 'the butcher.' But women still end up there."

The women who stay with us are for the most part proper and

well dressed. They have to be, for they pay at least a hundred dollars. But Dora says the really rich ones have their personal doctors come and do them privately in their mansions.

"Is that true?" I ask.

"You bet your ass. And the poor have ways too. But if you're poor the cure can be rough. I've known two women in my life who were all messed up inside from douching with lye."

It shocks and upsets me to learn how many lies the world allows and protects. Dora is right, referrals from other MDs are numerous, and a congressman's wife also sends us somebody. It takes a while for me to reconcile what is pretend from what is truth. It's as if a whole layer of drapery is lifted and I glimpse a secret society that is invisible to most people. By now I've thrown my own repentance overboard, but not my pledge to be the best nurse I can.

On Thursday evening, there's a silver anniversary party for Mom's cousin up in New Bloomfield. With my extra income, it is possible to rent a car for the occasion, so that no one will have to sit in the DeSoto's rumble seat and get bounced and wrinkled. Hazel and I leave Dora's car at the dealer on Cameron Street, where for three dollars a day we rent a Packard that is quite roomy.

I wear my nice gray dress, Mom ends up wearing her good old bottle green standby, while Hazel has a new dark brown skirt and a chiffon blouse with flowers embroidered on the cuffs, and she is crowned with one of the new little hats that perch down on the forehead like a bird's nest. Since she has married Joe, he gives her money for all of it. He's good that way. When I pull up in Mechanicsburg, Myrtle is waiting on the porch with a new black felt hat with a velvet ribbon that goes around the back of her head. I'm not sure if black felt really goes with pink silk and I tell her so. My remark irks her, that and the fact that she isn't the only one with something new. I make a big fuss over Hazel's blouse just for spite.

After the party, the sky has been dark for some time when I drop Mom and Myrtle back in Mechanicsburg. Sam is already in bed, but I go in to check on him, only so that driving home I won't have to worry if Hazel thinks I'm callous. But there must be something wrong with me. What mother would miss a chance to look in on her child, even if asleep? I just want to appear normal. I'd have checked on a patient, why not check on my child?

It's after ten when Hazel and I get back to Harrisburg, and we return the rented car to the dealer as prearranged, sliding the keys through the letter slot. Dora's DeSoto is parked alongside the building right where we left it. But as luck would have it, the engine won't turn over. Now we're stranded in our good clothes on Cameron Street, thin skirts blowing against our legs as we search our purses for nickels to call someone.

Just then a Studebaker comes up driven by a guy in a checked shirt, a black knit tie, and a brown felt hat. He offers to give our car a push with his car and parallel parks in behind us. The DeSoto's wheels rotate as he pushes us along the curb all the way to the corner but the car still won't start. The man finally gives up and puts his car in reverse, but more bad luck, his bumper has locked itself to ours. The man is clever; he figures out how to let the air out of the DeSoto's tires so that it sinks lower to the ground, and finally the two bumpers separate. Now not only will the DeSoto not start, but we have flat tires. The man laughs and invites us to his apartment for a sandwich. "No," I say. "It's almost eleven o'clock." But Hazel ignores me and says, "Sure, why not?" I can't believe how foxy she is while Joe waits at home with the baby.

The man's name is Dewey and he lives up on Verbeke Street, in a nice second-floor place. He makes ham sandwiches and serves us bottles of beer. I worry about the DeSoto and say it belongs to a friend and that I'm supposed to help her run an important errand the next day.

"Take my car!" Dewey says without a moment's hesitation.

I protest, but the next thing I know, Hazel and I are driving off in a car that belongs to a complete stranger. I drop her at home, then go back to Dora's. I can't believe the trusting nature of this man Dewey.

Dora is fascinated by the story of Dewey. This kind of craziness is right up her alley. "I hope you go out with him," she says the next day as we drive the patients back to Crampton. "He sounds perfect."

By afternoon our flat-tired DeSoto is fixed and I'm amazed at the can-do reliability of a good garage man. I'd marry one in a second, but they're always taken.

When I drop off the Studebaker, Dewey isn't home. I leave a note in his mailbox with a dollar for gas. I wonder how many other women have had the privilege of borrowing his car. I plan to thank him by baking an angel food cake.

Dewey phones two days later and invites me to dinner downtown at Santo's restaurant, a place known for their steaks. It turns out he's an insurance man and must be making pretty good money. My plan to bake him an angel food cake is spoiled when I learn Hazel has already dropped off an apple pie to thank him. I don't want him to think we're a family of baking nitwits. She's the one who gave him my phone number. "You'll do anything to get me hitched," I say, annoyed. She thinks this is hilarious.

Dewey picks me up wearing a natty suit and freshly blocked hat. A talker, his gift of gab eases my nerves at being with him. At the restaurant he seems to know everyone; free drinks appear, and several times patrons come by and trade jokes and talk about horse racing.

When he takes me home, we make plans to see each other the following week. He kisses me on the cheek and waits at the curb until I'm inside.

Dora is beside herself. "Tell me!" she shrieks. "Tell me!"

I give her the rundown.

"Oh, he has confidence," Dora says. "He's sure of himself. That's why people buy insurance from him. He's trustworthy."

On our next date, we drive up to Reservoir Park and, from the hillside, gaze down at the city below. We marvel at the pattern the streetlamps make and how the city has grown. "But Harrisburg will never be big like New York or Chicago," he says. "Because of the Susquehanna."

"Lots of cities are built along rivers," I say. "St. Louis for example."

"But this river is shallow and also extremely wide; two counties lie on either bank and don't cooperate well. Then there's the railroad yard; it runs parallel to the river in the bed of the old Swatara Creek. Only seven or eight blocks of streets can run north to south between the river and that no-man's land of railroad soot and freight. Only two streets run east and west, State and Market. They cut across the tracks and connect the hill section, but to keep growing the town would need a dozen east-west streets."

"Maybe one day the state will move the tracks. It is the capital after all."

"There's nowhere to put them. The eastern terrain rises too steep. Look how high we are now. It would cost millions."

"It's still a major city," I say.

"Putting the capital here was a compromise between Philadelphia and Pittsburgh, and though much was spent on the capital buildings, and civic buildings like the Zembo Mosque, the Eastern Star, the Y, churches, and factories, the city has no college or university. Young people with ideas leave."

"I don't blame them," I say. "But I once had a job down in Philly and as a city it wasn't much to brag about."

"Well, Philly has twenty-five colleges. Harrisburg—none."

I nod, feeling dumb. I didn't know that. We sit quietly for a while, nervous as our silence changes the mood.

I know that to confess I have a child might incur his farewell, but I want to be forthcoming, so finally, after much debate, I tell him about Sam. I needn't have worried; it turns out he has six children—five girls and one boy. He doesn't ask me any prying questions but offers how his own wife died giving birth to the sixth child and a few days later the flood washed away their home. Three of the children live in an orphanage now, two live with families who have taken them in, and the boy is down at the Milton Hershey Technical School.

"Don't you feel bad keeping your kids in an orphanage?" I ask.

He looks away. "I'm not much of a father. I like my kids, but to have all six living with me would be impossible. I'm not equipped. It's too late now anyway. The orphanage has ruined them."

"How can they be ruined?"

"It's been almost seven years now. They've been deprived. They grab and pinch and scheme and get into each other's business. Fight like cats and dogs. But then they make up again and are thick as thieves."

Suddenly out of nowhere, Dewey turns to me. "You don't have a high opinion of men, do you?"

"Why do you say that?" I ask, and wonder if he can read that in me.

"You seem skeptical when I show you affection." He flicks the lid of his lighter and puts his cigarette to the flame. I watch the blue smoke curl from his nostrils.

"No," I say finally. "I don't think the world of men. They've always made me suffer."

He gently removes a shred of tobacco from his tongue. "At the same time men must find you attractive."

"Most men look me over and walk away. They know I have no use for them. Or they dig, and I'm like a stubborn root that stops their shovel."

He clicks his teeth. Then he smiles, leans over, and kisses me on the mouth with an urgency that I find irresistible. I taste the cigarette and feel myself fold under his embrace, it's all so good. Though I yield, I think he senses that he can't possess me, that I never want to give up my will or power to a man again. That seems to make him want me more. His gentle manner allows me to confess. "I never married Sam's father," I say.

"It doesn't matter, none of it matters."

I spend the night at Dewey's apartment. He is by far the most unusual man I've ever met. I like the little things he does to get ready—dabs a bit of clove oil in his mouth, runs a barber's comb through his hair, and washes up with scented soap. Nothing about a man is more attractive to a woman than health, confidence, and a clean soapy smell. His hands are not the softest, but he has a gentle way of moving them. I'm glad I stayed over.

Coming home, I see a familiar big, navy blue Lincoln with a white chauffeur that pulls up in front of the Penn Harris Hotel. Dr. Crampton jumps out wearing a well-cut beige suit and dark shoes with spats. He carries himself well, light on his feet, and doesn't resemble any colored man I've ever seen. He enters the Esquire Bar. All the big muck-a-muck politicians go there. It surprises me that they let a colored man enter. He's certainly the only one.

So much has happened in the last few days my mind is swimming. In the afternoon Dora finally agrees to sit still so I can address her about some things, mainly the way she runs off and leaves the patients alone in the apartment. The other night she went to the Capitol Theater for a movie and didn't get home until midnight. Always high-spirited, lately she's become even wilder, more extravagant, less responsible. Maybe I'm just getting to see more sides of her, but the money seems to be making her reckless.

Dora admits she's tired of being on call and of having strangers in her home. She's eager to have Judy come but can't quite swing it yet. "If we took an extra girl or two every weekend," she says, "I'd soon have enough for a house. But I can't do it without you."

"I need to think about it," I say. "Don't pressure me."

So far about thirty-five women have stayed with us. I study their faces in the rearview mirror as I drive, looking for clues as to what they might be thinking. Sometimes they look confused. My favorite is still a sweet red-haired girl from Conestoga. She left a simple note on the supper tray stating, "Your vegetable soup is better than any I've ever tasted." When I drove her to the depot she hugged me good-bye.

There was also a coarse woman from New Cumberland who came in and said, "Show me where to park my stump." She wasn't as tough as she made out and afterwards sat bawling for hours. We don't get many like her. Dora says there's a colored nurse on Seventh Street who handles the rough ones.

9

Dewey takes me for outings several times a week. He likes to drive in the country, where the land is wide and the beautiful farms are rich with crops. As we pass, butterflies flit up from the wild-flower fields, bits of color and moving light.

When we get lost, Dewey says we are traveling by faith. "The senses sharpen on a faith drive," he says. "Anything can be a marker—houses, barns, a strange bend in the road, a twisted tree. Time moves differently on an unfamiliar path. It seems, in life, we are always being warned not to get lost, and yet it is in the risk of the unknown that you know you're fully alive. It grows dark, you're low on gas, everything is like a dream, and then suddenly something in you recognizes something in the landscape. You reach a familiar road and are on your way home again."

I never tell Dewey that I do some driving for Dr. Crampton, but people he collects insurance from inform him. Apparently I've been noticed waiting in Dora's car on more than one occasion, and as the news travels, someone tells Dewey, referring to me as "his girl." "All colored people know Dr. Crampton's business," Dewey says. "It takes work to keep even small secrets in that part of town and he is a figure of great interest."

When I tell Dora, she says Negroes possess superior knowledge about the personal lives of white people; so many work inside white homes, the secrets and trials of those who employ them get revealed. On the other hand, a white person will rarely visit the home of a Negro. Though my experience is limited, this insight doesn't strike me as all that odd. For how does one go about imposing on people who have so little? There just isn't occasion.

I tell her how it is possible to discern that it actually pleases Dewey that I'm involved with something illicit. It is evident that a streak of larceny runs through him, and the idea of doing anything outside the law brings him enjoyment. Perhaps I have a touch of that in my blood too.

But do I want more involvement? Dora speaks to Dr. Crampton and he asks to meet me. She says he'll send his car the next morning at eleven. Right now I can back out of any trouble saying, "I know nothing. Dora is responsible." But if I meet him—then what? Still, I could provide better for Sam and for Mom, move them to the city, also buy a house. Then there's the pit in my stomach that warns of trouble with the law. Should I ignore that? The indecision is exhausting.

I fret over the idea of working for the doctor. Do I really want to work for a colored man? For some reason, maybe because I am so conflicted, it occurs to me to pray to God for guidance. It's been a long time since I looked for God's or anyone's permission. Religion itself has never helped me. Like Pop I challenge God with my life, and if God doesn't like what I do he can strike me dead with a lightning bolt. But here and now, my confusion is great and I climb from my warm bed and kneel on the hardwood floor. I whisper to God that I'm at a crossroads and don't know what to do. I need money. These women need help. I'm worried about my nursing oath. My own repentance. I'm scared. If the direction I'm headed is wrong, I ask God to show me the right path instead.

When there is no message, I begin to accept that God just might have a different idea of right or wrong than we humans. There is a mystery here. God will not actually tell me anything. I've always been skeptical of people who claim to know what God wants them to do or who interpret things that have happened—good or bad—by saying, "It is God's will." How presumptuous to think you know or claim you know what God wants! I get up off my knees and crawl back into my warm bed.

The next morning Dr. Crampton's Lincoln pulls up outside our house, a white driver behind the wheel. Dora says you can travel the entire United States and find only a handful of colored men with white drivers. He holds the door open for me. The back is big as a cave, the seats soft leather.

At the doctor's house, we pull into the courtyard and I go to the back door. Frances, the woman with the curved spine, answers. She introduces herself and leads me through a narrow supply room, formerly the kitchen of the house, then on through a second room with an examination table and a metal chair. It's a typical doctor's setup—ground-floor offices, everything painted with white enamel including the glass of the windows in the exam room, living quarters upstairs and out of sight. Young doctors rarely set up this way anymore; they want privacy at home and prefer their practice to be in medical buildings.

Off the hallway at the front of the house are two large waiting rooms with colonial chairs lining the walls. The light is dim, but it's enough to reveal among the many periodicals copies of *Life*, *Look*, and *National Geographic*, and then I notice that the room is overflowing, practically bursting, with floral arrangements—pyramids of carnations, chrysanthemums, dozens of milk glass vases, roses of every hue, yellow, pink, and red. "The doctor turned sixty yesterday," Frances says matter-of-factly, but there is also a hint of pride. "He received eighty-two flower arrangements and more than four hundred cards. More come every year." She shows me her desk, which is at the back of the second room. Several large sprays of gladiolas line the floor, banked up against the base of the desk; three floral arrangements sit on top amid stacks of papers and a large appointment book.

We hear a door open at the top of the stairs and a man's footsteps begin to descend. "That's him now," she says and turns with anticipation. When Dr. Crampton enters a room, you take one look at him and know he is somebody. Tailored gray suit, trousers creased to perfection, a shirt collar crisp as a fresh piece of typing paper, and a pale blue tie anchored with a large diamond stickpin—all business, he won't take any guff. When he shakes my hand I feel an electric tingle in my toes. He commands respect. My feelings of intimidation grow intense; my knees tremble as he leads me into his office.

He sits behind a large desk with a magnificent set of fountain pens at the center. The room is filled with medical books and on one wall there's a small marble fireplace. I try to avert my eyes, but his face fascinates me. His skin is brown and a bit golden; it reminds me of the tannish shade that is found in the grooves of certain plums. His face is handsome and unlined, and you'd never know he was sixty but for a small pouch under each eye. Black don't crack, I think, and wonder where I picked that up.

"According to Dora you're a fine nurse," he says, steady, no-nonsense, his voice quiet, deep, powerful. I keep my gaze on him and try not to be tongue-tied, noticing how expertly his mustache is shaped. But I really don't know what to say.

"I understand you looked after Tom Nelly's mother?"

"Yes." I nod. A feeling of awe has overtaken me. He has a warmth and charisma I didn't expect to find. There's a strange combination of command and ease about him that is most attractive. You just know he's the boss.

"Tom's an old friend of mine—from even before he became county commissioner. Mrs. Nelly booted many a girl she thought wasn't up to par. It used to drive Tom crazy. But he tells me you are aces."

I smile, surprised to hear I've been discussed with Tom and by how frank and open it all sounds. "I liked her. She was from the old school."

"That she was."

"You knew her?"

"I was a guest at her table many times. Before she grew too frail."

It shocks me to learn that Mrs. Nelly had a colored man to dinner, but I realize this isn't just any colored man. Inside of me, I'm suddenly aware there's a feeling of hope: I'm being given an opportunity that doesn't come around every day. I can learn things from this man. He is unique in his offerings.

"Now, about the procedure, I suppose Dora's told you how important confidentiality is? The consequences are serious. Please read this."

He slides a parchment envelope across his desk. Inside, a newspaper clipping dated August 1935 describes the trial of a doctor down near Lancaster. This doctor performed illegal abortions in an old farmhouse. One operation went badly and the patient died. Afraid of what would happen, the doctor cut her body up and fed it into a wood chipper. The article ends by stating the doctor has been found guilty and he'll be sent to prison for punishment.

I'm not sure what Dr. Crampton wants me to say, but I somehow register that the crime is terrible.

"It happened four years ago," he says. "But unscrupulous people still operate on women every day. This is why my patients must receive hospital-quality care and I won't settle for less."

I'm stunned that Dora has the nerve to run things so loosely in the face of this precise decree.

"I want to keep the Monday, Wednesday schedule, and we'll have to set up a time so you won't overlap with Dora."

"But won't she and I be working together?" I ask.

"Oh, no. I'm bursting at the seams and need you to set up your own place. There's an apartment on Kelker Street I want you to take. I've already made the arrangements." He passes me an envelope with five ten-dollar bills and a set of keys. "This will help cover your moving expenses and get you set up."

The next thing I know, he's shaken my hand, and I'm back in the car on my way home. I'm exhilarated by the thought of so much change, and the time for doubt or reconsideration has passed. I've discovered one thing—I want to work for this man. He believes in me. I also run the math in my head. I'll be making sixty dollars a week!

Dora is worried at the news of our separation, for it means she will again have to shoulder the entire responsibility for her patients. I tell her about the newspaper clipping. It was never shown to her.

10

Two weeks later I make the move. The new apartment has its own side entrance and is on the second floor above an accountant's office. The move isn't too overwhelming, as I have no furniture, but for the first time in my life, I do have money to install a phone and buy sheets and towels and dishes. Dora and I work out an arrangement that allows me to purchase the DeSoto from her at half price in exchange for helping her to transport her own patients. She lives only three blocks away, so it's not difficult.

When I enter the brick courtyard at Dr. Crampton's my first solo day, Frances greets me and I follow her inside. "I put the girl upstairs until he's done," she whispers. "Wait in here," she says, guiding me to the small storage room. "This way no one left in the waiting room will see you." I perch alone on a step stool beside a percolator full of fresh coffee that Frances says I should try.

Dora warned me that a loyal group of colored women guard Dr. Crampton as their right. One of them, Jenny Johnston, lives up the block and cooks his meals, another cleans his house, another does laundry, and Frances coordinates them and everything in the office.

From my place on the stool I can listen through the door to a man speaking with Frances about his bill. He's charged two dollars for the visit, what doctors were making when I was a kid. Once she's sure the man has departed, Frances comes and fetches me and we watch from the side window as he climbs into a gray pickup truck and pulls away.

In a moment Dr. Crampton is at my side. He wears chocolate brown pants, a spotless white shirt, and an acid green tie. His greeting is curt and his manner businesslike. "The girl is upstairs. Go take her name and address, ask who she wants notified in case of an emergency. If she doesn't want to give it, tell her there can be no procedure. Then bring her down. Frances will show you the next part."

I climb the stairs to the second floor, where good rugs line the hallway. My mind is racing. I usually have some sense about things—what makes me thankful, what I dislike or resent, what saddens me or makes me glad, what makes me feel impoverished. But this is a new feeling. I am breaking the law. I am willingly breaking it. It both elates me and frightens me to death.

One door is ajar, and I enter a sitting room furnished with beautiful mahogany furniture and glass lamps with roses painted on them. A young woman waits there. She's in her mid-twenties and answers my questions directly and without hesitation, says she lives in Hummelstown, and in case of emergency gives the name of her sister who owns a farm outside Union Deposit. I offer her a throat lozenge; she declines and watches me unwrap one for myself. I use the candy to hide my nerves, but inside I'm far from calm.

We descend. Frances hands over a hospital gown and tells the woman to undress in the examination room. After a few minutes, I come in to find she's already lying on the table, her dress and coat neatly folded over a chair protecting her undergarments, shoes lined up against the baseboard. Her neatness is a clue to how she handles life's bigger problems.

The doctor comes in and motions for me to place her legs in the stirrups. "How long since you had your period?" he asks. "About nine weeks," she says. "I'd have come sooner but you didn't have any appointments."

"You're at the perfect time to have it," he says. His tone indicates there will be no idle chatter. Without further ado, he rolls his metal stool over to her and begins dilation. I try not to show embarrassment at the sight of her exposed vagina. The loudness of my heart beating is all I hear. He adjusts the light. Frances takes a syringe from the sterilizer and fills it with saline solution. The woman asks if she can see the needle.

"There's nothing to see," Crampton says.

With her free hand, Frances turns the woman's head away. She quietly hands Dr. Crampton the needle and the woman squeezes her eyes shut as he smoothly injects her cervix. After a minute he removes the dilator and rolls his chair away, and Frances tells her to get dressed. "Is that it?" the girl asks. "Yes," he says and nods in my direction. "You'll be staying with this lady until the fetus passes."

Outside the examination room, Dr. Crampton whispers, "Call if she has complications or if you have questions." He hands me a small brown envelope holding fifty dollars.

Once dressed, the woman follows me out to the car and I drive her back to Kelker Street. She settles into the extra bedroom at the back, which I've supplied with old towels and an enamel basin. "You can use the toilet to urinate or have bowel movements, but anything else must be passed into the basin for examination," I say. She stares at me in silence.

When night comes, I lie sleepless in my slip, ready to jump up in case she calls. I suddenly see the moral implications of everything I'm doing, how my mind has split in two. I learn that from here on in, my thoughts will be burdened with different versions of what I could say should we get caught. I act out these speeches in my head again and again.

By morning she's doubled up in pain. I examine the basin: it's empty. By noon she's passing blood and tissue. By three she's exhausted and sleeping. In the evening the fetus finally tears away. I remove the basin to the bathroom and transfer the pulpy tissue to a glass jar with preserving liquid. "Can I see it?" the woman asks when I bring her some weak tea and saltines. "There's nothing to see," I tell her, echoing what I heard at the office.

The next day her appetite recovers, and I bring her some tomato soup. "Try to rest and get your strength back," I say. In the evening we return, and Dr. Crampton examines the woman first, then in the other room removes the glass jar stowed in a cardboard carton. He is satisfied that the fetus has been fully expelled. With no stray pieces left inside her body, the woman is free to go. Upstairs another patient is waiting, a middle-aged woman with a snood. This time I don't feel as nervous, and while she is in the stirrups I secretly study the droopy crepe flesh of her thighs. It surprises me to find myself in charge of a woman who is so much older and an adult.

Back on Kelker Street, I watch everything like a hawk. I'm probably overdoing it, but I can't allow anything to go wrong. On Friday we return to the office and the woman checks out clean. I head home alone. The week's stress is suddenly released and I'm overcome with exhaustion. I fall into bed, where a new feeling rushes through me, a sort of dread mixed with terror, mixed with exhilaration. I got away with it. The world is getting bigger. I recognize that with lawlessness, a hint of madness comes and the excitement of possibility. How much luck does one person's life get granted?

On Saturday morning I awake from a nightmarish dream about the woman with the crepe flesh thighs. She is swimming naked in a lake with her lover. After watching her take his erection into her body, I know she will soon be pregnant. I bolt awake. The sheets are twisted, my heart is beating. I'm embarrassed, a rabbit on the run. There is no one I can admit this dream to.

After breakfast and a shower, I seal a fifty-dollar bill into a business envelope with a short note of thanks and address it to Tom Nelly. When I get to his building, it is open but his office is locked. I slide the payback through the mail slot. In one week of work I've paid off the loan for my entire nursing school tuition using only half of what I've made.

On Sunday Dewey and I pick Sam up for an outing. Mom is upset because the landlord has said he needs her house for his cousin to live in. She has ninety days to move. "Don't worry," I say. "I'll find you something in Harrisburg." Mom's eyes widen as if I've announced she's moving to Hong Kong.

11

Dewey and I take Sam down to the amusement park at Willow Mills. Sam is preoccupied and finally poses a question. "Since Dewey has an automobile," he says, "can I ride the bumper cars?"

I don't understand his logic. "What does one thing have to do with another?" I say. Sam then tells about the last time he was here. Apparently Mom wouldn't let him ride the bumper cars, saying they were dangerous and he wasn't old enough. Then Sam pointed to a boy from his class at school who was whizzing by in one. "But he knows how to ride it," Mom said. "His daddy has a car."

It makes me angry to think a nine-year-old boy must struggle with such explanations. Perhaps Mom is scared of bumper cars; she probably has no idea of how they work and didn't have the money for Sam to ride, but to answer as though Sam can't ride because he doesn't have a father is terrible and not a little hurtful.

We drop Sam back in Mechanicsburg and I feel guilty that Dora plans to bring her daughter, Judy, to live with her, when I have no plan for Sam. I wonder if Dewey has these regrets about his children. Whenever I ask, he looks frozen, but then after a moment just shrugs it off. It doesn't strike me that he is hard-hearted, just that having six children must be confusing. He told me that to accept some, only the younger ones for example, and not all of them is to injure them all. When I press him about other options he doesn't like it. "My children are staying put," he says. "It's too late."

The only way I know to overcome these sad feelings is to prepare for work, put on a fresh uniform, and whiten my duty shoes. The next day I scan the papers looking for a house in town that can be rented for Mom and Sam. After seeing the ridiculous rents, I decide to buy one instead. They are surprised when I tell them I've found one on Logan Street, that they will move at the end of the month and that I've already enrolled Sam in a city school.

12

With the attack on Pearl Harbor we are finally at war, just as Mr. Zimmerman predicted. Long days unfold without sleep. I now take two patients at a time, am raking in two hundred dollars a week, and am oddly charged-up from the success. Life is moving up. This must be what it feels like to be transformed like one of those traveling preachers who spend the night in a strange hotel, Wichita, or somewhere in Alabama, and out of desperation read Gideon's Bible and then somehow came through the eye of the needle.

With all the money I'm making, I am able to purchase the house on Logan Street for Mom with cash. She is beside herself with gratitude, saying, "I never dreamed I'd live in a house that was owned." Dora has also saved enough to buy a bungalow on the West Shore and says she'd like out of the business by summer. Crampton wants me to take up the slack by accepting an additional patient twice a week, but this apartment is too crowded. "It's a shame not to make the extra money," I tell Dewey. "I'm here anyway—in for a penny, in for a pound."

Dewey puts his head down and stares at the linoleum. "Why don't we buy a house together?" he says. "Why not just cut to the chase and get married?" My jaw drops open. He's caught me off guard. "You ought to close your mouth before a fly gets in there," he says. I turn my face so he can't see me struggle with my emotions.

The next weekend Dewey takes me down to York to meet his sister Elsie. She sizes me up like a head of cattle before an auction. But by the end of the visit she warms up—as though she thinks I can pull the plow. "You'll have your hands full with six children," she says. I nod. And Dewey changes the subject.

Afterwards we visit the Quincy home, the orphanage where three of his five daughters live. They are adolescents, desperate for attention, and it is also evident that they have internalized certain skeptical attitudes and irreverent, even sneaky ways, no doubt learned by necessity from their long stay in the inhospitable orphanage. You can see how they boast of petty advances and even act as each other's parents. I shudder to think about how much the routine of the orphanage reminds me of the state hospital. We sit in the visitors' room and Dewey tells them we're getting married.

"Will we come live with you?" the youngest asks right away.

"No," Dewey says. "There isn't room."

Their faces grow indifferent, and any excitement dies. The news is but a fact; it does not pertain to them.

Dewey and I return to Harrisburg in silence. Later we agree that one day soon we'll visit the two older girls, who are living with foster families, to tell them, and we'll also drive down to the Milton Hershey Technical School, where his son is a resident, but somehow I know we never will. They'll have to hear about our wedding from their younger sisters.

It's a difficult circumstance to accept, and I can see that Dewey does not want my involvement where his children are concerned. Not that I'd know what to do. The whole thing is awkward. I see they have been badly affected by institutional life and that Dewey, as a man, is incapable of managing their needs. It is all so bumbling and sad. If we are to marry I must accept his failure and these flaws, influence them wherever possible, and otherwise just accept them, just as he must accept my limitations. I feel the pull to make some kind of difference here, but in this case such notions are folly. It is impossible for me to raise six children plus Sam, while at the same time nurse patients.

Upon returning to our house, I go out into the back yard and sit on a swing Dewey has hung. The evening is mild and I gaze up through the branches of the pear tree crooked with age. So far most of our patients have not had good things to say about marriage. I feel panic and sudden caution. Dewey senses my mood and comes out to find me. I'm relieved he doesn't ask me questions. If it was Norm, he'd be all over me wanting to know what was wrong, making assumptions about my feelings, trying to give advice. Dewey stands quietly, and after a while I inhale and say, "Tell me about your wife."

He pauses and then nods. "Can we go into the kitchen?"

I sit at the table and he makes a pot of coffee. Then he joins me. "Now, I'm only going to tell you this stuff once, so pay attention."

He recounts growing up on a fruit farm down in York, running away at the end of the Great War for a brief career in the Navy, where he drank too much, and how his courtship and marriage to Addie were hastened by her first pregnancy. He says after five children, he wishes he'd have known about Dr. Crampton during her sixth pregnancy when her health failed. She died giving birth, and he didn't know how to manage without her. He says drink got the better of him. Whether or not that is an excuse, I don't know, but regardless, a few weeks later the flood came and washed away whatever thin chance he might have had to look after the children. "I was poorly equipped for the job anyway," he admits softly. "So it was a sad relief."

What Dewey doesn't say is what Addie was like. Did he love her? Did he weep at her death? Was he glad to go out without her? Could she bake a pie? Did she oversalt the stew? Was she fat or thin? Did he long for or recoil from her touch? I can't ask him those things. When I say, "I'd like to know more about Addie," he says, "Talking too much about people we've been with in the past only breeds trouble. She's passed away and let's leave it at that." I'm disappointed but also relieved that he doesn't want to discuss her. I felt her presence at the orphanage and carried it away with me, but when it's clear he's put her to rest, my melancholy departs.

I manage to shed a few pounds on my wedding diet and look for a dress to be married in. I work up my nerve and enter Mary Sachs, the venerable store where Mrs. Parrish used to shop for her fine clothes. Mary Sachs herself is European, born in Lithuania; her lady's store is the best in town. Once inside, I glance around shocked that there are cases of gloves and bags, a wall of lovely hats, but no clothes racks. A foreboding salesgirl greets me and asks what she may assist me with. "I need a dress," I say, like I'm a criminal confessing.

"Evening, afternoon, cocktail, morning?"

"Something I can wear to a wedding," I say.

I follow the girl to the salon at the back of the store and perch on a small satin sofa. She hands me a pad of paper. "Jot down anything you'd like to try."

An attractive girl emerges from behind some drapes wearing an ivory-colored dress with collar, cuffs, and belt made from emerald green striped fabric. Initials are embroidered on one shoulder. "Straight from New York," the salesgirl says. Three other models weave in and out, each time wearing a different dress. "Because of the war, colors are drab this year," the salesgirl explains. "Factories that make dye products for brighter colors are overseas and have been shut down or taken over for military supply."

Some other customers come in, wearing furs and velvet shoes. They sit across from me with their own pads of paper and jot notes as a parade of the most elegant clothes I've ever seen passes before us. I'm nervous in their presence but act as if I do this all the time.

Then a girl comes in wearing a smart powder blue dress with a matching jacket. "How much is that?" I whisper to the salesgirl. "That ensemble is eighty-five dollars." I almost gasp, but I know I must have it. At nearby Feller's Department Store, four spring coats could be had for that price. The salesgirl makes a good point that with all the shortages, better fabrics will be harder to come by. She also talks me into two lovely silk blouses at seventeen-fifty each. One of them has full sleeves that gather at the cuff and is modeled after one worn by Lucille Bremer in a film. The beauty of these clothes charges my senses and suddenly I'm like a horse at a racetrack ready to run. I can't stop myself. The money is rolling in; I may as well splurge, adding to my purchases a wide-brimmed straw hat for summer. It has beautiful brown netting and a band of pimiento-colored velvet at the edge. I feel intoxicated when I leave the store and nauseous from overspending. The new clothes make everything else in my closet look shabby. A hundred and forty dollars gone and right away I want to spend more. It's like a fever.

I show the dress to Mom and she says, "I'm so glad you're not trying to wear white." I don't know if she means because my reputation is spoiled or because she thinks white makes me look big. It really doesn't matter because as a nurse wearing white every day, I long for another color.

The wedding is a simple service, and afterwards Hazel and Joe throw a nice reception for us at their apartment. They now have three babies, each a year apart, which makes for a lot of commotion. Sam is also there, but Dewey has opted not to invite his own children. "If they see our lives, they'll just feel worse about their own," he says. I do not question him.

The very next day he and I begin looking for another house, this one for us. With the war on, prices have moved higher, the Depression is finally over, business is booming, and things are bustling as the new turnpike carries military trucks through and men are again earning fat paychecks in the steel mills.

We find the ideal house at 2311 North Third Street. It's big and brick with a sloping hill and nice foliage shielding it on either side. The neighborhood is beautiful, with large well-maintained homes and gardens, very fine, respectable. I never dreamed I'd afford a house uptown—and on my own wouldn't even have the nerve to look here—but Dewey convinces me we can. I pay $7,500 dollars for the house, in cash.

The first floor holds a living room with pocket doors that open onto a dining room with oak paneling and a built-in plate rack skirting high along the walls. There's a large kitchen in back, with pantry and breakfast room, plus a sunporch. The second floor has a full bathroom and three bedrooms and the third floor has three additional bedrooms and a half bath.

A brick pathway cuts through the rear garden to a wooden garage. It opens onto an alley where garbage and delivery trucks do their work without being seen from the street. I'll be able to come and go from here with little notice. With the additional space, I can increase the number of patients I handle to six a week, maybe more. "Who knows," I say, "maybe after a year or so of making money, I'll quit and we'll have all these rooms for your kids too." Dewey smiles and puts his arm around me.

· 13 ·

For a wedding gift, Dr. Crampton sends us a mahogany box lined with brown velvet, fitted to hold sterling silver place settings for twelve people. The forks, knives, and spoons are large and heavy and their extravagance embarrasses me.

"Let him spend," Dora says. "He's got plenty."

"I didn't even invite him. I don't want him to feel obligated or think that I'm needy," I say.

"It's better to poor-mouth him." She lights a cigarette and inhales. "You never want him to think you've got extra."

"Money is so personal," I say. "I don't want to take advantage."

"He knows how to handle that. Besides, he likes you. Don't you sense that?"

"Well, yes, but how long will he like me if I'm taking him for things?"

"It's a gift. You didn't ask. You merely said you were getting married. He did the rest, so what's your beef?"

"I've got no *beef*. None. But it does make me feel awkward. That's all."

Dora stares at me in a strange way. "I've never seen you go on so about accepting gifts," she says. "You can always hock it. Can't you use extra with Sam and your mother always asking for something?"

"Of course," I say, wiping my hands on my apron. "It's just that

I see the colored people frequently coming by the office to hit him up for money. Everyone needs or wants something. I don't want to be like that."

"Who cares! Jesus have mercy! I believe you are a little stuck on Dr. Crampton." She grins, delighted to think she's caught a glimpse of some secret.

"Don't be ridiculous," I say, sliding a tray of biscuits into the oven and slamming the hot door. "What would make you even *think* such a thing, let alone *say* it?"

"Well, all I know is you wouldn't be the first. A line of women swoon whenever he passes by. He's got that special thing, the aura of great tenderness that some men have. It connects the bones and tissue in his body and gives him a confidence and grace. He makes women feel alive between their thighs."

"Oh. That's so vulgar," I say, to steer the attention away from myself. "And *you* certainly seem to know all about it."

"I've felt it, yes, but I've never been susceptible. Do you know they say a confident man lives longer and that he lasts longer in bed?"

"Oh, Dora! If that's true, God help us all," I say, laughing.

"You never know!" Dora cries. "They say he prefers white women. That he even keeps a white woman in a house not far from here."

"Don't tell me," I say, setting a platter of meatloaf on the table.

"They say his mistress lives right over on Green Street. Keep watch and you might see his car there some night. You know there are some white women who prefer colored skin. Some people say all white women are curious about Negro men."

"Don't tell me any more," I plead. "I've got to work with the man. I don't want to know his personal business."

"We can't all act professional like you," Dora says, and her eyes shine with glee as she uncaps a bottle of beer and drinks. "Still, there's no telling what might happen at the end of a long shift."

"Stop now," I say. "I mean it."

But to myself I must admit I am attracted by his independence. You can't keep him down, and maybe, secretly, I want to be like that too, or at least think I am. A romantic attraction would be more than I could handle. But now, because of Dora and her dirty mind, his romantic life suddenly interests me and I drive by the houses on Green Street and try to figure out which one might hold his girlfriend. What kind of women does he like?

And the following week when we return to work, it annoys me to realize that I feel weak in my knees when he rises to give me a congratulatory hug. I thank him for the silverware and he says, "If you ever need anything else, let me know."

14

As head of the war rations board, Dr. Crampton publicly announces that this year he will not make his annual summer trip to Tyrone to see his brothers and nephew. "As our nation struggles to defend our very way of life, sacrifices are essential, and the gasoline needed for this trip is better used by our troops overseas."

Still, we take a few days' break and I use the time to get settled in our new house. It will be so much easier to handle the patients here. The week when we return to work, the wife of a prominent judge in Harrisburg refers a woman to us who turns out to be a student at Bryn Mawr. Her eyes are bright and everything about her manner says privilege. She talks about the war, the South Pacific, Hitler, and Stalin, almost to test me. Thank goodness I still copy things from the newspaper or I'd feel completely ignorant.

"Do you have a particular philosophy that enables you to do your job?" she asks out of the blue, catching me off guard.

"What do you mean?"

"Do you help women for a reason?" She props herself up on one elbow and sips tea.

I guard my thoughts; my tussle with God is nobody else's business. Besides, my ideas seem unformed and amateurish around her. I don't want to admit I've put these thoughts away, into a part of my mind where I store unsolvable dilemmas.

"Well, why do you do it?" she asks again.

"Maybe because I can," I reply.

She seems to like that answer, but I still feel that a judgment of me is taking place. Does her nose rise up just a sixteenth of an inch? Or do I imagine it? "Do you believe in women's equality?" she asks.

"Sure," I say. "But women aren't men."

She sinks down on the mattress as if to dismiss the notion that we have anything else in common. That attitude bothers me. I sense a shift in myself, a bit of fury rising. Who is she to judge me? I'm relieved when her time here is done, and I vow to pay more attention to current events.

A statewide election is coming up in a month, and the paper says Dr. Crampton has been named vice-chairman of the Dauphin County Republican Party. Tom Nelly is treasurer. They are both part of State Senator Harvey Taylor's machine, and Taylor runs the state. Dewey is amused that a man in Crampton's business carries the word *vice* in his title. Myrtle shows Crampton's picture to Mom. "I never imagined your boss to be colored," she says, echoing my own surprise with Dora. They know I work as his nurse but nothing about the true nature of our business. Mom's silence and lack of curiosity send me a disapproving message.

After supper Hazel and Joe stop by with the three boys, and I accept her offer to walk down to the drugstore to get them to pack us a carton of ice cream. Sam and the boys join us and run ahead. On the way home, Hazel pauses. "I need your help with something," she says, and quietly explains how she is expecting and that with three children already, she doesn't want another. I am startled. "You know about Dr. Crampton?" I ask.

"My doctor told me. At first I was surprised, but then it all made a certain sense."

"Does Mom know?"

"Of course not."

"And Joe?"

"He's progressive. He said to speak with you about it."

"Do you have any doubt?"

"The question I keep asking myself," Hazel says, "is how can I recognize a baby that should be born from one that shouldn't? Then I decide that only I can decide."

The next evening I speak to Dr. Crampton and tell him that it's important for me to help my sister. By working together so closely, for so long, I feel a friendship has grown between us, to the point that I can tell him anything and he will understand. He's become not just a boss but also a mentor. We both see firsthand, every day, how fallible people are.

The next weekend, on a Friday, I bring Hazel to the office and Dr. Crampton does the procedure at no charge. She stays with us overnight, and while Dewey goes out to play cards, we have a chance to talk for the first time in years. She admits to being very impressed by Dr. Crampton. "I can see how he respects your opinion and your work," she says.

We move on to other subjects. I tell her about Dewey's children and that he has given in to defeat on this part of his life. "He can't handle them," I tell her, and then I confess that while this weakness in him should repulse me, instead I'm rather moved by it. "It's difficult because though they don't say it, I don't think his children like me."

She nods her head. "Raising children is the hardest thing I've ever done," she says. "I see myself turning into Mom." We stay up half the night talking, and when she finally departs after her checkup, I am sad to see her go but also grateful to have found such a sister.

15

As the election nears, some viper writes in the paper that "Harvey Taylor is a stench in the nostrils of decent citizens of Dauphin County." None of us can believe the paper printed it. The article says that during the last election someone forged the names of the executive who runs the Girl Scouts and the assistant secretary of the chamber of commerce in order to cast their votes. Both were out of town. People speculate that the Taylor machine casts hundreds of phantom votes, and I'm sure it's true, but most politicians play tricks, otherwise they'd never get elected. The other fact of political life is that it's someone's job to throw mud on whoever is trying to govern.

Summer is upon us and I'd like to buy three electric fans to cool the house—one for each floor—but my ration book only allows one. I tell Crampton, and as a member of the war rations board, he gives me additional coupons. There's a thirty-six-year-old woman here who is grateful for the electric breeze. She says her husband is a shoe salesman and in thanks offers to send me a free pair.

Dewey is helpful when I'm tired. He boils the laundry, folds the towels, puts fresh blankets on the beds, and at night burns the dirty wads of Kotex and cotton gauze in the furnace. Not many men would tackle that. I have an account with the drugstore at Emerald and Third; they provide supplies in bulk and even deliver them into our garage off the alley. Dewey uses canvas tote bags to bring the supplies inside. In return, when some of his clients are short of cash, I advance him the money to pay the insurance company so their policies don't lapse. Everyone knows colored neighborhoods are the most difficult to collect from, but he says if he makes all his payments on time, the company will take notice and promote him. He keeps what he owes me on a card in his wallet and pays something toward it every week.

One weekend we invite Mom, Sam, and Myrtle over for Sunday

supper. When we are alone in the kitchen, Mom asks if I might finally bring Sam here to live with us. She can't handle him anymore. Mom then tells me that she has some other news. At that little doughnut shop near her house a "help wanted" was posted in the window, and the owner complained that he was having trouble finding someone. Why don't you apply? he jokes to Mom. To his astonishment Mom says she'll take him up on it.

She'll be the daytime manager. I never thought I'd see the day when my mother would earn a paycheck. She's pleased with herself to have found a job. Funny how owning some property has given her confidence.

I ask Crampton's advice about bringing Sam to live with us, partly as a way to let him know my plan. I expect him to raise an objection. But instead he agrees that Sam, who is almost thirteen, would benefit from living with his mother and having a man act as his father. He crosses to the sink, undoes his cuff links, and rolls up his sleeves to scrub for work.

"You know," I tell him, "when I was growing up, the women used to say you always favor a boy. But in Sam's case I don't think I've ever done that."

"Children are a lot more resilient than we give them credit for," he says. "When my own parents left me to be adopted by another man and his wife, I cried every night. But they turned out to be a gift. That man who adopted me had himself been poorly raised, but as a result, he was interested in raising children well. Sometimes early losses build character, give a person empathy, which later in life can burnish to a certain moral weight."

I can't tell if he really believes this. It's unlike him to refer to himself in such grand terms. In the end I decide he's just saying this to make me feel better. I'm curious to know more about his family, about the man and woman who raised him, but it doesn't feel proper to question him directly. I'll ask Frances sometime, or maybe one of the chauffeurs. He has three that rotate the job. Two are white and one is colored.

Crampton may be cultured and kind to me, but he's also a businessman and a politician, and therefore highly changeable—shrewd and eagle-eyed one minute, warm and generous the next. He knows I'm just as tough and can handle it when things get rough. By now we've been working together long enough, and are syncopated enough, that we can often read each other's thoughts. I know how to hand him the right dilator even before he asks for it. I know when to leave the room, what order to bring the girls in: young ones first; they grow more frightened the longer they wait. I know when he's had a bad day. I'll even wield the scalpel when need arises. He knows he has no worries with the women under my care; I'll have everything under control. I often tell him, "If there isn't a way, I'll make one."

Whatever Dr. Crampton's aims or motives are, I leave feeling affirmed and strong, and I try not to act sheepish when I bring the subject of Sam up with Dewey. As Dora points out, when I discuss it later with her, how can it not be heartbreaking for him to contemplate living with my son, when he himself has so vocally recognized that he can't possibly take his six children in? The thought of Sam living here is already nerve-wracking. He's at that age when boys ask questions. But Dewey deflects any conflict and says Sam should move in before the school year starts and that we'll deal with any problems as they arise. We designate one of the third-floor bedrooms as his and drive over to Mom's to deliver the news.

Once he is living here, I tell Sam it's extremely important that he not speak to the patients nor mention them to anyone else, that they come here for different reasons and we have a responsibility to protect their privacy. He accepts these restrictions.

Dora almost weeps with happiness when I tell her he's moved in. She hugs me and says, "You've managed it! After all the struggle, a husband, a home, a profession, and now this. Did you ever think you'd make it?"

Then, during his first week here, there is a knock at the front door and Sam answers. A woman in a stone-colored raincoat asks to speak with me and by the time I make it downstairs Sam's already invited her in.

"Can I help you?" I say. My manner is brusque.

"My daughter is in trouble," the woman says. "She's not married. I was hoping you might be willing to talk sense to her."

I'm irritated at the idea that this woman has decided to come up to my house in broad daylight. "The decision lies between you and your daughter," I say, as annoyed and uninterested as I can sound. "I don't advocate anything."

"Please," the woman begs.

"Go away," I say. "See the doctor if you need help. But don't show up here again." The woman quickly turns and leaves. When I close the door I see Sam still standing in the living room. "Don't ever let a stranger in here again," I say. "From now on only I answer the door."

16

Harrisburg has suddenly become a haven for servicemen. Within a twenty- or thirty-mile radius of the city stands Fort Indiantown Gap, the Navy depot in Mechanicsburg, the Army depot in New Cumberland, the Army Air Force post in Middletown, and the Army War College in Carlisle. Troop trains roll in and out of the station at all hours.

On the weekends the movie shows, restaurants, and bars are jumping with men in uniform. Dewey and I hardly go downtown for dinner, because even at the lousy pork chop place near the Senate Hotel we have to wait an hour for a table. One night we are returning home by way of Green Street and we see Dr. Crampton's big car pulled over to the curb driven by the colored chauffeur Togans. As we pass, Crampton gets out and we see him go up the walk of a handsome arts and crafts bungalow. My heart pounds. In the rearview mirror I watch the chauffeur pull away headed in the opposite direction.

Since then I've been driving past the bungalow every chance I get. One day I see an attractive woman with dark hair come out. She's pale and clutches an orange Chinese silk wrapper as she stoops to take the paper off the porch. I slow down to get a good look at her, but in a moment she's back inside. For some reason it pleases me to know that perhaps someone is loving Dr. Crampton, and is appreciating his rarity and his fine qualities.

Our business continues to boom and though often exhausted we work around the clock. They keep saying the war will only last a few more months, but with all the strangers in town, and all the men on the move, the number of women who find themselves in trouble has increased dramatically. I've gone from a few patients a week to over a dozen.

Dewey, who rarely has a day now when he hasn't been drinking, says in his insurance district at least ten whorehouses have opened on North Sixth and Seventh Streets, and that the conditions are deplorable. He says the war has broken down all color barriers and that whites and blacks are drinking together and that women are open about their business and can be had for as little as fifty cents following a dance to a jukebox.

Crampton and I handle any number of girls we know are fast. You can always tell—heavily rouged, tough-acting, smart-mouthed. The men are making so much money in the plants they don't know what to do with it, or they're in the service far from home and are lonely with a paycheck to spend.

It is good to have money and the things it can buy, but it comes at a price that is sometimes hard to see. Pop always used to say that when you acquire things, you start to know fear, because now you have something to lose. Though I'm proud to have been able to help the family, to buy my own home, to get an education and practice my profession, more frequently those accomplishments are accompanied by a feeling that something is about to go wrong. Despite the fact that I'm enjoying my prosperity and my work, I'm worried too much of the time and don't seem to have the peace of mind that other people do.

It's all moving too fast. The amount of money that is coming in is staggering. It makes me giddy and terrified all the same, for I have no idea how to manage it or what to spend it on. Still, I find myself wanting twice as much.

But there's no time to enjoy anything. I've got closets full of clothes that I've hardly worn. Last fall I bought a lovely mink coat, and though it got little use, it's already time to put it into cold storage. Sometimes when I'm alone, I put it on and admire myself in the mirror. The fur gives me broad shoulders, and I pull the notched collar up around my face and bury my hands in the sleeves. A woman wrote in the beauty column of the paper the other day that real mirrors were invented in Italy a little over four hundred years ago. Before that people could not really see for themselves what they looked like, except maybe in a pool of water—but for that you always had to look down at yourself. The discoveries of transparent glass, liquid mercury, and molten tin led to the invention of the looking glass. The article listed all the characters in history who never saw an accurate reflection of themselves—Cleopatra, Joan of Arc, even Christ.

When I look in the mirror and see my red eyes, puffy from fatigue, I stand amazed by my imperfections. How lucky Cleopatra was not to see herself. In those days beauty really was in the eye of the beholder. Then I realize that though I'm all dressed up, I have nowhere to go.

17

Harvey Taylor is sponsoring a bill in the senate to build more government office buildings. Crampton hates the idea, because the Capitol extension will tear down blocks of houses in which hundreds of colored families reside. Where will they go? The plan places government buildings right across the street from Crampton's own house. But none of it will happen while the war is on.

Dewey and I walk around in the direction of North Street to see what all the fuss is about. Naturally Dewey is concerned because the project will remove twenty-three acres from his insurance area. The blocks in question run from Third Street back to the railroad on Seventh. The homes are actually quite nice around there, as are the civic buildings—the old Central High School, the Wickensham School, the Phyllis Wheatley Y for colored women, all of which will come down. Crampton's house is only a few blocks away.

The tough streets along the railroad are entirely colored, and as we begin to approach I tell Dewey I don't want to be seen there snooping around in a mink coat. Just then one of the doors opens and a handsome, dark-skinned woman in a lavender dress comes out to the fence pulling a white sweater on. She greets Dewey by name and asks him if he can cover her for a few days while she gets her premium together. She makes a sad face and says her baby has been sick. Dewey grins and says, "You sure you ain't been playing the horses again?"

The woman lifts up her hand in extravagant surprise and says, "Mr. Krone, you know I don't bet no horses." Then Dewey says, "Well then maybe you got a new man you gotta look after." "Lord have mercy," the woman shrieks. "I never paid for a man in my life. And don't go spreading them stories in front of your wife."

The familiar way Dewey jokes with the woman displeases me. Speaking to her in that familiar way while I'm by his side implies my collusion or agreement. Many a true word is said in jest, as Pop used to say.

"How do you know she's my wife?" Dewey continues his bullshit.

"Everyone knows Mrs. Krone," the woman says, smiling at me. "She's always so stylish and works for Doctor Crampton."

I smile back, embarrassed to be wearing the fur, and am relieved when we part, turn, and head back toward the white part of the neighborhood.

"Didn't think *you'd* mind the colored section so much," Dewey says.

"It's not that I mind the colored section," I tell Dewey. "But I don't like stirring up talk when I have no business being over there, and the truth is, despite my work with Crampton and your insurance calls, they really don't appreciate us being in that part of town, any more than we do them in ours."

Dewey's banter with the woman lingers in my head and continues to annoy me. After a while I recognize it's because he doesn't really respect her. It also strikes me that as comfortable as Dewey can seem around colored people, he has never really taken to Dr. Crampton. Often he refers to him as the old black crow, and for a while it was easy for me to fall into such habits myself, saying things like "Did the old crow phone while I was out?" or "Keep an eye on things while I run this pie over to the crow." Then I start to feel ashamed in Dr. Crampton's presence, like I am Janus-faced. He treats me with such courtesy and has taught me so much.

I think about how much Dewey enjoyed seeing the house where Crampton's girlfriend lives. It also pleases him to tell me that in addition to abortion, he's heard Crampton makes a killing treating venereal disease. I come to realize that Dewey has begun to actively dismiss or deride Dr. Crampton, probably because it's difficult for him to find a way to feel better than him. He's actually quite envious of his position. The unflattering nickname of crow helps break Crampton down.

Most white people accept interactions with colored people, so long as they can walk away from the encounter and feel above them. That need to feel better than others is a terrible game most humans play—be it by salary, family, religion, age, looks, or the color of someone's skin. I wish I could be free of such pecking orders. I wish I had addressed this side of Dewey sooner.

He blathers on about how Harvey Taylor has gotten rich in the insurance business, selling insurance to the state. If the colored section is torn down and the state puts up office buildings, Taylor will probably write the state policies on those properties. He is also in the business of bonding state employees, eighty-five percent of them, according to Dewey. He's not doing anything illegal but his influence is astounding. He even affects the way judges are picked. His courtly manner, silver hair, long pointy nose, and glasses give him a fatherly air. When he smiles, his lips curve and you see his front and side teeth. He chews tobacco. He's the boss.

Crampton is mentioned in the newspaper as an honorary pallbearer for the funeral of Justin Carter, who for years has been the only colored lawyer serving Harrisburg. Though others have tried to practice law, attending rigorous schools, their bar exams seem to always come back "denied." They eventually leave town and practice somewhere else.

Carter was called upon by many in the Negro community and, around the time of the First World War, was a big deal in politics himself. When I get to the office, C. Sylvester Jackson is describing the funeral to Frances. I can see he relishes telling the story in front of me and is prideful when noting that Dr. Mordecai Johnson, the president of Howard University, came up from Washington to read the eulogy.

Frances says that Johnson is a friend of Crampton's and has dined at his house many times. Some big shot lawyers also attended: Homer Krieder, Sidney Friedman, and a judge by the name of Hargest who's sent us patients. A former state senator, William Earnest, also spoke, as did the district attorney Carl Shelley, also a close friend of Crampton's. He's a pint-sized prosecutor, and everyone in his circle openly calls him the "bantam rooster." He has also sent us patients on a couple of occasions.

I expect Crampton to be sad or melancholy after losing his friend Justin Carter, but he never mentions it and goes about business as usual.

Frances reports that so many calls are coming in they must refer many girls away. As always we suggest they go to Stanley Spencer up in Ashland. "Better to travel up to the coal regions, honey," Frances tells girls who balk at the distance, "than to the body shop in Steelton." They get the message.

Our patients are for the most part grateful and seem to look up to me, but we have a mean one here right now, a tough, yellow-haired blonde from Baltimore who begins to expel her fetus in the middle of the night. She's the type that wants to blame someone and so she's going to try and take it out on me.

Usually a woman who's a player is more furious at her predicament than any other type. It's some sort of injured pride: though she knew the score, she's now in a jam and wants to forget her part in it, forget that she too has instincts, that her black lingerie was bought for a reason. These women rarely admit their desire or efforts to run after men, or that they can get aroused, like we all can, over something as slight as the fit of his pants or the way he uses his hands when he's talking to someone.

I used to sympathize and commiserate with the plight of all women, but then one day I began to wonder: Why do we put up with it? And especially those tough ones? They have free agency. They can say no. Why are so many of us willing to enter bad situations? Why do so many of us find ourselves unable to leave? As I contemplate the women who demand too little respect, a dislike toward my own sex grows, and that increased lack of sympathy vexes me a great deal. Where does it come from? Is it a hard layer forming around my heart, or is it because I may be in the process of becoming one of them?

"If I ever get my hands on the weasel who knocked me up," the busty blonde says, squatting in the bathroom over the metal basin, "I'll cut his rod off."

I step out into the hallway for a moment and she begins to holler. "Hey! Nurse! While you're out there can you grab me a cigarette?"

We cannot call attention to the house, so we never turn the light on after midnight. We use flashlights instead. I come back in, hold the beam of light steady on the enamel pan to see what she is passing, and tell her smoking is not allowed.

"That's a lie, because I can smell your husband's cigarettes."

"Well, he didn't just have an abortion, did he?" I say, with efficient invective intended to let her know this is my house and I'm the boss.

"Screw you," she sneers.

"Hey!" I snap back. "I don't allow that kind of talk in my house."

"You think you're tough?" the blonde says, laughing. "Well, I'm tougher. I've been a stripper for more than fifteen years and I know all about men and money and bitches like you."

"And a lot of good it's done you," I say.

"Oh yeah? Well, I wouldn't want to be you for anything in the world." She hisses quickly through her teeth to show her disgust.

In my irritation, I grow very determined, fully enter the room, sit on the edge of the tub, shine the flashlight at the blood-filled pan. "Well, to tell you the truth," I say, cool as ice, "I wouldn't want to be you right now either."

She does not reply—just sucks her teeth against her tongue.

I act like I couldn't care less, but my tough heart pounds.

Once she is calm, I go to Dewey's room and bring her back a cigarette. She takes it without a thank-you.

18

Earlier this week a white Army private was murdered in a rooming house on North Seventh Street. It happened only a block from where Dewey and I walked a short time ago. Crampton in his role as chairman of the Negro Division of the Dauphin County Civil Defense Committee meets with the chief of police and the mayor and asks that the rooming house where the murder took place be padlocked. The paper quotes him. "Many of the buildings in that area are health menaces and should be condemned."

Dewey says, "It's all just smoke and mirrors and nothing will change. The mayor's office and the cops are all on the dole. Crampton's helping Taylor get the buildings padlocked so that the state can condemn them." Dewey says Crampton must be in some kind of deal to take this position.

Another story in the newspaper says that prostitutes have begun invading Harrisburg every Friday night for the weekend, hanging out in taprooms looking for intoxicated soldiers or war plant workers to roll. Apparently, at a bawdy house on Verbeke Street, a soldier from Indiantown Gap recently got syphilis and the U.S. Army lodged a formal complaint with the Harrisburg police. Since then that house has also been condemned and boarded up, but no arrests have followed. Supposedly the women are still out there working.

Dewey persuades me to join him for a drink at a bar where our car is parked, though I really don't feel like it. "C'mon," he says. "Just one to take the edge off." Over a glass of scotch he says the stories of crime in the colored neighborhood are being trumped up to help the state tear down the slum neighborhoods and that the *Patriot* and the *Telegraph* are both on the take. Whenever he drinks he becomes more conspiratorial about these things.

He orders another round and now I regret having agreed to stop at the bar. I think about how since I've known him there's been a progression to his drinking, and how he carries the expectation that I will always join him. At first he took me to ladylike places, the Alabama Inn or the Jupiter House. But as time has passed, we've graduated downward—Buffalo Nick's, the Shipoke Chophouse, the Mercury Tavern, Dexter's Red-Ace Bar and Grill, the Double Shot, Miss Dixie's Room, the Elmsford Inn, the Old Glory, the Palm House, Uncle Sam's, the Latin Pavilion, and the list goes on and on. At first I tried to keep up, and a few times they carried me out drunk along with him. I pretended that these were just "the good times" my life had lacked. I've since learned how to cut back, to avoid his parasitic friends or the "buyback" help of no-brain bartenders with nicknames like Tex, Slim, Honey Bun, Sugar Bear, Daddyo, Bingo, and Hairball. For a while his friends were dance hall types, men who escorted dames with muskrat coats or payday sailors on a spree, but lately he's not ashamed to put drinks back with filthy bums wearing whiskered jowls and crummy, foul-smelling pants. He resists my attempts to leave and sulks all the way home when I finally insist.

A few days later I ask Crampton about why he is cooperating with the Capitol extension plan. "I'll be honest with you, Mrs. K., because you deserve the truth and can be trusted. We already know we are going to lose. Anytime a colored community goes up against white business interests, they lose. So the trick is to see what you can get in exchange. If we cede the blocks that Harvey Taylor and the others want, we lose what? Run-down, ramshackle homes, some that haven't been updated since the Civil War. And what could we gain instead? Modern high-rise apartment buildings, clean and bright, with views of the city. Taylor has promised me that ten of the twenty-three acres will be set aside for residential use. But our housing projects can't be built without the funding for his office buildings. And Taylor can't finance office buildings until the land has been delivered. It's all a big package."

"What does he get out of it?"

"He'll insure the new properties, and our people will have the same number of units that they are losing, but the new ones will be far superior."

"What if the people prefer where they live now? What if they like their gardens and clotheslines and familiar streets?"

"Then they will lose everything. It's a bitter pill, Mrs. K. But they can't win against these forces. The same thing happened after World War One with the first capital extension. Only at that time nobody was in a position to cut a deal. In the end all that we gained was land for the Forster Street Y and the building that houses the Phyllis Wheatley Y.

"Helping them do in cooperation what they are prepared to do by force through eminent domain and eviction anyway also grants us protection for our work with patients, and the Seventh Ward will gain newly constructed housing."

I look at Crampton with a deeper respect. What a burden it must be to lead a group that is destined to lose. I also experience a deeper feeling of trust, for though I have confided much in him, he rarely confides anything in me. It is rare for white people to receive the confidence of colored people. Who can blame them?

The next week I have an early appointment with a dentist whose office is just off the square. From his window I see a dozen colored boys lined up outside Doutrich's waiting for it to open. I think maybe the store has a job opening for a stock boy or something. Then I see the Lincoln pull up and Dr. Crampton jumps out. The store manager unlocks the glass doors and everyone files in.

Frances tells me later that the boys are graduating from high school and that Crampton is buying them all suits. He does this every year, for without a suit they can't attend the ceremonies or look decent standing beside their white classmates. Each boy also gets a shirt, a tie, and a pair of shoes. On this day Doutrich's opens early so the boys can get in and out before the store officially opens. Colored people are not usually permitted to try on clothes in white stores.

A few days later Crampton is in the papers again, this time with regard to a conference on social needs being held at the Forster

Street YMCA. A probation officer, Jordan Ewell, is lined up to speak on juvenile delinquency, and to guarantee that as many boys as possible turn out, a free luncheon will be held, which Crampton is paying for. It amazes me to see how much social and civic funding our enterprise generates.

·　　**19**　　·

A woman in her thirties arrives, chestnut hair, a good figure, wearing smart brown felt gloves, matching shoes, a medium-quality crepe de chine dress printed with large green jungle leaves and on the collar a small gold pin engraved with her initials.

I tell Frances that the woman seems weak. When I touch her wrist to check for a pulse, my fingertips leave two white marks that take a while to fade. Crampton thinks she'll be all right. After the procedure I drive the woman home—along with four other patients. By midnight she starts to hemorrhage.

Her blood is thin and watery and unable to clot. It splashes like cranberry juice and I have it on my robe, my slippers, the floor in the bedroom and bathroom. We pack her with cotton. I tell her to apply pressure while I call for help. I am furious with myself for not speaking up more strongly when I suspected she wasn't well. To make matters worse, Sam is upstairs sleeping.

I feel panic.

The woman's blood is everywhere.

I call Crampton.

No answer.

"Take Sam over to Hazel's," I tell Dewey. Sam is groggy and confused but gets dressed and Dewey takes him down the back stairs so he doesn't see anything.

I phone Hazel, grateful that we've grown closer and that she knows firsthand the seriousness of our business. My call pulls her out of bed. I tell her of the emergency and say I've sent Sam and Dewey over to her house. "I'll put the porch light on," she says, "and I'll make a bed up for Sam in the den."

I call Dora.

She's at my door within ten minutes. Upon entering she drops her coat on the foyer floor. "My head feels like it's been smacked with a two-by-four," she says. It's clear she's sauced. When she sees the blood on me and follows me upstairs to the bathroom, she sobers up quickly.

I try Crampton again and thank God he answers. He's been out playing poker after some Shriners dinner. Immediately quick-witted and steady, Crampton knows from my voice I'm upset. "I'll send an ambulance at once," he says. "Make sure the other patients stay out of sight." While Dora sets about making all the beds, I hustle the women out through the kitchen to the back yard, where they hide in the old garage.

In minutes the ambulance is here. It arrives silently, no siren. By now the sick woman is splayed on the floor in a pool of blood and has stopped moving. She's weakly draped the crook of her arm over the rim of the bathtub. Her pale face holds a violet tint and rests sideways on her shoulder.

The ambulance attendants know when they see the amount of blood that it is too late. The police arrive next—also without siren. They search her room and pocketbook and question me. I tell them the woman phoned from downtown in response to a sign my girlfriend and I had posted saying we had an extra room to let. With the war on, it's not uncommon for people to take in lodgers. Police know boarders are often down on their luck; they're no doubt familiar with these bad endings. Acting as though she also lives here, Dora shows the amount of upset that seems appropriate—a hardened landlady's sadness, the kind where ruined bath towels bear consideration equal to a corpse. The police seem satisfied that we don't know her. They jot some notes for their report, and oddly, the woman's personal belongings are left behind.

Dewey drops Sam off with Hazel and waits up the street in the shadows until the police have gone and he can return. Silently he takes a shot of whiskey, then mops up the blood while I bring the other women back in from outside. They notice the blood on my robe and two of them begin weeping. Dora tends to all of them while I go and change.

I wonder what the night must have been like for them huddled behind the old DeSoto and stacks of medical supplies in a strange, unlit garage—their own bodies weak from the babies leaving them. Were they frightened by the police like I was? Did they strain for snatches of conversation, hear the creak of the oak stairs as the ambulance men carried the corpse down and out into the cold night air?

Could they see through the garage window how the sheet-draped stretcher glowed white in the moonlight? Could they hear the ambulance motor humming at the curb—the ghost of death behind the wheel? Could they hear the men cough and whisper as they closed the doors?

Once the women are resettled, Dora falls asleep on the couch and Dewey brings me a cup of tea. I almost weep at the kindness of that. It is well past five in the morning before we try to sleep. Down inside me, a worry gnaws, and I shiver with horror at having failed as a nurse. Could I have prevented that woman's horrible end?

And what about Sam? His sleep was disturbed. How will he fare at school tomorrow? Will he be as alert and attentive as he should be? Maybe that's why he's becoming so angry.

The morning is hideous. I prepare the patients' breakfast trays. Dora stands in the doorway and watches. My hands shake. She reads my mind. "Her death is not your fault, Verna," she says. "You are a superior nurse."

It's hard to explain just how much I need to hear that, but it isn't Dora's assurance I need, it is Dr. Crampton's. Dora scans the evening editions of the *Patriot* and *Telegraph*. No one writes of the death. I learn from Frances that Crampton had phoned his friend Paul Kunkel, head of surgery at the Harrisburg Hospital, who practically runs the place. The Kunkels are an old family and do mountains of public work. They are unequivocally respectable. No one questions or messes with them. Apparently Kunkel gave the ambulance a directive to keep the siren off. Someone also phoned the chief of police with similar instructions. I can see how everyone is in on it—maybe the newspaper too. Crampton has protection. The morgue took the poor woman's cold body, no questions asked.

Later Dewey stays with the patients and Dora comes with me to use the pay phone at the Harrisburger Hotel, where we call the emergency contact the woman gave. I don't give my name and stick to the story that the woman was a lodger who died on the premises.

The man at the other end owns a bar and restaurant near Lewistown; he is plenty shook up. "She was my bookkeeper." His voice chokes. "She had a long history of pernicious anemia. I should've stayed with her."

I tell him the woman's handbag, clothes, suede gloves, and shoes have been left and ask if we should mail them. He says no, not to mail them. By now he's gulping and sniffling openly into the phone. But he asks about the pin with the woman's initials. "Can you mail that back?"

"Of course."

We say good-bye.

I'm too tough to cry.

Back at home, I check on the other women. Dewey takes the handbag, shoes, and gloves and the lovely jungle green print dress out and burns them. None of us can imagine keeping her things, and it seems wrong to give them away.

When I return to Crampton's office with the other girls, he takes one look at me and leads me into his office. When the door is closed, he sits me down and puts his hand on my shoulder. "I know you couldn't save her," he says, "and that you did everything in your power to try." Because of the gentle way he speaks, I begin to cry. It comes out as sobs and I'm so embarrassed to be seen like this. He pulls me closer to him and I smell his spicy cologne. I am shocked. We both have a demeanor that won't permit such expressions. What would people say if they saw him lend me comfort this way? Though the fabric of his jacket is cool and soft, I pull back. But I am moved to know that he has sensed just how deeply I need his acquittal. Still, though I love him for coming to my aid, and no matter what he says, we both know I'm responsible. The poor woman died on my watch.

20

When Sam's sophomore year starts, I ask about his classes and he says, "You're not interested. You're never interested. So why pretend?" and he stomps off.

I learn from Dr. Crampton that Sam is trying out for the football team. "You know, Mrs. K., his husky size is very desirable, and he could eventually make varsity." Crampton, as the team's doctor, never makes mention that I work for him, but he takes an interest in Sam and is guiding him along. I'm grateful for that. Sam says all the boys on the football team think Crampton is the greatest. When one of them is having a problem he goes by Crampton's office. Crampton listens, no doubt in the same gifted way he listens to me, and afterwards offers his advice or help. He's sincere when he says, "The best cure you can give someone with a problem is to listen."

Through Crampton we get some tickets to the Negro USO, housed in the Forster Street YMCA, which at night has become a home away from home for black servicemen. Dr. Crampton knows when they have a good headliner, and so far we've seen Cab Calloway, Lena Horne, and Jimmie Lunceford. The soldiers there are swell jitterbuggers.

As a USO it's almost too successful. It threatens the Y's primary purpose of keeping young boys off the streets. To relieve the Y of the USO, Crampton with his friend C. Sylvester Jackson comes up with a plan to gain permission from the school board to let colored servicemen use the Penn Building at Seventh and Cumberland Streets to make a bigger USO.

When we go to the colored USO, I give Dewey strict rules about drinking. No way do I want to be sitting there like a couple of trashy drunks. The last time, C. Sylvester Jackson came over and said he'd like to meet my husband. C. Sylvester Jackson is interesting and always impeccably groomed. He and Dr. Crampton have known each other since they were boys but Jackson is more conservative. The only mad touch on his gray or black suits is a fresh red carnation in his lapel which I don't recall ever seeing him without. He manages some kind of estate for a wealthy family by the last name of Boyd, and he does Dr. Crampton's taxes and other accounting. "I've heard nice things about you helping folks so they don't lose their insurance," he says, shaking Dewey's hand. Dewey appreciates this gesture.

A few nights later we go out with Dewey's friends Scotty and Evelyn Albright. That night there is an upset that starts at the restaurant while we're waiting at the bar for a table, when everyone, including myself, foolishly begins to drink gin. Conversation turns to politics and a stranger seated at the bar asks who they are favoring in the election. Dewey shoots his mouth off. "Anyone but that SOB Carl Shelley," he says. The stranger laughs and buys us all a round of drinks. Dewey likes anyone who buys drinks. "Say, what's your name?" The stranger grins. "Pleased to meet you. I'm that SOB Carl Shelley." I could have crawled into a hole.

I don't remember what we eat, and after midnight, and several other bars, the men grow keen to visit a gambling den in the 1200 block of Market Street. Scotty knocks on the door's peephole and says we are friends. Inside a smelly room, a couple of dozen guys throw dice, dropping big money on a sheet of Masonite they use as a table. Evelyn and I are the only women, and they let us roll a few times, but we lose. The green-visored payout men add our money to their wads of cash, already thick enough to clog a drainpipe. It's all so seedy, and it shows how parts of town have really gone to the dogs. One never saw this kind of thing before the war.

The betting parlor sells grain alcohol, which Evelyn and I mix with ginger ale. We laugh as Dewey and Scotty lose all their cash, but for me the laughter is uneasy. Coming home, I grow sick. They stop the car. I stand streetside, feeling hellish, and with everything spinning begin to cry about the lost money and that I'm wearing an expensive dress from Mary Sachs but standing in the gutter. Evelyn parks herself on the curb and says, "Once in a while you have to let loose or life isn't worth living."

"That's horseshit," I say. And then I cry some more because I know I am ruining the evening with my seriousness. Again I recognize that feeling that something is going terribly wrong. Life has become too hectic and too fast. I can barely keep track of it all. Nothing seems to turn out the way I hope or plan.

Somehow we make it home and I tell Dewey the next day that I won't be going on any more drinking jaunts or visits to gambling dens. He shrugs.

·   **21**   ·

Sam tells me it's widely known on the team that Crampton will help them with their girlfriends if they need it. I keep silent. Is he baiting me? Up to now we've never spoken about the women staying in our house. He knows they're patients and that I'm the nurse. My manner in these dealings is discreet. He knows it's not his place to question.

Crampton's been in the papers a couple of times this week, cited as host for a sports banquet for basketball players; the war has drained a lot of money from the sports teams, and Crampton keeps them afloat. The second mention occurs because the Republicans have appointed Crampton as Negro division chairman of the Dewey-Bricker campaign with his friend C. Sylvester Jackson as secretary.

I've started wearing my hair a new way, rolled with rats in the front and in the back like Betty Hutton and the Andrews Sisters. It makes me look taller and lengthens my face. I buy a crepe blouse with sequins that I wear to the Forum to hear Sam's band play a special program to honor America. Sam is progressing from cornet to tuba and plays in the school marching band. He's on the football team as well, and at halftime he speedily changes uniforms, dons the tuba, and runs out on the field again to join the musicians. I hope these activities will help him develop some discipline; God knows we can't do much there. If one of us asks Sam a question he always answers with a sarcastic reply—to the point that we've stopped asking. But proud, we go to see him wearing the tuba in the Veterans Day parade. He marches across the State Street Bridge with all boys and old men; the rest are off fighting. Because of Sam's size, the tuba looks good on him.

Meanwhile Dewey is growing annoyed that I no longer want to go out drinking. With the exception of the USO, he's off on his own most nights and drinks more heavily. Sometimes upon waking in the morning, to ward off a hangover, he now takes a shot of whiskey. "Hair of the dog that bit me," he says. He gets annoyed that I'm always tied up with patients and I think he's jealous that I make so much money. Though he won't admit it, I also know how difficult it is for him having a sulking teenage boy around. Though he never mentions his own children, and we never visit them, I'm sure their circumstances must weigh heavily on him. But everything is an excuse to drink if you want it to be.

22

In the spring Crampton keeps his word and helps Sam get an after-school job as a locker attendant for City Island beach. The job begins on Memorial Day weekend. A lot of boys would like to get paid to spend the summer near the sandy beach and swimming in the river. The irony is that though Crampton's influence gets Sam the job, the beach is closed to colored people.

Sam is almost fifteen now and complains that our curtains are always closed and the house is always dark. He also complains that he can't bring friends home. I know these complaints are just an excuse for him to stomp off in a huff and then to go hang out at the pool hall under the Senate Theater.

Meanwhile I keep cautioning Dewey to set an example and slow his drinking. He nods and cuts back for a couple of days. But my reminders are growing more frequent and less effective.

He knows, after my decision that night gambling with Scotty and Evelyn, that I'm no longer willing to wake up with clothes that smell of smoke and floor mop disinfectant, the sour taste of alcohol in my mouth, and my pocketbook empty. I keep my word and refuse to go along. With the increase in our business, I'm too busy for late nights anyway.

Now when Dewey goes out on an errand downtown, I say, "Don't stop for anything."

"No," he promises. "I'm coming right home."

Sure he is.

I don't enjoy him touching me like I used to. When he wants love, I go through the motions and soon even that stops.

It is a chilly late morning in autumn when Dewey's daughter Sally comes by the house. "Your father isn't here," I tell her. "He's at work."

"It's you I've come to see," she says, and as I take in how grown up she's become, with lipstick and eyeliner, I already know what this is going to be about. She tells me the story of a marine who has run off to Parris Island with someone else and left her in trouble.

"Please. I need your help."

"What makes you think I can help?" I say.

"Pop told Freda what you do," she says.

I'm so mad at Dewey's big mouth I could punch him. But it's best not to say anything. Let Sally keep talking. See what she knows. "It's important that Pop not know," she says. "And it's even more important that neither Freda, Hennie, nor any of my sisters ever find out. If they do I'll never hear the end of it."

She's only twenty but has an edge of a much older woman, yet under the makeup and the tough talk, I see how sweet she is. I soften and make her some lunch and try to counsel her. Tell her what she's in for. "Are you sure you want to go through with this?" I say. She nods and lights a cigarette. We set a date for two weeks later. It's a weekend when Dewey will be on a fishing trip with some guys from the Legion. I am supposed to go along; when I beg off, it makes him angrier than when I decline to go to bars.

As he did with Hazel, Crampton performs the procedure on Friday at no charge, and Sally returns with me to stay at the house. I study her ways and manners and see she's coarse, unpolished, and far from innocent, but there is something about her I like. She seems to have a good heart. Her personal habits are deplorable, and I'm shocked when I enter her bedroom to see she's draped a sanitary napkin used side up across the waste bin because she's too lazy to go down the hall to the toilet. But I refuse to react, feeling she might be testing me, partly because of the deprivation she's known growing up.

Instead I speak with frank directness. "Sally, can you wrap that in paper so it can be disposed of properly," and once she has obeyed, and the room is tidy again, I sit on the edge of her bed. The experience with the doctor has left her emotional and weepy. She says she hasn't felt this bad since she lost her mother. And then the anger comes, waves of it; she calls her fellow a cunt chaser and every other filthy name in the book. I let her rant, and pity her.

By now, after hundreds of abortions, I've grown skilled at managing the anger of women, girls furious at their husbands or boyfriends for their predicament, not to mention those, like Sally, who've been jilted. "I thought he cared about me," they cry.

Some girls also resent the money they have to pay, some grow irritable from the physical pain, and some grieve for the baby they have decided to lose. I comfort Sally as best I can, and I sense that she likes my compassion. She is injured and needs nursing. When she says that she has a lot of pain, I give her an injection of a mild narcotic. What she really needs is to talk, so I just try to make her feel safe, and once the anger has lessened, I listen. When the drug takes effect, she, like many others, waxes philosophical.

"In every town there are men who hunt women," she says. "Some say they're lonely, some say they can't live without you, some pretend to be hurt until you fall for them. It's all bull. Just their damn instinct to reproduce."

I nod.

"The whole town knows who they are; they call them hosers, the cat's meow, or tomcats. Some say he's only sowing wild oats or putting another notch on his belt. They chuckle over his urges. Part of their enjoyment comes from believing civilization depends upon his pull to survive.

"These cocky men aren't rare or hidden," she says. "They're ordinary, law-abiding. They sit alone or in packs at the lunch counters, the filling stations, the bowling alleys. In daylight they watch where women go—the bank, the beauty parlor, the grocer, even church. Bob? Wilson? Leroy? Ed? They're not vampires but fine fellows. But just follow their eyes and notice how they size up her breasts, hips, legs, and face. And if you give them two fingers of whiskey they'll tell you quite openly which women they'd like to 'do.' "

I interrupt her. "Of course there are some men who act with restraint," I say, thinking of Murphy and Hazel's husband, Joe. "They speak with courtesy and respect, offer a word of caution to the men who go too far, deliver women from trouble. Maybe you can try to meet someone more like that."

"Yeah, but most lack the courage to run against the pack," Sally says. "Except if one of them makes an error like trying to screw another wolf's mother or sister."

I tell her that Dewey says one of the problems is that when a man publicly defends a woman against another man, one of the trio usually dies.

"What does he know about it?" she snaps.

"But women need to be responsible too," I say, not sure to what degree I can believe this but hoping she might stop feeling sorry for herself. "Time and again I've heard, 'One morning I woke up and *found* I was pregnant,' or 'The next thing I knew, a baby was on the way.' "

"I know what you're saying," Sally agrees. "Women play a part. I've seen it. They loosen their hair, push their titties up as they dance too close, whisper in his ear, and feel their own bodies hot with a want they later forget to mention. And many of these broads have allowed themselves to be bought. The lucky ones get marriage and houses to keep, the smart ones get diamond wristwatches and mink coats, others get restaurant meals, and girls at the bottom of the barrel, like me"—she begins to blubber like a baby—"all I got was a lousy glass of beer." I hold her and stroke her hair. When she's calm again, she looks at me through swollen eyes and says, "When we met you at the orphanage that first time, we figured you for a chump. We thought you were too green to see that our dad was a dog. He's not the worst of them, mind you, but he's still a dog. We knew you weren't a gold digger or you wouldn't have taken up with him in the first place. So we figured you for a chump. But now I see you're really very kind." I smile and tuck the quilt tighter around her. She closes her eyes and the drug pulls her into sleep.

I think about what Sally said about women being bought. For a long time I thought women took gifts because they had to give up their bodies, and I secretly believed that women's bodies were worth more than men's. Now I think it's because men control most resources, and many like to depend on illegitimate forms of power. From all the stories I've heard, I've come to believe that brute force may be essential for many men to get excited. Power over women fires them up, and for whatever reason, I think some men need this feeling of dominance to keep erections. Of course I keep these thoughts to myself.

Sally sleeps throughout the night but cries out periodically, so I stay awake and ponder on. Can the ability to dominate or control perhaps inspire copulation on both sides? Many women are in collusion here. I hear so much about what is wrong with men, but most women grow excited and demand or require their men to be heroes, breadwinners, or warriors. They want them confident, neolithic, and fiercely competitive. They expect a man to pay. They want him to lead. Make more money. Get promoted. Dress well. Some even ask if he's man enough to take them, for they know they like to submit. Also, the women who are beautiful have more currency than those like me who are plain.

But what about what I went through with Wertz? Or Sam's father? Also, what about what I've learned peering into the enamel basins filled with blood and tissue? I've witnessed some of the false cleverness that leads women to believe that nothing like this could ever happen to them. When I look into the basin and see what remains of life, I know that it is women who decide. But why do they have to make such choices? And how many women come to us to rid themselves of his children—but still expect their cash benefits?

A question emerges. Has my independence and earning power made me an oddity? Does it give me a unique vantage point to see these contradictions? I begin to think so. I've learned my resources mean I'm no longer dependent on men. Another question: might my independence be injuring Dewey? I can't think about that now.

23

It is August and I am driving on the West Shore heading back to Harrisburg. Suddenly cars begin to slow and start blowing their horns, then air raid sirens begin to wail. My first thought is that we are under some kind of attack, until the driver of a truck coming in the opposite direction slows down. "Heigh ho, sister!" he yells. "The war is over!"

Now traffic comes to a standstill. The entrance to the bridge backs up. All I can think of is that Sam may be leaving his job at City Island, and that he may climb up onto the Walnut Street Bridge and head into town. In frustration, I finally am forced to pull away from the bridge without being able to cross it or to spot him. How sad it is that Sam and I are so near each other at such a happy time but that we cannot find one another in the crowd.

Forget the bridges, I drive all the way up the West Shore to Clark's Ferry and catch the next boat across, thinking sadly that so many mothers have lost their sons in this war and I don't even really know mine.

Later I learn that Sam stayed downtown and that Market Square was packed shoulder to shoulder. The crowds were so thick in the streets that the buses couldn't get through and stopped running. Most of the stores and businesses closed, but every bar was full. At dawn Dewey returns home by hitching a ride on a sanitation truck. It was a big day for the Navy, so he's drunk. Sam comes in a while later. I sleep like I'm in a coma, so lonely it hurts. I wish I could have joined them to celebrate. But we are all so separate.

This week another serious hemorrhage occurs, a woman in her thirties from Wilmington, Delaware. Turns out she packed a pint of corn whiskey in among a half pound of rhinestone jewelry, and has polished off the entire bottle. She decides in the middle of the night that it's time to leave, and she wedges herself into her girdle and has her stockings half-clipped before she passes out. By the time I find her, the pressure from the girdle has made her lose a lot of blood. She too is admitted to the Harrisburg Hospital, no questions asked.

I keep playing a scenario in my mind: what if she, while intoxicated, had wandered outside half-dressed and been picked up by the police or seen by the neighbors? Luckily I awoke with a strange premonition, or she'd have also been a corpse. The experience leaves me plenty worried. I'm reminded of the other woman, the bookkeeper, the one who died.

24

If the war years have been good to the Taylorites, the postwar years are even better. Talk everywhere is about prosperity, contracts, mergers, capital buildings, bridges, shopping centers, and deals, deals, deals. The newspaper has doubled in size, thick with advertising for new cars, washing machines, and refrigerators. Passing time has burnished Harvey Taylor into a homespun, plain-talking granddaddy. The last election was a landslide with less than the usual number of cracked skulls, punched kidneys, and broken noses. In fact, Taylor's boys probably would've won without buying votes. Taylor's opponents watch it all, no doubt feeling baffled and helpless.

Crampton and another black doctor named Leonard Oxley, as co-chairs of a newly formed Forum Education Committee, bring in an inspirational speaker to the Wesley Union AME Church on Forster Street. The newspaper quotes Crampton's introduction: "During these uncertain postwar days, the youth of our community are now as never before in need of guidance and encouragement that tends toward the building of strong character." I show Dewey the quote and say that this applies not only to youth but to grown-up men as well. He sneers with disgust.

Now he's always late for supper or misses it altogether and I sit waiting. My patience turns to venom. I spit poison words like "Damn you!" and "Can't you ever draw a sober breath?"

He follows with "Jesus Christ! Can't you stop harping?"

One day, without telling him, I go to the car dealer and order a brand-new 1946 Oldsmobile. Because the factories in Detroit are retooling from the war and are so backed up with orders, it takes almost two months for the cream-colored car to be delivered. When Dewey comes home and sees it, he flies into a rage that gives me much pleasure. "How could you order something that big without telling me?" he says.

"I just felt like it," I say, coldly, and can hardly hide the condescension and spite in my voice. "And besides," I say, "*she* who pays the piper calls the tune."

That night he goes on a bender and again I regret all the times I went along with him when I shouldn't have, because now I realize that in his mind, by joining him, I have forfeited my right to be treated with respect. When I try to appeal to him to quit, he says, "You're not so clean. Don't get so high and mighty because you're no better than me."

It annoys me to realize that I want him to treat me well, like he used to, but in his eyes I'm like a piece of old linen, still useful and well spun but frayed and yellow, and he's craving the unworn white blindness of the new.

What is love?

A rescue?

Now whenever he wants to kiss me I feel humiliated and vindictive. When I bristle he says, "There's only a party when *you* want one."

Then he asks if he can borrow the Oldsmobile. "I'm not about to let a drinking man get behind the wheel of a brand-new car," I say with great gusto, having waited for this moment since the car was delivered.

He storms out in a rage.

Some of this I share with Dr. Crampton. He listens whenever I complain how I should have paid more attention to the signs—card playing, liquor, borrowing money. I leave out that it was such a relief not to be alone, and to be with a man who wasn't only interested in pawing after me. Aside from Murphy—and I never slept with him—Dewey was the first man who offered a partnership on what I thought were terms I could accept. I should have seen how his love was based on a happy-go-lucky irresponsibility.

What do you do when Cupid leaves the scene and you are left to manage a poison arrow straight to the heart? One afternoon while crossing by the Capitol I hear someone tooting his horn. It's Charles Dennis. It shocks me to recognize how powerful my attraction to him still is. He invites me to lunch, and we agree to meet again the following week. Only this time we check into a small hotel. Our lovemaking is as tender and passionate as when we started. We are both adulterers now, not just him, and it feels fair and just, particularly after all the disappointments with Dewey. A few weeks later it shocks me to learn I am expecting.

I drive over to Dora's. She is baking corn bread and the warm scent fills the kitchen. Her face is like a stone when I tell her. Not the reaction I expect. Even though I do not say that it's Sam's father who has made me pregnant—once again. It's not hard to figure out something is bothering her. Does she suspect I'm leaving a big part of the story out?

All afternoon her manner is closed and difficult. To fathom what could be troubling her seems impossible. She stands at the sink rinsing a head of Boston lettuce, and I watch in a trance while she separates each green leaf with her thumb and forefinger, releasing the black dirt at the core. I can't restrain myself any longer. "Tell me what's wrong!" I say.

"I don't know," she says. "I just don't know."

"Oh, come on. Just tell me."

We go back and forth; my lips press together waiting for her to speak.

"Well," she says, "Chet's overheard a bit of buzz among the colored men about Dewey. It's just trashy talk." Chet is a new guy Dora has been seeing. He has his own lawn care business. From the sound of Dora's voice I know I'm in trouble. Her hands are skittery with cigarettes and whatever is on her mind.

"What did he hear?"

"Can't say," she says. "I don't know the facts but Chet is due here for supper shortly."

"If you don't tell me I'll leave right now."

Dora waves her cigarette in the air. "I can't say another word. He'll tell you. Let him finish his supper first."

Needing to keep busy, I take over the cooking from her. "I don't feel like eating a bunch of cigarette ashes in my mashed potatoes," I say, rude as I can be. Just then Chet comes in.

"Hey, my goose girl," he says to Dora and pecks her cheek. I can see Dora enjoys looking at him and that with him she hides her crafty resourcefulness in a way I never can.

He greets me with a shake. His hands are battered from work and he needs a shave. His wavy hair is lightened by the sun. He washes up at the kitchen sink and we sit down to supper. Does he sense an ambush?

At supper his robust body fills the chair—a contrast to Dewey's slight frame. But unlike Dewey's, Chet's talk is dull—despite his having sailed the seven seas. He goes on and on about how a sea is really an ocean or vice versa, every sentence an eternity, "Arctic, Indian, North and South Pacific, North and South Atlantic, Antarctic."

He works on his supper with an appetite you'd expect from someone who's been tending lawns all day. We watch him eat every string bean, every bite of sausage.

"There's tension in this room like a telephone wire," he says at last.

Dora rises from the table and stands in the doorway. The way her fingers twitch with the cigarette at her hips, he knows she is juiced about something.

"I want you to tell Verna what you told me the other day," she says.

Chet stands up, a look of shock upon his face. "You shouldn'ta said nothing," he says. Now he sees her craftiness and opens his mouth but no words come out. It makes him mad to be cornered, and he goes outside onto the porch.

She follows him. "Tell her what you told me," Dora says, like an order.

"Damn it," he hollers. "Can't ever keep your big mouth shut." They fight. I too feel trapped and embarrassed to be listening to their rumble.

Dora finishes the argument by yelling, "She's expecting!" The dread in my stomach wraps itself around and around.

Chet gets into his truck and begins to leave but somehow Dora persuades him not to, and after endless whispering and pleading they come back in. They stand by the kitchen counter, he in front, she toward the back where the flour canisters sit.

So this big beefy guy, so at home with himself, who will probably be out of her life forever in another month, has the burden of telling. His voice is low and solemn. It costs him a lot to rat. I can't recall his words. Only their cut.

He explains how he works with a lot of colored men in lawn care. They talk. They say that there are a few women in the neighborhood who when they are short on cash slip the insurance man a little something extra so they can keep up their premium. He doesn't mention Dewey by name.

Chet apologizes for telling. I just sit and stare, unsure how to react. It is so naïve of me never to have suspected as much. I rise to take my leave and Dora offers to drive along with me, but I make it clear I'll manage. I feel like a zombie. I drive to Crampton's office. "I need to speak with you," I say.

We go into his office for privacy. His lovely brown face listens with concern. I am too bashful to ask for his help, but I finally say, "The way things stand with Dewey and his drinking, I can't go through with this pregnancy."

Crampton nods with understanding. "Let's arrange it right away," he says, "and we'll also do the test for syphilis."

I startle and sit up. I hear Chet's low voice—"Sometimes they slip the insurance man a little something extra."

Crampton sees I'm shocked. Reluctantly he tells me Dewey visited him about three or four months ago to be treated for syphilis.

The humiliation. Now I understand things I should never know and burn with rage. No wonder Dora insisted Chet tell me.

"How could you?" I ask Crampton.

"As a doctor, it's my job to keep people's secrets," he says, "even his. He explicitly stated there'd been no relations between you and him for quite some time."

Another wave of humiliation leaves me numb. I'm positively dying with shame. Is it better to let him think that I'm in relations with someone who cheats on me or let him know I was a cheater too? *He who tells even the smallest part of a secret loses his hold on the rest.* I can't think, can't speak, and stagger out.

It's lucky that Dewey is spending the night in Allentown at an insurance forum or I might kill him. It's such a relief to be home alone because I don't yet know how to handle myself. I weep over how wonderful the promise of our union was. How did it all go so wrong?

By the time he returns the next evening, I've gotten ahold of a plan. I've decided it's better to be suspected of the clap from one's husband than be known as an adulteress. In an act of revenge, I make him open his insurance books and show them to me. He's about four hundred dollars in arrears, with installment payouts due at the company in a few days.

"This time you can forget asking me for help," I say. "The bank is closed." He hangs his head like a wounded hound dog. Upstairs I count the cash in the cedar chest, lock it, and slip the key and the one for my safe deposit box in my bra.

At Crampton's the venereal smear test comes back from the lab. "You're lucky," he says. "Negative." We sit in silence. What does one say on such an occasion? It's all too sordid.

"I'm sorry, Verna," Dr. Crampton says at last. "I never meant to hurt you. It was a dilemma to know how to handle this. It called upon my deepest sense of ethics."

"It doesn't matter," I say. "Our marriage had already turned a corner and was headed down a one-way street."

"I'm sorry about that too," he says. "I wish there was a way to keep you from going through that."

On the day of my procedure, Dora comes along to the office to act as my nurse. I close my mind. Take sedation. I don't want to re-member my legs in the air, the hands of my employer, the pain of disappointment.

· 25 ·

No doubt everyone in town learns Dewey was fired. With the money I had been advancing him, his rate of lapsed policies was probably lower than any other agent's in a colored neighborhood. People there are always short, and thanks to me Dewey had man-aged to float them.

When I cut off his credit, I was full of vengeance. As the weeks pass, I begin to wonder if I should never have gone into nursing with Crampton, should have stayed poor, pretended to be frail and feminine so Dewey could feel strong. Why do men when faced with strong women allow themselves to become children? Is that what women fear when they allow men to lead? Is it better to let him think you are reliant upon him? That's what Buckley's young bride Liz did, and she ended up with a refrigerator full of piss.

With my pocketbook closed, the insurance payments grew overdue, and when he notifies the company that he is going to be a little late, they waste no time. Insurance companies know everything, and this one probably overlooked his antics, and the fact that his cash flow came from abortions, so long as the money came in. But once the payments slow, they smell trouble, and a white insurance man run amok in a colored neighborhood is trouble; they want no part of him.

After a week he sets about looking for another job, but the mass of soldiers returning makes work impossible to find. On the one hand, I feel sorry for him and again often wonder, if I hadn't advanced him so much cash, would he have remained more responsible to his business? But on the other hand, he's brought this upon himself.

Again, in frustration, I turn to Dr. Crampton for help. I've already forgiven him for secretly treating Dewey. I sit facing his desk and he puts everything aside while I explain my confusion and worry. It is a relief to have someone's full attention, and Crampton makes me feel like I'm the most important person in the world.

"Mrs. K., you need to look at Dewey as a businesswoman might," he says. "Then he emerges as both an asset—emptying the trash, burning the Kotex, and most important giving you cover as a married housewife—and a liability—out of your sight he drinks to extreme, whores around, and shoots his mouth off in any barroom. If you throw him out, you raise suspicion, and few people here have anything good to say about a divorcée. He's also eligible for half of your assets. And if things get ugly, he could cause you a lot of damage. The best you can do is clip his wings and hope he finds another job."

The honesty is a cold slap. But I'm grateful. Still, my anger burns. At home it shows up in the way I fold a brown grocery bag, the way I set a coffee cup in the sink, and the way my heels thump the floor when I walk. Dewey lies on the couch for hours listening to radio jingles and waiting for the storm to pass. He has never been mean or sulky, and if he is angry at me for refusing him the cash, he never shows it.

One morning, with no patients in the house and Sam out at football practice, I'm surprised when Dewey asks me to sit at the kitchen table and says he needs to discuss something with me. "Been thinking about my next move," he says, his tone bright and open, as if he's just emerged from the darkness to discover he prefers light.

"And?"

"Well, I've come upon a solution."

"Oh?"

"I'd like to try my hand at growing peaches."

"Peaches?"

Dewey was raised on a fruit farm, but I've never heard of someone escaping the tough work of farm life only to return to it—except maybe rich people, gentlemen farmers, that sort of thing. Dewey seems like such a city person. How proudly he wore the charcoal suit of the insurance man. Typical of Dewey when he brings up something out of the blue, he already has a farm in mind. He's heard of one an hour north of Harrisburg in the town of Halifax. I feel resistance; not about to spend a dime on him again. Dewey has brought his troubles upon himself and I'm blameless here.

But then I discuss it with Dr. Crampton. "Do you think on this matter your position against Dewey is too strong?" he asks. "Mrs. K., I learned a long time ago that it is possible to go through every day with bitterness over something. Bigotry. Poverty. Hatred. I've seen people consumed by how unfair life is, how much suffering is brought to bear. People often imply I should be angry over something. But why? When I have no proof of malice? I don't like to form opinions in my head of things which I cannot prove. And even if there is malice, forgiveness heals me."

I tell him that there is a bitterness in my heart that I just can't overcome. "So you feel your position is just?" He tilts his head to one side and listens with compassion. Again, I have that feeling of being important and understood.

"I can look any judge square in the eye if that question is put."

"Well, then stay with your convictions," Crampton says. "Stay right with them." But something in his tone, his relaxed demeanor, annoys me and won't let me rest.

"If you told me to view him with my new businesswoman's perspective and instructed me to behave differently, I would. But on my own I'll never consent to his wishes again."

"Well, hold fast to your ideals," Crampton repeats and smiles. Again, something in his response rankles me. My fury is stoked. The heat burns. I am right, I am correct, I haven't erred in the way Dewey has, and yet I am miserable. All evening I fume and at bedtime toss and turn, feeling ill at ease. If I am right, why do I feel so rotten? Then I realize that if I don't change my thinking, my anger will continue to poison me. My anger begins to detach as I begin to contemplate how to move through my marriage with tolerance and indifference—as a strategy.

The next morning I call upon Crampton and say I've decided to buy the farm for Dewey. Crampton has a habit, when pleased with a decision, of smiling in a way that makes the corners of his eyes crinkle. "That's quite a reversal," he says. "Yesterday you were seething. It sounded like you would punish Dewey for the rest of his life."

"That's exactly right. He needed to pay for what he did."

"And now?"

"Now I feel like it's not my place to keep judging him. I've let my dissatisfaction be known, and that is that. If I hold on to this anger it will eat me up."

"And letting go of that bile has brought you peace? Maybe even happiness?"

"Yes. I feel much lighter."

I've always been in awe of Dr. Crampton, but now he has again taught me something new: forgiveness isn't for an offender's benefit, but for my own. And you can't wait around for justice before you forgive. Otherwise it isn't forgiveness. Something else happens with this epiphany; my conscience awakes and I decide that it's no longer wise to see Charles Dennis.

Crampton and I talk some more about the farm. I am able to look at Dewey sensibly, to see his flaws and make plans accordingly. As Crampton confirms, if Dewey moves to the country, the work of a farm might keep him from the bars and out of my way. He'll benefit from the fresh air and the planting of trees, and if he gets loaded, he'll be shooting his mouth off to a bunch of soused farmers and not to the cagey drinkers in town. If he passes out it will be in a hayfield and not in Market Square. I'll stay in town, but Sam and I can come up on the weekends, where physical labor might also teach Sam something useful. Most importantly, it is time for Dewey to get on with things. Losing his insurance practice was humiliating and no one wants a spouse whose career is spoiled.

I ask Dewey to make arrangements, and late one morning we drive along the Susquehanna, past the stone railroad bridge, its shadows crisp as strokes from a calligrapher's pen. A freight train passes slowly overhead. We crane our necks—orange, brown, and green boxcars, but no caboose in sight. Soon the road inclines away from the river and up over Peter's Mountain, the steep roadway winding to gain altitude. At the top, the view over the valley is splendid, the air scented and fresh. We descend to the other side until a jumble of odd buildings marks the perimeter of the town of Halifax.

At the side of the road, a man Dewey knows is waiting, and we follow his car down a twisted lane to a small white farmhouse in the center of a valley with a red barn and a pond banked by willow trees. A small summerhouse, like the one Mrs. Wertz used to cook in, connects to a breezeway attached to the main house, where the kitchen runs the length and breadth of the ground floor. The old windows need replacing, the only heat comes from an iron wood-stove, and upstairs we find three bedrooms but no bath. We go outside and tour the land. Up on the ridge, dense woods cover a dozen acres and below that there are plenty of open fields to plant orchards and grow some other crops, 110 acres in all. The man requests $7,500.

"Is this what you really want?" I ask Dewey. He smiles.

I pay for the farm with cash, the same amount that I paid for the house on Third Street. We take immediate possession. Dewey sets to work repairing the house and the barn and we hire a plumber to build an indoor bathroom. I buy one hundred saplings—seventy peach, thirty apple—with a few cherries and plums thrown in. When the trees are delivered Dewey sets to work digging holes to plant them.

On Saturday mornings Sam and I drive up. I bake pies, cook pot roast, and fix stew that during the remainder of the week Dewey can heat up for supper. Sam helps plant the orchard, but from the get-go, he hates the place. I know he isn't a farmboy. He carried on when Mom and Myrtle needed his help to plant a victory garden during the war, but I imagine he'll get used to it and benefit from the experience.

Despite his disdain, he helps Dewey clear a lot of timber at the back of the property. I try to sell the wood locally, but no one wants to buy. Then I run into Tom Nelly. So many years have passed since I looked after his mother, but I will always remember him as the man who helped me get to nursing school. We chat for a minute about old times, and I ask if he knows of anyone who might be interested in the lumber. "Well, seeing that it's yours, and that your credit is so honorable, I'm sure the county can find some use for it," he says. He sends an inspector up the next morning and by afternoon they've cut me a check for five hundred dollars, double what the wood is worth and ten times the amount he loaned me for nursing school. That's politics.

In August it grows hot, and on the drive up to Halifax, Sam tells me he isn't going to help on the farm anymore, saying football practice is about to start and the coach has already told him he'll have no trouble making varsity. It's one of those moments I imagine many parents have, when they speak without enough consideration for their children's point of view. I underestimate now that a smart-alecky teenager is like a barn full of wet hay: combustion can come at any moment.

"Football is a waste of time," I say, thoughtlessly. "You ought to put that effort into your studies." I think it's important to demonstrate that I am in charge, not him. In an effort to form an alliance with Dewey, when we arrive at the farm I expose Sam's plans. Dewey has been drinking and joins me in my intolerance. "You're not playing football," he says. "You're staying here to work the orchard."

From the redness of Sam's face, I can see his anger. That evening, after a tense day when he and Dewey together work to mow a field of timothy and a field of alfalfa, the football argument erupts again. Dewey grows frustrated and curses. Sam gets sore. "You're not a real farmer," he says. "She only bought you this place to make it look like you have a job."

Dewey smacks Sam upside the head and a fight breaks out. Hazel has come up and she and I are canning in the summerhouse. We come running at their shouts. Sam is big and has gotten the better of Dewey, wrestling him to the ground. By coincidence a neighbor named Russ Hoover has just stopped by, and he jumps from his truck to break it up. Sam is still enraged and turns and runs off into a cornfield. As dusk comes, I get into my car and drive down the lane searching for him between the corn rows. He remains hidden and must have either lain down or exited from the road on the other side of the field. As night comes, I have no choice but to stop looking.

Later I learn that Sam has indeed made his way out of the corn to the main road and hitched a ride down to Harrisburg. In the morning I drive to the city to see if he might have returned to Third Street, but Mom swears she hasn't seen him. He's disappeared without a trace. Now my concern and anger mix to retribution. "If he thinks he's teaching me a lesson," I say, "just wait until he runs out of money."

Four days later. Still no word.

On the sixth day a short letter arrives. In it Sam says he's joined the Army.

At sixteen he is underage. How has he managed to join? Should I try to get him out? I ask everyone I know for advice. Dewey, with his pride injured, won't discuss it. I cut him slack, thinking it must not have been easy for him losing his wife, home, and six children. Maybe he's bitter at the idea of a conflict over football when much bigger issues have been foisted onto his own children. He says the Army is the best place for him. Mom says if I get him released, he'll be welcome to live with her again. Dora says, "Write him at once and patch things up."

I again seek counsel from Dr. Crampton. "Sam's fortitude in asserting himself is necessary," he says. "I hope you won't think me callous if I tell you I've gotten to know Sam a tiny bit when he played football and he will come through. Which is better for him, that he feel like he can chart his own course, or that he return home, where neither of his parents know how to help him?"

"I've done the best I can," I say. "My whole life has been a struggle."

"I don't say that to hurt you," Dr. Crampton says, and pats the back of my hand. "And Sam has an air about him that everybody likes. He will prevail, and who knows, maybe the Army is just what he needs."

I turn my face away to hide the tears streaming down my cheeks. Crampton's voice softens. "Mrs. K., if you get him out of this jam, you'll be getting him out of things the rest of his life. Write him and say, 'Should you decide to come home, you will always have a place here.' "

That night I write the letter, adding, "I hope you find what it is you want and that you won't regret your decision. As your mother, I'm at least grateful the war is over so you won't be shipped to battle." My insides spin like a wheel as I seal the envelope.

26

Somehow the seasons pass and the political climate changes with them. Crampton is still in good standing, but the Taylor boys can't really move with total abandon anymore. The next election is upon us and gets off to a bitter start. A group of men calling themselves the "fighting five" will try to oust Harvey Taylor. A young Negro doctor named Joseph Randall has been recruited and he joins them in trying to splinter away as much of Crampton's colored vote as possible. For the first time in all his years in politics, Crampton is vulnerable. He's also about to turn seventy.

Together with his friend C. Sylvester Jackson, he decides to organize a group of the leading colored businessmen into a social club, along the lines of the all-white Harrisburg Better Business Association and the Rotary Club. A special memorial membership is created for Justin Carter, whose absence as the only colored lawyer in town is still felt. The other core members are Charles Erwin, a florist with a shop in the Congressional Hotel; a dentist, Slim Emmanuel, the first colored man in town to own an electric drill; Shepard Simmons, who operates three dry cleaning stores, two that cater to whites and one to colored; and Oscar Williams, who owns a cut-rate store on Seventh Street that sells patent medicines, sickroom supplies, cigars, magazines, colored cosmetics—a place where people always linger to chat about colored news, the stuff not found in papers, newsreels, or on the radio. There are also the undertakers, the venerable Hooper and the recently opened Leftwich, both of whom Crampton helped with seed money, and Duke Jefferson, a hotel doorman at the Penn-Harris who himself also owns the Jefferson Hotel in the Seventh Ward, where Negro out-of-town guests stay. Jefferson also holds the title to two Negro tourist homes in Atlantic City, though reports are that the rooms are quite a ways back from the beach. Core members also include Nathan Jasper, who runs the Plantation House Restaurant, which features colored waitresses in hoop skirts and serves a white-only trade; Doctors Green, Moore, and Oxley, the other colored general practitioners in the city; and Dr. Richard Brown, a historian and high school teacher who was recently voted onto the school board, the second colored man to serve on the board since William Howard Day in 1878.

On the outskirts of the group are another dentist, Red Walls, known as Hard-hearted Red, who some say would cheat a mattress of its filling; Otis Pillsbury, who owns a Negro burlesque house where colored girls are said to dance in their nightgowns; Alger Wesley, who runs a colored-owned beauty supply and catering company and who often buys leftover flowers from banquets in the white hotels, reselling them to dress up Negro affairs; and lastly, at the outermost edge, are the Reverends Cook, Johnson, Pervis, and Polk, who can pay no dues but are useful in spreading information.

Under the stewardship of Dr. Crampton, the group sets up a civic agenda, as well as a social calendar of poker games and picnics, and plans an annual dance where wives can get dressed up and fox-trot. The group calls itself the "21 Club" after the twenty-one original founding members.

As the election heats up, Dr. Crampton asks me to step into his office one evening. "We've got to be more careful," he says. "It's important that you aren't seen overspending right now. No furs. No new cars. Our every move is being watched."

To be told your daily life is under scrutiny would alarm anyone. But given our line of work it is nerve-wracking.

"This whole thing has me furious," Crampton continues. "Harvey Taylor is in for a tussle, and that has put him in a panic. He's calling all the boys in and making new demands on them. He even asked us about any women we might be seeing, to make sure some lady isn't going to trip them up."

"How many names did you give?" I ask.

My delivery stops Dr. Crampton cold. Then he realizes I'm joking and breaks into an enormous grin. "I didn't tell him nothing,"

Dr. Crampton says. "But I'm sixty-nine years old and any Casanova dreams I might once have had are now on hold." He shakes his head and begins to grin again. "Mrs. K., I never knew you to be so funny." That I could make him laugh pleases me without measure.

But in another moment we are back to the matters at hand. "Do you think we should stop?" I ask. "Quit while we are ahead?"

"I've done nothing but ponder that same question," Crampton says. "But what do we gain? If Taylor loses, we'll have to stop anyway. But if he wins, I'll have a chance to make sure the machine does right by the Seventh Ward. I can make sure the housing projects get built for the people who will be displaced. There isn't another leader coming up who knows what I know to wrangle with them. I know where they're vulnerable and can hold them accountable; they can't win this election without our cash."

Frances tells me later that the machine has requested Dr. Crampton stop using white chauffeurs and that he also stop wearing spats. "They want to look respectful and conservative but also modern and up-to-date. They say spats are old-fashioned and that since the war, no one is wearing them."

But our business continues unchallenged. Dr. Crampton also begins to do the procedure in a new way. Instead of saline solution we now inject the women with a clear gel that is being shipped from Germany, in a tube with a plain white label. It acts about twelve hours quicker, and the fetus detaches cleaner and with less risk. It's an illegal import, which somehow gets delivered by a guy directly from the loading dock in Newark, New Jersey.

Meanwhile Dewey and I hardly see each other. For the most part he stays up on the farm and I stay here in town. Again, I worry that money has corrupted us, that it has fueled Dewey's decline. I average between five and seven hundred a week now, about thirty grand a year, three times more than the average doctor or lawyer makes. But it never seems like there is enough saved or that we can take time off. On more than one occasion Crampton and I revisit our talk of quitting but decide we have to keep going.

The hardest part, now that I can't spend as much, is figuring out ways to stash the cash. I'm terrible at keeping track of it all; I don't balance my checkbook, and thousands of dollars fill the bottom of the cedar chest. I also keep some hidden in the attic, and in the summerhouse on the farm. Because it's illicit, we can't put it in the bank—no stocks, bonds, or certificates. With the farm, the house on Third Street, the house for Mom, I'm at the limit of how much property I can show. A few times now I've given small amounts of money to Dewey's children—first Sally, then the others. But they began to fight over it, each believing the others had received more.

I think about how I used to lie awake and imagine dressers stuffed with cash, but I could not have guessed the high cost of having my dreams fulfilled.

This feeling of mocking frustration, of failure even, is compounded when I get a postcard from Sam saying he is being sent to Korea. I go to the bookstore and look in an atlas to see where that is exactly; I find a country on a peninsula connected to China. On one side lies the Yellow Sea, on the other the Sea of Japan. I think about that little baby I left behind so long ago and imagine him coming ashore and having to find his way in a strange country. As I leave the bookstore my role in Sam's absence overwhelms me, and the only way I know to distract myself is to spend money.

New dress styles are everywhere, with full skirts and long hems. Mary Sachs has printed a card with the names and pronunciations of all the new fabrics that have become available—organza, satin, baldachin, chiffon, façonné, taffeta, jacquard. There haven't been such luxurious goods for years. Against Crampton's advice I continue to buy, beginning with a royal blue ribbon suit that's worn over a royal blue satin slip, a jade-colored silk dress with black embroidery on the cuffs and belt and my monogram over a pocket on the hip, and a navy crepe dress with a lilac sash and matching bow at the scooped bodice, several full skirts, an array of blouses—one of them a cream-colored blouse with a tie at the collar—hats, and gloves. I've also bought dozens of pairs of shoes.

Why is it if you've ever struggled with your weight, people always remember you at your heaviest? Recently Aunt Varnie saw me and said, "Are you keeping the weight off?" I looked down at my hard-won figure and said, "I'm a size twelve. I think so."

One afternoon, while I go to Lemoyne to open yet another bank account in my mother's name, I run into Norm Trexler. It's been years since I last saw him, and how lucky that I've just come from having my hair done. "You look prosperous," he says—and we chat banalities for a moment. I tell him that I've had a postcard from Sam and that they are sending him to Korea, and that as a mother I'm concerned. "Well, lucky him," Norm says. "There's no fighting there, and he'll get a chance to see the world." Then he throws in the kicker. "I heard a while back the insurance outfit fired your husband."

"Oh? No!" I say. "He quit. We bought a farm and are growing peaches now. In fact our first crop is due this summer."

Norm ignores my effort to change the subject and tells me about his friend Oyster Jones, who'd headed the maintenance department at the Haywood House Hotel. "He'd spent so many years working his way up to that position, and one night he was arrested for shooting craps. The hotel fired him the very next day, no questions asked."

"Gambling is a serious vice," I say, as though I've never done it.

"Well, maybe if we get reform in government, that can be addressed. The fighting five look to take this election, and I'll say this right to your face. I know you are hooked up with Harvey Taylor, but the sooner we get rid of him the better."

I look at my watch and tell Norm I'm late for an appointment. I begin to cross the street but he calls after me, "Hey, Verna. Thanks for the memories." He kind of sings it after me like he's Bob Hope, and it's embarrassing to see people turning to look. Then I realize he's changed the lyrics and said "Thanks for your mammaries." Disgust overtakes me. He's being hoggish and vulgar to humiliate me. What a payback. Thank goodness I don't carry a gun or I'd have turned and shot him dead in the middle of Market Street.

27

The pressure to earn cash for the election continues to consume us. It's one thing to work hard because you want to, but when you *have* to, that takes its toll.

The fighting five are gaining ground and they have put the Republicans on the defensive for the first time in decades. During the spring primary, a ruckus erupts at the Seventh Ward voting station when Charles Franklin, a colored poll watcher, whom everyone calls Nibs, speaks to voters waiting on line, "encouraging" them to vote the Taylor ticket. If the primary is won, Nibs promises to go around and give each voter two dollars. Many Negroes feel the government is rigged against them and that they may as well get something for their vote.

But the fighting five send an attorney to monitor the poll and he grows outraged to see Nibs soliciting. Nibs grows outraged at being snooped on by a white lawyer and things get lively when he kicks the lawyer in the pants. Probably such high-jinks occur in every election, but the fighting five play them up in the newspapers. They also publish a list of "phantom" voters who somehow manage to show up at the polls and vote though they are deceased or living out of town. As summer nears the debate grows feverish.

In an attempt to give Joseph Randall some political credibility, the fighting five appoint him to run as a substitute legislator from the city district. It's another attempt to gain some of the Negro vote from Crampton. In his acceptance speech, Randall says he is a maverick leading a minority group with no representatives or voice in local government, a jab to Crampton's chin. He refers to the Republicans as the well-lubricated Taylor machine and pledges to beat them or at least frighten them toward a change of attitude.

Crampton looks exhausted. Socializing with the twenty-one Negro business leaders in the 21 Club means hosting late-night dinners and poker parties. Talk is that Randall is annoyed not to be included.

Another attempt to keep the colored vote from dividing requires the formation of an all-Negro unit of the Army reserves, the first of its kind in central Pennsylvania. A big ceremony is hosted by Crampton at the Forster Street Y and speakers include Calvin "Hap" Franks, a war hero and former football player with political aspirations, and Franklin Moore, my old boss from the Penn-Harris Hotel. He tells the reserve members that the world has made more progress in the last 250 years than in the entire 5,750 years before the founding of America. He says the prime ingredients for freedom are ideas, manpower, and money.

And money for the election is indeed pouring in, but Crampton says it's being spent by the machine twice as fast. We increase the number of procedures and enlist a colored woman named Laura Waters up on Jefferson Street to house some of the extra patients. Her husband is a young Republican and loyal to the machine.

We are averaging fifteen to twenty procedures a week, and with Sam gone I convert his bedroom and also add extra beds to the living and dining rooms. As we work, Crampton barely says a word. His movements are clear and precise, but it is obvious he is trying to conserve his strength. Tough as an old turkey, he works with little sleep and tries to act unconcerned about the election and the threat that Joseph Randall poses. Only Frances and I comment on the strain.

Despite our grueling schedule, Crampton doesn't miss a single William Penn football game. The boys expect him to be there and they know his dedication to them is stalwart.

One afternoon, as I cross Market Square, I notice that the gray cone-shaped public address speakers that were temporarily attached to the front of the *Patriot* building to broadcast the World Series are now being used to air election speeches. Usually I don't bother with such stuff, but I overhear a man call to someone, saying, "That's Joseph Randall speaking." Randall's powerful voice echoes off the buildings. Some listeners actually cheer when he says the Taylor machine has destroyed the principles of American democracy and that after sixteen years they should be ousted. He calls Taylorism filthy and cites a litany of complaints. It surprises me to see how well Randall is received. I suddenly comprehend just how much trouble Crampton is in.

As the election nears, Randall is frequently on the radio and one day he reads letters from several Negro pastors stating how scholarships for needy boys in their parish have been misappropriated by Taylor and his cronies. Naturally this stirs people up and Randall promises them all sorts of change. Times are shifting. Negroes sense this. In the old days, if a colored person spoke as boldly as Randall, he'd have soon been silenced. Had Crampton ever spoken out in this fashion, made such demands, become a pebble in Harvey Taylor's shoe, Taylor would have simply changed shoes.

A week before the voters go to the polls, Randall phones every member of the 21 Club to inform them that he's acquired several acres of property up in Perry County and that he plans to open a colored country club there. He invites them to join the Blue Mountain Club and says it will provide an additional place to hold weddings and other social functions, currently held at the Forster Street YMCA.

On the night before the election, I am at the office when Joseph Randall delivers his final election speech. Crampton and I take a break from doing procedures and stand in his office by the radio listening to the broadcast. Randall gives a rousing speech, vows to eliminate corruption, and says the community needs to get rid of the stranglehold that Taylor's gigantic monster machine has over them. His last words are "The era of the Uncle Tom is over."

Crampton brings his fist down on the radio, his eyes half-shut with fury. "Damn him!" I can feel his frustrated anger emanate from every pore. Though I've never seen this forceful side of him before, it doesn't surprise me.

His anger and tension are so palpable it feels like a tornado has just passed through the office. Such upset will make our work with patients difficult if not impossible. I'm not sure how I can comfort him but it seems like something I have to do. Without allowing myself to ponder or become self-conscious I cross over to where he stands with his back to me and place my hands on his shoulders. I can feel his surprise.

"You've got to relax," I say in my firmest calming voice. Taking charge, I press my fingers into his knotted muscles. "Take a deep breath," I say.

To my surprise he complies and for him to do so lets me know my efforts provide some relief that he must also recognize is necessary if we are to get our work done. "Exhale."

Though he has in the past often given me a little hug or a peck of a kiss, I've never actually touched him before. I tell myself it is strange—yes, but also perfectly natural.

"Inhale."

I tell myself that as a nurse, it is my job to come to the aid of another person in distress, to provide them with aid, and if I can be of service then that is also my duty. "You are exhausted," I say and as he continues deep breathing, I work the deep tissues of his shoulders. After a few moments his muscles soften and he starts to relax.

"Thank you, Mrs. K. I think I'm okay now," he says suddenly, standing up straight and moving a step beyond my reach. He recovers his professional demeanor and without turning to look at me he says, "Can you tell Frances we are ready to get started. And bring the first patient down."

"Yes, Doctor." I say.

There are six patients to handle and thankfully all their procedures run smoothly. He is strangely focused and calm as he works, and also a little detached, as if his earlier outburst has caused him to retreat into himself. At the end of the night, just before I depart with the women, I pause in the doorway of his office. "Don't let mudslingers bait you," I say. "Remember, Joseph Randall can't deliver that housing project."

He looks up from the paperwork on his desk. "Mrs. K., I wish I had a dozen more like you."

I smile, knowing that is his way of saying thank you.

The next day the fighting five are defeated with a ballot so close a recount is ordered. The Taylor machine wins by a hair, but everyone senses they will never again enjoy the degree of power they've had over the last score of years. And despite winning in Pennsylvania, the Republicans are kept from the White House as Truman is reelected.

28

With our first-ever peach crop ripening, Dewey works hard to prepare for the picking and has redeemed himself with responsibility. Throughout July the weather is perfect for peaches, lots of slow steady rain at night and hot, clear sun in the morning. On weekends we go out to the orchard several times a day and just stand there witnessing the miracle. One weekend Dewey's daughter Sally drives up with a young man she's been dating. We make a picnic and sit joking and laughing on blankets under the trees. Overhead, the well-formed peaches hang ripening, and everyone says it's the best growing season in a decade.

The beauty of the orchard helps take some of the sting out of what the crop has cost us as people. I think of Sam and wish that he could come home from Korea and also witness the bounty. Maybe if he saw this majestic fruit suspended from the trees that he helped plant, he wouldn't be so bitter and could forgive me for not being a better mother. Maybe he'd understand I did the best I could and it would all be different. I go down the lane to check the mail and by coincidence a card from Sam is in the box as though he were reading my mind. The card is brief.

August 1949

We are on a train bound for Kwangju. The cars are beat-up with springs shooting through the worn-out seats. There are so many floorboards missing you can count the railway ties below, and half the windows were shot out when the Japs left here. As the train moves, the wind rushes in, and you never get warm. The only toilets are holes you have to squat over. For the past forty years the Japs have terrorized this place in occupation and the old trains were torn apart by them when they were driven out. When we arrive in Kwangju, we'll join M Company, Third Battalion, 20th Infantry Regiment, 6th Division, which is a tank company. I'm in the heavy weapon division.

The fellows who've been here a while say that letters that are too long get censored, so I'm sending this with a fellow who's heading back to the States. He said he'll post it from there. Hope you are well.

Sam

I'm told that some outfits require soldiers to write home once a month. I wonder if that's the case with Sam or if he's writing voluntarily.

It is the ninth of August, and Dewey is back in the saddle again. He's brought in a couple of early, big, juicy samples for us to taste and announces that the full picking will be ready to commence tomorrow. I've already arranged three days off from work, the porch is stacked with brand-new bushel baskets, and Dewey has hired an ex-con named Leo to help pick. Mom and Hazel both come up from Harrisburg to spend the night and we are excited, sleepless, anticipating the feel of our small knives slicing through the flesh of the peaches to free them of their stones.

In the morning Mom cooks a big country breakfast—bacon, eggs, hotcakes—then we hurry the dishes and tie our aprons and scarves around our hair before setting to work in the orchard, shoulders, backs, thighs climbing, lifting, stretching on ladders in the perfect sunshine, plucking down the luscious fruit. Dewey inspects every basket for bruises and instructs us on how to move them properly. "Never dump or pour peaches," he instructs. "Always transfer them by hand."

Then, in the late afternoon, Mom and I have just finished the last load of canning in the summerhouse and are in the middle of scalding jars for the next day when the sky darkens with a rumble. We each take a different window and watch big fat drops of rain begin to plop down into the dirt. Leo runs in laughing and says the rain will give the fruit a good wash. But the wind starts to howl and a strange lightning begins to fork through the heavy air. Like many people raised on farms, Mom grows tense and shivers; she's seen her share of barn fires caused by lightning. "Don't worry," I say, "both the house and barn have lightning rods." She doesn't relax. How wise she is.

There's a popping sound, like rocks thrown against the house, handfuls of rocks. We scramble out to stand under the breezeway. The rain has turned to the largest hail any of us has ever seen. It pounds the ground and the roof overhead, like frozen buckshot, a good five minutes of torture until the grass is ankle deep in ice. Then as quickly as it began, it stops. The sky lightens to a pale yellow and warmer air presses the storm away.

We know the orchard cannot withstand such an onslaught. We run through the slush, the jagged pieces of ice crushing like gravel underfoot, a field of cold white diamonds in hot August. You can scoop them up with your hands.

Water is dripping from the tree branches and it sounds like the orchard is alive. Twigs lie ripped away and clusters of leaves scatter about. The sky brightens and a steamy heat begins to envelop us, and then we see. The hail has been a curse. The heavy shards have savaged the peaches, tearing through their tender skins and leaving fine razor cuts. They hang leaking juice. Big fat horseflies appear out of nowhere. It is clear there won't be time to pick a full orchard before the fruit rots.

Dewey's face is unmoving, his lips rest together. The whole thing is so painful we can't look at each other. We stand in shame and stare at the sky, watching as it clears.

"Now the sun will mock us," Leo says, and then the two men, already exhausted from picking all day, test their resolve and begin to pick again. Hazel, Mom, and I also hurry to fill baskets. We realize that if we move fast enough, more of the fruit can be saved. When the handcart is stacked with damaged fruit, we turn and wheel it to the summerhouse without a word. As dusk comes we stoke the fire in the range and with weary joint and muscle begin our morning's chore all over again. The summerhouse only has one dim overhead bulb, and without the daylight coming through the windows, it's not as easy to see our work.

Nightfall comes, and under a shimmering cobalt sky, Dewey and Leo finally call it quits. Meanwhile Hazel and Mom keep canning while I go inside the main house to fix everyone a late supper of scrambled eggs. Though I am too tired for baking, I quickly roll out a peach pie, crimp it the way Murphy showed me so many years ago, and put it in the oven. Leo comes in silent and goes to wash up, but Dewey stays behind at the orchard's edge and in the light of the moon I can see him lower himself down to the ground. He takes an empty canvas sack and wraps it around his face.

When supper is on the table, I go to the screen door. Mom catches my arm. "Leave him be," she says. "Food won't help him now."

At the table Leo says grace and we begin our meal, passing the platter around. We keep silent. The crickets sing. Out in the distance we know Dewey is still seated on the wet, black grass. Forks scrape porcelain. We chew with tasteless appetite, eggs twice in one day but no energy to roast meat. After supper we cut the pie and listlessly eat, already sick of sweet things. Mom, Hazel, and I wash up in the kitchen while Leo plays solitaire at the table. We each continue to steal glances outside to see if Dewey is still sitting out there on the ground. The breeze stirs the curtains, moths flit by the window screens, and in the glowing night you can still just make out the motionless form, head bent and wrapped in the grain sack, arms crossed over knees, hands loosely curled into fists.

In the morning he is gone and I know he can be found in the bar of the Fisherville Hotel. It's one of the few times in our married life I don't begrudge him a drink, though I sense that now all bets will be off. We have plenty of peaches put up for winter but none to sell. Another year with no income on the crop—another failure for Dewey.

29

A seventeen-year-old girl slipped out of the house sometime after midnight. I can't believe I didn't hear her go. She'd given an emergency address down in York, but the phone number does not work. Crampton decides that he wants Togans, now his only chauffeur, to drive me down to try and find the girl's home. He has a hunch that her address is correct. Dewey is up at the farm, and Hazel isn't home, so I call Dewey's daughter Sally and ask her if she would be willing to come over and stay with the other four patients. She agrees and is in fact flattered to be asked.

Togans picks me up, and by the time we reach the highway there's a mist and the roads are slick. From the front seat he senses my nerves are ajangle over the missing girl, and so to fill the time, he makes idle conversation, glancing back at me in the rearview mirror from time to time. He is an attractive man, trim and nearing fifty, with a reddish tint to his dark skin that Frances says comes from some Cherokee blood. He is an interesting talker with an eye for what's important. He tells me how while driving on long stretches he likes to hum a song his brother taught him more than thirty years ago. The song repeats the phrase "Don't worry, baby, I'm gonna come back home."

His brother memorized the song while working a night shift in a munitions factory during the First World War. He'd return home at dawn, sleep all day, and Togans, a twelve-year-old, ten years younger than his brother, would rush home from school each day to wake him like a bell. One evening a six-foot length of steel snapped loose from a gearbox. It sliced the artery in his brother's throat, permanently silencing his song. The foreman found him crumpled at the side of the machine.

Doctor Crampton visited the grieving family and promised young Togans a job driving just as soon as he finished school. After the funeral, the owner of the munitions plant also came by their house and offered to send Togans to college someday. But the offer never materialized and anyway, Togans says, the idea of moving ahead on his brother's hard luck disturbed him. He failed the college entrance exam by two points, and he confesses that he didn't consider himself college material anyway. "I liked cars, and to run around," he says. I don't have the heart to tell him that many college boys like those things too. It seems important for him to keep that distinction in his mind.

We emerge from the flat farmland and are nearing York when I ask Togans to pull over at a café and filling station along the road. A young boy with pink ears, astonished at the sight of the shiny black car, runs out from the garage, his mouth agape. He freezes when Togans tells him to fill the tank and check the water and the oil. For a second he shifts from one foot to another and I wonder if he will obey. His hands are cracked from the cold and embedded with engine grime, and he wipes them on his overalls before hurrying to the pump to get started.

The café is fashioned from an old railroad car, and its silver shine looks inviting. Inside, the place is deserted, just the hiss of a coffee urn with a low level of brown liquid in the tube. The song

Togans spoke about nervously runs through my head as I scout for some sign of a bathroom. "Don't worry, baby, I'm gonna come back home." From the back of the empty room there is a loud bang and I see a woman has kicked the scuff guard of the kitchen door to enter. Her elbows are skewed outward as she carries a rack of steaming water glasses. The sight of me standing there startles her. "Washroom's around back," she says, and points to a key hanging from a small wooden board by the cash register.

I go back out to Togans, give him a ten-dollar bill. The boy has lifted the hood of the Lincoln, and its insides steam in the cool air like the organs of a body with the skin pulled back. I tell Togans to take the change that is left from the gas and go inside to get us two Dixie cups of coffee from the woman, then I head around back to the dingy toilet. I'm almost finished and am washing my hands when I hear someone knocking on a door somewhere outside, and in the distance I recognize Togans's voice. "But that's double what it says inside." I hear a woman's voice but can't make out what she is saying. I exit and see Togans is speaking with the waitress at the back door of the restaurant.

"What's the trouble?" I ask.

Togans politely informs me that two Dixie cups of coffee to be taken away now cost sixty cents, not thirty cents as it says inside. "That's ridiculous," I say.

"I didn't know you two were together," the woman says. "I wouldn't have made him come around back." I'm stunned that the woman is speaking to me as if Togans isn't even there. "The coffee costs thirty cents," she says quietly. "You can't be too careful. We try to discourage trouble here."

Togans hands the woman the money and takes the two containers, and without speaking I follow him back around to the car.

Neither of us discusses what has just happened. Not in the least. We sip the bitter coffee trying to pretend our trip has not been altered.

By the time we get to the missing girl's address it is almost noon. The house is yellow brick, small and ordinary. Togans waits while I ring the bell. An older woman, her hair neatly pinned back, answers. "May I help you?" She is wearing an apron with cherries printed on it.

We speak for a few minutes while I ascertain that she is indeed, as I suspect, the girl's mother. She believes her daughter is at the home of a friend and has no idea her girl has traveled all the way to Harrisburg. When I tell her what for, and how she's run off, adding that without proper medical care her daughter could go into shock and die, the woman grows pale and begins to shake. "I knew something wasn't right," she says. It is soon clear she doesn't think much of me or my service; she adopts an attitude, as though it were also my fault that her daughter had gotten pregnant.

Reluctantly, and probably feeling nervous about her neighbors, she invites me in, while she calls the friend's house where her daughter is supposedly staying. I stand beside a small couch, upholstered in colonial fabric, and listen to them speak. The mother grows angry and is on the verge of tears. "What should I tell her to do?" she asks me with her hand over the receiver. "Tell her to go to the nearest hospital right now and say she began to bleed. Under no circumstance say she had any procedure."

"What if they ask if she's pregnant?" the mother asks.

"Teach her to lie," I say.

It surprises me to recognize the pang of pleasure that I experience in making the facetious remark. Where does that come from? What is it about this situation that provokes me? Then I recognize that what I am responding to in this mother is a sense I perceive that she believes her middle-class propriety renders her superior. Pop always said middle-class observances are responsible for much of the suffering of the world; the rich can do as they please because they can afford the consequences, and the poor are also free because they have nothing to lose.

Everything about this woman from the fruit printed on her apron to the minutemen covering her couch annoys me in its effort to illustrate something convincingly respectable. Do I resent it because I've compromised my own reputation to help her daughter maintain this façade? I'm not sure I understand my reaction entirely, but I am relieved when our business with their household is finished and Togans delivers the Lincoln onto the main road again, headed back toward Harrisburg.

30

By evening Togans and I have returned and Dr. Crampton is relieved to hear we located the girl. His adopted brother Frederick has just arrived on a visit from California, so I can only quickly whisper the outcome to him and then head off. Tonight yet another testimonial dinner to honor Crampton is being held and Frederick has traveled across the country to attend. This time Crampton is being honored for fifty years of service to Harrisburg.

The two "brothers" reunited, one white, one black, is a good story, and the morning paper has devoted an entire column to the visit, with an accompanying photograph. It says Frederick is an engineer who has just retired from a big concrete manufacturing company out of Chicago and moved to San Mateo, California. His work took him around the nation, and in our region he helped design the Army Depot in New Cumberland, as well as the Pennsylvania turnpike tunnels through the Allegheny Mountains.

The article goes on to tell how in 1884 Fred's father, Colonel Lucius Copeland, adopted Charles Crampton. Charles was five at the time; Fred was two. The article describes Colonel Copeland as a famous lecturer on the Chautauqua circuit who himself had quite a story to tell: his father had died in the Mexican-American War during the Battle of Buena Vista, his mother had died shortly after, and as a nine-year-old boy Lucius Copeland was bound out to a tyrannical uncle in upstate New York. At fifteen he ran away, but six years of mistreatment had formed within him an appetite for justice and a lifelong sympathy for any underdog. He served in the Civil War, where he advanced quickly to the rank of colonel, and after becoming first a newspaper reporter and later a well-known lecturer, even speaking at the White House for Benjamin Harrison, he settled in Harrisburg. According to the article, the title of his most famous speech was "The Plight of the Negro," with whom he heavily identified.

The paper doesn't mention that Dr. Crampton's real father had been a slave in Maryland owned by a family named Hanck. Frances tells me that. She says Crampton's father was freed by the Emancipation Proclamation, went to Baltimore, where he joined the Navy and served on the battleship *Appomattox*. After the war he migrated north to Harrisburg, where he found work as Colonel Copeland's stable master. When he decided to move his family west to Tyrone, so that he could work on the railroad, the colonel offered to adopt one of his children. Frances says many wealthy families adopted Negro children during Reconstruction.

Before we begin working, I tell Dr. Crampton I read his story in the news, and it pleases him. He tells me he was lucky, that he grew up in the glow of the colonel's spotlight and received firsthand instruction in public oration. From a shelf in his office, he pulls out a scrapbook and shows me a newspaper clipping from 1899 that tells how he delivered the graduation speech to his class at Central High School. "That was quite an accomplishment for a Negro in 1899," he says. "Mrs. K., have you ever heard real oratory?"

I tell how the summer I turned eleven, Aunt Varnie took me to some Chautauqua meetings, and once we even took the train down to Mount Gretna and spent the night. Inside the enormous hot tents, men sat in jackets, fanning their faces with hats. Women in boned corsets, slathered with perspiration, breezed themselves with cardboard fans printed with advertisements stapled to flat wooden handles. Aunt Varnie and Uncle Mose enjoyed the meeting's message of temperance and clean living and believed the programs to be educational and an aid to human decency. Before moving pictures and radio, this was entertainment. I don't tell Crampton, but I always thought oratory relied too heavily on exaggeration and melodrama to make its points. Hunger is always bigger, work harder, beatings bring one to the point of death, and misery stretches beyond endurance.

While Crampton is upstairs I take a closer look at the scrapbook. There are clippings and photos showing him laying the foundation for the Negro Y with a gold shovel, raising money to send children to Camp Inglenook, receiving an honorary degree from Lincoln University, hosting sports banquets, leading the mayor on a tour of the Seventh Ward. There are pictures of him at various functions of the Forster Street Y.

There are articles about the big fire that burned down the state Capitol in 1896. The fire department, like something from the Keystone Cops, went to the wrong address. All the students from Central High School, including young Crampton and Copeland, ran out to form a bucket brigade. It was snowing and raining and the article notes how some onlookers had holes burned in their umbrellas from flying embers. It is still the largest fire Harrisburg has ever seen, and the whole town watched as the dome of the old Capitol collapsed in a volcano of sparks. The building would take nine years to rebuild.

What surprises me about the scrapbook is that I can't imagine Crampton still cutting all this stuff out and saving it. Then I realize that he may have begun the book, but it is Frances who keeps it alive and up to date, using cuticle scissors to meticulously cut articles whenever they appear.

There are photos of Crampton being honored with plaques, citations, lifetime achievement awards; holding silver cups; receiving a black leather medical bag and even a morris chair. One photo shows the Copelands with Fred and Crampton; it was taken in a studio as they went off to college. A receipt shows Crampton's tuition was sixty dollars a year and that he paid Mrs. Copeland back. There is one whole section devoted to the death of Colonel Copeland in 1904 while on a lecture tour in Illinois. It was front-page news. "Frederick Copeland and a close family friend Charles Crampton raced across the big four railroad system to Chicago to meet the Colonel's casket."

When Crampton comes back down he's surprised to see me still looking at the book. "We better get started," he says. "The patients are waiting and I want to take dinner with Fred."

Later Frances tells me that Frederick is staying in a suite at the Penn Harris Hotel and that a Negro visitor in a white hotel is unheard of in Harrisburg, and even Crampton, who is permitted to enter and drink in the hotel's Esquire Bar, can't be served in the dining room. So Fred orders room service, Dr. Crampton meets him there, and everyone in the Seventh Ward talks about how the colored cooks are selecting the biggest lobsters and finest steaks to serve, while the waiters draw straws to see who'll get to serve meals to the two brothers.

· 31 ·

I read somewhere that the human life can be boiled down to three questions. Who am I? Where did I come from? And where am I going? The last question is the most mysterious. Where am I going? Where do I want to go? Where do I think I should be going? How do I plan for the future? What if I find out that where I am, or who I am, is not really where or what I want to be at all? Why do thoughts of the future come with so much distress? What if I could let go of worry about the future and just be happy wherever I find myself? I've begun to think about the word *happiness*. How does one know one is happy? What I thought would make me happy—marriage, a home, money—only leave me feeling I must be pursuing the wrong things and haven't figured out what I *do* want. I've decided the pursuit of happiness is a foolish goal, for like all feelings, happiness comes and goes like the weather.

Frances has been out with a cold the past two days. It's the first time I can ever remember her missing work. She's getting up there in years and the office has been getting to be too much for her. Crampton has recently recognized that some things have been slipping, and he's hired a young colored girl named Daphne Monroe, fresh out of high school, to take over the accounting, record keeping, and billing. Daphne is a bundle of energy, and though a chatterbox, she soon has the office reorganized. But it has lost some of the calm reverence that Frances always maintained.

Crampton has been doing a lot of public appearances lately. When Frances returns to work, she invites me to attend the Capitol Street Baptist Church on Sunday, where Crampton is slated as "distinguished speaker." Crampton serves on the board of directors for the church—also for the Second Baptist Church and the AME church—but he usually only attends on holidays.

"Please be punctual," Frances says to me. "It's a very strict Baptist church. They close the doors at nine a.m. sharp."

I wear a plain beige dress and matching coat, a short string of pearls, and a new small feathered hat with a net veil. I sit in a pew halfway back, the only white person there. How often is Dr. Crampton the only colored man in a sea of whites? Yet as Dewey once noted, how rare it is for a white person to be the only white person among Negroes.

At nine o'clock sharp the organ begins a slow introduction to the hymn "In the Upper Room." Then the beat picks up and a dozen men, the deacons, dressed in dark suits, walk two by two, down the aisle. They're followed by the deaconesses, a dozen women wearing white suits, white hats, with white pocketbooks

dangling from their elbows. Pinned to their bosoms are fleshy or-
chid corsages, which later I find out Crampton has bought for
them. Frances is a deaconess and despite her spine's curvature and
her age, she keeps perfect step with the other women, her white
gloves spotlessly moving in rhythm.

The formality of the procession prevents her from looking in
my direction. The group settles into the front pew, and the preacher
welcomes them and gives a blessing. Crampton, wearing a custom-
tailored pearl gray suit, sits to the left of the altar.

The preacher delivers a rousing sermon about the need to take
young children to church. He gets fired up. "You all don't hear me,"
he hollers. There are hallelujahs and amens. "You all don't hear
me!" he shouts louder. Then he sermonizes for more than thirty
minutes about the importance of not letting young people down
and how the church can help with that.

Once he has finished, a stout, coffee-colored woman rises up
and sings "How Great Thou Art," with a bracing power that rattles
the stained glass windows. Afterward we bow our heads in prayer,
then Crampton proceeds to the podium. "How honored I am to
appear before you," he says and thanks the congregation for the invitation. His presence holds energy and force, but he is not bom-
bastic like the preacher. Everyone is now awake and taking notice.
His talk centers on the importance of community. "We need to love
one another," he says, "for we are all intertwined." Amens ring out.

He speaks with gratitude of the many day-to-day blessings in
our lives and says how lucky we are to live in a land that is free.
Many nod and verbally agree. I imagine him fifty years earlier, class
orator, charming the crowd at his high school. The tone of the talk
shifts. "Lately the unity and fabric of our community have been
threatened by the negative and harsh methods practiced by some
during the past election," he says. "I urge you not to fall prey to
such un-Christian and divisive tactics and to remain tall and proud.
My brothers and sisters, we can never reach our full potential if we
divide against one another. We must be an example to our youth."

The congregation expresses their approval, clapping and saying amen, throughout the remainder of his message.

When the service ends, a crowd gathers around Crampton and follows him out the side door. He disappears before I can even say hello. It's obvious that his visit to the church is an attempt to reaffirm his position as *the* community leader. His presence suggests that he must have sustained quite a bit of damage during the election. Before the fighting five, I don't think most people had stopped to imagine local politics without Crampton or Taylor.

Frances invites me to a potluck supper in the church basement. She's baked a large pan of crispy breaded chicken. I'm trying to stay slim and don't want to look like a greedy white person, so I only take a small plate. Frances introduces me around and everyone is friendly and polite. I am struck by the strong feeling of joy and acceptance and long for these qualities in a white church.

32

We currently have a distressing case on our hands, a girl who has had improper relations with her brother. "When you return home," I counsel her, "tell somebody close, a minister, your parents, a friend. Tell him if he tries it again, you'll go right to the police."

But this girl is different. It upsets her to be "giving up" her brother's child. She says she's in love with him.

I tell her it's improper and criminal, but she'll have none of it. "How can you judge me," she says, "when what you do is criminal?" Her words anger me. I've never seen the like. Her brother is the one who brought her in—a thin frame, leaning on one hip, a blank, stupid face. He's the one insisting she lose the baby. She behaves as if she's mentally deranged and it feels like a wise thing not to trust her.

It's strange how I can play cards with Hazel, take a brief nap, and the next day feel rested and refreshed, but staying up to monitor this girl exhausts me. It's a relief when her final checkup is complete and her brother takes her away. I phone Dora and she says, "You hear about sinful stuff like that but never believe you'll encounter it."

"This girl seemed like she was being held by a force that is evil beyond belief," I say. Dora understands.

I'd like to tell Dewey about it, but he and I hardly spend any time together anymore. He's ghostly and sullen, and when we are in each other's presence we really don't know what to say to one another. I get so lonely that my resolve weakens and one day I call Charles Dennis. Several years have passed since I vowed not to see him, and he's never learned about the consequences of the last time—or the outcome of the pregnancy. He sounds happy to hear from me. I talk real sweet and it isn't difficult to do because I still feel something for him. We agree to meet for lunch at the Magnolia-Spot Tea Room on the West Shore. After lunch we take a room at the Brice Inn and spend the rest of the afternoon in bed. The inn is much nicer than the drafty old cabins we used to meet in. We are both adulterers again, and after twenty years it surprises us to discover that a strong attraction still exists when we touch each other.

He's also surprised when I tell him Sam has been in the service for almost four years. Then I turn peevish and say that Sam is coming home on leave and has mentioned that he'd like to pay a call on Charles. "What for?" Charles asks, propping himself up on the mattress.

"He's growing curious. He shares your last name, after all."

"I can't have it," Charles says, lighting a cigarette. "I can't take this now."

"That's how I felt when I was pregnant with him."

He takes a pull on the cigarette and studies me. "Can't you talk some sense into him?"

"Since he's been in the service my influence has passed. I can't stand in the way of what he wants."

"What does he want?"

"Well, his Army pay is low and he probably needs some money."

"This is blackmail, just like before." He stands, pulling on his pants.

I keep calm. "Can't blame him. Every boy would like to know his father."

"How much are you looking for?" he asks.

"Two hundred. For each of us."

He gives me the fish-eye. "You're quite a piece of work," he says, shaking his head in disbelief.

"So are you," I reply. "It's me that kept a roof over Sam's head all these years. Fed him. Clothed him. I can count on one hand the number of times you came around or gave us anything."

"The Depression was killing me."

"Oh? Was there a Depression? Who knew? We were living like kings."

"Well, you're making big money now."

"What does that have to do with anything? Maybe you ought to go home to your wife and ask her to help you sort it out."

He sits on the corner of the mattress and smokes. In the mirror I can see him watching as I climb out of bed, wrapping the sheet around me. I begin to dress in the fading afternoon light.

"You're bold as brass now," he says. "You've lost all tenderness."

I smile and lower my guard. "Experience is the mother of wisdom," I say, and cross the room in my slip to take a drag from his cigarette.

"I never meant to hurt you," he says, and places his hands upon my waist. He pulls me close and rests his cheek on my stomach. "If things had worked out I would have married you."

"As my Pop used to say, there's cold comfort in that."

We rest like that, in silence, me standing, and him sitting with his arms around me. "I'll write you a check," he says finally. "No. I'll give you cash."

"Are you afraid to give me a check?" I ask.

"Yes," he says.

"Well, then four hundred cash is fine."

"I'll make it five, but I don't want to see that boy." I smooth his face and he hugs me tighter.

As I drive home by myself with the money, I do not understand why it was so important to get it. I don't like the idea of using Sam in this way, but we've been at a disadvantage with Charles for too long. I know what kind of women do these things, and I like to think I'm not one of them. But with a man who's never taken full responsibility for the feelings he stirs in me, it's at least something.

·   33   ·

Sam arrives home on leave, in his khaki uniform, carrying a duffel bag on his shoulder, just like in the movies. I pick him up at the station. He grows annoyed to learn a patient is staying in his old room and that only the small room off the kitchen is vacant. I didn't think he'd care, but he does.

Dewey comes down from the farm to meet us for dinner. I've already warned him on the phone not to get drunk during Sam's visit.

"Well, you look like a soldier," he says when he sees Sam.

The three of us go out for our meal and afterwards, not to be a wet blanket, I agree when Sam suggests we stop at the Maple Grove nightclub at Maclay and Sixth. The joint is not nearly as crowded as it was before the war, and I'm surprised to see how shabby everything looks. It's a mixed crowd, colored and white, something we all thought would change back after the war but in certain quarters seems to be here to stay. We sit at the bar and order drinks, and

Dewey whoops out the names of his friends and seems to know everyone who's sitting nearby.

Sam's visit passes quickly. We don't discuss anything of importance; I wish we could be comfortable with each other, sit down and talk frankly, but we're both guarded. He's received his orders and is being sent back to Korea. In the afternoon I take him to the station, where he will head across the country to catch a boat in Oakland, California. Our parting reflects the strain of the entire visit.

Other soldiers stand nearby, so we shyly just say, "So long," and "See you." I push fifty dollars in his pocket but I don't mention it comes from the money I wheedled out of Charles. Sam thanks me and climbs aboard the train. He's all grown up now and suddenly I feel old.

As I drive back home in this melancholy mood, I recall when Sam was a baby, how I fought to break free from motherhood so that I could help us get by, and now I feel that the price of that decision will never be paid.

I think about the summer before he ran away from home. He'd just turned fifteen and Crampton had gotten him that job as locker attendant at City Island beach. One war has ended, but the conflict between us remains unresolved.

BOOK

Three

• 1 •

Every town has a man who is permitted to break the law. His chief duty is to engage the sins of his fellow citizens by supplying them with substances or services that they are desperate for. He rarely breaks the law on his own behalf but profits well from the type of human weaknesses that can never be tempered. He snares many a citizen in his own vice, knows what secrets lie beyond the town green and which sins grip the banker, the politician, or the priest. His breaking of the law is overlooked because he makes life simpler for everyone, and he protects the town from greater effort to procure, and even greater shame.

Every blue moon a man will appear who makes his name as a crusader, a reformer, an angel of righteousness against this other man's business. The status he receives as defender of virtue inoculates him against temptation and sets him apart from other men. Such a man was Huette Dowling.

In 1951 Crampton's friend Carl Shelley decides to step down as district attorney. He's held the office since 1939 and the paper says in that time he oversaw 16,618 cases, winning eighty-nine percent of them. Talk is that Shelley will be made a judge soon.

The new district attorney, Huette Dowling, who's been an assistant to Shelley, is a staunch Catholic who went to Catholic High School in Harrisburg, then followed in the typical local route of Dickinson Law College in Carlisle. Dewey says that as a result of never having been anywhere, Dowling suffers from those acute Pennsylvania maladies known as pettiness and envy. These attitudes are prevalent around the state capital and must be avoided.

The glory days of the Taylor machine are coming to a close. Everywhere the changes are visible. The era of backslapping testimonial dinners is ending. The last one honors Harvey Taylor himself. He's just recovered from a mysterious illness that, though duly reported in the paper, is never identified. Dewey says it was probably piles. There are twelve hundred people in attendance at the banquet, a gathering so large, they hold it at the Zembo Mosque. The planning takes weeks. Taylor is presented with a new four-door Cadillac to thank him for his public service, while Mrs. Taylor takes home a brand-new radio. Needless to say, a dinner with that much flash and swagger causes a tremendous amount of backlash from his opponents. Dewey and the other cynics say Taylor rigged the whole thing as a publicity stunt because he wanted a new Cadillac but didn't want to pay for it. He knows he has to milk the cow while he still can.

Crampton and I again discuss slowing down, even quitting our business. I worry that we might be growing more vulnerable, but Crampton says as long as Taylor is in office, we have our protection. So we continue. And the designs for the new Seventh Ward housing are on the drawing boards. When I come to the office, he and C. Sylvester often sit poring over proposals and blueprints.

A few months pass and a new "secret" version of the Capitol extension plan is unveiled by the machine. This time the blocks to be demolished have been extended even further northward—all the way over to Forster Street. In fact, the entire south side of the street is to be torn away and Forster Street will be widened to six lanes feeding onto a new bridge heading over to the West Shore. Crampton is livid, not just because his own home and office will face the traffic, but because the acreage previously allotted for his Negro housing plan has been greatly reduced.

To make matters worse, the state legislature votes to call the new span the Harvey Taylor Bridge, the first time in state history that a civic project is named for a politician still in office. The outcries are tremendous, and somehow we know that an act so arrogantly grand can't possibly go unchallenged. The smell of a fight is in the air.

The Seventh Ward is the hive of upset over the scheme. Half the ward stand to lose their homes, and they perceive Crampton as the man who allowed it to happen. People have been given but sixty days to move, then the entire neighborhood will be erased. The paper is full of hardship stories, and it reports, as Crampton noted, that many of the houses were built just after the Civil War. Some tenants pay only thirty dollars a month and such low rents can't be duplicated.

Advancing a plan that will remove so much Negro housing almost guarantees that Randall will take the next election, and when Crampton complains, the answer comes back from the boys on high.

"Don't worry. He won't win."

2

In June 1951, Laura Randall, the wife of Joseph Randall, is arrested at their country club in Perry County. Dr. Randall is on duty at the Air Force Hospital in Middletown that day, and Mrs. Randall is managing the lodge-style café.

At lunchtime the sheriff and a posse of squad cars line up along the highway before swooping down on the club and arresting fourteen members, including Mrs. Randall, who is charged with making illegal liquor sales.

The entire group is held overnight in the Perry County Jail. Randall isn't present, but he arrives that evening with an attorney and stays up all night waiting to see the judge. The next morning the sheriff decides to arrest him as well, but he is quickly released on bail and does not spend any time in jail.

Back in Harrisburg, the Seventh Ward, home to most of those arrested, buzzes with frenzied gossip. The talk is that the Taylor machine, and particularly Crampton, is behind the arrests and is getting even for Randall's participation in the 1948 fighting five election campaign. His arrest is sure to sideline Randall for the upcoming 1952 vote. Many people are also furious that Laura Randall is embroiled. At forty, she's tall, dignified, and well dressed, and is correctly perceived as a decent churchgoing lady who doesn't deserve to be smeared.

Since its founding several years ago, Randall has applied and reapplied for state approval to gain a license to sell liquor at the club and has every time been denied by the state liquor authority. Harvey Taylor controls the state liquor authority, and his agency officials claim a quota system has overextended new permits. Meanwhile Randall has made a list of places that have opened since his country club—and that have gotten licenses to sell drinks. He rightly claims discrimination.

Country clubs need to sell liquor to stay in business, and when weddings or dances are held there, he's forced to make underhanded deals, with bottles of booze presold in vague catering contracts and then served from the trunks of cars parked outside. In the bar and café, the lack of permit is slyly bypassed by selling two-for-a-nickel hard pretzels at twenty-five cents apiece: their high price is warranted in that they come with a "free" shot of whiskey. The police hear about this variance and decide it violates the law, hence the move to arrest Mrs. Randall.

It is well known that a few days prior to the arrest, Crampton visited the club and bought one of the "expensive" pretzels and drank the shot. But nothing linking him or the machine to the arrest is proven. I suspect that either someone connected to Taylor prompts the arrest, or that Perry County law enforcement wants to show its weight to a group of uppity Negroes in their "country club." Perhaps the two are in it together.

Randall's incensed to have his good wife publicly humiliated. And in a furious backlash, many Negroes rally around them. Even Dewey says the Republicans had better watch their tactics or in the next election there will be an even bigger defection of voters. Already the number of Negroes who voice support for Adlai Stevenson has everyone concerned.

I myself don't believe Crampton is involved in Randall's arrest. In all the years I've known him, I've never seen him publicly put another colored man in a bad light. Even when Randall openly challenged him, he turned the other cheek. He's well versed in the dangers of divide-and-conquer tactics and believes that any rift among Negroes played out in front of whites is ultimately bad for all of them. Many times I've heard him say, "You don't bring the race up by tearing each other down."

A few days later Dr. Randall stuns everyone by filing a lawsuit against the State of Pennsylvania. A Negro suing state government is unheard of. In his suit he challenges the quota system for the licensing of liquor, saying that the manner in which licenses are denied is discriminatory and unconstitutional. "Half a million Negroes are counted in the quota," the newspaper reports from his court documents, "but they are not welcome nor permitted membership in the clubs issued licenses under the quota."

Meanwhile the eviction process begins in the Seventh Ward; trucks are loaded, women howl and are finally pulled from their doorframes, while crestfallen children stand forlorn watching it all be taken, somehow knowing they are losing something vital that will never be regained. So far, the only housing provisions made are for seventy units up on Allison Hill. Over two hundred families vie for those seventy units. None of Crampton's housing projects has been announced for downtown. Of the evicted, the hardest hit are low wage earners with three or four children. A lot of newer apartments won't even allow children, hoping to keep the poorest Negroes out. The director of the Harrisburg Housing Authority, Melville Smith, is quoted in the paper saying, "The situation is serious and the city itself is in no position to provide adequate housing projects, being hemmed in as it is by the river, the railroads, and the 'first-class' townships and boroughs on its boundaries."

On wealthy Front Street, during construction of the newly opened Harvey Taylor Bridge, an enormous red brick mansion stands in the path of the roadway leading to the span. The entire three-story structure is jacked up and turned sideways—at the tax-payers' expense—so that it doesn't need to be demolished. Try explaining that to your constituents when they face the wrecking ball and are being forced from their homes.

It is clear from the rise in crime in the city that Negroes are angry and are growing more difficult to control. In an effort to appease them, on Lincoln's birthday the charges against Joseph Randall are dropped. His record is still clean, he can still pursue politics, while Laura Randall, in a compromise, takes the fall and pleads guilty. She's fined two hundred dollars.

In March, Dr. Crampton is pictured in the paper with a huge birthday cake. The caption under the photograph reads, "Doc takes the cake." Two former athletes, Jack Zehring and Red Olewine, present it to him. Both presenters are white, and the picture is accompanied by a flattering article.

A few weeks later, the annual Forster Street Y drive begins and, as is now the custom, Crampton heads the blue team and William Reeves the red. This year they again seek to obtain eight hundred new members who will pledge their support. While I wait for Crampton to finish some calls so we can begin our work, C. Sylvester Jackson comes by to do the annual audits for the Y's budget. A couple of card tables are quickly unfolded where he can work, and the office is now overcrowded.

Crampton steps out of his office. "I'll be with you in a few more minutes, Mrs. K. I just need to finish up here."

I nod. C. Sylvester calls him over and shows him a yellow legal pad where he's been making notes.

"Bill Evans says the boiler shut down. For two days they had no hot water for showers. I used up the reserve fund last month fixing the pool, so I'm afraid I had to tap next month's payroll fund. Bill says he wrote the Central Y and the national office to see if they'll help but the letter just got posted yesterday."

"Is it fixed?"

"Yes. Water's good and hot. I called Green Brothers. They said it's twenty-five years old and only a matter of time before she goes out again."

"What's it cost?"

Jackson shows him the yellow legal pad. "You ain't gonna like it."

Crampton eyes the figures but shows no emotion. "I'd better get back and finish those calls. Mrs. K., I'm sorry to keep you hanging here." I let him know I have no plans and don't mind waiting. He returns to his office.

"Why do they have two Ys anyway?" Daphne Monroe asks, from behind the desk where she is organizing files.

"Harrisburg is really a thinly disguised southern city," C. Sylvester answers. "It sits only thirty-eight miles above the Mason-Dixon line."

Frances interjects. "That's not why. It's simply good for our boys to have a place to go that is all theirs."

"But it's so expensive," Daphne says. "Just so boys can play basketball." This time they both ignore her.

We can hear Dr. Crampton's voice coming from his office. "Hello. This is Dr. Crampton, I'm calling to ask for your help in supporting the Forster Street Y." The next call must be to someone he knows in another social context, for he's a bit more familiar. "Hello, Charles Crampton here calling to pester you again." Frances shakes her head. "It's tough sledding this year." I nod. I've already bought supporting memberships for Dewey, Sam, and myself, but once I learned the drive was sluggish, I bought additional memberships for Mom, Myrtle, and Hazel. They will never know that they are full-fledged members of the colored Y, and I print my phone number and address on the records to ensure they can't be called upon.

Daphne asks what year the Y was started. C. Sylvester Jackson designates himself the group historian. "In nineteen twenty. That year the Central Y won a grant from the National YMCA to construct a main facility," he says. "Ten percent of the grant money was set aside with a mandate to create a separate colored branch. Over the next ten years, Dr. Crampton somehow acquired the site and began planning a building at a price well above our sliver of the pie. The board members and the fund-raising committee were impatient and nervous at the delay and the price tag. 'Why does it have to be brick?' they'd say. 'Why such a big pool?' Crampton stared them all down and shut them up by saying, 'When our boys walk through those doors, we don't want them to feel like second-class citizens.'

"Over the next decade the Y met in temporary rented spaces, while Dr. Crampton worked like a man possessed to raise additional money from business leaders and to put aside money from his own pocket."

"It came together just in the nick of time," Frances says. "A few months later and the Depression would have put a stop to it all."

C. Sylvester glares at Frances. "*Woman*, you walking on my story."

"This ain't *your* story," she says. "This story is about the power of the Lord and belongs to all of us. I was born in eighteen seventy-two, and if you'd have told me as a young girl that colored men would someday have their own Y, I'd have laughed in your face."

"She's right," C. Sylvester says. "Except for churches, we never had a community or civic building before. And you can see for yourself it was quite *fancy*—Tudor-style, handmade brick, and windows with leaded panes."

"We checked on it every day while it was being built," Frances says. "Knowing it was for our children."

"It was me that handed over the spade at the ground-breaking," Jackson says. "The shovel was painted gold with a red ribbon tied on it. Dr. Crampton himself placed the cornerstone. Everyone in town was there.

"And during the Depression, even when things were tight, he made sure the Phyllis Wheatley YWCA got a permanent home for the girls too. And that money had to be raised *entirely* from scratch. Don't tell him I told you, but most of that money came from his own bankroll, and he's been the Y's chair ever since."

"Doesn't he ever get tired?" Daphne asks.

"Lord, child." Frances laughs. "Nothing can lick that man."

"You have to understand him," C. Sylvester says. "He's built a legacy. The Y is a monument that will live on long after he's gone."

"There won't ever be another like him," Frances says. "He's like *Moses* leading his people."

We all grow quiet and listen as Crampton begins another call in his office. "Butch? It's me, Charlie. I need you and Cora to help."

Frances shakes her head again.

For the first time in history, the red fund-raising team led by Reeves beats the blue fund-raising team led by Crampton. Reeves raises eight hundred and fifty dollars while Crampton brings in only three hundred and fifty. The defeat is embarrassing but really underscores how the Capitol extension is damaging the old man's popularity. Negroes being forced out of the neighborhood don't join the Y, and those that stay are fed up.

To make matters worse, C. Sylvester Jackson, who serves on the statewide executive committee for the YMCA, says there's talk about opening the downtown Central Y to both white and colored members. He and Crampton believe the move is a tactic by the state to acquire the Forster Street Y site for a new Labor and Industry office building, thereby expanding the Capitol extension even further. Plans are also being discussed to open new modern facilities out in the growing suburbs, where ever more white people seem to be moving. No one believes colored boys will get the same privileges if they join the white Central Y, and they will have to travel much farther to use it. It's growing clearer to everyone that Negroes living anywhere near the Capitol will no longer be tolerated.

Crampton needs to do something to show his support for the families the state is evicting. So to shame Taylor and the machine, he announces that he is putting up five thousand dollars of his own money to start an investment fund to guarantee the construction of the apartment dwellings for families being forced to move. He projects that fifty thousand dollars will be needed to start, and in order to raise the funds, he challenges by name nine other business leaders, urging them to come forward and match his gift. C. Sylvester Jackson quickly obliges with money from the Boyd estate.

Meanwhile, in June, the temperature soars to ninety-five degrees. The city is a furnace and for the first time it's decided that the City Island beach will be open to Negroes—a move that is a half-hearted attempt to appease both them for the loss of their homes and the police commissioner, who has numerous reports that the heat is making everyone dangerously restless. On Sunday Joseph Randall visits every colored church in Harrisburg, saying that thanks to him Negro children can now swim on City Island. He instructs them to wear respectable bathing attire and to follow the rules and behave so they won't look trashy. Crampton is furious to have his act be appropriated in this way.

As the weeks pass, the embarrassment grows as not a single additional person puts up any matching money for Crampton's housing fund. And soon it will be time to raise money for the Y all over again.

Within a few weeks of the Harvey Taylor Bridge's opening, there's a drizzle and a truck spins out of control, jumps up onto the walkway, and snaps the railing. The driver is thrown over the side. He falls forty feet. The river is so shallow there that he hits his head on the riverbed and is instantly killed. People begin to say the Harvey Taylor Bridge is jinxed.

One Monday evening I park my car and am about to open the back door to the office when a Negro man in a gray business suit comes out. He nods as he passes me on the stoop. I recognize his face from the paper. It is Joseph Randall.

"What was he doing here?" I ask Frances. She shrugs.

When I ask Crampton the same question, he tells me he's reaching across the partisan aisle to unify the Negro vote. No fighting five faction has emerged this election and the opposing Democrats are unorganized. He says Taylor and the machine have decided to ask Randall to join them.

"How is that going to work?" I ask with much skepticism. I can see the query annoys Crampton.

"We've offered him the title Interracial Consultant to the Dauphin County Republicans, and he has accepted."

It annoys me to see Dr. Crampton compromising himself. "Randall has done nothing but smear you and Taylor," I say. "He's broadcast all those terrible remarks on the radio. If it was me I'd say to hell with him."

"He's working for us now," Crampton says. "He'll do as he's told."

We argue the new plan for a good ten minutes. I tell Dr. Crampton that it's impossible for me to put aside my reservations, that I think he's playing with fire.

"Mrs. K., by bringing him to our camp we weaken him and the opposition. It will be impossible for him to ever rejoin the Democrats."

I dig in, continuing to raise my objections, something I've never done before. "Randall cannot be trusted," I say, "any more than Taylor." I also tell Crampton that I'm concerned for his safety and that I can't help but feel he's making a terrible mistake. He really dislikes my interference, and he grows more determined, defending the move with worn-out phrases like "Politics makes strange bedfellows."

"But he called you an Uncle Tom," I say—a last-ditch effort to persuade him.

Crampton looks stricken. He grows curt and his voice drops with anger to a long, flat monotone. "Mrs. K., you are skilled at many things, but politics is not one of them. You'll have to trust that I know what I'm doing."

His rebuke stings sharper than anything he's ever said to me. He's discounting my opinion and my caution, and his condescending method works, for I close my mouth, end the conversation, and set about getting ready for our evening's task.

3

The paper says that the conflict in Korea is escalating and has bogged down. Apparently they also have rain so heavy that no fighting is taking place. The men sit bone wet in tents or foxholes. Sam sends a short postcard asking me to try and round up some used clothes for refugees. They especially need women's things. Mom promises a couple of old dresses, but Myrtle snaps them up for her church rummage sale. I say who needs the donations more, some fat-ass church in Camp Hill or our soldiers who are at war? Myrtle says it's not likely the soldiers will be wearing Mom's dresses.

Meanwhile Dewey's daughter Sally announces she plans to marry the young man she brought up to the peach orchard. She's not the first of Dewey's children to marry; the two oldest girls and the son who went to the Milton Hershey Technical School and whom I've only met twice, all have married either out of state or through elopement. Sally's is the first wedding that we are invited to attend. As her stepmother, I want to represent her well, so I decide to have a dress custom made, ordering fabric from New York and hiring an excellent seamstress, who sketches out patterns on cloth with a large black pencil like Mom used to.

During a fitting, the seamstress, who is colored and has learned I work for Dr. Crampton, begins to complain while holding a mouthful of pins. She says, "He simply hasn't done enough for his people."

"I don't get involved in politics," I say.

She persists. "Some people have a little name they call him."

"Oh?"

"Uncle."

A few years ago no one would have dared say that—and to a white customer who works for Crampton. I grow uncomfortable standing there being pinned into the dress.

"Since the war, Crampton has only gotten jobs in the Capitol for a few Negroes," the woman continues. "All for the high-yaller wives of his friends. I make clothes for these women and I hear how they got their jobs."

"You should discuss that with Dr. Crampton," I say.

The woman grows silent and finishes her work. I can feel her disdain.

How dare she be angry? Doesn't she know she's lucky to have me as a customer? When the work is done, I put on my clothes and leave as quickly as possible.

A week later I return to pick up the finished dress. After a tense final fitting, I find the total owed to be much higher than originally quoted.

"A lot more handwork was needed," the woman says. "More than I expected." She busies herself with some bolts of cloth. "You don't have to take the dress," she adds, and her arrogance is infuriating.

I tell her, "I can shop at Mary Sachs for less."

"But that's not custom work."

"But it's from New York."

"You added a beaded neckline and cuffs. That's not cheap."

"I also bought my own fabric."

"Look," the woman says with contempt. "If you don't want it, I'll put it in the window and sell it to someone else."

The wedding is in two days and I need the dress—not to mention that it's my fabric. I open my pocketbook, withdraw the money, and put it on the counter. "You won't get any more business from me," I say.

"Well, you're only here because you expect me to work on the cheap."

Her words infuriate. No colored person has ever spoken to me that way. A tense moment passes, then I pick up the dress and leave. Climbing into my car, I play the scene over and over in my head. How dare she? I'll report the incident to Crampton. Let him know that she called him an Uncle Tom. But by afternoon my head has cooled, and I don't mention anything about the encounter to Crampton. He'd probably just send her a fruit basket anyway.

Then I begin to feel ashamed, because what the seamstress says is true. I'd gone there expecting her to sew on the cheap. It's embarrassing to have been caught; I feel I'm no different from the stingy white patients who come to Crampton for his free aspirin and liniment. I'm forty-two years old and suddenly aware that despite my life's hardships, I've enjoyed certain privileges not open to all, not the least of which is the opportunity to feel better than someone whose skin is darker than mine. The shame burns, because I've deceived myself that it is otherwise, and because I now must recognize how much I resent having my advantage over a Negro questioned.

The custom-made dress is a big hit at the wedding. Sally's husband seems different than when we met him at the farm and turns out to be a loud, big talker. All of Dewey's children are there; most of them we haven't seen in years, and yet they treat us both with courtesy and respect. Starting families of their own is maturing them, and they are getting on with things. It seems like they hold no grudges against their drinking daddy and me, the second wife who replaced their mother. Talk about forgiveness.

In the powder room, I secretly give Sally an envelope with five hundred dollars in it. "Use this for a down payment on a house," I say.

The next day I ask Frances to explain how the colored jobs at the Capitol are distributed or acquired. She admits a lot of factors are at play, saying many professional men, no matter how dark their own skin, marry light-skinned wives for status. That status carries over into the workplace, because Crampton can't just send anyone to work at the Capitol. If he sends the wrong person to a job, it can close the door on those who come next. A colored worker's skills can't just be good, they must be impeccable and withstand extra scrutiny. There's also the necessity to afford nice clothes, dresses, shoes, hats, and gloves. The wives of Crampton's friends can do that and are often college-educated, with an attractive deportment that doesn't inspire unpleasantness—a certain calm to handle bad re-marks, to handle the pressure when some white clerks get ugly, wor-rying Negroes might be out to take their jobs.

· **4** ·

The paper announces Huette Dowling is prosecuting a man across the river in Marysville named Edward Smalansky. They say he performed an illegal operation on a twenty-nine-year-old woman named Elizabeth Wright. She lived at 381 Third Street in Steelton and died while being rushed to the Harrisburg Hospital an hour after he operated on her. Smalansky has no medical training what-soever. He works in the bridge and construction department of Bethlehem Steel. Mrs. Wright leaves three children behind.

At the office everything is worry. Frances can barely sit still and jumps every time the phone rings with someone wanting an ap-pointment. "Let's just hope our girls come through okay," she says.

Luckily Daphne Monroe, who has grown more businesslike and efficient, is doing more of the important work, but she openly com-plains that she needs better compensation. "I just gave you an extra fifty dollars," Crampton snaps. "That was last month and my mother's been sick," Daphne says. No doubt he'll throw some more money at her just to get her to shut up.

In late August Dr. Crampton takes his annual trip out to Ty-rone, to see his brothers Benjamin and Ulysses. "The trip used to play them out," Frances tells me. "There aren't no hotels for colored men to stay between here and there. A couple of times they stopped at the home of another colored doctor, and Togans slept in the car with a gun, one eye open all night worrying about vandals. That part of the state has Klan, and a big, new car driven by colored men is something they notice. But the state turnpike makes the trip faster; they can easily do it in a day."

Two weeks later a patient is vexed and says she resents paying two hundred dollars for our service. I'm surprised. Our fee has always been a hundred, and my cut, fifty. If anyone pays extra, Crampton gives me a bonus. I ask the other women who come for procedures this week and learn that all of them are now paying two hundred dollars, and a few have paid even more. It angers me that Crampton hasn't cut me in or even told me. "I wish I had a dozen more like you," indeed.

The climate of deceit spreads my dissatisfaction. Sure, he has political expenses and a staff, and though those colored women are fiercely loyal, they work him over. He'll come downstairs and Daphne will say, "Doc, I need a new pair of eyeglasses." Then Jenny Johnston pops in and says, "I heard they got beautiful pork chops at Broad Street and they'd make you a nice supper, but I'm a little short." Then Laura Randall, who handles the extra patients, comes by and says, "My shoes have holes, Doc. Can't you help me?" He snarls and growls, "What do you think I am, a money tree?" Or he mocks them: "Why don't you just get a fur coat while you're at it?" The women love this and laugh. "Dr. C., you know how much we do for you." And he almost always gives in. Only Frances never asks for anything. I think she too secretly loves him and would never take advantage.

As the days pass, the temperature of my dissatisfaction climbs. How petty I become. These women work him over for extras but I do the lion's share of the work. Every night I lie awake with the patients in my own house.

I finally confront Crampton. "Women are complaining about the higher cost," I say, "and I have to deal with these complaints."

"What do you want?" he asks, tapping his desktop with an envelope.

"A bigger cut."

The expression on his face shows that my request disgusts him. My heart pounds at the delay.

"Do you think you deserve it?"

"They stay under my roof. I cook and change bed linens and sit up with them every night."

"I know what you do," he snaps.

"Well, I think I at least deserve to know when prices change, and to be included in better compensation."

"I'll think about it," he says.

I feel guilt, but I deserve to be treated fairly. I also want the extra money. All night things are tense between us. His manner is professional but curt. One woman has a peculiar inflammation, and rather than inject her with solution, he has me assist him in a D & C. After we finish and I clean up the exam room, he stands on the landing about to retire for the night. "Starting next week—a hundred a head," he says without emotion, and turns to go upstairs.

My ears pound because this is twice what I expected to get. "Thank you," I say after him. He does not pause or respond, his weary feet just keep climbing. The reaction makes me feel hollow inside. He's treating me like I'm some greedy bitch. He sees the patients for half an hour, I'm stuck with them all week. They live in my house. Keep me up at night.

Being treated fairly was supposed to appease me but it doesn't. I feel small and petty for gaining this equity. I keep telling myself that it's simply business, that I deserve extra income too, and that it's my right to be treated with fairness and justice. But when I wake up in the middle of the night my victory makes me cringe.

I've demanded justice from a man who stoically has refused to buckle under a lifetime of injustice, based solely on what some people have decided is the misfortune of having been born with dark skin. As with the seamstress, I've felt it was my right to determine in my head how justice toward me should appear to them. How presumptuous. I am white. How can I expect to define justice and reality for people who've endured slavery, and a system of laws and permissions that abetted it?

The seamstress, fueled by her anger, fought back at my perceived superiority. She showed me how she resented her implied lower status. But Dr. Crampton has conceded to my wishes for more money. He has overthrown stinginess. His fairness says he won't collude in his own diminishment, or to the moral deformity of the past. I lie awake with a splitting headache feeling guilty and ashamed. Eventually I come to see those feelings are not so much because of greed, but for feeling entitled. To imagine that I deserve to be treated justly by him when in our land he himself does not fully enjoy the same rights. But perhaps he can be just, because he has already forgiven me and my entire race. I push these thoughts from my mind. The money is mine to keep. I asked for it, and deserve it. I'm being rewarded. I can't take on all the struggles of the world. Let the people whom they affect fight them.

By dawn my throbbing headache finally begins to fade.

5

In October Senator Richard Nixon comes to town as part of his whistle-stop tour. He speaks from the steps of the Capitol and the radio says twenty thousand people turn out to hear him. Harvey Taylor, Dr. Crampton, and the rest of the muck-a-mucks spend time in the senator's railroad car. As a result Crampton is late and I have four girls waiting to be examined. He's brisk because he's expected at a football game. At one point he almost growls.

"Don't snap at me because you're packing too much into one day," I say. He looks surprised and neither of us can quite believe I've spoken to him that way. He is very courteous after that.

Three days later it's Eisenhower's turn to stump Harrisburg. Dewey's daughter Sally and I have planned to meet so I can take her to lunch for her birthday. Traffic is unbearable. We park on lower

Fifth Street, which is as close as we can get, then walk the rest of the way to the Colonial House.

Over our club sandwiches, we talk like girlfriends, pleased that we've been able to overcome some of the obstacles between us. She confirms what I had always suspected, that she disliked me up until she needed my help with her abortion. Even then she was testing me by leaving her dirty sanitary napkin lying around my nice clean room. "Then I started to feel rotten for my behavior," she says. "And as the years go by, I can't thank you enough for the way you've helped us all by looking after Pop."

Afterwards we do some shopping. I buy her a skirt at Feller's, and then she takes her leave, catching the bus back uptown, while I head over to Mary Sachs by myself. There I purchase a navy crepe dress with ivory satin grosgrain woven at the bodice, hideously expensive, but as the salesgirls all agree, it will never go out of style. Then I go over to Worth's and drop another hundred dollars on a flat-brimmed navy suede hat, a pair of long black gloves, silk stockings, and two pairs of shoes. I can't stop spending.

Eisenhower arrives by train, gives a speech, and then waves his way down Market Street. The whole town comes to a standstill, and I, burdened with half a dozen shopping bags, wait among a hundred thousand other people trying to get a look. Mamie is tiny with a full bosom; she wears a nicely tailored cardigan suit. Crampton is with a group riding in one of the cars and I also recognize Carl Shelley, Tom Nelly, and of course Harvey Taylor.

Then with only a few days to go before the election, as I have feared, Joseph Randall begins to play his hand. Dramatically, he resigns from the interracial post that Crampton and Taylor have awarded him. He does not, however, resign from the Republican Party. He then goes on the radio to urge the Negro Republicans of the Seventh Ward to go against their party and support Adlai Stevenson, saying, "Negroes can no longer sacrifice principle for friendship or depend upon promise or hearsay. The day of the Uncle Tom has passed." There is now no doubt in anyone's mind whom Randall is referring to.

There is no feeling of vindication on my part. No sense of "I told you so." In his office Crampton looks downcast, like a guilty child. "You were right, Mrs. K.," he says. "Taylor is apoplectic. I should have listened to you." His words are dispirited in their generosity and offer me no consolation or pleasure.

"They plan to bring him down," Frances whispers to me in the supply room. "I've seen colored men in trouble before. They plan to bring him down."

At the foot of Forster Street the Harvey Taylor Bridge stands lit at night, glowing with arrogance. All the blocks on the opposite side of Forster leading up to the bridge are now condemned and boarded up—an entire neighborhood and its beloved community vanquished, to be replaced by state office buildings, as well as an archive and museum that we need like a hole in the head.

Crampton grows ever more irritable and is not as steady as he should be. He's put on at least fifteen pounds and his face is all jowls. One night at a huge Republican rally that shakes the Chestnut Street auditorium, Crampton stands on the platform with Harvey Taylor, the governor, and the rest of their posse, and they all look haggard, as if none of them is sure what is going on anymore. The many years in power have worn them down.

Sally moves to a nice three-bedroom bungalow out in the Allison Hill area and she says many white families who live there are furious to have Negroes moving in. The white residents even tried to buy the remaining plots of land and turn them into parks. But the city has a problem on its hands and prevents these sales, for the displaced people have to relocate somewhere, and since no one wants them moving farther uptown, the hill is the only alternative. Dr. Brown, the first Negro to head the school board since the late 1800s, is affluent; he buys a corner lot up in the Allison Hill section and begins to build a new house. His arrival upsets the residents there to the point that someone burns a cross in his yard. Some whites come out on Brown's behalf, but once construction begins on the house, it suffers so much vandalism that Dr. Brown and his friends begin to sleep there every night with loaded shotguns.

Crampton continues to try and find support for his housing project, but after all this time, the only one who has put up any money is C. Sylvester Jackson. Crampton says we must now process as many patients as possible, for he intends to put up the entire fifty thousand himself. He's socking every bit of cash away.

On his seventy-fourth birthday there is for the first time in years no mention of him in the newspaper, and only a dozen floral tributes are delivered. I run into Tom Nelly in front of the Senate Hotel, and because of a forceful wind blowing off the river, we duck into the lobby. "Tom, tell it to me straight," I say.

"Well, Crampton has angered Taylor and the machine by speaking to the newspapers about putting up his own money for public housing, hoping to pressure the state to match funds. He spoke to reporters about state business without consulting Taylor and that is verboten."

Tom says if things don't improve between the two of them, Taylor won't ask Crampton to be a part of the election campaign for '56. "Taylor is scouring every dark face he meets, looking for a replacement. He wants a new man to pull the Negro vote. Given Crampton's age, and his declining popularity with Negroes," Tom says, "there's little incentive to hold out an olive branch."

"But Crampton and Taylor are the same age," I say. "And Taylor could never have won any election without Crampton delivering his votes."

"I know, I know," Tom says, "but Crampton's days are numbered."

6

A week later an Internal Revenue Service official informs Dr. Crampton that he's under investigation for tax evasion. A lien is placed against his home, automobile, and bank accounts. They publicly announce the case in the *Patriot Evening News*. Everyone is shocked to read that Crampton owes Uncle Sam one hundred thousand dollars.

When I arrive at his office, Frances says, "Mrs. K., I been trying to call you. The doctor has canceled all procedures scheduled for tonight."

"Is he around?" I ask.

She points to his closed office door. "See if you can talk to him," she whispers.

I cautiously knock and then enter. He sits alone at his desk with the lamp on, the evening paper open to the story. "Not a good day," he says, his facial muscles tight. It's the first time in all our years of working together that I've seen him with his tie loosened. "They say I owe taxes from 1939 to 1945."

"How do they figure?"

"They've been monitoring my spending against the income on my tax forms. The numbers don't match."

"They can't possibly hold you accountable all the way back to 'thirty-nine."

"The whole thing is a setup. I've hired an attorney—Manny Kraus. I intend to fight."

"Why don't you take a few days off? Go fishing. See your family up in Tyrone. Get some rest."

"I must keep up appearances. Look like I'm unbowed."

"Can you win?"

"I don't know. I only hope now you'll take my advice. Keep your money out of sight. Stop buying them expensive clothes."

Although he's canceled our patients for the evening, I remind him that there are still four girls waiting out in the car to be examined.

He looks defeated. "Bring them in," he says. "Bring them in."

7

The annual Forster Y membership drive is on again. Dr. Crampton is sulking, and his injury can be openly felt. This year he doesn't make a single fund-raising phone call, and his silence seems to say, I'll show you all. Let someone else keep young Negroes off the street. Let someone else shoulder the expense and effort. The drive yields only ninety-three new members, a far cry from the goal of eight hundred. Crampton is credited with only three of the new memberships and raises only eighty dollars.

The Y now faces an enormous deficit and has begun to cut its hours, programs, and staff. Crampton can't bail them out this time. His assets are frozen. Talk is that Huette Dowling is behind the IRS action.

In defiance, Crampton raises our fee for procedures yet again, to a nerve-wracking three hundred dollars. "We should stop," I say. "This is crazy." But even with the new rate, there is no dip in women who book appointments. This time I don't ask for a bigger cut.

I've never seen Crampton so sullen. He barely speaks and no longer confides in me or Frances. He plods along like a tired old mule. The only place where he comes to life is at the William Penn football games. There he projects an invincible façade of defiantly mustered vigor infused with artificial cheerfulness. Those close to him aren't fooled, and that makes it all seem pitiful and sad. We know his effort is backed by the gallons of antacid he drinks to keep his stomach down.

He continues to champion the housing project for Negroes, if for no other reason than to prove that he's not an Uncle Tom. But it's as if something inside him has finally broken loose and he's become what he so long avoided being—a pebble in Harvey Taylor's shoe.

C. Sylvester Jackson is at the office daily. He and Crampton speak listlessly about low-income housing as they draft plans to try and persuade the state to come up with alternative ideas. It's unlikely anything will change. They know white people don't like formerly cooperative Negroes who suddenly start to infiltrate their neighborhoods, speak their minds, and ask for things.

In a strange twist, the Dauphin County Medical Society announces a tribute to five doctors who have each given fifty years of service to the town. Crampton is one of them. We all hope that having the spotlight on his years of service will prop up his popularity and perhaps soften the need to punish him.

But on the day of the dinner, the *Patriot News* announces that the evening's keynote speaker has been changed and will now be Huette Dowling. His topic: What happens when in the everyday practice of medicine doctors find themselves at odds with the law.

We are all astonished at the way Dowling has persuaded the scheduled keynote speaker, Dr. William K. McBride, to step aside and snagged the spot for himself. Dowling is not a doctor, not even a member of the Dauphin County Medical Society. But he is on the board of directors of the Goodwill Industries, the Boys Club of Harrisburg, the Boy Scouts of America, and the Knights of Columbus, and most importantly, he is also on the advisory board of the Harrisburg and Polyclinic Hospitals. Apparently he has called many governing members of the medical society's board personally to request permission to deliver the keynote speech at the dinner. I don't know if he calls Paul Kunkel, but there are few men in any town who would have the courage to stand in the way of a district attorney this overzealous.

On the day of the dinner, Crampton appears stalwart, but Frances says he spent most of the day locked in his office, and for courage he puts away half a fifth of bourbon before shuffling off to join the banquet. Dowling's speech turns out to be about doctors getting sued and how medical practitioners can navigate the legal system—

not about doctors who engage in criminal acts. Did he have a change of heart or did Paul Kunkel persuade him to change his speech at the last minute? We wonder.

Crampton and four other doctors are presented with plaques. In his brief turn at the podium, Crampton recalls that in his life he's been lucky enough to have shaken the hands of two presidents. "The first occasion, with Teddy Roosevelt, took place near the beginning of my medical career, when Roosevelt came through Harrisburg in nineteen-oh-six. I admired Roosevelt because not long before, he'd invited Booker Washington to dine at the White House. The second president whose hand has met mine is our current one, Dwight D. Eisenhower. Our country's president is popular throughout our great state of Pennsylvania because his people came from Elizabethville. They know us and we know them. Spending his leisure time on his farm in Gettysburg, just thirty minutes from here, he is a good friend to our city. I'm greatly honored to still be in service to the community under his watch and I thank the Medical Society of Dauphin County for recognizing me."

His words are met with polite applause.

8

Pusan, South Korea
May 31, 1953

Dear Mom and Dewey,

Arrived here safely aboard the USS General Breckenridge *after many days at sea. First I was in Yong-Dong Po, now I'm back here in Pusan.*

With the war on, the situation is very tense, but a lot has changed for the better since I was here in '48. The people seem to have more old vehicles and they don't look as hungry. They are geniuses at making things out of nothing. On a street corner some guy was building a bus. He had an old motor and was building the frame and steering column from a salvaged metal drum. I recently saw a worn-out tire on a truck that must have had a hole in it. To repair it they put a bolt in the hole and tightened it against two washers and a nut. In the villages they take the ends off of tin beer cans, flatten them out, and make shingles for the roof.

Going down the road, we pass bags of rice in the lane next to us. In the rice paddies nothing seems to have changed. The women do the planting and the men who aren't off fighting stand with the oxen and watch them. At times you'll see water running along the street—sewer water—and women will be out washing their clothes in it. They still do all their fertilizing with human waste and as you can imagine it makes the air unpleasant. The waste gets deposited in what are called honey-wells and these are drawn from and spread on the fields. You see the farmers—men and women—with a wood frame strapped to their backs and they attach a barrel to that filled with waste. They load the barrel as full as possible, as with anything they carry—firewood, etc. The muscles on their legs are like balls of iron. They grow the largest carrots, strawberries, turnips, melons of all kinds, but we get daily warnings not to touch any of them because of worms and dysentery.

There is a culvert where you drive into the railhead and here the orphans come to bum clothes or rags. One kid has his leg cut off below the knee, and he uses a tree branch as a crutch. After a while you get to know them, and they you, although un-like last time, we are under orders not to fraternize.

Again, Mom, I'm sorry to burden you, but if there's any way you could round up more clothes and send them, the people here would greatly appreciate it. The women especially are moving away from their traditional way of dressing and adopting our western ways. This can only help our cause.

I have to close now because we have a 9:00 curfew and I have to report to my barracks. Please give my best to Gram, Hazel, and Myrtle. Talk is they may send us down to a place called Tong Nae and I'll write to you from there. Meanwhile if you want to write me please use the APO box I left you.

Love, Sam

I finish this letter and can't believe he's written all this to me and not Myrtle. I can't believe my eyes. At the bottom, he's actually signed it with "Love." How could something so small feel like such a blessing?

9

We do as many procedures as possible. There is no pleasure in our work and I pity the girls who aren't getting to see Crampton in his prime. But a girl is staying here whose sister went to see Sherwood Raymond in Newark. He charged her a thousand dollars for an abortion and treated her like dirt. I hear Dr. Levine in New York lectures the girls that they should "marry the guy" before he agrees to do a needle scrape. So in comparison we shine.

Frances says Crampton eats little and goes through a quart of bourbon in two days. Since the IRS trouble he's short on cash and has had to let Daphne Monroe go. He leans on someone in the Capitol—someone with a past he wants to forget—and makes him find Daphne a clerical job. It's soon apparent that Frances can't handle the office alone anymore, so Daphne Monroe, grateful for her new job, agrees to return for a few hours in the evenings to help out with paperwork.

I stop by Mom's house to bring her a couple of boxes of strawberries and pick up some old clothes she collected for Korea. A colored man I hired to clip her hedges and pull the weeds up around the curb is there—it angers me to see Buckley lounging on the porch, the hired man at work only a few feet away, just like when we were kids—I'd hack the metal blade against the weeds and he'd loaf like the country squire.

"You go down to work in their neighborhood," he jokes, loud enough for the man to hear. "Now I guess they're coming up here to work in ours." His eyes glitter like fool's gold.

I'm angry and snap at Mom. "Get that son-of-a-b. off that porch while the hired man is here," I say.

Mom gets flustered. She's never stood up to Buck. But she knows I mean business and goes to call him in. He knows I'm behind it and curses up a storm. He drives his old mud-splattered truck off in a huff.

Once Buck is gone and things calm down, Myrtle pulls up in a new car. I read Sam's letter out loud to Mom and make sure Myrtle is in earshot, proud to show that my son writes me as well as her. Halfway through Myrtle bolts out and runs for the bathroom. "The thought of all that human waste growing food makes me have to upchuck," she says.

"Oh, stop making such a production," I call after her.

"Myrtle's always been delicate," Mom says.

Myrtle returns ten minutes later, but I've finished reading. "I'm just so glad Sam doesn't write stuff like that to me," she says.

I mail a second box of clothing to Sam. It's expensive but perhaps we can win the war by showing our kindness.

10

In July Dora invites me to an anniversary party for her cousin down in New Cumberland. "You have to come," she says. "I haven't seen you in ages." I wear an expensive new brown dress with an orange sash and when I walk into the room I find myself standing directly in front of a small, shriveled-up couple. They look familiar and we blink at each other like ghosts from the past. I suddenly recognize them—Mr. and Mrs. Wertz. How many years have passed since I arrived at their farm in New Cumberland to milk their cows? They're both so old and shrunken, I hardly know what to say.

It turns out Dora's cousin is married to Mr. Wertz's niece; we had no idea. After almost thirty years, I feel nothing except a certain freedom, and that makes me strangely happy to see them again. We talk about the old days on the farm and how hard life was. They are poor now and have moved to the county home to spend their final days. I ask about Penny. Sadly they tell me that five years ago Penny was caught in a rainstorm without a coat and came down with pneumonia. "The good Lord finally took her to heaven," Mrs. Wertz says.

When we say farewell, Mr. Wertz takes my hand and holds my forearm for emphasis. He looks away from my eyes and then the most astonishing thing happens. He begins to cry. I can't believe it. Is he crying over remembering what he and I did to her? Is he crying because he's sorry? Is he crying for Penny? Is he crying because time has passed and the old days are forgotten? For all of it? I'll always wonder.

11

A large picture of Crampton appears in the sports section. He and a young doctor named Don Freedman in their roles as Pennsylvania Athletic Commission physicians will conduct the examinations on two boxers, Freddie Beshore, a native of Harrisburg, and a black fighter named Art Henri, who comes from New York. The two will duke it out Thursday night at the Hershey Arena. As the pro bono medical examiner, Crampton has always made himself available to discuss boxing bouts, wrestling matches, stock car races, or any other sporting spectacle that has come to Harrisburg. His good will has paid off and probably explains why his photograph has so frequently been found on the sports page. Crampton's political friends may have turned their backs on him, but his friends in sports haven't.

Our relief at the positive story is short-lived, for the boxing commission orders a recheck of the fighters whom Crampton okayed. They bring in a third doctor who they say is "independent." They say this sort of thing happens all the time, but under the circumstances it is humiliating and implies that Crampton either acted irresponsibly or is incompetent. Having his medical skill and authority questioned is more than he can stand. For the first time, even in public he drops his bluster and looks angry and defeated.

"Isn't there anything you can do, Mrs. Krone?" Frances asks me. Her voice is raspy and pleading. She knows I have no influence over anything, and she is only asking me because she doesn't know what else to do. "I wish there was," I say.

12

In October the evening paper announces that Crampton is being removed from his post as deputy secretary of health and that he's taking on a full-time job as supervisor of public health education. Lest people think it's a promotion, the paper says his salary will be cut from $6,654 to $4,500. To rub it in, the health secretary makes a public statement implying there are questions about his time card. "Dr. Crampton will now be expected to put in thirty-seven and a half hours a week like everyone else."

If you lie down with dogs you get fleas. But in politics you've got to lie down with men who are worse than dogs, and you come away with worse than fleas. I've spent my whole life anxiously scrutinizing and enduring illegitimate forms of power—to use Mrs. Pierce's term. I always look to see who has that power, for I know it is they who keep people separated. I'm finally learning.

The mood at the office is glum. Crampton no longer jokes or has any bounce in his step. The girls who come for procedures grow more wide-eyed and seem younger than they once did. Or is it because we are so much older? There is little I can do to comfort them. It is a sad business.

· 13 ·

October 22, 1953
Pusan, South Korea

Dear Mom and Dewey,

I've just come back from patrol duty and am bone tired. Yesterday we were assigned a half-ton truck and drove through miles of rice paddies. There are a lot more oxen now than five years ago.

The orphan who likes me, the one missing his leg, calls me Big Poppy. We give him C rations for helping with the chores and he tries to peddle homemade whiskey, blended as fine as any from Kentucky, with labels that the kids paint by hand. We mostly keep our distance for we aren't supposed to fraternize with any locals.

I'm sending this letter with my buddy Doogy, who is going back to the States. He said he'd mail it from San Francisco and we can avoid the censors that way. Mom, thank you for sending the clothes. They were greatly appreciated.

Love, Sam

14

Three weeks following his demotion, on November 7, 1953, while rushing to keep up with his schedule, Dr. Crampton suffers a heart attack. The evening paper reports Crampton's illness on the sports page. "It's like watching an old lion get destroyed," Frances says, weeping.

They say he'll be confined to bed for three to six weeks but that he's unusually agile for a man his age. It also says he'll miss his first football game in thirty-five years if William Penn plays Williamsport today. Frances says the story pleases him and he keeps the clipping by his hospital bed.

I don't visit the hospital. I tell Frances that in nursing school we learned not to visit heart patients because it gives them excitement and fatigue. But the real reason I don't go is that I don't want to witness his defeat. I imagine it as a dangerous thing, growing larger in his solar plexus, a grapefruit-sized knot that will tighten with bottled-up force until his heart explodes.

Five patients were with me when he was stricken, and not knowing what to do, I called Paul Kunkel. He said to bring the girls to the hospital and he would check them out. Luckily they were all fine.

15

It's strange to suddenly have so much time on my hands.

Ten days pass.

I catch up on my rest. In the morning I sit at the kitchen table and watch the birds. There is one particular holly bush that shakes under their weight.

On hearing the news about Crampton, his adopted brother Frederick Copeland arrives by airplane from California. Figuring that Fred's presence will be beneficial, I prepare a gallon jar of fruit salad and bring it to the hospital.

Dr. Crampton is asleep, so I sit in the day room with Fred. "Now, I hope you'll talk sense into Charlie," he says, "and not let him start up on the operations again." It turns out he knows all about our business. "As brothers, Charlie and I have few secrets," he says. "He started doing these things before the First World War. Back then there weren't many ways for colored doctors to make money—same as now. In practically every larger town I've ever visited there is someone like him offering service to women who know where to look. More often than not they are colored."

Fred reminisces about the days when he and Crampton played opposite ends on the Central High football team. "Classmates called us 'the chessmen.' One black. One white. Back then Charlie's charisma had these women chasing after him. He was wildly popular. And he always had the most extraordinary confidence.

"When we were in college, some weekends I'd leave New Haven and go down to visit him in Washington. He'd always know where to find the best crab boats, and we'd sit at dockside tables on empty packing crates banging boiled crab meat out with wooden mallets, while the thick-armed Negresses would hover over to serve him, clear up, and dump the broken shells into the Potomac.

"He also knew where to go for undiluted grain pressings, the fattest oyster po'boys, hair pomade that wouldn't go rancid, and tailors who would cut waistcoats for students at half the usual price. He also knew which brothels would take us in just before dawn, after the last of the senators, wholesale merchants, and Virginia gentlemen had been cleared."

I try to pretend I'm not shocked.

"My father, the colonel, came from a line of people that goes back to the *Mayflower*. But his experience of being 'bound out' to his uncle made him feel like Oliver Twist. As a result, he developed a lifelong compassion for anyone disenfranchised, particularly Negroes, and their point of view. In the years after the Civil War, Lucius became a reporter first in New York, then Chicago. He interviewed dozens of Negroes for a series of articles on Reconstruction.

"A special bond always existed between my father and little Charlie. As Charlie matured they'd fish together, and both were avid readers. Charlie, like Lucius, was always memorizing things. He has my father's way with words and also developed into a great speaker.

"In nineteen-oh-three, just as Charles and I were finishing college, Lucius took sick in Illinois. He was on a speaking tour and caught a chill and a fever. He died the very next day. Charlie and I met my father's body in Chicago. The funeral in Harrisburg was enormous, lines of carriages, huge floral tributes. Lucius was quite a celebrity here. His grave lies in the old cemetery up on Allison Hill. You know, until she died, Charlie always remembered to send my mother two dozen roses on her birthday. She'd fret all morning over their arrival, mutter to herself that he'd probably forgotten, saying that was the peril of raising colored children. Then when the flowers would finally arrive, her face would beam."

Two days later the hospital discharges Dr. Crampton. Recuperating at home strengthens him. Frances stays with him around the clock and says the phone won't stop ringing with women calling to find out how the doctor is doing and when he will resume procedures.

After another week Fred returns to California. Before he goes Frances pulls him aside: "Please talk sense to him, Fred. If he starts doing procedures again there will be nothing but trouble."

"Charlie has never been afraid of trouble," Fred says. "The last few months have been rough but his luck is about to change."

Crampton looks remarkably trim and fit in expensive robe and pajamas. We take lunch together and he says, "Once the holidays are over I'd like to get back to work." I nod.

The long rest has done him good. He attends a basketball game at William Penn, and when he walks into the gymnasium, the crowd rises to their feet and cheers. Tears roll down his face.

I keep thinking about what Fred said. But I've learned that Fred is a talker. Crampton's luck remains to be tested.

16

It is November of 1954, and when the police arrive to arrest me, Dr. Crampton's cautious voice lingers in my head. "If anyone ever questions you, size them up, but don't give them any answers." I follow the advice and speak as little as possible. I also remain lying down the entire time.

One of the cops has rifled my bureau and found a hidden stash of cash. "There's eight grand here. Enough to buy a house." They count the thirteen beds, two in the living room, two in the dining room, eight among the upstairs bedrooms, and a cot in the hallway. I wonder if they will notice the rubber sheets protecting the mattresses, but they're too dumb to look. "Why all the beds?"

"I have six stepchildren and a son of my own."

As if on cue, Sally enters the house. She's parked her car in the alley and comes in the back through the kitchen. She stops dead at the sight of the cops and knows at once that we are in some kind of trouble.

"Sally, can you drop by later?" I say. "We're in the middle of something."

Sally is shrewd. She knows a scrape when she sees it. "Of course," she says. "I just wanted to tell you I've left a casserole of macaroni and cheese on the back of the stove." Her exit is brisk—before they can think to question her—back out through the kitchen, the way she came in. I know as soon as she gets to the telephone she'll burn the wires calling her siblings with the gossip.

One policeman whips out a folding notebook. "How old are you?"

"What does that have to do with anything?" I say.

The other cop demands to inspect the cellar. Dewey leads him down and I thank God that there are no patients in the house. The day before six women were here recovering. I pray that Dewey has remembered to burn all the used Kotex in the furnace. I breathe deeply to try and stop the throbbing in my head. The men return up the stairs and I'm relieved to see they've found nothing.

"I don't understand this," I say. "Who has made such a charge?"

"I dunno," the smaller cop says, "but Huette Dowling's a Catholic and will try this case with everything he's got."

"Yeah, sister." The other one grins. "He aims to put you out of business."

"I'm not your sister," I snap. "And Dowling is a sap."

"He's the DA and wants you brought in."

I tell them about my back injury and bluff them by invoking the name of Harvey Taylor. They won't mess with him if they know what's good for them.

Once I invoke Taylor's name, the taller cop speaks softer and is more precise. He says there will be a hearing in a couple of days. He is nervous and trips over the doorsill as they leave, carrying the basins, syringes, and one box of Kotex, but leaving the cash, which lets me know I've won the round.

Dewey and I are leery of using the phone to call anyone. We sit and whisper to each other.

"It's a setup," he says. "Gotta be."

"Where the hell is our protection?"

He buttons his overcoat. "I'm going downtown to see what the buzz on the street is." I know for Dewey the buzz on the street can only be found in a barroom. "Keep your big mouth shut in case they tail you," I warn. "And if you get drunk don't bother coming home."

The door slams.

Alone in the empty house, I feel my toughness dissolve. I sit in the dark and nervously wait for what will happen next. I've been arrested. How will Mom react? Hazel will understand—anyone who's been a patient gets it—but Myrtle? She's so howlingly moral, and she will delight in any opportunity to belittle me. I've never before thought of myself as especially bad, but now, for the rest of my life, I'll be known as someone who ended up on the wrong side of the law.

How did I allow this to happen?

Sally calls in the evening. I tell her that she shouldn't speak too openly over the telephone. She understands that there might be people listening in. I thank her for the macaroni and cheese and say how much I appreciate not having to cook supper. I do not say that because of nerves I've eaten almost the entire casserole myself.

After midnight Dewey returns home fairly sober and with news. Apparently Dr. Crampton was arrested and taken out of his house in full sight of a dozen colored boys who flocked down from the Forster Street YMCA. They stood on the curb and watched him be escorted in handcuffs to the police car. I shudder at the thought. He's a father figure to so many of them. There are so few Negro leaders. I wonder how the Y will manage to stay open.

I thank God that I've outfoxed the police, but in the morning they return. "Orders are to bring you downtown," the short one says. "Spine or no spine, Dowling is insisting."

· 17 ·

We enter the courthouse through the basement and stop at a dingy office for fingerprints and photographs to be taken. The elevator brings us upstairs to a waiting room outside the chamber where the charges will be entered.

Dr. Crampton's gaze meets mine as I enter, but we do not acknowledge each other. The pupils of his bloodshot eyes are like two black peppercorns waiting to be cracked.

The room is lined with pale tables and shaded lights that give a green tint to the cigar-smoky plaster ceiling. I take a seat on the far side of the room. There we sit on opposite shores and wait. Every few minutes the windows rattle in their frames from the wind blowing off the river.

The thought of Dr. Crampton sitting dignified and erect on a wooden bench overnight is upsetting. He needs a shave. Using my peripheral vision I study him as though I'm looking at a stranger. The lines of dark purple ink have bled from his fingertips to the top of his hands. A smudge mars his crisp white shirtcuff, and that tiny bit of untidiness seems sadder to me than anything else.

A bald-headed bailiff enters with a stack of files. "Hey, Doc. I heard you were here and I wanted to wish you well," he says.

"Thank you." Dr. Crampton gives a tired nod.

The bailiff lingers a moment. "You know my brother used to be on the William Penn track team. His name is Will Cahill."

"A fine sprinter," Dr. Crampton says and offers a tired smile. "He could run."

"You remember him? That's more than twenty years."

"Of course," Dr. Crampton says. "Will was one skinny fellow."

"Well, he's big as a moose now and don't run that way no more. Works at the mattress factory down in Lemoyne. He must weigh two fifty, at least."

"Well, tell him I said hello."

"Oh, I will. He'll be tickled you remember." The bailiff begins to leave and then pauses in the doorway. "Doc, I hope you come through this okay."

Dr. Crampton nods.

Other faces appear in the doorway from time to time. They've all heard the old boy has been brought in and want to see for themselves.

After a while another clerk comes through, taking a break from her department, moving slowly like an old cat, patent leather belt slack around her waist, a steno pad tucked beneath her arm. A cigarette flicks to the corner of her mouth as she lights and leans against the radiator. She may have been a patient at one time. I realize over the past few years that all women have begun to seem like patients.

Then the doors swing open and Carl B. Shelley strides through, unbuttoning his tweed jacket to reveal a spicy necktie. He's shorter and rounder than I remember, and he's lost much of his hair. He greets Crampton and they whisper for a few moments. Then Shelley comes over and introduces himself. "I'll be handling your case," he says.

"I hope we're in good hands," I say.

"I remember you," Shelley says, breaking into a smile, pleased to show his excellent memory. "You're married to that fellow who was drunk in the bar downtown."

"Don't remind me," I say, my cheeks turning red. It's true, Dewey spoke ill of Shelley because of the publicity he garnered raiding bars with a sledgehammer.

"That day your husband told everyone in the bar that they shouldn't vote for that son of a bitch Carl Shelley, not knowing I was sitting right there beside him." I wince and endure it. "I hope you won't hold that against me," I say. "Fiddlesticks!" Shelley says and removes his spectacles and wipes his eyes. "It was hilarious! That's one of my best stories."

Then he returns to Crampton's side of the room and they go off into the far corner and whisper until one of the court officers tells us it's time to see the judge. I gather my things and they both wait to let me pass through the doorway first. Inside the chamber, huge murals of battle scenes do combat over our heads, and above the judge's bench the blindfolded figure of justice is painted.

Huette Dowling is not present. A young man from the DA's office represents him and stands by the opposing table. At first glance he appears natty and well groomed, but his black leather oxfords are scuffed, the heels worn uneven from poor posture. The shoes make him seem juvenile and careless, the type of fellow who puts a yo-yo in his breast pocket.

We stay standing until the judge gathers his robes at the knee and climbs the platform to his chair.

"How's the football team doing, Doc?" he asks, settling into his chair and opening a file on his desk.

"Better than I am, at the moment," Crampton replies.

"We'll see to that in a moment. Hello, Carl." Shelley nods but remains silent as the judge begins to study the documents.

He asks the young man from the DA's office to explain the charges. In a thin, nasal voice he says the people of the commonwealth are bringing charges alleging that on the second of August, Dr. Crampton with my assistance performed an illegal abortion.

The final word echoes in the empty courtroom. Hearing it spoken so plainly in public is a shock.

When it's our turn, Shelley rises and speaks directly to the judge. "Dr. Crampton is one of Harrisburg's leading citizens," he says. "A great man. A pillar of the community. Such charges can ruin an innocent man's life. I ask that the word *abortion* be stricken from the record." I see that it's not just his diminutive height but also his direct manner and cocky courtroom style that have earned him the nickname "the bantam rooster."

The judge thinks for a moment then orders the word struck from the record. "To ease the damage from those newspaper boys, we'll keep using the charge 'illegal surgery.' "

My stomach drops at the thought that we'll be in the newspaper. In a flash I imagine everyone I know—Mom, Myrtle, Dora, Charles Dennis, Dewey's children—reading of my arrest in the paper.

"Mrs. Krone, you are named codefendant with Dr. Crampton. How do you plead?"

"Not guilty," I say, following Crampton's lead and trying to sound earnest.

The judge announces that a third party by the name of Emanuel Franzone is also being charged and that his plea of not guilty has been registered in Luzerne County but is being accepted here. All of the charges are being brought by a woman named Violet Hauze. Crampton and I glance at each other and he gives the slightest shrug. I raise my eyebrows to indicate the name is unrecognizable. A hearing gets scheduled for the twenty-ninth of November. Bail is set for each of us, including the mysterious Mr. Franzone, at a thousand dollars.

Shelley advises us not to put up cash or our own property so that we don't look too prosperous and to show that we have trusted friends. A longtime buddy of Dewey's, who owns the Emerald Street Bar and Grill just around the corner from our house, agrees to sign for us. Then we're told state law prohibits liquor establishments from putting up bail money. In a quandary I use the phone booth in the lobby to call Hazel and ask for her help.

"You gave us the down payment," she says. "Without you we wouldn't even have a house. I'll call the bank holding our mortgage right away."

A couple more hours pass. Crampton's bail is put up by his closest friend, C. Sylvester Jackson, who arrives in tandem with Hazel and Joe. She hugs and kisses me and for the first time I fight to keep back the emotion pulling at my throat. Once the bank papers are entered into the record and everything is signed and delivered, we are free to go. Joe needs to return to work and Hazel leaves to drop him off. "I'll call you later," she says.

I follow Crampton out across the marble lobby of the courthouse. "The whole thing hangs on some girl from the coal regions," he whispers. "She's had a lover's quarrel with this guy Franzone. Do you recall the name Violet Hauze?" I shake my head. "When Shelley was DA he'd make this kind of horseshit disappear. But Dowling—that Catholic jackass plans to give us a ride."

A sportswriter named Walt Tremain approaches. "Just heard the news, Doc. Got anything I can quote?"

"Say these allegations have fallen on my head like a ton of bricks. Go write that."

"That's good. Anything else?"

"I'm innocent of all charges."

"You're getting a raw deal here, Doc. A raw deal. Anything off the record?"

Crampton lights a cigar. "That's how people in this town show their gratitude." He turns and exits through the revolving door.

Outside, the square white columns of the Dauphin County Courthouse line up on either side of him. Crampton spies Togans waiting at the curb with the Lincoln. Togans comes up the steps and takes Dr. Crampton's arm, leading him across the wet slate, which despite a sprinkling of salt is already beginning to freeze. The two men navigate the dark plaza together, one foot in front of the other. They do not offer me a ride or even ask if I have one. Though there is no call for it—as I was the one who sat apart from Crampton in the courthouse—my feelings are still hurt. Have I too already outlived my usefulness? I walk around to the front of the building and find Dewey. We go home and wait for the evening paper.

·   **18**   ·

The Harrisburg Patriot
November 14, 1954

Dr. C. Crampton, 75, a former deputy State Health Department secretary, was free under $1,000 bail last night on a charge of performing an illegal operation on Aug. 2.

"These allegations are like a pile of bricks falling on my head," said Dr. Crampton, who has practiced medicine in Capitol City for 48 years. "Further," he added, "I'm innocent of all charges." When contacted last night at his home Dr. Crampton said he has retained as his counsel Carl B. Shelley, former Dauphin County District Attorney.

Dist. Atty. Huette F. Dowling yesterday announced the arrest of Dr. Crampton, together with an uptown housewife and the owner of a Morrisville dental laboratory. All charged with the same offense the others are.

Mrs. Verna Krone of Third Street near Emerald, and Emanuel Joseph Franzone, 38, of Morrisville.

Dowling said the operation was allegedly performed Aug. 2 in the Doctor's office at 600 Forster Street, and that the patient was Miss Violet Hauze, 27 of Morrisville, employed by Franzone as a dental technician.

Both Dr. Crampton and Mrs. Krone denied the charges after Miss Hauze identified them to State Police. Miss Hauze was arrested by Luzerne County authorities on a charge of conspiracy to secure an illegal operation. She is free under $1,000 bail for appearance before the January Grand Jury.

The district attorney said Dist. Atty. Louis Feldman of Luzerne County told him in October Miss Hauze had given him a signed statement concerning the operation.

After the surgery, the woman said she was taken by Mrs. Krone, a practical nurse, to

Mrs. Krone's apartment on N. 3rd St., the
district attorney said. Two days later Miss
Hauze was returned to Crampton's office and
then to Morrisville by Franzone, Dowling said.
The operation cost $200, he said.

Mrs. Krone was also released on $1,000 bail
yesterday. Franzone was served with an
information yesterday in Morrisville. The
hearings are scheduled for Nov. 29 in Alderman
Joseph Demma's office.

Dr. Crampton, a Capitol City native, is
vice chairman of the Dauphin County Republican
Organization and is on leave without pay as a
public health educator. He is a member of the
board of directors at the Forster St. YMCA and
has been medical trainer for some 20 years at
William Penn High School. He is a former
president of the State Dental, Medical and
Pharmaceutical Association.

19

It pleases me to see that by my refusing to answer the cop's question about age, mine is the only one that does not appear in the newspaper. I'm also pleased to see Crampton's quote. But I do not appreciate being referred to as an uptown housewife. They should have said I was a licensed practical nurse.

The phone rings nonstop as news of our arrest travels in connecting patterns like flat ice crystals across a window pane. The conversations are brief and stilted, with warnings to be careful about what gets spoken, as the phone lines may not be private. That surprises everyone. I warn Dewey as well, saying, "I'm not going to jail because some drunk couldn't keep his big mouth shut."

The days pass. I begin to grind my teeth at night. I awake in the mornings with a splitting headache. The time on my hands allows me to dwell on all the stories I've heard over the years. In my memory I see a parade of faces; all the women we treated over the years march there.

I always imagined trouble would come from a patient with complications, a hemorrhage or a death. But no. We are being charged by a woman with no complications. She's alive because we did a good job. I wonder if she knows how many butchers are out there.

A meeting with Carl Shelley is scheduled for Friday evening. On the phone his secretary says Happy Thanksgiving before hanging up. Is she joking? At night my head thrashes on the pillow. In the morning Mom calls. "I'm eating Thanksgiving dinner with Hazel and Joe. You and Dewey are invited." I decline. She does not mention the arrest. For once I'm glad that she avoids the personal.

The holiday creeps in like a fog bank. Dewey goes to Fisherville to drink and I don't care. A wild pheasant is waiting in the freezer and I defrost it and roast it with some yams. I sit at the table alone and rest my head on my arms. I'm filled with self-pity. Have yourself a merry little Thanksgiving. I detest myself for these maudlin feelings. I should keep busy, write down what I remember about the case.

Dewey returns home fairly sober and sits down to eat his supper while I, nervous and jumpy, scrape dishes and put leftovers away. Hazel calls toward bedtime with bland talk that would put any wiretapper to sleep—turkey stuffing, pumpkin pie, and which of her boys liked which dish. A neighbor's son was in a school play. He wanted to play an Indian like Squanto and was disappointed when they cast him as Miles Standish. She sewed him a costume with a rope belt. Joe took the boys to the Turkey Day game. She says the coaching and medical staff, as well as all the members of the team, were present. I know that's her foxy, coded way of telling me that Crampton was there. I wonder if Carl Shelley told him to appear at the game so that he would foster the illusion of being unflappable. It's a relief to have Shelley on our side.

On Friday I set my hair and look for something to wear to the meeting. There are dozens of cotton day dresses here at the farm but nothing suitable for town. Toward evening we set out for Harrisburg. At my house on Third Street I scan my wardrobe. I select a charcoal gray suit and a mink coat. We exit through the back door. We are locking up when the nosy woman from next door sticks her head out. "How are your patience holding out?" she calls over the fence, raising her painted eyebrows like a vaudeville vamp. She emphasizes the word *patience* so that it has double meaning. Her smug grin lets me know she's seen the paper.

"Couldn't be better, thank you," I say. I quickly cross the alleyway where Dewey has the car door open and waiting.

Traffic flows smoothly on account of the holiday, and we're downtown in record time. Since the arrest Dewey has been trying to be supportive, but he's jumpy, gets on my nerves. I want nothing from him and he knows it.

Above the town square, the third floor of the *Patriot* building is lit up in preparation for tomorrow's news. Just a few days ago, in that same room, my own name was being typeset.

A few doors down, the marquee of the Senate Theater announces that last year's smash *White Christmas* will be returning—maybe I'll have time to see it this year—and around the corner, the passing of Thanksgiving is marked by the Christmas decorations that have sprung up in the shop windows. Since the war ended, the holidays arrive earlier every year. On Market Street, outside Pomeroy's Department Store, a half-dozen cars float blue exhaust up into the streetlights as they double-park and idle.

"The merchants' association won't let them be ticketed anymore," Dewey says.

"They have to let them be," I reply. "There's nowhere to park."
For the thousandth time we lament how tearing out the trolleys has
only made traffic worse. "A lot of people don't shop downtown anymore," I say. "They go to Klein Village or Colonial Park."

We drive around the Capitol, look in the windows of Mary
Sachs and Worth's, then at last it's time to head over to Shelley's office. He's located in a big townhouse facing the river. Like everything else in Harrisburg, even Front Street looks to be in decline.
Many of the grand houses are being sold and converted to commer-
cial use; the Capitol extension project has changed their zoning.

A blustery wind hurries me up the walk and I enter through a
heavy leaded-glass door. "We're in the back office, Verna." I follow
Shelley's voice down a black-and-white-checked marble hallway to a
wide room with walnut paneling. He comes around an enormous
carved desk, shakes my hand, then tucks his thumbs into his suspenders like a middle-aged cherub.

Dr. Crampton rises from a wing chair by the fireplace. He gives
me a peck on the cheek. I am shocked at how haggard he looks. His
face has lost much of its definition. Choked by sudden emotion,
neither one of us can speak. For the first time in fifteen years we are
free from our bond of work.

Shelley takes my coat. "Have a spot of Irish," he says.

Crampton says he hasn't touched alcohol since his heart attack.
"Nonsense," Shelley says, "whiskey's the best thing for your heart."
He fetches three water glasses and pours an inch for each of us.

We toast "to happiness" and sip. The wall is lined with old photos: young Shelley in France wearing leggings and a flat helmet,
later standing on the steps of the old courthouse in a straw boater.
There are also some more recent photos; one shows him shaking
hands with Richard Nixon at the State Potato Growers banquet.
"Every Republican in Pennsylvania shook hands with Nixon that
day," Shelley says, following my gaze. "It was dogwork getting him
on Eisenhower's ticket and he was grateful. He knew it was Harvey

Taylor that put him over and he thanked us in a speech broadcast over national radio."

We nod and sip our drinks.

"I don't understand how we were arrested," I say. "Isn't Taylor supposed to protect us?"

"It's all pretty dumb," Shelley says. "But what I've been able to find out is that this girl Violet is playing smoochie-pie with this guy Franzone. He knocks her up. He gets her out of trouble. All is well. A few weeks later there's a lover's quarrel. She decides he's gonna pay. She tells the police he forced her to get herself fixed. Bingo. The problem here is Huette Dowling. When I was DA I never put that kind of chow mein on the witness stand. But Dowling's a Catholic. He's anti-Taylor and he's also got it in for the two of you. He knows how many women come to town. He also knows Crampton brings the Negro vote that keeps Taylor in office. The judge is on our side. They've struck the word *abortion* from the court documents, which is a big deal. The cops even had to retype the arrest papers; the newspapers have to print it that way too or it's libel. Now it's important, Verna, that you not make statements of any kind."

"Don't worry," Crampton says. "She knows how to keep her mouth shut."

He and I agree that it is a tremendous piece of luck that our arrests took place at a time when there were no patients in the office or at my house. A day earlier the women recovering there would have all gone to jail with us. There was a case like that in Kansas a few years back.

"I wouldn't be surprised if Dowling planned it this way," Shelley says. "They don't want to be arresting aborted women. What if one of them dies in custody, or if one of them turns out to be someone they know?"

"I've done some checking up in Hazelton," Shelley continues. "While he's been fooling around with Hauze, that dog Franzone also has a wife and children at home. That won't play well on the witness stand."

I begin to relax as the whiskey takes effect. Shelley tells Crampton that it is imperative that he mend his relationship with Harvey Taylor. Crampton shouts, "I've got a knife the length of Forster Street stuck between my shoulder blades. They didn't tear down a white neighborhood to build the Harvey Taylor Bridge." Then he starts to snarl. "I've done favors for every rat bastard from the police chief on down. Where's my protection?"

"Dowling's a pious Catholic," Shelley says. "He'd throw jaywalkers in jail if he could."

"So where's our Catholic contingent?" Crampton's eyes burn with anger. "The Knights of Columbus? The Italians? The Rotary? I've helped more Catholic women in my life than Dowling has ever met."

"You're going to get off," Shelley says. "There is no way to make these charges stick. But we have to follow due process. The machine is behind you, but you've got to patch things up with Taylor."

It's been a long time since Crampton has had to openly ask for personal help. His life has been methodically planned to collect favors, not beg them. "There's barely a colored man in this town who doesn't blame me for the destruction of downtown. They want to know how come whenever the state expands the capital, it always demolishes colored neighborhoods. They did the same thing after World War One." What Crampton says is true.

"You can't be arrogant here," Shelley says.

"They'll all blame me."

"You can't ignore Taylor. We need him as a character witness."

"Did I ignore him when I fixed his 'cousin'?" Crampton snaps. "Or all the others? No one has done more for Taylor and the community than me."

The conversation ends. Crampton sits dejected. We finish our drinks. "We'll have more of these meetings, Mrs. K. This is just preliminary for us to meet and touch base." The visit comes to an end and it surprises me how little we have actually accomplished. In a moment I'm heading back down the walkway to the car.

"You smell like whiskey," Dewey says as I settle into the passenger seat.

"Shoe's on the other foot," I say quietly. Dewey heads the car back uptown in the direction of the farm. Outside only a few people brave the icy sidewalks. Inside the yellow-lit houses families are at dinner. I wonder what it must be like to be so normal. I think of Sam and wonder what he would make of all this. Halfway to Halifax we stop for a roast beef supper at the Triangle Inn. The night seems endless. I miss my job and my sense of purpose. The meeting has left me realizing that the destruction of our work and livelihood is permanent.

20

A few days later I come down from the farm to take Mom to her dentist in New Cumberland. Thank goodness, a mission—I'm still a nurse after all. Later on, at a luncheonette near Camp Hill, we're almost finished eating grilled cheese sandwiches when a face from the past enters the diner. It's been several years since I last saw Norm Trexler; he looks almost the same. A blowsy blonde accompanies him and they take stools at the counter. Mom and I finish and pay our check and as we make our way to the door he looks up and sees me. "Hey! Hey!" he hollers. "Look who's here. I've been reading about you in the papers."

I smile and nod my head. He greets Mom, shakes her hand, and then turns his attention back to me. "I never thought I'd see you in the soup." I keep my face blank and Mom follows me toward the door. "Aren't you going to say hello?" he calls after me. We keep walking. "Well, I can see you haven't changed." His voice rises. "Maybe this mess will straighten you out!"

Mom steps back, turns, and waves her pocketbook at Norm. "Don't you speak to her that way," she says. "No wonder she didn't want to be with you. Now just keep your nose out of our business." She turns again and follows me out the door.

I am flabbergasted. It is the first time I can ever remember my mother defending me, and she refers to my troubles as "our" business. It shocks me beyond words.

· **21** ·

Shelley has lined up thirty-eight character witnesses for our trial. Harvey Taylor won't come, but he's made sure other Republicans will be there. I don't know if Crampton patched things up with him or not. What is important to me is that Shelley has agreed that I won't be called to the witness stand.

While we wait for the trial to begin, time weighs heavy on me. Sometimes I feel relieved not to do the procedures anymore. It's a luxury not to have to worry about lights at night, a knock at the door, or who might bleed to death. But the trial has a new kind of worry, and though I'm free of making beds, sterilizing syringes, or unclogging toilets, I'm still awake in the middle of the night worrying about what is to come.

Out of concern for impartiality, Dowling requests a judge be sent from outside the county. He cites the personal remarks about the sports teams made when Crampton and I had our bail set. As a result, a judge by the name of Snyder is coming from Bedford County.

In the evening Dewey tells me Joseph Randall is on the radio. He's being interviewed for community reaction to the trial. He says, "Public office and tenure do not entitle trusted leaders to break the law." I think about Crampton. He's sure to be upset. Randall is becoming the new leader.

22

The trial is beginning and I can't keep food down. At the court-house Frances pulls me aside, dying to tell me something. "I set a full breakfast in front of him and he left his plate untouched. Then, when he thought I wasn't looking, he went to the cupboard and poured whiskey in his cup. I helped him on with his coat and gave him a handful of peppermints. And he was about to walk through the side door where Togans had the Lincoln waiting, when the phone rang. It was the wife of his brother Frederick Copeland call-ing to say that last night Fred was rushed to the hospital with chest pains and was dead by the time the ambulance reached the door. Fred's wife feels just awful calling with such news on the first day of the trial, but she didn't want the old man to hear about it from someone else."

Frances continues, "He didn't react. He just thanked her, put the phone down on the stand, and turned to go to the car. It was like watching a zombie or a robot. Do you think it's a bad omen, Mrs. K.?"

"It's a coincidence," I say, refusing to be spooked. "Not an omen or a sign." But inside I feel shaken and undone.

Crampton wears a gray flannel suit and sits dull and stiff at the defense table while Dowling turns down eight potential jurors and Shelley says no to seven. One is dismissed by the judge. By the end they've gone through twenty-eight people before they have twelve they like—seven men and five women. We're exhausted from listen-ing to all of it, and it's late in the day. We can't believe it when the judge orders Dowling and Shelley to make their opening remarks. We want to go home, but it's clear that Judge Snyder plans to get back to Bedford County without delay.

People crowd the courtroom. Hazel sits near the back, while Dewey and Dora flank me on either side. For the first time I see

Franzone; he looks seedy. Dowling tells the jury that Franzone paid a hundred dollars when he made the appointment and a second hundred when he brought Violet in. I'm sure Violet is also present but somehow I haven't yet spotted her. It's almost seven o'clock when the court is finally adjourned for the day.

In the morning the paper carries news of the trial on the front page, and our names are printed yet again. For a second day I can't keep my breakfast down.

The next day begins with Dowling objecting to the number of well-wishers who lean over the rail to pat Crampton's shoulder or shake his hand—mostly boosters or professional men who've played on the sports teams at one time or another. Judge Snyder shoots Dowling down and says they are harmless and don't seem to be interrupting the trial in any way.

When they call Violet Hauze to the stand, she wears a plain beige suit and her hair is neatly combed. Her face seems familiar but I really can't remember her. When she talks, her voice is unpolished and has a gruff quality characteristic of the coal regions. She tells how she is a divorcée who earned twenty dollars a week working in the dental lab with Franzone. Shelley gets her to admit that their sexual acts took place on a couch in the office. "How acrobatic" is his understated reply. "Certainly not what you'd expect to see in a dental lab."

Dowling objects.

Violet Hauze continues and gives a fairly accurate story of her trip to Harrisburg. She is the first one to use the word *abortion*. The crowd rustles. Shelley asks her if she can remember the house she stayed in while she recovered. She can't. It was dark. Then he asks if the nurse who tended her is in the courtroom. She gazes out at us and my heart skips a beat. "No," she says, failing to spot me. I'm wearing a black velvet hat and a loden coat with a red fox collar, and she probably doesn't recognize me out of my white uniform.

At recess we huddle in a private office Shelley has procured. "She's the kind of girl who chews gum while she's getting it," he says.

After the break Franzone takes the stand. Though it isn't noon yet, he already has a five-o'clock shadow and his overall appearance is one of darkness. A trained dental technician, he makes false teeth and hired Hauze to work as his secretary. He admits to being married with three children at the time he began a sexual relationship with her, and he relates how when Violet became ill, he brought her to several doctors and together they learned she was pregnant. "So many examinations," Shelley notes with skepticism. "Just to learn she was with child?"

On the second of August, Franzone says, he brought Hauze to Harrisburg to see Dr. Crampton. "I heard he did abortions from a fellow at the American Legion," he says. He also shows a parking ticket issued that day and Shelley notes it was only just paid last week. "I guess one doesn't want to look like a scofflaw when one is going to trial." Shelley chuckles. Dowling objects.

In late September, Franzone says, he broke up with Violet Hauze. She blackmailed him, threatened to tell his wife if he didn't give her money, and though he tried to appease her, bought her some jewelry, she was bitter and felt used. She came to his house; they fought on the front porch and in the street. As a result, Mrs. Franzone learned of their relationship. With no other weapon, Violet Hauze went to the police and told them she was forced to have an illegal abortion.

Next comes a whole slew of questions about the procedure itself. Franzone lies and says he stayed in the room during the procedure—a total inaccuracy. No outsider was ever allowed to remain in the examination room. When Shelley cross-examines Franzone, he asks for details about equipment used during the procedure, and Franzone vaguely describes what he saw. "Your answers seem to focus more on Miss Hauze's anatomy than on any actual medical procedure," Shelley says dryly.

When Franzone finally leaves the stand, another recess is called. Hazel waits in line at the refreshment stand to buy me a paper cup of coffee. "Those people are nothing but trash," she says.

When we return to the courtroom, Brigadier General J. Calvin Frank is sworn in. A state legislator, "Hap" Frank, as he is commonly known, is scheduled to leave town on a business trip and thus is being permitted to offer his character testimony ahead of all others. He wears a military uniform and is quite convincing when he says Dr. Crampton is one of the most dedicated medical men he's ever met. He cites Crampton's tireless work on behalf of athletes around the city, particularly the sports teams of William Penn High School and those at Harrisburg Tech before that. He tells how Crampton built the teams, helped boys get into and through college, and then put any number of them into business. "He worked like a dog to help me become a state legislator," he adds.

Dowling asks Frank if he has any idea where the money that Dr. Crampton was spreading like manure came from. "Yes, I do," Frank says. "It came from his own pocket." That gets a laugh from the spectators.

"And do you know how the money got into his pocket?" Dowling persists.

"Yes," Frank replies. "He earned it." More laughs.

The questions continue, but Frank is wily and at ease. And when he finally leaves the witness box he makes a show of crossing over to Crampton and shaking his hand. "Thank you for all you've done," he says loudly.

Dowling shouts an objection. The judge sustains it.

In the evening Joseph Randall is on the radio again. He doesn't mention Crampton by name but says, "The days of the old-fashioned political boss are over. Our city needs representation beyond the power of one man."

The next day in the courthouse hallway, Frances and I huddle and dissect the speech. I've never seen her so angry. "Is Joseph Randall going to take a dozen colored boys down to Doutrich's and buy them suits for their graduation? Will he put up money to keep the doors of the Y open?" We agree he won't.

The toll on Crampton is tremendous. It's painful for him to see the Negroes divide into two camps—the group loyal to him, and the voters Randall is courting, who are younger, impatient, downright disgusted with the slow pace of change. Dewey says there's a third category too, those that don't give a damn except to sell their votes to the highest bidder.

The trial continues and Shelley begins to call the other character witnesses for Dr. Crampton, including the sheriff, the city school superintendent, several police detectives, the director of the Central YMCA, doctors, teachers, coaches, ministers, politicians, and Franklin Moore, a personal friend of Crampton's and my old boss from the Penn-Harris Hotel. Together their testimonies create an impressive portrait of Dr. Crampton and his lifelong contributions to the city. Dr. Paul Kunkel, our friend from the hospital, also takes the stand. I admire that, particularly since he has helped us out of many a medical emergency. Another hospital administrator, Dr. Harvey Smith, also appears. It's clear the medical men see Crampton as a role model for community service.

The trial enters its fifth day. We are restless. Dr. Fritchey from the Polyclinic Hospital spends the entire morning going over charts to explain how eggs are fertilized. Then, just before lunch recess, a man we've never seen before causes a ruckus. He stands up at the back of the room and shouts that Crampton is guilty of killing and that everyone in town knows it. The tipstaff moves quickly to eject the man, and as he is being hustled out, he mutters some other stuff that I can't make out. Hazel sits nearby and later tells me he said, "A coon who kills white babies ought to be locked up." Once in the hallway, he begins to recite the Lord's Prayer.

Shelley believes the heckler was planted by Dowling, and after lunch, as I'm coming out of the ladies' room, Shelley comes rushing over and takes my elbow. "I want you to go home right now. Don't delay. Just go home at once. If you stay they're going to try and call you as a witness."

I turn and, coolly as I can manage it, exit the courthouse and grab the first taxi. My heart is racing. It all happens so fast there isn't time for questions.

Later I learn that someone in the DA's office tipped Shelley off to the plan. It's not legal to call me to the stand, and the judge would never allow it, but the commotion that would erupt if Dowling tried would have led to all kinds of questions in the minds of the jurors.

Shenanigans.

In the evening an assistant in Shelley's office comes by the house to tell me Shelley says the coast is clear and that I can return to court the next morning, when Dr. Crampton is scheduled to take the stand. I have no idea what wranglings have taken place, but I'm impressed that Shelley still has loyal friends in the DA's office.

Day six, a special Saturday session. As Crampton is sworn in, he acts composed but I can see the toll the trial and Fred's death have taken on him. He wears a navy serge suit and a red and blue striped necktie.

Dowling is formal and a bit cool as he asks Crampton about Violet Hauze. Crampton says she showed up at his office complaining of abdominal cramps and that she'd already been to see five other doctors. "She said the last one inserted a tube and told her to go home and be quiet for three days and she would be all right." He explains that he examined her for damage, did a smear, found signs of nonpregnancy, and tried to get her to go to the Harrisburg Hospital.

Crampton says that when she refused to go to the hospital, he finally persuaded her to stay with me, so that she would be under the supervision of a nurse and that he could see her again the next day without having to travel back and forth to Hazelton. He explains how he injected her hip with penicillin to try and stop the organisms that might be giving her pain. Mention of the penicillin injection and the "organisms" is intended to imply that Hauze came to him for treatment of venereal disease—not pregnancy.

"She stayed in the home of my private nurse for two days," Crampton says, "then returned for a final dose of penicillin. Then I advised her to return to Hazelton and find a physician there for further treatment."

As I sit and listen to Crampton lie, I'm so grateful not to have to testify, for I would be sitting up there doing the same thing. After Crampton finishes the story, Dowling asks dozens of questions, but Crampton's elusiveness is well rehearsed, and finally Dowling removes his black-framed glasses and rubs the bridge of his nose.

Crampton is asked to explain the remark he made to the reporter on the morning after his arrest when he said, "That's what you get for doing favors for people." Crampton sits unblinking. Then there's a fire in his eyes. "What I meant and what I mean is that I'm vice-chairman of the State Republican Party, and that having served my post so well for so many years, I should be treated a little more fairly."

The judge, who seems tired and eager to be home sleeping in his own bed, calls an end to the questions, saying, "The district attorney is being circumlocutory." The judge says he's heard enough and instructs Shelley and Dowling to begin their closing remarks. You can just feel Dowling's anger as he protests and wrestles with the judge over the decision to conclude things so soon. He loses.

During his final remarks, Dowling again reconstructs the events as he sees them, and his narrative is pretty accurate. He concludes by describing Crampton as someone who intentionally deceives the authorities and skirts the law, and he says, "The facts speak for themselves."

Shelley in his closing is more colorful and concise, but he questions the facts as presented by Dowling. "Who knows how a woman who's been handled by so many doctors can accurately comprehend their effect on her body?" He finishes his conclusion with a superior statement. "The people of Luzerne County ought to wash their dirty linen at home and not in Dauphin County." The local spectators roar with laughter and his remarks are followed with light applause. Since the jurors are all from Dauphin County, he wants to appeal to their local pride, reinforcing their prejudice that Hazelton is an inferior backwater.

The judge instructs the jury to begin their deliberation. While they are deciding, one of them, a middle-aged woman, takes sick and asks to be dismissed. It is rumored that she is upset by the nature and content of the trial. The remaining eleven jurors stay sequestered for more than ten hours, and finally a special night session is requested.

At eleven p.m. the judge calls them in and demands a verdict. It is clear now that he does not intend to spend another night in Harrisburg.

The foreman states how ten of them believe Crampton is innocent, but one believes he is guilty. The result—a hung jury.

This is quite a blow for Crampton. Quite a blow for me. We are in shock. A new trial is quickly put on the calendar for March. Shelley tries to bolster us. "Retrials always hurt the prosecution. The longer this drags on, the better." But somehow we cannot be cheered. We sense that Crampton's lucky days are over.

· 23 ·

A week passes. It is late January and the phone rings. "Will you be on your farm at around noon?" Crampton asks without mentioning his name.

"Yes," I reply.

"I'll be by," he says.

"The roads are loose," I start to say, but he's already gone and I lower the receiver back to its cradle.

Our lane is deeply rutted with tire marks left by the tractor. Snow is banked on either side, and muddy water splashes the shiny black paint and chrome fenders of the Lincoln as it lumbers into view of the farmhouse. I direct Togans to park under the breezeway.

Crampton gets out and greets me with a pat on the back and a peck on the cheek. The dog won't stop barking. "She's not used to them expensive cars," I joke.

Crampton turns and gazes out at the fields stretching back from the house. He deeply inhales the fresh air. At my request, Dewey has gone to Fisherville, but before he took off I had him light a fire in the range of the summerhouse so Togans can wait there and have a nap—leaving Crampton and me to talk in private. Having Dr. Crampton visit my home for the first time makes me nervous, but he seems perfectly at ease as we enter. While he settles into the padded rocker, I lift the lid from the kettle and ladle chicken potpie into soup plates.

The table is already set with biscuits, chowchow, pickled eggs, and beets. I fill a third soup plate with potpie, invert another plate over it, and carry a tray over to Togans in the summerhouse. When I return, Dr. Crampton and I sit together and eat. A silence enfolds us, different from any silence we've ever known.

Outside, a pair of winter birds fly past the window and perch on the clothesline between some frozen overalls. We watch them with interest. Dr. Crampton slices the last potato with his fork, scrapes the bottom of his plate, and insists on another helping.

"The one holdout on the jury was a man named Raymond Mc-Garvey," he says at last. "He lives up on Eighteenth Street and knows Dowling from Catholic High School. But we can't prove anything was rigged. Shelley is planning the new trial. He wants a witness from my office to take the stand but Frances is too old and nervous. She also can't bring herself to construct anything that isn't true. Instead, Daphne Monroe will say she took Franzone's phone call. With her personality, she'll make the account pretty entertaining. She'll claim Franzone needed to bring Violet to Harrisburg because Hazelton is filled with small-town gossip. After that, Louis Wright, the lab technician, will say that he was sent a test to determine if Hauze had a venereal disease—as well as pregnancy—and that indeed there was infection."

I nod as I contemplate the lies and am caught off guard when Crampton says, "Mrs. K., during this trial, I'd like you to take the stand and testify. Shelley says it is to our advantage."

At last, the reason for Crampton's personal visit is clear, and an anxious feeling grips me. His political authority has slipped away. He is desperate now. The only respect he still commands is for who he used to be. It goes beyond sadness to see him this way. I stand to clear the plates and bring out a lemon sponge pie. He accepts a piece. His lips press together and he stares at me as I serve the dessert.

"I don't want to go to jail," I say, taking my chair again, "but we've done nothing wrong and do not deserve to be tried. If Dowling questions me, I'll tell him what he can do with his crusading piety. If you want me to take the stand, I will, but I've made up my mind that if I do I'm going to tell everything. They can throw me out for contempt of court. And I will keep talking. I'll spill it all before I let myself be cross-examined by him."

Crampton looks stricken. "Well, you are *white*," he says bitterly. "You can afford to take bigger chances."

His words cut me like a knife. He's reduced himself to using race to make a point. "That isn't fair," I say.

"No, you're right. It *isn't* fair." His voice is rich with the inversion of sarcasm. But then, like a skilled politician, he switches gears and smiles. "So how about we end this conversation now, and you show me a bit of the farm?"

I willingly agree, happy to change the subject. On the landing at the top of the cellar stairs some old boots are stored for the hired men who come to pick fruit. Crampton pulls on a pair and follows me outside to the rear of the house. At the summit, acres of winter-barren peach trees spread before us. We amble down between the rows, their cobby tops flattened so that when the leaves return in summer more ripening sun is admitted between the branches.

"Dewey says to prune well is an art," I say. "His father was a fruit grower down in York County."

"It's impressive."

The gray trunks stand in neat order beneath the winter sky, and when there's a gust of wind, they tremble and drop clumps of snow to the ground. The air is frigid, and as we circle back around toward the house, Crampton seems unsteady and I reach out to hold his arm. His eyes meet mine for an instant but quickly look away. The fury contained there is palpable.

Perhaps because I feel I have wronged him, I say, "Do you know I've kept a list of all the women who have been patients over the years?"

His eyebrows lift with surprise. "I always told you never to keep records."

"I know."

"What if they find them? It's a sure way to go to jail." His tone is strict.

I feel annoyed that he is annoyed.

"I want you to turn them over to me," he says.

"I can't." The frustration mounts in my body. It seems improbable to both of us that I can behave with such stubbornness.

"Very well, but just know you've got a tiger by the tail."

Back at the house he changes shoes and without another word exits to the breezeway, where Togans holds the car door for him. He turns to give me a quick wave, cold as the day, then climbs in.

I step in front of Togans and hold the door for a moment. "Why didn't we stop sooner?" I ask, tears forming in my eyes. "Before an ending like this? Why did we think we were untouchable?"

My emotion startles him. But in a beat he has recovered. "Because we were," he says calmly, and pulls the door closed. I stand watching as the Lincoln departs slowly, bouncing down the lane.

I feel something else slipping away, the sense of connection with another—of being made to feel whole through, what? Through need?

That same evening one of our removed cousins, Emily Strine, who is friends with Myrtle, calls to ask if we've received an invitation to her sister's wedding. We have. "Now that Myrtle tells me there will be another trial," she says, "would you be upset if I asked you not to attend? I don't like to ask, but I just don't want anything to take attention away from the bride. I hope you understand," she says.

"Yeah, of course," I say, and agree to sit this one out.

Afterwards I'm so angry I slam the dinner dishes in the sink. After all I've done for Myrtle and those inbred cousins. Now suddenly they're society people? I felt like saying to Emily Strine, "Since when don't marriage and abortion mix? They did in your case." Maybe she still believes that what Dr. Crampton did to her wasn't really abortion.

The next day I go to the drugstore for some aspirin, but it's really an excuse to escape the house. Up to now the farm has been my refuge. How much more difficult it would have been to keep up the pace of the abortions or lately the exhaustion of the trial without it. It offers me a place to put my thoughts in order, only now I feel a little trapped here. I don't know what to do with my time, and when I'm upset, the quiet hours just drag by. I feel like I could sleep for fifty years.

Crampton must have been feeling the same sort of restlessness, because I learn he's made several overnight trips to Philadelphia and one to Reading. He also makes a winter trip to see his family out in Tyrone. He returns on February 19, 1955, and when Frances arrives at the office early and lets herself in, she is startled to find him asleep on one of the waiting room sofas, still in his clothes.

Right away she begins to suspect something must have gone wrong on the trip. She doesn't wake him but goes to make coffee, and every time the percolator shoots hot water up into the glass knob, she feels dread. When the coffee is done, she pours him a cup and brings it to him, only to find he's gone upstairs and left his overcoat lying on the floor, still warm from being used as a blanket.

At the landing she listens to the sound of the shower running in the upstairs bathroom. In the meantime Jenny Johnston drops off his breakfast, kept warm on a metal thermal plate. It has a hollow center that she fills with boiling water through a screw cap on the edge of the rim.

When Crampton comes down, he is freshly dressed and smelling of soap. He removes the lid from the breakfast plate—the usual, three eggs over easy, bacon, scrapple, and a couple of buttermilk biscuits. He pours syrup on the scrapple, cuts the eggs into pieces so that the yolks run. Then his head drops and his shoulders slump over the newspaper lying to his left. Frances finds him unconscious—another heart attack. She quickly calls an ambulance.

·   24   ·

Now our second trial is rescheduled for June. Meanwhile Dowling's first term as DA is almost up, but any chance that he will be defeated is unlikely, as he enjoys a popular lead.

This time I visit the hospital, but Dr. Crampton is asleep, so I sit in the waiting room with Frances.

"Is there anyone we should call?" I ask.

"Not that I can think of," she says.

"What about the woman on Green Street?"

"That's just talk, Mrs. K."

"But I saw him going in there once."

"That's just talk started years ago. Leave it alone."

I feel ashamed to have brought it up. I realize Frances may not even know if the rumors were true. Just then Togans comes in, and we both descend on him to ask about what happened on their trip to Tyrone.

Togans describes the excursion as very typical until the return home. They drove out of Tyrone as always on the township road headed for the highway, but Crampton had other ideas. "I want to get off of this road," he said. "Take the other one." Togans argued, "Doc, that ain't the way to Capitol City."

"Just do as I say," Crampton told him.

"That trip always lays heavy on him," Frances added. "He's from the city. The country makes him sad."

Togans has a way of storytelling that reminds me of Pop. They both use their hands in the same way. His descriptions are precise and vivid, and he's not about to be rushed. When he talks, I feel the dank mountain air, the mist that obscures the polish of the Lincoln's massive hood, the roadway as the fields curve away. He says a few scarecrows still guard the rows of neat brown stubble, their ragged heads weighted with icicles.

In the town of Bald Eagle, Crampton has him take a left to go up the mountain. Togans looks at him in the rearview mirror and says, "Doc. This weather." Crampton leans back with no reply.

"Since his heart trouble he's been moody," Togans says. "I don't want to upset him. He closes his eyes like he's dreaming of spring, like he's smelling mayblossoms. His eyes shut to what he doesn't want to see—the low-lying clouds hanging yellow and dark over a grove of black walnut trees. I know he must be thinking there is precious little time."

"His doctors say he'll make a full recovery," Frances interjects.

"You know him. He don't put store in doctors. I think he's dreaming of spring, knowing his summers are spent."

They wind up and around the mountain, and a fine, silty snow starts to angle down. By the time they coast through Bald Eagle, the snow is swirling across the road like sand. "It's a town of crooked frame houses, a secondhand store, and an eating place with a greasy fan and a chalked-up menu on the outside," Togans says, "but everything's closed down tight." On the outskirts, a three-story brick factory stands next to a low juke joint. A hand-lettered sign is nailed to the clapboard announcing a player piano inside. It too is closed. "And we're not about to go there anyway." Then Crampton says make a left, and all of a sudden Togans knows where he wants to go.

"I see our car reflected in the windows as we pass," he says. "The Lincoln looks gray in the falling snow."

Up and back and around a junkyard stacked with rusted automobiles they climb, and then onto a long, blank stretch lined with telephone poles. They drive in fifteen minutes what should have taken five. The road is slick. Evergreen woods come in on either side and the old man whisks the cellophane from a cigar and bites off the end. "Now there's fog on the windows, the heater's blowin', and he starts with that thick smoke so I can barely see."

"A cigar calms him," Frances says.

Soon the paved road yields to gravel. For two miles they jolt and bounce their way along; the white fir branches, hanging low with powder, brush the sides and top of the Lincoln.

"He's going to the park," Frances says, and tells me about a public park outside Tyrone that Dr. Crampton gave money for, where Negro families, including his own, could go and have summer picnics. Togans says that the sign bearing the old man's name is still there, but that joking vandals have removed the RE from RECREATION PARK, so that it now reads CREATION PARK. Togans winks. "Lovebirds like to go up there and neck."

When the car stops, the old man says he will only be a minute and insists Togans remain. "He's dressed for town, trousers the shade of light-brown egg custard, with breaks so deep the two-inch cuffs drape over his shoelaces and grow wet with snow. This is one day when he oughta be wearing spats. His wingtips shift around the icy ruts. He wanted his family to see him dressed. Let them know he can still strut."

Togans details the park in the wilderness, picnic tables at one end, and alongside them a great field for sports. He watches as Dr. Crampton walks to the center of the clearing and stops. My own imagination takes over. I picture Dr. Crampton standing in the open, the cold coming through the soles of his shoes, coming up from the frozen ground, and sinking back down again through the chilling layers of mud, shale, and granite that make the mountain. He stands inhaling the smell of woods, dirt, and decay, wheezing as he attempts to relight his cigar. Snowflakes extinguish each sputtering flame, and on his third try, no doubt with the sour taste of tobacco still on his tongue, he throws the cigar and the wooden matches to the ground. "Now, I never saw the old man mishandle a smoke except during an election," Togans says.

He describes how the old man just stands there snorting, dignified, erect, his chin high despite the wet snow crystals that drop behind his glasses. In my mind I see his eyelids close, and through the darkness he listens to the furious white flutter of falling snow, like the wings of a hundred thousand crystal butterflies. The desire to visit the land he's helped buy must have overwhelmed him. Only a handful of colored men in all of North America have ever had land named after them. It is a great accomplishment.

The snow falling without fail, pelting his coat, the flakes gathering wet between his collar and neck. That's when Togans tugs at his sleeve. "Doc, doc, you all right?" The old man is dazed. He's startled to see Togans right beside him. He hasn't even heard him approach. "Doc. You been standing in that spot for half an hour," Togans says.

The old man blinks. Then blinks again. "My toes are numb," he says, and licks his lips several times. "We oughta go back to the car."

Togans, as on the day I saw them at the courthouse, takes Crampton by the arm and leads him back. They make small steps until, like the drip of warm honey, circulation returns to the old man's feet. His blue silk tie is water-stained but in the middle his diamond stickpin still reigns in its empire setting. They cross the frozen ground to the Lincoln. "Let's go to the barbershop," the old man says. "I need to say good-bye to Ben." His voice is so tired Togans doesn't have the heart to trample the request.

They wind their way back along the same roads, their previous tire marks already gone. "I try to make small talk to lift his spirits. Tell him how in the paper the other day, they showed Eisenhower getting out of a car just like this one." The old man does not reply.

They turn south at the sign for Tyrone, and the asphalt on Main Street is white with ice. At the shop, the old man's nephew runs out in his barber coat, a comb in one hand, scissors in the other. He is alarmed, telling them that his niece phoned more than an hour ago. "Where you been?" His nephew's breath puffs clouds in the cold air. Around them, snow shovels scrape the sidewalk and children throw snowballs.

"Business," the old man says. He searches his pocket, then unwraps another cigar.

Togans says Sherman has a foxy sense of humor. "What's her name?" he asks.

"Any women who chased me are long gone," Crampton says. Then he notices two men peering out from behind the plate glass window, one wrapped in a cape, his hair half cut. There is nothing left to say. Sherman leans his forearms on the iced roof of the car. He tells the old man the storm's bad. Asks why they don't stay another night?

Togans reports that the old man says he has to get back to relieve Frances of running things. Frances purses her lips at the remark.

Togans tells how the old man asks his nephew if he needs anything. Then, as their tires spit snow down Main Street, they hear Sherman calling after, imploring them to take the turnpike.

After the first few hours, the storm worsens but there are no places for Negroes to stop. Theirs is practically the only car on the road in either direction. They creep along the frozen turnpike for a couple of hours. They come around a long even bend and up ahead a yellow flashing light is blinking. A snowplow stands stalled in the middle of the road.

"They hit something," Togans says.

A husky man in a quilted hunting vest is poking the rear fender with a crowbar. It's a really heavy dump truck, fitted with a plowing blade. As they pull alongside, another man comes from around the front end. I can just imagine the two workers standing there looking at the strange travelers in their snow-challenged big car, like they are something born of the storm. They've probably never seen two colored men in a new car before, let alone a Lincoln.

The old man rolls down his window. "I'm a doctor," he calls out. "Can I help?"

"Ain't nobody can help that dog," the man with the crowbar shouts. Then they see between the truck's massive double tires and its fender the body of a large collie. Flush against the splash guard, bloody fur and bunched-up paws are wedged against a crushed skull. The driver explains how he felt her go under, but it was too late. He says she kept barking the whole time. The other man explains how they couldn't slow up and that they're supposed to have cleared to the county line by now.

Dr. Crampton takes out his pocket watch and says he also has to keep moving. "The road up ahead hasn't seen a plow all day," the driver says. "Even in a car like this you'll have a devil of a time. The state pays us to plow. Better wait for us to lead."

"We'll manage," the old man replies.

"You'll sit crying if you don't make it."

"We'll manage," he says again. He motions Togans to move. They glide on into the storm. About half a mile down they hit a frozen patch and their wheels begin to spin. They stop moving and Togans hits the gas pedal until their tires smoke the ice. Then the old man takes the wheel while Togans gets out to push. After a while they have no choice but are forced to wait for the snowplow. They sit with the motor running and the wipers flapping and eat the roast pork sandwiches that Crampton's niece Laura has packed.

Another hour passes. Darkness is coming early, and the storm is getting worse. All of a sudden they can hear the snowplow coming up behind them. They expect the men will stop and help, but before Togans can get out, the plow speeds up and drives right past, banking a waist-high wall of snow up against the car.

Now they're really stuck. Unable to open the driver's side door, Togans crawls across the seat to exit from the passenger side. The car is now walled in on three sides—back, front, and side. Togans remembers an old folding army field shovel he has stowed in the trunk. Using that, he starts to dig. When he stops for a break, Dr. Crampton gets out and starts to shovel. "He's so mad I can hear him cursing a blue streak," Togans says.

Frances looks alarmed. "He has a heart condition," she says. "He can't shovel snow."

"Well, you should have seen him. Between the two of us it took less than an hour and we got out, and we drove the rest of the way straight through. He was tired from the trip and all the shoveling. It was after two a.m. when I brought him in, and he was fine except one of his arms was sore. He told me to leave his bag by his office, that he wanted to sit a while and check his mail before climbing the stairs. When I left him he was at his desk sorting envelopes."

25

Crampton is released from the hospital a day before his seventy-sixth birthday. I stop by the office to bring him a pair of slippers. Outside, on the front stoop, a few pitiful flower arrangements sit facing Forster Street, their bright petals blowing in the cold wind, a far cry from the fifty or sixty arrangements he received on the birthday before his disgrace. Frances says he won't allow them to be brought into the house. "He wants to shame the whole town for what's happening to him."

Inside, Crampton sits behind his desk wearing an old red wool bathrobe, eating a roll of Ritz crackers and a jar of olives stuffed with pimientos. "That's quite a feast," I say. He keeps chewing and doesn't respond, even when I wish him a happy birthday. I sit with him and chatter about nothing. His eyes are swollen and glassy; the cracker crumbs stick to his lips.

After half an hour I take my leave and head over to Mary Sachs. She says in her thick Lithuanian accent, "I haven't seen you for a while. But you're still on my list of regulars." I wonder what one has to do to get taken off her list of regulars. Stop spending, I suppose. Spring clothes are everywhere and I'm suddenly struck with a desire to change everything about myself. I'm sitting at a hat table, trying on a celery green straw trimmed with violets, when one of the shop-girls walks by and says, "You have a fat face."

I am stunned. Furious. How dare she? I'm about to make a scene. Get her fired. Storm out. But she is smiling and displays no malice. Then I realize that what she said was "You have a hat face." I suddenly realize that this time new clothes won't help me. I've grown too emotional and touchy; I need to be wrapped in layers of cotton wool.

Dr. Crampton's decline spreads gloom over everything. Because I no longer have a job, self-pity moves in and it just keeps growing and spreading through my mind. One day I sit and tally all the mistakes I've made with Sam—my failures as a mother. It feels like all my life I've been either too weak or too bossy. When I'm bossy, I get upset because people won't follow me. But if I sit back and wait for others to look after me, I get upset when they don't step up to take charge or they do things wrong.

Then I focus on Dewey and all the money he's lost to slot machines, all the washed-out holes in the rutted lane that he never fills. He just takes the tractor and cuts around them. The farm is too much work; it's no wonder young people don't want to farm anymore. Some of the nicest places are being broken up into lots, whole neighborhoods of ugly little houses—or car dealerships. I lie awake at night and weep over the sadness of it all.

26

One day while at the beauty shop, I read in a magazine the definition for a prayer: "Please God, pay attention to me." The thought strikes me as useful, and it comes at a good time because Sam has just written to say he'd like to come home on leave.

He arrives on a blustery day in the middle of April. You'd never know it was spring. He looks healthy and fit and so grown up his hair is thinning a bit.

I've warned Dewey to keep his mouth shut about the trial. Sam doesn't know about it or the arrest. I want to keep it that way. On his second day we take a walk around the farm—almost the same walk I took with Crampton. Behind the house we stop in front of the plot, twenty by thirty feet long, where in summer our vegetables grow. Its clods of dark brown earth show where the soil has been turned. Windowpanes of the seedling beds have been left out all winter and are warping. Sam notices. We move on. I'm not in the mood to discuss Dewey's irresponsibility.

Sam knows Crampton has been ill and that as a result I haven't been working. Money is tight, but still I give him fifty dollars when he asks. I think of all the money I've spent on crepe dresses, silk blouses, alpaca coats, boxes of shoes, and Paris hats, many of them never worn. I've squandered thousands of dollars on those things. Now I've learned I'm most happy in a cotton dress, one I can wear up to the attic or down to the barn.

The hung jury weighs on my mind and there's a part of me that would like to tell Sam, but there's another part that knows he already isn't too happy with me, and I simply can't bear his judgment. In the afternoon the muscles in my neck twist like knots and I go upstairs to lie on my bed with an icepack on my forehead.

Dewey and Sam stay downstairs and talk, not knowing their

voices carry up through the heat register and that I secretly listen.
The topic is how much servicemen like to drink.

Sam describes a group of career men called twenty-seven-day
soldiers. They are models of decorum, efficiency, and duty, but
when they draw their pay at the end of the month, they go on
drinking binges that last until their pay is gone, usually three days,
and then they are back for twenty-seven days. "Then they are some
of the best soldiers you could ever hope to find. The officers understand who these men are and make sure their posts are covered for
the three days after payday. A career in the military can be tedious,
and it is tough to find hard men who can go the mile, particularly
in peacetime. The officers know that when a twenty-seven-day soldier returns from a bender, he will be grateful for the understanding
and liberty, and repay it with loyal and expert duty for the rest of
the month. Some of them are the very backbone of the Army, with
a code of honor to outperform." No doubt their high accomplishments during their sober days help justify their next payday binge.

Then Sam describes another kind of drunk, the type who needs a
drink in order to function. He is less predictable than the twenty-
seven-day soldier, hides liquor around the post, ties it to tree
branches, buries it in holes, sticks it in the latrine or up in the rafters
of the barracks. You can't leave anything with alcohol unattended
around him. Aftershave lotion, hair tonic, mouthwash, rubbing
alcohol—all disappear when he passes by. Even the big bottles of
vanilla extract in the mess hall kitchen are kept under lock and key
because their alcohol content draws these men like a magnet.

"I've never been desperate enough to steal a drink," Sam states,
matter-of-factly. Dewey says that when he was in the Navy he never
needed to steal because they were always well supplied with military
rotgut. Sam says in Korea the booze shipments are sometimes late
getting to the men on the front or are of inferior quality. On one
occasion they receive several cases of bad Spanish brandy that Sam
says "could take a coat of paint off a tank." They drink it anyway.

At other times, when the booze runs out and new shipments are delayed, they drink medical alcohol cut with cans of grapefruit juice, and once they even polished off a case of Aqua Velva. Sam says he burped up the perfume for days afterward.

How disgusting. I can't imagine wanting to poison yourself like that. I feel sorry for the men who need to drink in order to fight. Is it loneliness? Fear? Do they drink just to get through the ordeal? The newspapers and the politicians call them heroes but give no account of what it takes for many of them to maintain their courage. In the military there's obviously a strong link between bravery and alcohol.

As Sam and Dewey talk, their voices grow loud. They're drinking hard cider, and when the stories grow foul, I just keep lying there and listening as though it were a play. Sam tells how they call their flat fabric service hats cunt caps because of their shape. The word revolts me. Sam continues. "We live in tents or Quonset huts. Sleep in cots twenty-four to thirty-two rows. At night the pine shrubs outside the perimeter fence are full of women and their pimps, who whistle to get our attention. Often they're pimped by brothers or even husbands. You can get to know the girls for a pack of cigarettes. You see all kinds of things. One fellow gave a girl his undershirt and they did it on the ground with the snow falling all around them. One guard at the motor pool carried a woman on his back over to a deuce and a half—what we call a two-and-a-half-ton truck—and had his way with her in the back."

Sam says he shacked up with one woman for several months. She did his laundry and ironed his uniforms. One day he saw how she pressed them so perfectly: she took water in her mouth and spit it out on the clothes to make steam.

"I had one buddy who fathered a baby with a Korean woman. They had an argument and he broke up with her. She came to the post and pushed the baby into the arms of another soldier and then ran away. The father of the baby was annoyed that the other soldier had accepted the child, but the other fellow didn't know what else to do. He was decent and couldn't handle a woman who was so angry and upset." Dewey and Sam laugh.

Somehow, with the help of an officer and some cash, the baby got returned to the mother and no doubt she looks after it still: some things never change. Even in a country so different from America, women prove themselves to be just as resilient as men.

Sam then says, "I had more than my share of women because of the clothes Mom sent. I traded them for favors."

A sharp blade cuts into my heart. Humanitarian aid? Just lies.

"When she sent that second box, I was like a king!" I hear his glass slam down. "Hey, isn't there anything to drink in this dump, besides hard cider?" Sam's big-shot words are beginning to slur.

"Well," Dewey says, the voice of a banker giving away free mortgages, "why don't we nip over to Fisherville and see what the boys are up to?"

"We can't stay long," Sam says. "We promised to take her to supper."

"Her." They refer to me as "her," as though I were just another stupid bitch whom they can use and toss around.

I hear the engine of the old pickup turn over; the doors slam, the clutch releases, the gears shift, and the sputtering motor grows faint as it carries them out and down the lane.

In my whole lifetime, I've never been so angry. I lie in bed and watch the evening shadows change patterns on the walls, their brightness fading as the sun goes down. The men fail to return in time to take "her" to dinner.

How to describe the anger? A volcano? TNT? A hydrogen bomb? Pop used to say, "Anger is the wind that blows out the light of the mind," and as I lie there, my mind, like the walls of the room, grows pitch-black. The world is not a safe place.

My whole body sinks into the mattress and after an hour my neck kinks from clenching my jaw and lying prone for so long. This is my cue to pull myself up and get out of bed. In the cellar I find a cardboard box and I bring it up to our bedroom and fill it with Dewey's things. I take them to the spare room and dump them all out onto the bed, then go back for the remainder. In about half an hour I've moved all of Dewey's stuff from what had been our bedroom. The room is now mine.

I go down to the kitchen and boil a pot of coffee. I light a cigarette and throw the match in the sink. I shuffle a deck of cards and am on my fifth game of solitaire when I hear the truck chugging down the lane. I snap on the outdoor light.

When Dewey crawls out of the truck I am waiting for him, standing under the naked bulb hanging over the breezeway.

Dewey's eyes are bloodshot, the stink and smoke of the barroom still cling to him, and he chomps a toothpick in the corner of his yellowed teeth. "Aw, now don't get sore," he says. "The kid's home on leave and I wanted to show him a good time."

The bell rings. The match is on.

"I oughta bust your jaw," I say.

His eyes widen. "Well, I'll be goddamned. So we had a couple of drinks."

I let him take the first step toward me and the house. "Come any closer and they'll carry you off in a pine box."

He freezes. He knows I mean business.

Under his breath he curses me with threats of hell and damnation.

Sam is worse off than Dewey. He's holding himself up with the door of the truck, his hair hanging over his forehead. "Mom, whatsa matter? Don't you wanna go to dinner?"

"It's midnight, you jackass."

"We can go to town for chop suey," Sam says, his tongue thick and wet. "Chop suey joints are open all night. I'll buy you a whole bucket of chop suey."

"I'm washing my hands of you," I say. "Get that through your thick skulls."

"We can all get rump steak. The place by the depot," Sam pleads. "Pounded out. With onions. Have some laughs."

"Yeah, and the laughs are all on me."

"I know what is what," Dewey pipes up, his eyes beady and glistening from drink. "You want to run us ragged, don't you? Well, don't get all high-and-mighty, goddamn it." Dewey smiles as he smoothes down a shock of hair standing up on the back of his scalp. "You're not clean. You're crooked too."

"That's enough," I say.

"They'll slam you into the pokey. You and your darkie doctor."

"Shut up."

"You can't escape. They'll slit your throat."

I swing my arm. I feel my palm make contact with Dewey's face. He falls to one side and stays where he fell.

"You bitch," he hollers from the ground. "You hard-assed bitch. You can't slap me around in front of him."

Sam lurches forward and steadies himself on the hood of the truck, blocking one of the headlights. "Mom. We didn't do nothing. Why're you being so awful?"

"Shut up," I say. "I've had enough."

"Mom. Whatsa matter?" Sam seems on the verge of tears. His eyes are dopey, limp-lidded, and swollen.

"You four-flusher," I holler at Dewey's body where he lies supine in the grass. "You just want to stir things up now that he's home and you have an audience."

"I know what is what," Dewey says weakly from the ground. "Why don't you lay off and come clean? Tell your boy the truth about the racket. Tell him what they've done to you. Tell him why you aren't working no more."

"And why don't you call your children and tell them the truth about yourself?" I say with as much venom as I can produce.

"Whatsa matter?" Sam says. "What racket?" Sam's eyes open large with emotion and fright, and drunken tears begin rolling down his cheeks. "Mom, why can't you ever level with me?"

"I'm going to bed," I say, feeling shaky in my knees. "You two sleep it off. Just not in my house. I won't have you messing up the rugs."

"Tell me the truth," Sam blubbers after me. "Just once."

"He'll tell you," I say, gesturing toward the ground. "He's your buddy, not me."

"Mom," Sam bawls. "Why can't we ever get along? Why can't you be like a real mom?" His voice fades off into the night.

I turn without answering and go back into the house. So now he wants to be friends and it's supposed to be all right? Maybe I can collect some more clothes for him.

At the moment I'm not in the deal. Their game can go on without me. I don't care what anyone does. To hell with them. I sit up thinking about how to make this horrible pain go away. I want to split my rib cage open and cut out my heart. Let Dewey figure out how to explain the trial. None of it is any of Sam's business. But in a way they have won. I've resorted to slapping Dewey, just like Norm once slapped me. There's no victory in that.

The next day they are sober. But I'm the one who feels like hell. In my forties, I can't get by on jangled nerves and no sleep like I used to. Sam is sheepish and polite and does not ask me any questions about the trial or the arrest. I have no idea if Dewey has filled him in or not. In the afternoon Sam says Myrtle has invited him for dinner and that he might even spend the night at her place. His leave is almost over.

·   27   ·

The new trial is nothing but a circus. Crampton sits at the defense table like an old water buffalo caged at the zoo. Once again a steady stream of visitors—members of the William Penn football team, cronies from politics, patients, and lifelong acquaintances—lean over the banister to wish him well. Last time around he looked indignant and angry; this time he looks humiliated, his eyes puffy, and does not seem to comprehend everything.

The jury selection goes smoothly and they schedule a special night session to move things along. Dowling is riding a wave of popularity following his landslide reelection as district attorney, but I think he looks ridiculous for attacking such an old man.

On the day the trial begins, Shelley and his assistant plead with me to take the stand. They remind me of a pair of wood rats scratching in the root cellar. "It will end things," they say. "You can talk about nursing, let them know you were like a regular nurse."

"All right," I say quietly, "I'll take the stand."

Their faces look pleased.

"But if you put me up there I intend to tell everything I know. I'll name names. All of them."

"You can't spill your guts. They'll lock you up for contempt of court."

"Let them. I'm still gonna keep talking."

"Be reasonable," Shelley pleads. "If you pull a stunt like that you'll ruin everything."

"You want a show? Well, I'll give you a spectacle. I've got a ledger full of names and I'll admit it for evidence. I'll hand it to the newspapers. We did five thousand abortions. Anyone who came and had one will be found out—along with anyone who abetted them. That means the police department, the mayor's office, the hospitals, the churches, and even the White House. Big names are written there, including yours."

Shelley looks stunned. "Mrs. Krone, be reasonable." Then he pauses, curtly snaps his briefcase shut, and says he has to go. As he leaves the room, he looks back at me and says, "Mrs. K., I've never met one quite like you."

After my grandstanding, I'm so agitated and upset that food won't stay down. But I've made up my mind. I'm not bluffing. I will not take the stand without exposing everybody.

28

That afternoon, unbeknownst to anyone, Shelley meets with the judge and tells him I am at wit's end. He says I am about to come undone, and that I have evidence that could affect the entire state legislature. He tells him how far-reaching my knowledge is.

Apparently the judge does not like what he hears one bit. Like Judge Snyder before him, he's eager to see this case end and to get back to his own county. This trial is almost over. He does not want any large messes or explosions to clean up. He does not want to be swallowed up in the eye of a hurricane. He does not allow such things to happen on his bench.

Shelley catches me as I enter the lobby following the break. "Guess what?" he says, his voice half whispering. "The judge has just exonerated you from the case."

I stare back at him.

"You're off. Free."

Back inside the courtroom, we rise while the judge enters. Right away he announces my exoneration. The room erupts with astonishment at the news and the judge quickly restores order. Dowling doesn't look up but sits at his table and shuffles papers with a scornful face.

Crampton stares straight ahead, his eye sockets so deep they remind me of egg cups. Later during recess he passes me in the hallway. His lips pull back to bare his teeth, like he's trying to avoid spitting at me. "Congratulations," he whispers. "But you should have stuck with me. We could have had full jury acquittal. Now you'll always live with doubt in people's minds."

That the prosecutor's case is falling apart is irrelevant. What Dr. Crampton sees is his own control diminishing. "Exoneration suggests deal making," he says. "Joseph Randall will have a field day. I can't believe you'd want it this way."

I lower my head. "I'm sorry," I say, then turn and walk on.

29

My exoneration is reported in the next day's paper. It should feel like an anvil has been removed from my neck, but it doesn't. Crampton's words make it feel like cheating. Why? My threats were more truthful and direct than lying. But what I didn't realize is that Dr. Crampton still thinks he has a political career. It's a delusion. He's seventy-six. He's finished. What bothers me most is his perception that I have done something to harm him. I decide not to attend the trial anymore.

On Saturday Crampton's case goes to the jury. According to the paper, he has thirty-one character witnesses this time, with added testimony from the lab technician and from Daphne Monroe. The latter is said to have been pretty entertaining, sassing Dowling and playing up how Violet Hauze—a woman she never met—was troubled and confused.

I'm feeling cut off from everything. In the evening, for a distraction, Dewey and I go to play cards over at Sally's house. She bakes macaroni and cheese again, and every half hour gets up between hands of pinochle to call the courthouse to ask about the verdict. When no verdict has been reached she sits back down. I marvel at her energy. Since marrying and starting a family she's proven herself a good mother and has begun a side business of making sock-monkey dolls that she sells to local stores. While we play pinochle she simultaneously sews a sock monkey, and rocks her baby's cradle with her foot. She does all of this as if it's the most natural thing in the world and her industry and enterprise impress me.

It's almost one a.m. when the night clerk finally tells us Dr. Crampton has been found not guilty. The jury deliberated for over ten hours. I get up from the table and go to phone him. The line is busy. I try several more times but am never able to get through.

In the morning Frances picks up. "I'm sorry, Mrs. K., but the doctor has stepped out." Crampton is correct, she really can't tell a good lie, and from her fumbling I know he is standing right there.

· 3o ·

Another hot summer. I try to figure out how to occupy my days. I've stopped reading the newspaper except to look for grocery coupons. It's all lies. I'm still more interested in what the paper can't write—the unprintable stories. But people can't bear to read those.

I spend an afternoon at Mom's house. And while she's lying down to take a nap I spot a letter from Sam to Myrtle lying on the back of a kitchen counter.

July 24, 1955
Ft. Knox, Kentucky

Dear Myrtle,

Thanks for the birthday card. I cashed the money order and am using it to make some much needed repairs to my car. Your gift came just in the nick of time as I'm short of cash. Me and another fellow were on our way to Knoxville on a Saturday afternoon and had a car accident. The left rear tire blew out and I lost control of the wheel. We skidded off the road into a freshly plowed field. The car flipped over and the weight of the battery pulled the floorboards apart, splashing battery acid all over us. Luckily none of it got into our eyes. We were shook up, but there wasn't a scratch on us. The farmer whose field it was brought his tractor around and pulled the car upright. We towed it to the road but couldn't get it to start. We fiddled with it for more than an hour and finally hitched a ride into town to find a mechanic.

By the time we got to Knoxville, the sun was going down and the garages were all closed. We spent the night in a pool hall and in the morning I went out to try and find breakfast— hoping for bacon, eggs, and coffee. Main Street on a Sunday morning was white with sunlight, but everything was closed. I was wearing a pair of brown serge pants I had custom-tailored in Korea and as I walked I felt a cool breeze. I looked down to find two flaps of fabric loose around my shins and flapping with every step. You see, the stitching on the bottom seams was made of a plastic fiber and the battery acid had eaten through. I was a sorry sight indeed. Eventually we found a fellow who would fix the car and we headed back to the base, our pockets and our stomachs empty.

> *Well, that's all for now.*
> *Sam*

P.S. Thanks for telling me about the outcome of the trial—you know I'd never hear it from her.

The letter upsets me. I even believe Myrtle left it there on purpose so that I would read it. At least it's clear that someone has told him about the trial, but to be referred to as "her" again makes me angry. And on top of that he's spending his days drinking.

31

Just before Labor Day I get a phone call from Dr. Crampton. I'm delighted when he says he's feeling better and asks if I can come see him in the afternoon. The invitation pleases me, and he makes no mention of the trial. Perhaps we can turn the page and start fresh.

At three o'clock I arrive at his house, toting a peck of our best peaches as a gift. I ring the bell and wait. Ring again. No answer. Frances must have gone home for the day. I go over to Leftridge's cut-rate store and use the pay phone. After five rings he answers. "Didn't hear you," he says. "I'll be waiting."

He's leaning against the back door as I return. I see that he actually needs the doorframe to give him support. A crusty old pair of navy trousers clings to him, while an unpressed, half-tucked white shirt is a background for a poorly knotted necktie with stains on it. He reaches his hand out to pat me on the cheek, and I can see his hands shake, his nails are long, and he smells like sour milk.

Inside he shuffles past an old photograph left lying on the radiator, a picture of a lovely young girl, her hair piled up on her head, a string of pearls on her creamy neck. He doubles back and takes the picture and puts it on the coffee table in front of him. When he sits down on the sofa, I can see he is suffering from edema, his ankles swollen to twice their normal size. His breath is short and shallow. He talks about working again and asks me if I can get some girls lined up.

"Where's Frances?"

"I let her go," he says. "She's too old to run the office now."

Light pours in through the venetian blinds and highlights the stubble on his chin. It's horrible to see him like this, as though I'm speaking to an entirely different human being. I begin to wonder how much medication he is on. He looks at the picture of the girl. "Mrs. Krone, have you ever lost somebody that you never got over?"

"Yes," I say. "More than once."

"Maybe that binds us."

"Maybe," I say. "I know the suffering it causes."

"Yes," he says.

I nod. "Who was she?" I ask.

"Her name is Lucy."

"What happened to her?"

"She died."

"With child?" I ask, wondering if this might be the catalyst that began his foray into abortions.

Crampton looks at me askance. "No. She died of polio."

"I'm sorry," I say. "I just assumed."

"What?"

"That you were . . . in love."

Crampton stares at me; the sunlight through the blinds makes stripes across the floor. "Yes, there was great love between us, Mrs. K., but not in the way you think. Why does everyone always assume colored men lust for white women? In this case it would have been incest. Lucy was Colonel Copeland's daughter, sister to Fred, and to me. While I was growing up, she did much to let me know I was wanted, needed, and appreciated as part of the Copeland family. Colonel Copeland recognized that I had brains and talent, and that he could edify himself and practice his beliefs by supporting me. I don't mean in a selfish way, for he always treated me well, with empathy and kindness. But in his mind I was still a Negro, in need of his benevolence. Lucy was different.

"One has a different relationship with siblings," he says. "Your influence on one another has more impact. Lucy wielded none of her father's good intentions. Her speech and actions were always the same whether she was addressing Fred or myself. She loved us both equally. I drew my greatest strength from her ordinary way of seeing me, and from her kindness and equanimity. I spent the rest of my life trying to find someone like her.

"Mrs. K., you and I share something like that. We have a unique relationship. Professional but resonant."

"Yes," I agree, wishing it were possible to add something more profound. I regret my inability to express devotion.

As if reading my mind he says, "That's what I always liked about you, Mrs. K. You didn't care what anyone else thought. You were willing to chart an unconventional course. I'm happy to be resuming our work. It defies the small mind. The people like Huette Dowling."

"But," I say, my voice suddenly unsteady, "I just . . . I just can't do it anymore."

My words catch Crampton off guard. It feels like the room is lost in time. The oxygen gets extracted.

"The trial, it's taken something out of me, robbed me of courage. It's more than I can bear." My throat quivers. "I don't have it in me to do it again."

"I understand," he says, and we sit across from each other and the silence grows.

Suddenly I am torn by what I cannot express, a fifteen-year storm of tenderness, our feelings of mutual respect and admiration. I should go to sit beside him on the sofa and put my arms around him, protect him from the great floodwaters about to pull him under. He's grown weary, and his ragged helplessness is as visible as cracks in the earth. I should comfort him, trace the chart of his dark skin, stop at all the injuries. I should follow him home to high ground, move in with him, and hold him in my cool arms as I nurse him back to strength. I should thank him for being the great human who gave me my best chance, who taught me what I was capable of. Instead, whatever sobs lie between my heart and my voice go dying.

I've seen white women who've been ruined by colored men and I'll be damned if I'm one of them. There is thirst and there is hunger in our land. Dr. Crampton is dying and soon they will finish him. Already the Negroes he represents smell the blood. Many have waited for this day—the fall of Uncle Tom. The price of friendship is dear. It can ruin your life.

For fifteen years we've labored together and kept each other's secrets. But now I retreat into my white propriety, the same propriety that exonerated me, the same propriety I've always thumbed my nose at—when it suited my life or pocketbook to do so.

He senses the change. He senses something far beneath the surface with his ultrasensitive sonar. For a moment his face looks deflated. Then he marshals his strength.

"Risk is risk," he says, "but something in me has also changed. I no longer care about the money or the politics or helping my people, or that I'm no longer considered a credit to my race. They can't seem to remember the work I've done. I know they call me an Uncle Tom, but I don't care, because people who say that have never known the thrill and terror of being the first one to go through the door. They don't understand. I'm at peace, because in my heart I did my best for the times for which I was chosen, and I got there first.

"And I don't care about the goddamned IRS. They can't put me in chains. My first calling has always been to be a doctor. Politics was second. As a doctor, I'll keep doing procedures, because men like Dowling are frightening those who might take my place. Well, they can't frighten me.

"What Huette Dowling can't stand is that he can't find a way to exercise superiority over me, and that causes him distress. He can't beat me—can't dismiss me as just another nigger.

"But what Huette Dowling does or doesn't do no longer concerns me. I am not his victim. He does not matter. Small men are not important. What is important is my calling as a doctor. And if I don't start doing procedures again, women will die. I can't allow personal fear to place me in collusion with Dowling. If I save even one woman's life, my work is worthwhile."

The silence returns. We sit and blink at one another. "Well," I say, with uncertainty, "all in good time. All in good time."

Crampton knows by the sound of my words that I'm patronizing him. "Well, Mrs. K., don't let an old man take up your whole day," he says and chuckles. "Let me show you to the door." I protest, but he insists on getting up and shuffling his feet across the carpet behind me as I gather up my pocketbook. When we get the screen door open, he pats my back. "You remember how I used to say I wish I had a dozen like you, Mrs. K.? Now you know why. Because I knew one day I'd lose you."

I nod and smile and exit onto the stoop. Halfway to my car I turn to look back at him. He is still standing in the doorway watching me go. My jaw aches. We both know that we will never see each other again.

• 32 •

It is late afternoon. August. The height of yet another peach season. I can't get Dewey on the phone. I call Hazel. She knows from my voice I'm upset and agrees to accompany me back to the farm. When we get to Halifax, a sign is propped at the end of the lane—no peaches today. I already know what to expect. The breezeway is stacked with baskets of ripe fruit and Dewey is nowhere to be found. He's sold a bushel or two and taken the money.

A blind rage engulfs me.

I can't stand that he is getting away with it.

It isn't like me to go berserk, but a fury overtakes me and something inside me snaps. I grab the long-handled shovel and begin swinging it at every peach basket in sight. I can't stop. I smash the fruit. I smash his skull. I smash the babies. The ones in Korea and all around the world. I smash the women who bore them. Who will never know love. I smash my son. Born to such bitterness. A child who doesn't write. I smash Dr. Crampton. For what the dogs have done to him. For my beloved nursing career now ended. I smash for what I've become. A victim. Yet again.

As my fury subsides, Hazel yanks the shovel away. She wraps her arms around me. We stand holding on to each other under the breezeway, among broken baskets and smashed peaches.

33

Under the orders of a doctor I've consulted, referred to me by a physician at the Harrisburg Hospital, I've come here to the clinic for a rest. But so far all I do is wonder at the lack of progress mental science has made in all the years of medicine. So much has changed in the fifteen years since I became a nurse, and yet there are some areas that are still in the stone age. I think selling medical theories of how the human mind works is not that different from selling pencil shavings as though they were smoking tobacco. Given how little they understand, they ought to hawk psychiatry on television with cars, electric fans, S&H Green Stamps, soda pop, and cigarettes.

I used to copy items from the newspapers; now I run from them. Papers profess to rely on "fact" to ply their trade, but much of their fact is really something blue, immoral, or violent. Such revelations bore me now. Newspapers give people an illusion that they know what is going on, but their accounts bear no relation to what I've seen with my own two eyes. They imply iniquity is random, rare, or strange. They write as though they're a moral force shocked by it all.

I now know unconventional acts are common, frequent, and normal, and I can say that little of what human beings do surprises me anymore. I think newspaper people must share this chasm; the weariness that comes from the gap between what they see and know and what they can write about. My work with Crampton would in most people's eyes taint any claim to respectability I might make, but like Crampton I am no longer inviting others to comment on what is right or wrong in my world.

Sometimes I lie awake at night and wonder, Was I dealt this hand or did I choose it? Should I not have rejected the curse of poverty? The only way I saw to escape it was through illegal acts. Was I wrong to want to free women from the sort of misery I suffered at the hands of men—to want to even the score?

I escape going to jail only to find myself in another kind of jail, one where I can't stop my mind from burning. The things I tended, the things I cared about are gone. The unstoppable calendar pages keep turning. The days and people we know all get swept away. Were they ever real? Who believed the life one was living would not last forever?

Among the things Sam left behind for storage is an envelope of pictures of the girls he knew in Korea—some wearing the dresses I sent for war relief. No doubt many hoped he would marry them. Sometimes I get so angry I could light a match to their images, but they are Sam's history to destroy, not mine.

I'm really two people now. The one who says, C'mon, let's get busy, and the one who can't do anything. There is no duty now. My nursing days really are over. For fifteen years I ran my own hospital. Now what?

When the thought of no work or purpose finally sinks in, I spend hours at the farm looking out the window at the crows in the cornfield or noticing the way their feet grip the hot telephone wires. I can't seem to want to get myself to do anything. Sometimes I go through the motions—bake a pie, roast a piece of meat—but everything seems off somehow, like someone gently resting their fingers on a phonograph record. I sit in the kitchen and stare.

It becomes clear my life was growing more troubled when I stop getting out of bed in the morning. At first I think—I'll just let myself sleep in, take the extra rest, I'll be better off. What happens is the longer I stay in bed, the less I want to get up. Soon I don't rise until afternoon—forget morning—don't bother getting dressed, stay in a housecoat and slippers, then head back to bed. The only meals I rig are eggs, toast, cereal. The weeks wear on. I know this is a deeper kind of trouble. Dewey knows it too.

A nervous breakdown?

I started to bawl over nothing. It scares the hell out of us both. I've always been the strong one, the one in charge. No one knows I'm here resting and the staff isn't sure how to help me because I won't agree to any of their methods. Shock treatments? No, thank you. Doses of narcotics? No, thank you. Warm hydro baths? Okay. At least they are relaxing. People from the country understand madness. They know from doing the same hard work day after day, year after year. They see it every day in nature—chickens that peck each other in a too-tight pen, dogs that chase the same skunk two days in a row, cows that disappear down avoidable sinkholes. I think of Grandma Peffer. How she'd butter toast with the thinnest scraps of grease, or if there were pancakes, she'd dole out only one spoon of syrup. Rancid butter was also saved for guests. She'd hide her food if there was a knock at the door.

Dewey visits every few days. "The water pump broke down over the weekend," he says. "It cost eleven dollars to fix." He asks again if he can use the car. He claims the truck is having problems. "I'm not about to have my car smashed up," I say. "The truck is good enough." He curses me under his breath before leaving.

Sam doesn't know I am here resting; if he did I wonder if he would write or even visit. He's still stationed in Kentucky, and does send a postcard to Myrtle. She puts it in an envelope and forwards it to Halifax. It's the ugliest card I've ever seen, a big barracks in Fort Knox connected by catwalks to another old building. It doesn't look that different from this place. On the card Sam writes Myrtle that things are going well except for shipments of tainted or really fatty beef that certain packinghouses unload on their military contracts. He says it's disgraceful to treat servicemen that way.

I think of Sam. Despite not having a real father or an education—

or a real mother, for that matter—somehow, he's finding his way. The Army has taken him to Korea twice and all over America, even the West Coast—to Washington State, California, Texas. Soon, he says, they're sending him to Germany. It's given him an education, an occupation as mess sergeant, taught him the skills of a meat cutter, offered him a roof over his head, a regular paycheck, three squares a day. One has to marvel at the resiliency of a child grown up—especially an unwanted one. I must forgive him because my indifference when he was young helped make him the way he is today. There is no other way.

Just as I'm making that decision, Dewey comes in. There is a hint of excitement in him, which means something is up. He hands me the *Harrisburg Patriot* and points to a photograph on the front page. It reads: DR. CRAMPTON DEAD AT 76.

34

When I was a child, loss was like an autumn leaf being carried downstream. I thought if one could just run swiftly enough, losses could be regained. As I matured the stream widened, the current grew stronger. Suddenly the losses weren't just leaves or branches but small bushes, one's innocence, my favorite schoolbooks, and even my ability to see; blind by the time I became an adult, I found that loss grew into a powerful, wide river; deep, swift, muddy, it swept away my past, my youth, and left me with a child who couldn't yet swim. Then I realized that there was no riverbank to climb up to, that what we're swimming in is not a river at all but an enormous gulf along the curve of a continent. I can and must choose either to get swept out to sea by the grief of it all, or to swim for as long as my body can endure.

All of a sudden I know that there is nothing wrong with me. It's just that my grief started early anticipating this season of mourning.

· 35 ·

Dr. Crampton's viewing is held at the Hooper Funeral Home just a block from his house. The area is now a construction zone, as the houses on the entire south side of Forster Street are demolished to make way for the Capitol extension project. Crampton's funeral will be the last in the old neighborhood. Even Hooper's is pulling out and moving up to the hill.

About twenty-five people gather in the outer parlor. Frances hugs me as though I'm a long-lost prodigal daughter. Daphne Monroe lets out a squeal and wraps her arms around my neck. They take me around, introduce me to members of Crampton's family—a niece named Laura, two brothers, Benjamin and Ulysses, who own the barbershop in Tyrone. The family plans to take his body with them after the funeral. This surprises me. Except for college, he lived his entire life in Harrisburg. "They feel this city has destroyed him," Frances says. "It does not deserve his grave."

Harrison, the nephew from Sewickley out near Pittsburgh, sits apart from the Tyrone clan. He's also a doctor, impeccably dressed, and Crampton favored him, even sent him to medical school. He says he remembers meeting me before and greets me warmly. He tells me a story about the time a couple of years ago when Crampton hosted Joe Louis for supper. Frances tells me later the talk is that Harrison came to town in Crampton's final days and that the old man gave him shopping bags full of money. "Do you believe that?" I ask. "It's all just talk," she says.

I know Harrison was Dr. Crampton's favorite relative, but I

can't imagine shopping bags full of money. Prior to the arrest we'd worked nonstop because his bills were outrageous. Still he somehow managed to have a new Lincoln each year, even after the IRS came calling. How? Was it money stashed for the housing project?

A photo album and scrapbook are set out on a table in the hallway for people to look at. It's the same album I once saw in his office: Crampton as a young man at Howard University, the sloped slate roof of a campus building in the background; Crampton laying groundwork for the Y, standing in black tie at the podium for the testimonial dinners in his honor, shaking hands with Ethel Waters and, more recently, Richard Nixon.

In the scrapbook: yellowed newspaper clippings, his oration to the high school class of 1899, a notice that he's setting up practice in 1905, his honorary degree from Lincoln University dated 1944. There is even a yellowed carbon copy of the last will and testament of Lucius Copeland, folded to the page that says, "and to Charles H. Crampton, so long a member of my family, I leave a hundred dollars, fifty books which he may choose from my library, and any of my fishing poles and clothes he cares to keep."

No doubt, more than fifty years later, some of Copeland's books are still inside 600 Forster Street a few doors down. I wonder what will become of them now. Alone at the table, I unfold Copeland's will. Then I see how his real children, Fred and Lucy, received a townhouse each, along with a thousand dollars. So much for the myth of equality.

On the last page of the book, his obituary is newly pasted. It does not mention his disgrace, the IRS, the trial, the other humiliations. Death has relieved the newspaper from telling the truth. I realize suddenly that Dr. Crampton died a year to the day of our arrest. That makes him a man who lived a year too long; every town has one.

Frances comes over. "His body wasn't even cold before the bank sealed off the house," she says. "They refuse to allow anyone to enter. During his final days, I came back to help him. He was sick and irrational, and I know he wouldn'ta let me go if he were well. He wasn't himself no more. On the last day, I was so upset at his passing—and they were rushing us out of the house—that I forgot my best blue cardigan on the back of my chair. They won't let me go back to get it, or the lipstick in my desk drawer either. I even took myself down to the bank office to ask the manager.

"The only reason we have these is because I took them home a few days earlier." Frances smooths down the cover of the scrapbook she's faithfully maintained for so many years. I wonder if she'll cry, but she's quiet and strong. "Togans was at the garage having the Lincoln serviced. The police stopped him as he was crossing the State Street Bridge. They pulled him from the car, insulted him, and left him standing on the bridge. It wasn't until he walked back here that he even found out Dr. Crampton had passed. The police never told him. They probably been waiting months to get their hands on that car."

I nod my head in sympathy. What to say? I recognize they'd never treat the staff of a white politician this way, even one in disgrace. "Mrs. K., there's not much time left," Frances says, and gently touches my forearm with her cotton glove. "You might want to go in and see him now."

To the rear of the parlor is a set of double doors that people have taken turns entering. I pass inside and allow my eyes to adjust to the strange, eerie glow from a pair of marble floor lamps. C. Sylvester Jackson occupies a green velvet slipper chair at the old man's feet. He slowly rises as I draw near, seeming more like a ghost than a man. He and I have never spoken a great deal over the years, but we passed each other in the hallway often and there is no doubt he was Crampton's best friend, so trusted that he even kept the old man's books.

I step closer to the edge of the coffin. The mahogany wood has silver fittings; the box is lined in blue with a white lace pillow. Dr. Crampton's face is smooth and tight and he looks years younger than when I last saw him. He wears a navy suit and a spotless, well-starched white cotton shirt. His tie is gold with a fine blue stripe—one I've never seen before. A peach-colored rose is held in his folded hands.

"Charlie would be so pleased to know you are here," Mr. Jackson says, placing his hand on my shoulder. "There aren't many people he respected as much as you."

"Well, he was quite a man," I say, my voice tight.

"You know we were both brown boys growing up in white households. Him with the Copelands, me with the Boyds. But Crampton went after things. He had unheard-of confidence. I just kept accounting records and was like a secretary, but not him. He wanted to lead. In the end, I think that's what hurt him so much. He never rightly estimated the loneliness of leadership. How being an example to others never allowed him to be totally at home with them. The burden of authority. He found out, like so many before him, that money and power are only temporary things, and when they go, they don't guarantee that people will stick by you."

I nod and say how my father used to quote Gray's elegy: "the paths of glory lead but to the grave." I struggle to act professional in the grip of my sudden grief. I must act like a nurse—peppermint crisp. Yet, as I stare down at him, I wish I could gain more control. "I'm a nurse," I whisper to Jackson. "And because of him a real one. He saw God was spare in giving me the things that girls trade on—grace, a nice figure, a fine dowry. I loved him because he was proof that it was possible to invent oneself—live up to one's potential." Tears make a noose of my throat and I struggle to keep them from spilling.

C. Sylvester Jackson pats my arm with understanding. Oh, why did I think it was going to be easier after he died?

I embrace Mr. Jackson, then turn and exit.

36

Dr. Crampton's funeral is held at the brand-new Capitol Street Baptist Church on Thirteenth and Cumberland. Here it is clear to what degree his late disgrace has erased the good deeds of his life, for the church is half-empty. Just a short time ago the crowd would have spilled out onto the sidewalk and blocked the street.

There is no sign of any politician: there are no longer any votes to be had. Even Dora stays home.

But the service begins, and the deaconesses in white—God bless them—pass up the aisle, weathered faces stoic. They know their duty. Under the modern fluorescent lights, their procession doesn't seem as elegant as it did in the old church downtown—another loss attributed to Crampton. Still the women move with dignified comportment.

One of them rises, goes to the front, and sings a moving version of "His Eye Is on the Sparrow." C. Sylvester Jackson sits in the front pew and openly weeps.

The minister conducts a brief service, saying, "I marvel that God never gets tired of challenging humans with trouble. Maybe we pray in hopes of negotiating the unfairness of it all. But God always wins because though we end up losing everything on earth we love, we return home to him." He recites some additional scripture and concludes by saying, "In death, Dr. Crampton's dignity lies intact."

Then he points out Don Freedman, the young doctor who used to assist Crampton on the sports teams. "I've just learned that Dr. Freedman is working on erecting a plaque at William Penn High School to honor Dr. Crampton for all his years of service there." A few of us applaud and some say amen. A few years earlier and they'd have probably named the entire athletic field after him.

There is a final organ interlude, then another old woman gets up and sings the Lord's Prayer. Her voice is powerful and moving. Don

Freedman has managed to round up a few players from the sports teams to act as pallbearers. They move into place and hoist the casket onto their shoulders; as the organ plays in the background, they deliver Dr. Crampton's body out to the hearse. Togans sits behind the wheel, his cheeks streaked with tears. The Hoopers have hired him to drive the hearse to Tyrone. "Don't worry, baby, I'll soon be coming home." While watching all these rites being carried out, I sense a new determination in myself. The grief at Crampton's demise is not a permanent illness. I must only forgive to move on.

We exit the building and move to our cars, tying scarves to protect ourselves from a blustery wind. I invite Frances to ride with me but she has other offers. When all the cars have lined up, we slowly follow the hearse as it carries Dr. Crampton down his beloved Forster Street for the last time. The procession passes the colored YMCA, boarded up now, slated for demolition to make way for the new Labor and Industry building. The sidewalk around the Y is empty, trash-strewn, and without a single boy in sight.

Dr. Crampton's house at the corner of Sixth Street is also boarded up, and a wooden barrier has been set across the driveway with a sign saying Keep Out. Again, not a soul anywhere.

The paper says the state has claimed the house for back taxes and that soon it will be demolished to widen the access road that links Sixth to Forster Street. Is that why the IRS came after him? To get at the land his house sits upon?

A block further down, a group of men stand outside the cigar store where Crampton used to buy his Cuban specials. Some lean against the building and some are gathered near the fireplug. They grow still and watch as the hearse glides past. A couple of them remove their hats, and a few nod their heads. They know another page of Harrisburg history is turning.

At Front Street I make a left away from the other cars and head upriver toward my house. The rest of the procession continues, west toward Tyrone, crossing the Susquehanna and the bitter span of the Harvey Taylor Bridge.

37

January 13, 1956. The front page of the newspaper shows a photograph of a pretty twenty-year-old girl from Lebanon named Jacqueline Smith. She'd gone to New York to become a fashion illustrator and died there in a botched abortion. So far her body has not been found, which means that no one can be charged with her murder.

Her boyfriend, who is twenty-four, found and paid the man who did the operation. The man, a hospital worker but never a doctor, performed the abortion in the boyfriend's apartment on Christmas Eve. Something went wrong and the boyfriend stood helplessly by as the girl lay dying. The abortionist in a panic called a Mexican doctor he knew to come over. By the time the Mexican doctor made the scene, the girl was already dead.

The Mexican doctor, in the United States for only two months, was afraid to become involved and left the scene immediately. What to do with the body? In a frenzy, the abortionist put her in the bathtub and then spent the next few hours into Christmas morning cutting her corpse up into fifty small pieces. The boyfriend watched. Together they wrapped the body parts in Christmas wrapping paper as though they were presents, then left them in trash bins all around the city. They got rid of the rest of her in pails and other containers that they poured into sewers at night.

She was due home to visit her family on Christmas day. The family phoned and phoned, wondering if she'd changed her plans. On the thirtieth of December her father came to New York looking for her. He went to the police.

When the Mexican doctor read of her disappearance in the newspaper, his heart went out to the father and he came forward to turn the other two in. At first the boyfriend lied, saying the girl stabbed herself Japanese style because he was breaking up with her.

Later he confessed to helping her get the abortion and explained how her body was mutilated and disposed of.

When the police finally arrested the abortionist this week, they found eight hundred medical instruments in his apartment, stolen from various jobs, including several small medical amputation saws that cut through bone.

Lebanon—hometown of this pretty young girl, Jacqueline Smith—is only an hour-long ride from here. The boyfriend says they'd heard about Dr. Crampton from a friend and tried to call Harrisburg for an appointment, but the number was disconnected. I cry the rest of the afternoon.

· **38** ·

Myrtle has another postcard from Sam. It announces that he has been shipped out of America and is now stationed in Germany.

It shows a peaceful valley with little houses and people in folk costume. Myrtle is fairly modest when she shows me the card. Not her usual trumpet and fanfare.

I've begun to notice an odd habit in myself. Whenever I talk about people or gossip about their faults, a short while later I notice the same bad qualities in myself. This strikes me with Myrtle more than anyone else. How cheap she is, how she wants to be the center of attention, a leader. Do we only notice in others what we know to be true within ourselves?

39

February 1956. The *Patriot* reports another young woman has recently died—Doris Silver, a twenty-two-year-old girl from Philadelphia. Her mother, Gertrude, age forty-nine, helped her procure the abortion. It was performed by a bartender and his wife, a beautician. The daughter, whom the paper refers to as an heiress, was brought to the bartender's apartment and the procedure he performed killed her.

The bartender, his wife, and Mrs. Silver have all been on trial for the past few days. The couple has been issued a prison sentence. Mrs. Silver, however, though guilty, is not sent to jail. The judge says, "The memory of this dreadful tragedy will be substantial and overwhelming punishment."

We could have saved this girl too. But I don't cry about it this time. I'm regaining my strength and taking stock. I'm recognizing that the service we provided saved lives. It wasn't just about cash or convenience. Since Crampton's death, my purpose has been compromised. It would benefit me to find another doctor who needs a nurse—or I could do volunteer work. But volunteer work is for women like Myrtle. Amaranth, Eastern Star, Bird Watcher's Club—they're for housewives who like to tell you how much charity work they do.

If I am to return to usefulness, I must return to the idea of how to be useful. In its simplest form, that means I must do useful things. But what? A farmer may be depressed but he still has to milk the cows every day. I must find a purpose equally demanding.

It is unseasonably warm. When I return from having my hair done, Dewey sits with his friend Hickey on the edge of the breezeway, a row of half-empty liquor bottles between them. They are clearly drunk or Dewey would have made some attempt to hide the evidence. "We're having a party," Hickey says. I walk over and kick the liquor bottles off the porch. "Well, the party's over."

I go inside and into my room, I get on my knees and pray to God to help me to change this situation and myself.

·   40   ·

It is April 1956, and the contents of Crampton's house are being auctioned off; the demolition of the house is only a few days away. A crowd has gathered on Forster Street to watch the sale. C. Sylvester Jackson sees me and comes over. We chat for a few moments. "People always flock to auctions," he says, "lured by the hope of a bargain, or just to learn clues about another person's life. Watching someone's possessions scatter off in all directions is a rehearsal for our own fate." He tells me they've canceled the plans for the new Negro housing, but he says he's fighting on. "If I can get even one building put up I'll put his name on it," he says, before moving to peer into some more boxes. I stand there and watch the crowd milling about. One strange man stands next to me and tells me outright he'd never buy something owned by a colored man. But most don't care—if the price is right. And many who are present actually knew Dr. Crampton and would like a keepsake.

Frances arrives in a fine car driven by local boxer Billy Gray. He drops her at the curb, and people instantly rise and begin offering her their folding seats. Someone hands her a bottle of soda. They call her Miss Frances. Once she's settled, she sees me and blows me a kiss from her shaky old palm.

The auction commences: china, glassware, a few paintings; the rest of the art, the really good works, remain mysteriously unaccounted for. There are linens and furniture, his beautiful mahogany bedroom set, and things I've never seen before: punch bowls, humidors, plaid wool blankets. And things I wonder about—the pen set from his desk, the fruit bowl with the Egyptian motifs. Togans sits beside me for a spell and I mention this to him. "You know his nephew took bags of money and objects," he says. By now the story is probably a legend in what's left of the Seventh Ward.

A box containing Frances's sweater is put on the stand and a buzz goes through the crowd not to bid on it. Her withered hand is the only bid, but she waits until they've knocked the price down from a dollar to fifty cents.

The man who says he'd never buy anything from a colored man ends up buying a box of books. I wonder if any of the fifty titles from Lucius Copeland's library are in it. The rugs bring a good price, as does the Philco television set. Then they bring out racks of his clothes. There must be fifty suits. I'm tempted to bid on one, to hold on to a piece of him, but they are sold in lots and I wouldn't have the nerve anyway.

The crowd grows still when the auctioneer hefts up a mysterious white bag. No one can believe it when they announce it's a bag full of dirty laundry. "Who'd auction off a dead man's soiled wash?" a man in front of me mutters. It is shocking, I have to agree. But the bank is running things and they don't care. No one moves to buy the bag, and then Frances stands up, her voice shaky with anger. "You gimme that bag," she says, her voice clear and distinct. "And you oughta be ashamed."

"Minimum bid's a quarter, ma'am," the auctioneer says.

"Gimme that bag this instant," she says. "Have you lost all respect?" The man stands frozen, then nods his head and the bag is passed back to her—no charge.

The last thing to be sold is the office medical equipment: examination table, sterilizer, tools. To my left, the old geezer who said he wouldn't buy anything colored, looks at me and smirks. "Why don't you bid on those?" It's his way of letting on that he knows who I am.

"Oh, heavens," I say, dry as toast, "I wouldn't know what to do with them." His little squirrelly eyes shine and his face twists.

When the auction ends, the crowd begins to slowly disperse,

but some linger a bit too, recognizing that an era has passed. I see Frances begin to struggle toward the sidewalk with the laundry bag like a beetle carrying a leaf. Togans hurries to her aid. "Miss Frances, what you gonna do with them old clothes?" he says.

"I'm gonna wash 'em, honey. I have to. It just isn't right."

41

In the afternoon Hazel, Mom, and Myrtle drive up to the farm in Myrtle's new Oldsmobile, and we spend the afternoon preparing supper. For the first time I start feeling like my old self. It reminds me of when we were small and would all pitch in to help do work.

Myrtle admits to me she's had another letter from Sam. She's like a sister to him but it makes me angry that he writes her but doesn't drop me a line, not even a postcard. Myrtle takes it out of her pocketbook and I try to bury my jealousy. "He's doing well for himself," Mom says.

Heidelberg, West Germany
June 19, 1956

Dear Myrtle,

I've been transferred from the 6th Army Cavalry regiment to Heidelberg, where I'm chef to General John M. Williams and his wife, Eileen. They are both in their early sixties though she's a bit older than him. He is chief of staff of G-2 intelligence at the Pentagon. General Williams graduated West Point in 1925 and he was in the 1936 Olympics as an equestrian rider for the Army. She's a nice, classy woman from Wyoming who knows a great deal about etiquette, can speak on world affairs, and is a good hostess. Every morning after breakfast we meet and go over the day's menu. The general's favorite dish is chicken noodle casserole. They host a dinner party for ten to twelve people every couple weeks and sometimes she has women in for card parties in the afternoon.

At the dinner parties, they bring me in from the kitchen, and they have introduced me to a few senators and congressmen, including Flynn from Scranton (who waxes his mustache, wears a cape, and carries a cane) and Wainwright from New York, and a German general who was in charge of intelligence for Hitler.

Heidelberg is a beautiful old city with a university and a big castle on the hill that dates to the Middle Ages. My first week here, I bought a turquoise and ivory '54 Chevy very cheap from a guy who was going back to the States. Thank you for sending the extra money. I've got plenty of cash now because American dollars have a lot of value here. Through a friend I met a nice girl named Elsa who works in a department store. On my day off we take short trips. I was teaching her to drive the car and she said, "Oh, this is easy." The next thing I know we hit a wood fence. Luckily the car is fine.

Hope this finds you and Gram well.

Sam

42

At the drugstore in Millersburg, a nice-looking man in a suit and tie comes in to speak to the druggist. He says he's trying to find someone to look after his ailing mother. Hovering by the mouthwash and dental cream, I listen while the druggist says he'll keep his ears open.

"Who was that man?" I ask, as I pay.

"Neal Troutman," the druggist says. "His family owns the car dealership outside of town. Their mother is elderly and suffers from dementia."

A bell goes off in my head. I speed home to change, putting on a gray skirt and white blouse. Neal is in the office when I enter the auto showroom and he stands up as though I'm a customer. When he finds out I'm there about his mother, we both sit down and he tells me of her deteriorating condition. After a while he asks if I'd be willing to meet her. "Sure," I say, and follow him outside, where he takes one of the brand-new cars off the lot. We drive over to the house, a modern ranch only a few blocks away. Mrs. Troutman sits in an armchair by the window.

"Mother, this is Mrs. Krone. She's going to take you out today."

I hadn't expected to start today, just to make inquiries. But she's spry, already up and getting her sweater. Neal hands me a small leather coin purse. "For expenses. Fill up with gas, take her for a drive and some lunch. She likes to go to the market. Buy whatever is needed. Treat yourself too."

The next thing I know we are on the road. She's a sweet lady but keeps repeating herself and needs help counting money. When I see that the coin purse holds thirty dollars, I decide it would be better if I keep hold of it. We have lunch at Hap Martin's restaurant in Penbroke, then stop at the market, then buy an ice cream cone.

I tell Mrs. Troutman how we used to sell our peaches to an ice cream stand out on the highway near Halifax. From the first weeks of August into early September, they'd make soft peach ice cream using our tree-ripened fruit. The ice cream would tube out of the refrigeration machine onto a cake cone, piling upward into a peak with a tiny loop curled at the top. It was the most beautiful shade of peach and on a hot evening your mouth would water waiting for the owner to slide back the little screen door to hand you a napkin-wrapped cone.

In June they made fresh strawberry, in July black raspberry, and in any season you could get delicious vanilla. Last year the family that built the place sold it and the new owner changed everything; the new machines no longer accept fresh fruit. Instead, they use a flavored mix. It tastes artificial, not like real peaches. I asked the man why he did it and he said, "These machines are being placed in every town across America. They allow for a wider profit margin and cut down on preparation time."

I say to Mrs. Troutman, "In summer the cars and trucks are still piled there three deep. Some people will eat anything, but I never stop. I only wish I'd have known in advance that the last fresh peach cone I ate there would be my last. I'd have paid closer attention and appreciated it more."

I can tell that Mrs. Troutman feels as sad as I do about the change. "I wonder how he spends that extra time," she says. "Making ice cream that tastes good is such a fine calling."

When we return to the house, I give the coin purse back to Neal and say, "I hope we weren't too hard on it. Lunch was bought, and gas was a dollar twenty."

"Oh, don't worry about that," he says. "Mother hasn't looked so content in a while." He hands me a twenty-dollar bill for my trouble and asks me to come back again the day after tomorrow. On the way home I start to sing. I'm working again.

On Saturday Neal asks me if I would take his mother to church the next morning. She attends the Methodist Church in Halifax. There's a visiting preacher that day, who is well intentioned but dull as gray paint. The congregation is sweet—I see a few faces I recognize from shops—but everything seems to be happening by rote. The hymns still move me, however, and while Mrs. Troutman can't remember what she had for breakfast, she remembers every word of "The Old Rugged Cross." She also brought some coins from the powder box on her bedroom bureau to put in the collection plate. How did she remember to do that?

The minister asks us to pray for those who are needier than ourselves and for some reason I pray for Sam. I don't necessarily believe that he is needier than me, but something prompts me toward him—as though he may be in trouble. Afterwards, it feels like a burden has been lifted. I leave church feeling clean, or cleaner than I have in a while, a bit lighter in my step.

Following the service I take Mrs. Troutman for a drive. She is oddly talkative and tells me a story of her youth. She once went with a Mercersburg cousin to visit a logging camp in a forest somewhere in northern Pennsylvania. It was a sort of summer excursion, extra tents pitched, everyone helping out with chores, and there was swimming and banjo playing. The vacationing group sat down to a lazy supper, tired from their day's activities, passing plates of food, congenial with the late sun streaming down in shafts between the trees.

But their laughter and good cheer were broken by a piercing train whistle, then a horrible stretched-out screech of metal. Less than a quarter of a mile away, a speeding locomotive derailed, skidding the passenger cars off the track at full speed, smashing them into the forest, where they uprooted giant trees and crushed and slammed against each other before coming to rest in a hideous silence.

Many were killed. Broken bodies, dressed in their traveling clothes, were scattered about. In shock, the survivors began to crawl from the wreckage. Some were trapped and their moans and eerie cries carrying through the woods frightened everyone. "Imagine," Mrs. Troutman said, her voice breaking with emotion. "One minute they are seated on leather train seats moving toward their des-tination, and the next they are flung into the forest, to find themselves sitting on logs. The twisted metal smokes behind them, forever to blame for ruining their lives." Mrs. Troutman weeps openly now and tells me the experience changed her forever. "It was the contrast of the pleasant outing, innocent and warm, crashing into the horror of the death of ordinary people, all of it happening in the middle of the forest. It haunted me. I couldn't sleep. I still see the bloody faces. I remember an arm, separated from someone inside the crumpled cars, its hand still clad in a fine lady's glove. I've never taken life for granted since that day, and I have never told anyone this before, but I've also never fully trusted God since then either. I simply couldn't. It was all too frightening." With my free hand I unsnap her pocketbook and hand her a lace handkerchief. She wipes her eyes and dabs her nose. "Have you ever questioned God?" she asks.

The question catches me off guard.

"At times," I say. "At times."

· 43 ·

It is Thanksgiving weekend. On the farm the warmth of an Indian summer has passed and what remains is the sour smell of the idled cider press standing amid the black walnut trees. The branches rise up into the autumn vapor looking like they've been burned in a fire. A bit more than a year has passed since Crampton's death—two since our arrest. As if to mock me, a photograph of our prosecutor looks out at me from the morning pages of the *Harrisburg Patriot*. He is doing some kind of charity work and is standing beside a nun wearing a habit.

A new tenant is moving into the upstairs apartment on Third Street, so all week long Dewey and I have been scrubbing to get things ready. I've been debating whether to convert the second floor into an apartment as well. We no longer need so much space and could manage well with the first floor alone. This would provide us with some extra income and cover the taxes.

This morning I take a pie over to Dora for her birthday and decide to drive along Derry Street to have a look at the old house that was home to the Pierce School of Nursing. Mrs. Pierce sold the business a few years ago and the building has been converted to a funeral home. It looks the same except that her lovely garden has been paved over to make room for more parking.

Driving along Derry Street, I see how much the neighborhood has changed. One small storefront building has been converted to a church, and a cloth banner hangs in front that says, "Bible Study now. You are welcome." I drive on, but the message stays in my head. For some reason I make a U-turn and go back to pull into the parking lot. Inside, a small group are just taking their seats in a circle of chairs. The preacher, a little gnome of a man, notices me standing in the doorway and comes over. "Sister . . . sister . . . So glad you are here." His voice has a lilting Pennsylvania Dutch accent. "Today we are looking at the Book of Job."

There is an upright piano along one wall, and when a hymn is played, the group gets up and begins to clap and join in. It reminds me of when we were children and would sing hymns to keep warm, our feet propped up against the woodstove. After the song we settle down again and begin to read from the Book of Job. The preacher tells us that many people think it is the most difficult book to accept. Job is faithful to God and yet has to be tested. He loses everything—wife, children, property, friends. He grows ill, and though he pleads with God and questions him, through all the trials his faith remains unchanged. I listen with wonderment, amazed at how well I understand the lesson.

Afterwards there is a brief prayer and people come over to introduce themselves. They laugh and talk and tell me how glad they are that I have joined them. Have I joined them? One thing is certain, I have never felt so comfortable in a church before. I leave feeling ten years younger.

44

All my furniture and personal things from town have been trans-ferred up here to the farm. A tenant appeared for the ground floor of the Harrisburg house as well, so I've decided the extra income will be useful. I go through boxes of stuff—clothes and household items and Sam's toys, his cornet, a few old letters from Charles from when I still thought he was single and would marry me. I also find a postcard from Murphy dated 1928, when he went on a trip to Baltimore, and a snapshot of me holding Sam, where I turn my head in shame so no one will see it's me holding a baby born out of wedlock. There are a couple of birthday cards, and a Mother's Day telegram from Sam dated 1949 that I will never part with.

Dewey's brother Harry and his wife, Emma, are visiting from Thurmont, Maryland. Harry's presence is annoying. He's a tight-wad and Dewey jokes that Harry and Emma could go to Florida and back on a ten-dollar bill. Dewey will be on his best behavior while they visit, given that Harry is a minister. He is assigned to a new church not far from the one where Dewey and I were married. When speaking to me, Harry turns every conversation into a ser-mon, and he'll say things like, "When you see something wicked, Verna, what do you do? You simply stomp it out!" I think he be-lieves me to be fallen because of my work with Crampton.

He knows about our work but delivers his message somewhat indirectly because he knows I once helped his daughter Margaret get a procedure. Cast not the first stone, I say.

It seems to me he represents the two things that I most resent about organized religion and that comprise two of its biggest of-fenses to Christianity—being pious and believing one knows what God intends. That's what appeals to me most about the preacher down at the little church on Derry Street: he is so humble. I look forward to going there every Sunday.

45

My forty-eighth birthday, and I'm at the clothesline, hanging up pillowcases and a couple of blankets. The wet clothes are heavy and I am propping a notched plank under the middle of the line to keep things off the ground when I spot Sam coming down the lane in his dark uniform. It takes me a moment to get used to the idea. It seems like we ought to run and greet each other like people do in the movies, but it doesn't happen. Instead I stroll partway up the lane to greet him and we say hello. Over the past three years I can see he's become a real man. He's heavier but the weight looks solid and becoming on him. "I was going to call but decided to surprise you instead. I went by Third Street, but no one answered, and the woman next door said you were living up here full-time now."

"Yes, the entire house is rented out."

"I can't believe how the city is tore up. I don't recognize it. All the neighborhoods around the Capitol have been bulldozed."

"They're going to ruin the whole thing," I say. "Dewey kept saying there was nowhere for Negroes to go but uptown, and he's right. Whole sections are being taken over. I ought to sell Mom's house on Logan Street but already it has lost half its value. It's the scheme that finally did Crampton in." Sam slings his duffel bag over his shoulder and we turn toward the house.

"I hitched a ride on a furniture truck to get here," he says.

We come into the kitchen and I fry him some eggs and bacon. He is starved and eats like a wolf. I tell him he can have the small bedroom at the end of the upstairs hallway. "Dewey still uses the other one."

Sam nods. "I hope you don't mind my coming unannounced?"

"No," I say. "It's good to see you. I thought you had six more months on your tour of duty."

"They cut it short."

"How come?"

"They told me I should visit my mother on her birthday."

"I'll just bet they did." I smile, pleased that he remembers.

He goes upstairs to sleep. He's been traveling for days, and his coming home remains a mystery. Without prying, I can tell something has happened.

In the morning I go to Harry Hampton's farm and pick up some fresh sausage. When I return I ask Sam if he's hungry. He says he's eaten some leftovers he found in the fridge. "How were they?" I ask.

"Unseasoned," he says. "Not your best cooking."

"That's because they were scraps and trimmings I'd cooked down for the dog." Dewey comes in just then and begins to howl with laughter that Sam has eaten the dog's food. Sam joins in, his chest and belly shaking. He likes making Dewey laugh, and for a moment it feels like we are a family.

Later in the day Sam comes out to sit with me in the summerhouse, where I'm canning tomatoes.

"Thanks for getting the sausage. It was good."

"I'm sure it's hard to come by overseas."

"Well, actually, it was the Germans who brought sausage to Pennsylvania in the first place."

"Oh, of course." I continue my work, scalding tomatoes, slipping off the skins to cold-pack them. Again, there is that dull, awkward edge, the nervousness that arrives whenever Sam and I are alone and try to carry on a conversation. We never seem to be really talking about what we should be talking about, but neither of us really knows what that is.

"Mom, is everything okay now?" he asks, and suddenly there is a change. His directness catches me off guard. "I mean with the trial and all."

"Things are fine." The silence continues. Sam takes an unpeeled tomato and begins to eat it as though it were an apple. He eats two of them, one right after the other, salt and pepper sprinkling the tabletop. I notice that he's stuffing his mouth full and has no patience to taste anything. I make no comment. But his directness sinks in, and I crave some connection with him, some hint that we are blood relatives.

"Why are you here?" I ask him. "How did it happen?"

"It's just the way the military does stuff."

"You were a chef to the general. Did something go wrong?"

"No." He lifts his head and looks out the window. "It's not like that. I'm here because of a girl I was seeing. I asked her to marry me."

I lift my head at the news. "And?"

"Well, she said yes."

It feels like a chasm opens between us. His life is moving along on one side while mine continues on the other. A marriage, it can't be. Yet he's old enough; I wish I could have known; for some reason I'm tongue-tied again. The struggle resumes. My heart won't unclench.

He pauses for a moment, trying to compose himself, his emotions visible to me for the first time. He swallows and then begins to speak again. "We applied for the license, her wedding dress was being made, General Williams and his wife invited us in for tea so they could meet her. Mrs. Williams said I have good taste in girls. It's all set to move ahead. Elsa is so happy. But then the Army sends me a notice: our application for marriage has been denied. A couple of days later I get orders to ship back here. I go to see the general. I'm confused and desperate and ask for his help. He promises to see what is going on, but I get the sense that he knows this is not normal. Then the next day he calls me in and says there is nothing he can do to help, that it's a problem caused by Elsa's father. He's not a politician, but somehow he dabbles in politics, he's friendly to Russian ideas. He's been arrested for protesting and stuff and they say that he's a Communist.

"Then Elsa and I find out that the government has done a whole investigation behind our backs. They've called in all my American friends, as well as her German ones, and they question them. Every one of them is sworn to secrecy and they are threatened about what will happen to them if they speak of it. No one breathes a word to us. Imagine, we've gone out with them during the whole investigation and no one says a word to us. It's crazy.

"Now that I'm back here in the States, there is no one to look after her. The guys who were my buddies are afraid to get involved on account of their careers. Their wives and girlfriends look the other way. They drive by her walking along the road and never offer her a lift."

"Maybe it's for the best," I say. "Suppose you had married. A situation like that can't be good for a family or your career."

"You don't understand," he says, his voice wavering. "She's six months pregnant."

I sit in silence and take in the information. Sam's face looks scared—more like the boy who ran away from home twelve years ago. My son is in distress and I'm not sure how I can comfort him. He's never confided in me before. And I'm going to be a grandmother.

"How do we fight this?" I say.

"I don't know," Sam says. "I don't know. Those other women who were our friends, they drive past her on the road now without stopping and they see she's walking alone and pregnant."

I lie awake the whole night thinking about Elsa. Even if her family is involved with the Russians, in less than ninety days I'll be a grandmother and won't get to see my grandchild. I can't shake my anguish. The important thing is for him to give her hope. With him gone she may try to do something desperate.

In the morning we go into town to take Mom out to lunch. We are all stunned to see the toll urban "renewal" is taking on the city. Now they have finished tearing down Dr. Crampton's house and the Forster Street YMCA. I wonder if the politicians feel any shame when they look at the acres of wasteland they've created.

We drive around and notice that colored families are now to be seen as far north as Boas Street. One family has taken the house right next door to where Mrs. Nelly used to live, and Mom has seen some Negroes only a block away. Whites are moving out; nice houses turn run-down overnight. "People with no jobs or low wages, no pensions, no retirement can't afford to maintain these properties," I say. "Everything is going to hell."

Over the next few days Sam and I spend more time together but the distance between us cannot be erased overnight. We're invited to dinner by Myrtle, who now lives in a stone ranch house in an affluent section of Camp Hill. As we pull up, I see that in Sam's honor, she has turned on the small fountain by her front door. It's lit by a spotlight with turning colors—amber, pink, aqua, and green. It's sort of beautiful but also causes me to sneer at the wastefulness of the thing, the artificial grandness, so far removed from nature and the cabin of our childhood. Who is Myrtle trying to impress?

We enter and I stop dead in my tracks when I see Buckley sitting on a sectional sofa. It's been years since our paths crossed. He wears a white T-shirt and some workpants and looks out of place in Myrtle's fancy living room with its lavender walls. I haven't laid eyes on him in years. He looks bad, jaundiced, old, with teeth missing. His profligate ways are catching up to him. He sees Sam and rises to shake hands. Then he sees me and says, "Oh, shit," like he always does, as though he's fit to judge me. He turns quickly away and lumbers out of the room in the direction of the kitchen. "What a greeting," Sam says.

"He was always that way," I say. "Even as a kid."

At the supper table Myrtle serves chicken corn soup. Buckley is absent. Myrtle says he's wrecked his car, lost his trailer, and now has no home. She's letting him stay with her and has set up a cot in what she calls her "Florida room," really just a glorified sunporch. She won't allow him to smoke in the house, so he sits in the enclosed box with louvered glass panels that he cranks open, and puffs away.

Later on I go to use the bathroom; it has two pink sinks and a square tub; the counters are all trimmed with gray Formica to match the wall tiles. Coming back down the hall, I peer into Myrtle's bedroom, and sitting at the center of the bed with its back against the pillows is one of the old china head dolls I bought so many years ago. It was Myrtle who broke the other one, but it figures she'd find a way to end up with the good one anyway. She probably bamboozled Hazel to give it to her.

During the meal I'm jealous of the easy way Sam speaks to Myrtle. He talks about Germany, the boat trip across the ocean, the dinners he cooked for the general, how you can pick up acres of land for a song in Germany, how cheap it is to have a suit made there, how an American dollar goes far; the sourdough bread, the pastries, the Oktoberfest—all this gets discussed. He can tell her all that. But he won't tell me.

Then I realize he doesn't mention Elsa. Only I know that.

· 46 ·

Hours have been spent by Sam and Elsa collecting letters of character reference for themselves. Hers are in German of course but there's a WAC in Heidelberg who speaks both languages and Sam has asked her to help translate them. This time when he resubmits the paperwork requesting a license to be married, he discloses her pregnancy. The Pentagon sends an official report, formally typed, that emphatically states applicant's request has been *denied*.

Sam is despondent, and to take his mind off his troubles, Dewey invites him to the Legion. I tag along. We sit up half the night playing cards with some soldiers on leave. We drink grain pressings mixed with cider, though I take only a few sips. While serving in the military, Sam has become quite a good card player. My pot grows too, and I come out a couple of dollars ahead, though Sam and Dewey chide me for playing too conservatively. The two of them like to throw money around, take fat risks, bluff big. Then a sort of irritating thought begins to enter my head at the waste of their carelessness: what if someone from the little church on Derry Street were to see me? I want to move with a new crowd. For a moment I feel ashamed, but then I catch myself. As a Christian can't I play cards? Can't I take a drink of grain alcohol? Suddenly, for the first time in years, I hear Pop's voice in my head: "Too much virtue can hurt you."

It can not only hurt me but others too if I become too intolerant of their weaknesses. For so many years I've battled Dewey over his drinking, fought hard fights. Nothing's changed. Suddenly I see that it's not something I can change. In fact, forcing my will upon him will only make matters worse. A great veil is lifted. I see that the only thing that might transform anything is kindness. Perhaps courtesy could be added to that. To practice those things means something in myself has to be given away. Right there in the smoky bar room of the American Legion, I decide to make it a new goal of my life, to wake each day and see if I can accept Sam and Dewey not for what I want them to be but for the way they really are.

The next morning I give Sam fifty dollars to send to Elsa. It takes almost a fortnight for a red and blue air mail envelope to arrive for Sam with a letter from her inside written in broken English. Folded separately on a smaller piece of paper is a note with my name on it. She thanks me for the money and for standing by them in their time of trouble. The simplicity of the note touches me.

Later in the day I drive Sam down to Harrisburg and we have dinner with Hazel and Joe. Sam talks a blue streak, saying that the best thing he ever did was get out of Harrisburg and make a career in the military, and that he doesn't know where he'd have ended up if he'd stayed. The remark annoys me, as does his blather, but then I recognize that, as with Myrtle, he hasn't said a word to them about Elsa. I'm still the only one who knows that.

The next morning I'm cutting grocery coupons from the paper when Sam comes in, pours a cup of coffee, and sits across from me. "I was wondering if you could tell me about my father," he says.

"What about him?" I reply, my hackles rising.

Sam begins to ask questions—how we met, how long did we go out together, that sort of thing. I answer as best I can, and when I don't want to respond to something I say, "It's so long ago I really don't remember much." In truth, I remember every shadow and line.

Sam seems satisfied with what I tell him and rises to put his coffee mug in the sink. In the doorway he turns and asks one last question. "I guess what I really want to know is was he decent?"

I put the scissors down on the table, their sharp edges splayed open like a dancer's legs. "All I can say is he wasn't the worst of them."

Sam nods and leaves me to my work. Then after he's gone, and I sink back into the silence of being alone, I think about all those families I see when I go to church. They appear united in a way ours could never be. Why is it that our family just can't seem to stand closeness?

Sam's questions stir a resentment toward Charles Dennis, for yet again his actions affect my life as I'm forced to explain and be held accountable for the things he—not I—did twenty years ago. I decide it's time to call Charles—if for no other reason than that we need a new tractor on the farm. It's been a while, but why not call? He owes me plenty for raising his son.

He's happy to get my call, he says, and we agree to meet the next day for lunch. I wear my good pink silk dress; he has on a navy suit with a shirt and bow tie. He looks the same but his hair is grayer.

We drive down to Gettysburg for lunch. No one knows us there. The town looks kind of polished now that Eisenhower comes up from Washington to spend his weekends at his farm on the outskirts of town. We stop at a nice restaurant and order chicken. After we finish we linger over coffee, and I tell Charles that he is going to be a grandfather. His face is puzzled; he doesn't know how to respond.

"The reason I called is to let you know that Sam is home on leave, and as he is contemplating what it means to become a father, he has been asking questions about you. He's eager to meet."

Charles squirms. "After all these years I don't think it's a good idea."

"But he's curious," I say. "I'm not sure I can keep him at bay."

"What is it you want?" His voice is growing irritated.

"What do you mean?" I ask, my tone bland.

"You're blackmailing me again. I can tell."

I smile. "Am I? Well, maybe. But if you'd rather speak to Sam and the baby directly, I can always just step back."

"How much do you want?"

"A thousand."

His face turns purple. But I don't flinch and sip my coffee like I haven't a care in the world. Later we drive over to the L & M Motel and take a room for the afternoon. In bed he behaves as though he's still wild-crazy about me, but I know he's just reliving a time when he was young. I go through the motions but watch everything from a distance, from high up in the corner of the room. I know this is the last time we will ever lie together.

Afterwards we go to his bank and he withdraws the money. I come home and scrub my skin until it is raw.

47

Sam is sullen and sits in a chair and mopes. He fills Dewey's ashtray with cigarette butts and sometimes walks out to the breezeway and just stands staring at the horizon. I know he's worrying about Elsa.

I find his mood affects me too. It's odd how many people I've helped not to have babies, and now my whole body aches to hold a grandchild. I try to let these feelings go and just get on with what needs to be done—fixing supper, putting up my hair, sweeping out the summerhouse.

During lunch Dewey and I bicker about how much fertilizer we've been buying, and I suspect he's ordering more than we need and getting a kickback to drink with. Sam lingers at the table after Dewey goes back out to the orchard. "Why did you ever marry him?" he asks.

"I really can't remember," I say, clearing the dishes.

"Well, did he propose on one knee?"

"Heavens no," I say. "Although he did like a proper setting for things. It might have been among the white roses in the garden of the Hershey Hotel. Even then he was crazy for gardens and we used to go there during the war. But you'll have to ask him."

"When did Dewey start drinking?"

I pause at the kitchen sink and look out the window at the fir trees lining the ridge. Part of me wants to keep silent—it's none of Sam's business—and part of me wants to tell him the truth, to speak like we are closer than we are. "His decline into booze happened fast," I say. "I was too busy and tired to notice or care. Then it was too late. The seeds were planted long before I met him. You just don't notice it as much when someone is young. Sometimes I used to feel like he was reacting to me. The money I earned made his pay look paltry. It also made his efforts to work unnecessary. For a long time I believed the money I made led to his destruction, but now I've come to believe it would have happened anyway. He's just a drunk."

Sam looks surprised. I don't think he expected me to be so blunt. He seems unsure of how to reply.

One thing I've noticed is how over the past few weeks it has grown easier for the two of us to be in the same room together. I know why he's pensive and anxious, and he knows I understand. A few times, when I'm out working as a nurse for Mrs. Troutman, he goes with Dewey to Fisherville. At first I feel a pang of jealousy, but he doesn't return drunk, and I figure it's just a way for him to keep from being pent up. I try to practice love and forgive him; after all, with few exceptions, no one has the right to impose their will on someone else's life.

Then at long last, his orders from the Army arrive. He's being assigned as mess sergeant to the officers' club in Fort Myer, Virginia, which is only a couple of hours south of here outside of Washington, D.C.

·   48   ·

As the holidays approach Sam comes home on the weekends, and with Dewey we take drives through the countryside, enjoying the winter scenery like some kind of snow travelers. Sometimes we also take Mom along and drive back through Perry County to pass by our old cabin. Nothing has changed; the old building still sits on a bluff above the stream—the same stream that Delia, Pop's daughter, forded with her husband, John, in their big, fine car when they came out from St. Louis so many years ago. You'd never know that there has been a bigger war, that a depression came and went, that Prohibition was repealed, or that court trials and arrests have marked our lives.

Another thing I notice is that the ease I'm beginning to experience with Sam is carrying over to Mom, like she's felt it too, and we're all too tired to keep our resentments alive.

"What do you think ever happened to John and Delia?" I ask her.

"I don't know," she says. "They lost touch once we moved to Mechanicsburg. Sometimes things just disappear. I think they thought I made a big mistake in not letting them take you. And maybe it's true."

"What makes you say that now?" I ask.

"I don't know," she says. "I guess it's because of the hardships you've had to live through. Maybe going with them would have given you an easier time of it."

"Well, it's too late to worry about it now," I say. "We all did the best we could." There's even a hint of comfort in these blank words.

When we drop Mom off at her house on Logan Street it is possible to see how the neighborhood is growing more and more neglected. You can see colored people hanging out on their paint-peeling porches, the sound of their radios coming from the house, playing way too loud. We don't openly speak of it, but I know the change on the streets is saddening her and that soon I will have to move her.

Just before Christmas, Elsa writes me a German holiday card and thanks me for the twenty dollars I mailed to her. She addresses me as "Dear Mom," and like the sentimental fool I seem to be developing into, I have to wipe my eyes on my apron after that.

Her English is hard to read, but whenever she writes she tells me a bit more about how she is filing her papers to challenge her denied visa and obtaining letters of character reference from family, friends, and former teachers. She also tells me she likes Nat King Cole and the movie *The Glenn Miller Story.* She says Sam told her all about the farm and our life over here and that she looks forward to the day when she can come to America. She apologizes for all the trouble she is causing.

Again, it just astounds me that I who have helped so many women avoid the burdens of motherhood should be so captivated by the thought of becoming a grandmother. Why is this baby so important? Why do I suddenly crave to see life renewed? Perhaps being a grandmother offers the hope of being needed again. Perhaps I will adapt to anything provided I am needed. I recall the simplicity of that simple question Hazel posed so many years ago: how does one tell the difference between babies that should be born and those that shouldn't? The thought haunts me now.

On the weekends Sam's hair stays rumpled and he sleeps a lot. Is it because he's relieved to have a break from Army routine, or is he gripped by the blues? I suspect it's the latter. Sometimes he grows ornery, but I just ignore him.

49

In a letter from the Pentagon dated February 25, 1959, Sam and Elsa's application for marriage has again been denied. When Sam arrives at the farm for the weekend, he gets out of his car and I can see that he is more than a little upset. He doesn't know what to do and finally just sits down at the table and writes a ten-page letter to Elsa. She'll be upset too. I pity her.

The weekend is long and arduous with a cold rain. We feel cooped up but no one wants to suggest that we go and do something. On Sunday morning I put a roast in the oven on low heat, leave a note for Sam and Dewey, then jump in the car and go to Harrisburg for the ten o'clock service at the little church on Derry Street, where I say prayers for us all. Afterward I tell the little Dutch minister how much I enjoyed his service, and he asks me if I might consider becoming an official member of the congregation. I smile at the question but don't answer. It seems to me that I want to belong to things—until I'm asked to join them. It's something in my mental composition, a need to question a group that openly recruits, a moral unwillingness to condone or endorse the power of any authority—even a church.

He brings me into his office and asks me to tell him about my life. I do. All of it. Everything. Good, bad, awful. I think I shock him but he listens.

When I am finished he sits staring at me, studying my face.

Then he reaches into a small box of Bibles sitting on a shelf by his desk. Inside he writes, "Come and take choice of all my library and so beguile thy sorrow. Read with humility, simplicity, and faith, and seek not at any time the fame of being learned." After that he writes, "You are forgiven."

"You don't understand," I say. "I don't need to be forgiven. I don't regret helping those women in need. I can't atone for that."

He sits blinking. The silence grows. "There are some things that go beyond my knowledge and skill to minister in the gospel, things that go beyond all mortal reasoning. I ask you to converse with God on this. His spirit will guide you as to your future course. Perhaps there will be some insight or actions to make your decisions clear. Perhaps not. But please, keep this book as the Lord's gift." Before he hands it back to me, he takes his pen and crosses out "You are forgiven." Underneath that he writes, "God is your counsel—only his voice can decide." The minister hugs me good-bye. "Please come back," he says.

When I return to the farm, the dog is outside, the screen door is unlatched, and the gas can for the tractor has been left sitting out in the rain with the cap off. The tractor is still there, but the truck is gone. I know that Sam and Dewey have gone to Fisherville.

When they return it is almost four; I've eaten Sunday dinner by myself and put the leftover roast away. The drinks they pursued all afternoon have left them jolly, and my annoyance strikes them as funny. When Dewey sees I won't join in their cheer, he loses his cool.

"Aw, what's eating you?" he says.

"I thought we were through with all this. Well, I'll be goddamned if I'm willing to support a couple of drunks in my house again, neither one who can keep a family."

Both of them look at each other and shut up.

The next few weeks pass without incident, and in the middle of March Sam phones me from Fort Myer with news from Elsa that she's given birth to a baby girl. Again, her letter took almost a fortnight to reach the States, so already I've been a grandmother for almost two weeks. Sam is beside himself, and we both grow emotional on the phone. When I hang up I sit and sob, my body aching to hold that baby.

That night I toss and turn, scheming for a plan to end this misery. I've got to do something to help. In the morning I rise and dress in a good navy crepe suit, heels, hat, and gloves. I drive downtown. Many streets are blocked off and there is all sorts of craziness on the sidewalks. Then I realize it is St. Patrick's Day. I can't get close to the Capitol, parking is impossible, so I pull my car into a service station and leave it for an oil change. I walk to the congressional offices and roam the marble hallways until I find Congressman Mumma's office.

"Congressman Mumma won't be available at all today," the secretary says.

"Please," I tell her. "I only need a minute."

"You don't have an appointment to see him, and even if you did have one, he's backed up because of marching in the parade."

"Please," I say again, using my most gentle pleading voice. "My business is urgent."

"Well, you can't just walk in here," she says, blinking. "He's very busy."

I can see that playing nice isn't going to get me anywhere. "Well, so am I," I say, leaning on her desk. "Now listen. Why don't you stop being so difficult and just pick up that phone, buzz the congressman, and tell him Verna Krone would like to see him. Tell him he'll remember me because I'm an old friend of Dr. Crampton's— and we once transacted some business together."

She knows now I'm not playing and must have some authority to be speaking in this manner. She purses her lips and picks up the phone.

In a few moments I'm being ushered into Mumma's office. "Well now," he says in his best folksy politician's voice. "I didn't expect to see you today."

I'm glad he picks up the ball to be friendly and I don't have to remind him of the favors Crampton and I did for him. I get right to the point and lay out Elsa and Sam's story. "I want to sponsor her to come here," I say. "And I want you to file the papers and make it happen."

Mumma hems and haws for a moment but then comprehends that I know all about politicians and their bullshit and will not be deterred.

"Well, I suppose one of the boys could check into it."

"Do whatever it takes," I say, "but make it happen." If the power of my knowledge over certain events in his life is a threat, he feels it. I hand him a letter I've written detailing Sam's rank and serial number and all the information I have on Elsa. My visit is over. Mumma shakes my hand and nervously walks me to the elevator, and I get the feeling it's less of a courtesy than a desire to make sure I'm really gone.

"I'll work on it," he says, as the elevator begins to close. "I can see you mean business."

Three days later forms arrive from the government. As a sponsor I'm required to list all my assets. I write:

House at 2311 North Third Street, Harrisburg
House on Logan Street, Harrisburg
110 acre fruit farm, RD #1, Halifax
Government bonds
Bank account at Dauphin Deposit
American Harvester Tractor, '56 Chevrolet truck,
     '57 Olds automobile
Life experience—
And my greatest asset: if there isn't a way, I make one.

50

It is September 5, 1959, an overly warm day, when Elsa steps off the plane at Idlewild Airport in New York. She wears a navy blue wool suit, too heavy for the temperature, which hovers in the nineties. She greets me with a hug and kiss, as I welcome her. "I'm so glad you're tall," I say, and marvel at her beauty.

"I must tell you, Mom," she says, shyly self-conscious of speaking English, "thank you for all you do to make this day happen." I smile, and Sam smiles too. He knows Elsa's plane ticket was paid for from the thousand dollars Charles Dennis gave me that last time we met.

The baby is wearing wool tights and cries from the heat. We undress her in the car and put her in a little cotton dress, but she keeps crying. I'm sure the trip and all the new faces are confusing. "They say the air pressure on planes can bother their ears," Sam offers. We stop at a restaurant on the way home, and Elsa is surprised when they put glasses of ice water down. Sam says it's an American custom; they don't do that in Europe. I can see he is assuming the role of navigator—helping to make the transition for Elsa and the baby. Over lunch he tells her that he's scheduled a preacher to marry them on Saturday. "I have my wedding dress packed all in my suitcase," Elsa says. The baby begins to cry again, as though she were expressing the heightened emotions for all of us. People stare with disapproval at the noise, until we pay our check and hurry back to my car. If only we could explain to those perfect strangers how much time and effort have gone into delivering the cry of that baby.

51

Elsa and the baby are now asleep upstairs in the big bedroom over the kitchen, and it's all I can do to keep myself from leaving my spot at the table here in the summerhouse to go inside and check on them.

Already I know the baby has changed everything. There is something about finally seeing the proof that I am a grandmother that makes me stand prouder, as though the maturity, wisdom, and hard work of my life have finally been tallied in my favor.

I lift my head and see Sam standing in the doorway. "Mom," he says, his voice faltering with shyness. "I just want to say thank you for everything you did to help."

"It's nothing that any mother wouldn't have done," I say, and stare down at my freckled forearms protruding from my sleeves. My heart beats wildly as I rub the backs of my hands—the same hands that know how to hoist a bushel of peaches, seal a canning jar, or bake a pie as good as I was taught. The same hands that know how to scald milk pails or medical equipment, insert a cervix dilator or a syringe. For the first time I feel the respect of my son being bestowed upon me. I know he is admiring my skill.

"Skill, that ancient and legitimate form of power."

Practical—as they taught it at the Pierce School of Nursing.

I am taken by surprise and almost overwhelmed when he leans in and kisses my cheek. For a split second, Pop flashes before my eyes and I recall how our people don't hug or kiss.

Later, when Sam has gone to join his new family in a nap, it is my turn to stand in the bedroom door and look at them. A late summer breeze is stirring the leaves outside the window, and when I study the baby sleeping in her crib, I think about the power of life. I can't believe when I hold her small warm body in my arms how much she means to all of us. I can't help but think of all the unborn whose mothers don't know what to do with them, and here is one that has made such a difference. A baby can be a terror, it can be a dream. All I can do is weep for it all, the confusion, the mystery, and the bittersweet miracle.

Afterword

As a child, my grandmother Verna Krone would every Sunday drive from her farm in Dauphin County, Pennsylvania, to our home in Fairfax County, Virginia—a trip of about three hours. Yes, the story of *The Blue Orchard* was inspired by real events.

Our Virginia neighborhood was extremely modest, a development of weather-beaten, repetitious working-class houses, where men in white T-shirts worked on their cars, sliding out from under them to have a cigarette, or drink from a can of Budweiser or Schlitz. The chore-worn women were young, could not afford to follow fashion except to tease their hair and paint their nails, and they stayed home during the week because in those days most families had but one car that the men took to work.

When Verna arrived, her presence on our drab street caused notice. When her large Oldsmobile pulled into our driveway she'd toot the horn with a few quick heralds and we'd come running. For with her came excitement. Both adults and children in the neighborhood watched from yards or windows as she stepped from the car; she always wore Sunday clothes of good quality, never without jewelry, hat, and gloves, and often a fur.

She'd open the trunk of her car and it was a cornucopia, brimming with whatever the season bore: cantaloupes, peaches, strawberries, pumpkins, apples, venison, scrapple, homemade sausage, wreaths of evergreen or dried corn husk, and extravagant ribbon-wrapped boxes containing dolls and dresses for my sister Annette; shirts, toys, and candy for me; and usually something for my parents as well. Who was this strange woman? Why did she not resemble anyone else we knew?

I sometimes ponder what my grandmother would make of this

book were she alive to read it. She did in fact read the first fifty or so pages, or rather I read them to her, and she knew all the facts of the research I'd done. She was amazed that so many of the stories she'd told me over the years had been captured. She seemed excited at the prospect of being the subject of a book, but at the same time she struggled to hide her apprehension. She was an intensely secretive person and could not help but be conflicted that the events of her private life were being set down on paper and would one day be known to anyone willing to pick up a book.

If I had a fact wrong, she'd correct it, and prior to her death, she accompanied me to the state archives, the courthouses, the historical societies, to read history—the original newspaper accounts and county court records. Often a particular detail or fact would jog her memory and then even more information would spill out. By this time, she was in her eighties, and I think at a point where this life review and self-sleuthing brought her some sort of validation. She told me that during the trials almost forty years earlier, she'd been so upset that she amazingly only looked at the first newspaper account of the arrest and ignored the rest completely.

While conducting research, I often stayed with her overnight; sometimes I'd pack three or even four interviews into a day, and when I returned in the evening, she'd have supper waiting and we'd go over all the details of what I'd learned that day. I'd say things like "Did you ever hear Dr. Crampton was raised by a white family?" "You know . . . why yes. I did hear that," she'd reply, her face alight with memory and surprise. "Funny, but I don't recall who they were."

In speaking to people about the project I often felt somewhat duplicitous in that I rarely revealed my own connection. When I did admit my grandmother's involvement, the interview felt strained, people began holding back, worried that they might get some fact or detail wrong, like they were deferring to my expertise, or that they might say something that would offend me or discredit my grandmother.

The nature of her work was also a well-guarded secret in our own family. Not even my mother knew. My father and his mother had a very complicated relationship, and though they had deep love and genuine caring for each other, there were also often subtle strains of contention. Growing up, I could never understand it. To my young mind, the source of the tension often seemed to be my father, but when I'd question him he'd simply say, "Someday I'll tell you everything." The line was both an annoyance and an intrigue.

I was twenty-five years old before my father finally revealed the roots of their trouble. It was a shock to learn of her secret life, and yet finally the contradictions, incongruities, and mystery of her ways began to make sense. To me she was always fascinating and complicated. She was a nurse, a farm woman, but also knew luxury and extravagant clothes; spent money wildly one moment, was acutely frugal the next; was cynical about the law, human nature, politics, and yet had a great wit that accompanied her stubborn, world-mocking viewpoint. How had she acquired so many facets? When I learned of her illicit involvements, the multiple sides of her personality finally clicked into place; they were born of an unusual and particular life experience. I also developed an empathy and compassion for my father, understanding for the first time the circumstances under which he had been raised.

There were several reasons that finally led me to attempt to write about their lives. First, I began to recognize that I was the only person interested enough to gather all of the pieces, and second I saw that the story was often being interpreted in ways that weren't accurate—never by my grandmother—but by others whom I asked: aunts, cousins, and of course, my father, who told a less than savory version. My grandmother's account of things turned out to be very accurate, and whatever research I did always bore her out.

Verna was a precise and calibrating storyteller and had no use for people who distorted the truth or told tall tales. (Something Dewey did all the time and with great relish.) What intrigued me most was whenever her vivid narrative grew vague, for then I always knew some deeper secret or shame was lurking, often a worry about how I would view her (usually over some detail that didn't affect me at all). Lastly, I decided to write it because it was a history of race and abortion in America that wasn't getting told. In this book, I wasn't interested in taking a position for or against, but I was simply fascinated by the truth, and the way historical fact informed the era that led to *Roe v. Wade*.

Though I began this book while working at *The New York Times*, and from that environment could see its journalistic possibilities (everyone with whom I discussed the story said it must be a nonfiction book), I always knew the book would be a novel. I wasn't interested in simply reporting fact; I wanted not just to re-create the physical world of a bygone era but also to capture the emotional intensity of these lives. I needed to imagine language and record experience in a way that only fiction allows. I also made a pledge to Verna and in my head to the men and women who had inhabited the bland, hard-won houses of our Virginia neighborhood: I would write a true-account book involving difficult American subjects that they could access and perhaps even find compelling to read.

From growing up in Virginia, I will always feel a strong affinity for southern culture and language—particularly that of the working class. I think the prose of this book, as does all my writing, has a distinctly southern ring. We grew up listening to Conway Twitty, Loretta Lynn, Elvis, Patsy Cline, and of course Johnny Cash, and the depiction of humility and ordinary life that prevailed in country music at that time still holds a sincere quality that I find very attractive. My southern affinity also gave me a useful perch from which to view Pennsylvania.

More research followed. I took a leave from my job at the newspaper and using microfilm during one two-year period, I looked at the Harrisburg newspapers from 1890 to 1960, which enabled me to piece together just how deep Dr. Crampton's involvement in politics was. It never ceased to amaze me just how much collusion there was among the town, the government, the medical community, and the local and state police. That interdependence also showed (along with his adopted family's pedigree) just how Dr. Crampton managed to get away with such a flagrant violation of legal and racial restrictions. It was also fascinating to discover to what extent this group of state politicians was significantly empowered by the money that Dr. Crampton and my grandmother generated. Eventually that crooked machine would end up influencing national politics when they secured the spot for Nixon on the Eisenhower ticket of 1952. And Nixon never forgot it; in the early 1970s around the time of the Watergate scandal and *Roe v. Wade*, he hosted state legislator Harvey Taylor in the Oval Office when Taylor was in his nineties. Taylor asked to sit behind the presidential desk, and Nixon allowed him to.

Looking back, if someone had told me *The Blue Orchard* would take more than a decade to research and write, and then take another handful of years to find its way to publication, I would probably have never attempted it, and certainly not for my first novel. (I offer this aside as a balm of encouragement for anyone currently involved in a long research project who feels the deforming pressure of judgment on the time that our efforts take us—just keep working!)

In the end, through writing *The Blue Orchard,* my life has been enriched in any number of ways. Most important, it has helped me to understand the manner of my own family; how this huge secret was under the surface of many a family exchange. It also made me see that when we as children sense a mystery or palpable puzzle, it often does have a source.

My wish is for this book to grant a tiny bit of license, or provide a small measuring instrument, to help chart the water of truth within every life and age. For we need to do our very best thinking when telling and recording the stories of our families. And the questions we pose are not merely for accuracy, but more importantly for discovery; to better comprehend the circumstances that shape the people we've known and loved and who've had influence over us.

In closing I wish to extend my gratitude to you the reader for picking up *The Blue Orchard* and giving it your valuable time and best consideration.

Jackson Taylor
New York City
April 6, 2009

Acknowledgments

With profound gratitude for my mother, whose tenacity and certainty defy all circumstance, and for my father, who never missed a day's work in his life and who finally set the story free.

With special thanks to the incomparable Marie Ponsot, whose instruction, knowledge and example grant sterling dividends that keep splitting and multiplying.

With special thanks to Tom Cocotos, whose fine eye imagines and illustrates a world that is beautiful, essential, and exceptional.

With extreme gratitude to Martha Sandlin, a dear friend of proven worth who has blessed me on many occasions with her exquisite intelligence, and who so kindly gave time to my first tentative draft.

With thanks for the dedication and skill of a literary agent who is both wise and principled: Ryan Fischer-Harbage.

And the chain of good fortune that links me with him to Mediabistro, to Carmen Scheidel, to Sue Rosen, to The PEN Prison Writing Program, to The New School, and on and on . . .

To a most magnanimous editor, Sulay Hernandez, her fine colleagues Shawna Lietzke, publicist Jessica Roth, and publisher Stacey Creamer; and copyeditor Peg Haller.

Thanks to some solid teachers and advisers—Brett Kennedy, Abigail Thomas, Joan Silber, Karen Braziller, Claudia Menza, Rosemarie Santini, Deborah Brodie, and my first creative writing teacher, Kevin Pilkington—and some exceptional people who lent me their sharp eyes: Meg McGuire, Rosie Hayes, John Aiello, Joyce Fuller, Hettie Jones, and the impeccable Vincent Cannariato. And some fine angels who granted me kindness and counsel: Sharon Stea, William Finn, Ultra Violet, Martin Hyatt, Susan Shapiro, Ira Silverberg, Nan Graham, Jane Friedman, Rita Andreopoulos, and Sarah Paley.

To the research libraries and their staff:

Sarah Lawrence College, whose dedicated enterprising team
    of librarians ordered cartons of microfilm from
    universities all around the country.
Columbia University, which lent advice and also ordered
    film.
Esme Bahm, the Moorland Springarn Research Center at
    Howard University
Barbara Williams, Library at Hahnemann College,
    Philadelphia
The New York City Public Library
The Cumberland County Historical Society
The Dauphin County Historical Society

Special thanks to *The Patriot News*, Harrisburg, Pennsylvania;
the Penn Harris Hotel; the YMCA; Dr. Frank DeLee, who granted
me permission to use excerpts from his uncle's work; and Carol at
the Dauphin County Courthouse.

With gratitude to my amazing New School colleagues: Bob
Kerrey, David Lehman, Elizabeth Dickey, Elissa Tenny, Scott Berry,
Patricia Underwood, Nick Allanach, Celesti Colds-Fechter, Almaz
Zelleke, Thelma Armstrong, and of course, Robert Polito, who
inspires and leads by a vision born from his endless passion for lit-
erature; with special thanks to Lori-Lynn Turner and Leah Iannone,
who lend celerity and grace to all they do.

Gratitude for a group of research assistants detailed and superior
in every way: Steven Hobbs, Jennifer Fortin, Eric Taylor, Nick
Burd, Antonio Aiello, Kristin Fahlbusch, Timothy Small.

To my sister Annette, for a lifetime of generosity.

Citizens of Harrisburg and its environs:

The Reverend Billy Gray; Laura (Pam) Randall; James S.
Togans; Marshall Waters; Harriette Braxton; Mr. & Mrs. Horatio

Leftwich; Millicent Hooper; Andy Robinson; Mrs. Helen McBride; Dr. Don Freedman; Dr. Claude Nichols; William Byers; Dr. Walter and Jeanne Kirker; Dr. Minster Kunkel; Dr. William Tyler Douglas Jr; Helena Oxley; Barton Fields; Dr. I. O. Silver; Mary Scheffer; Howard Clemens Sr.; Spencer Nauman Jr.; Bob Nation; Louisa France; Gardner Thomas; Mrs. Russell K. Patterson; Fitzhugh Shelley; Fran Hasselman; M. Harvey Taylor III; Cecil Franklin; Hon. William Lipsitt; Dr. Marilyn Mahon; Legree Daniels; Oscar Daniels; Dr. Wilson Everhart; Marianne Leitner; Mrs. Janet Eswein; Mrs. Grace Balkema; Mrs. Caroline Willoughby; Hon. Clarence Morrison; Mrs. Spencer Norman; Stanley Lawson; Roy Zimmerman; Judge Robert Woodside; Emily Rine; Gladys and Lester Gross; Mrs. Henry Raffensburger; Dr. Gerald G. Eggart; Robert Christ II; Eleanor Byers; Leslie McCreath; Margaret Bruchey; George Love; Ursula and Lish Crampton; Pat Greenwald; Verna Eckert; Leila Washington; Raymond S. McGarvey; Paul Beers; Jim Rollins Jr.; Lonnie Moore; Hazel Pannebakker; Virgie Hosler.

TOUCHSTONE
READING GROUP GUIDE

THE BLUE ORCHARD

For Discussion

1. In the Prologue, Verna candidly describes herself and the circumstances of her arrest, even admitting some of her flaws. What was your impression of her after reading the Prologue? In what ways did this initial introduction of Verna influence how you viewed her throughout the story?

2. Compare Verna's opinion of Dr. Crampton before she meets him to her view of him during their first encounter. How does their relationship change over the years, both on a professional and a personal level?

3. When Verna finds out Dora is assisting Dr. Crampton with abortions, she tells her that what she is doing is wrong and cites the nursing manual oath. Why does Verna then decide to work for Dr. Crampton? How does she regard the legal implications of what she's doing?

4. Verna admits to Dewey, "I don't think the world of men. They've always made me suffer" (page 160). Discuss Verna's encounters and relationships with the various men in her life—Mr. Wertz, Murphy, Charles Dennis, Norm, and Dewey. Why does she continue to see Charles Dennis throughout the years despite his deception?

5. Share your thoughts on how marriage is portrayed in the novel. Why does Verna marry Dewey? At one point in the narrative she says, "I weep over how wonderful the promise of our union was. How did it all go so wrong?" (page 215). What factors contributed to the decline of their marriage?

6. What motivates Verna to succeed? Why is she able to rise above her circumstances in a way that her mother was never able to do? How much is Verna impacted by her mother's attitude toward Buckley versus her daughters?

7. The time period in which *The Blue Orchard* is set was one of intense change in America and a precursor of the Civil Rights movement and *Roe v. Wade*. Discuss the social, racial, and political aspects of the time.

8. How did Dr. Crampton rise to such a position of prominence in Harrisburg? What led to his downfall? In what ways does Verna benefit from Dr. Crampton's political connections?

9. Why does Verna leave Sam to be raised by her mother? After she learns that Sam has run away and joined the Army, she says to Dr. Crampton, "I've done the best I can" (page 223). What is your opinion of Verna as a mother? How do you think Verna would answer the question of whether or not she was a good mother?

10. "I think about how I used to lie awake and imagine dressers stuffed with cash, but I could not have guessed the high cost of having my dreams fulfilled," says Verna (page 227). What, if anything, do you think she would do differently if given the chance? Why does Verna continue to spend so extravagantly even after Dr. Crampton advises her against it?

11. Why does Verna insist she'll reveal the names in the ledger if she's called to the witness stand? Did she do the right thing by accepting exoneration from the case or, as Dr. Crampton suggested, will she have to live with doubt in people's minds since she was not acquitted by a jury? How is Verna changed by the trial?

12. When Verna destroys Dewey's bushels of peaches, she says, "I smash for what I've become. A victim. Yet again" (page 343). Why does she see herself as a victim? What emotional impact does losing her profession have on Verna?

13. Why is Verna so determined to unite Sam with Elsa? Why is it important for her to bring her grandchild to America?

14. Does knowing that *The Blue Orchard* is based on the life of the author's grandmother, Verna Krone, alter your perception of the story? How so? What is your overall impression of the novel and of Verna in particular?

You say in the novel's afterword that if you had known it would take you a decade to complete *The Blue Orchard*, you might never have started it. What kept you working on it all those years?

The inherent mystery was an engine. It had momentous strength and pulled me along. Perhaps others who have pursued family secrets will know what I mean, and perhaps the reader while turning the pages of the book will sense some of the curiosity and excitement I felt while making discovery.

The Blue Orchard is based on your grandmother's life. Why was it important for you to share Verna's story?

The lives of people we come from are filled with exquisite, concrete clues that can be examined to understand childhood, the world, and ourselves, and to recognize how many ways we resemble the rest of our species. The study of the real record adds perspective to the ways anyone might look at the youth of their parents or grandparents.

During the years of research, the historian's voice in me kept questioning: How? Why? My grandmother wasn't easily impressed by people, so I wanted to know the nature of this man who'd earned so much respect.

Verna overcame many obstacles to rise from poverty and become an independent woman of means. How unique was she for the time?

I like to imagine that she was somewhat unique for the illicit nature of her work, but leafing through her ledger and record, it amazes me still to see how many women were involved in the act of procurement. In that sense even though underground, they were hardly unique.

What challenges did you encounter while researching and writing the novel? What can you tell us about the process of blending fact and fiction?

The biggest obstacle was learning the name of the family who raised Dr. Crampton. Though I was given at least a half a dozen leads by various sources, that always referred to the wealthy, august families of Harrisburg, none of these leads panned out. I'd spend weeks tracking down one of these "descendants." They were often quite elderly, living in nursing homes or under the care of their children. I'd introduce myself and the project and ask if Dr. Crampton might have been raised in their family. In voices shaky with age they'd say things like, "Well I never heard that," or "If he was raised by us and was as prominent as you say, I think I would have known." Though a few pondered that it might have been possible, not a single person could remember or confirm.

Earlier in the century there had been a fire in the records office at Howard University, where Dr. Crampton had earned his medical degree, so no records remained, but finally a wonderful librarian at the Moorland-Springarn Research Center found a scrap of paper dated 1903, with a Harrisburg address for Dr. Crampton on it. That led to a deed search which eventually revealed what had so long been forgotten. This significant bit of research took two years to complete.

As for blending fact and fiction? Hmmm . . . I'd say it's about proportion, the unusual phrase or detail, and working with and against the rule of probability. One of the things that helped me most was that I read every page of the *Harrisburg Patriot* from 1900 to 1960. That helped me see that the daily march of history is really much more subtle and revealing than the big iconic moments.

How did you make certain to present an honest portrait of Verna, both her good qualities and her flaws? Was there ever a tendency to gloss over certain aspects or incidents?

Verna could be deeply reflective about herself. I tried to weigh out and imagine those personal ruminations. It is also important for any writer to recognize that it is never going to be possible to tell "the" truth. The best we can aspire to is "a" truth, or a version of the truth as we might happen to see it.

You have said that for many years the nature of Verna's work was a well-guarded secret. How have your family members re-acted to *The Blue Orchard* and seeing her story in print?
It's been varied. Some see it as a validation—I like to hope that my version of the truth has perhaps given them a sense of freedom. Some are ambivalent; some see it as a violation or a betrayal.

What can you tell us about the novel's title and why it was selected?
It's a metaphor that hovers over certain scenes of the book.

Abortion is still a sensitive subject in this country for people on both sides of the issue. Do you expect that the book will spark conversations about it?
My guess is that the arguments on abortion will continue uninter-rupted and that most debaters will maintain their position. The subject stirs tremendous reaction in groups of our citizens—with often ill-considered consequence, blinding force, and violence. Such fervor deserves question.

One of the judges I interviewed, who as a young lawyer had helped the attorneys prepare the defense for Dr. Crampton, told me that he believed a major benefit of the 1973 *Roe v. Wade* decision was that it allowed for a clear separation between church and state as endorsed by our founding government documents. I thought that was interesting. It made me conscious of how many politicians defy that separation between church and state to curry favor with voters.

Another surprise was the discovery that no really definitive history of abortion in America has ever been written—and yet from colonial times forward there are accounts and records of all this activity—and in most states the practice was not illegal until the mid 1800s. A good deal of my time was spent reading whatever I could find on the subject.

This research, challenged my sort of simplistic, cinematic sense of history, particularly of the 1930s through '50s, and the blanket historical statements frequently used to define a period. Often the only contrast given to the lives of women, was the fluctuation between a kind of short-lived but plucky Rosie the Riveter wartime apparition, and a prison of idealized middle-class domestic perfection largely drawn from television or advertising. It interested me to find that women in those times were more nuanced, decisive, and resourceful than certain narratives might have you think. Also, I came to understand how often the men were also wrestling with the confines of their role as breadwinner, hero, leader, benefactor, leader, and daddy.

Senators, congressmen, clergy, and White House administrators were among the people who referred women to Dr. Crampton. What would the ramifications have been if Verna had revealed the thousand of names in the ledger during the trial?

Verna told me that the judge would have probably thrown all of it out for contempt of court but that she intended to keep talking no matter what the judge said. There was something about the size of this quagmire that made it ungovernable. Perhaps we see the similar scale and problem when in our time a bank favorably restructures the failed debt of a large developer! But who knows, perhaps if some of the roots of voter gain for President Nixon or President Eisenhower had been revealed during an election, American history would look very different. . . .

How would you describe *The Blue Orchard*—and Verna—to people who have not yet read it?

It's a novel about a woman who wrestles with adversity amid a particular time and history that is difficult for our country to come to terms with.

Will your next novel be rooted in history? What can you tell us about it?

It's closer to our time, is set in Italy, has an urbane and highly literary narrator, concerns the break-up of a peppery marriage—the terrible contract that decrees marriage—and forgive me . . . I don't intend to sound coy . . . but I'm still unknotting my intentions for the rest.